MARCIA ARMANDI

THE HAUNTING OF BLACKWATER

THE HAUNTING OF BLACKWATER

MARCIA ARMANDI

CITY OWL
PRESS

THE HAUNTING OF BLACKWATER
By Marcia Armandi

CITY OWL PRESS
www.cityowlpress.com

Cover Design by MiblArt. All stock photos licensed appropriately.

Edited by Lisa Green and Jessica Shearer.

For information on subsidiary rights, please contact the publisher at info@cityowlpress.com.

Print Edition ISBN: 978-1-64898-411-2

Digital Edition ISBN: 978-1-64898-412-9

Printed in the United States of America

To Angelo and Leopoldo. Your sacrifices will never be forgotten.

CHAPTER 1
FATE

London, England, 1937

Lina's dreams of a new life came to a halt the day her father was shot at Lydney Railway Station on his way to Blackwater manor, in Coleford. His death had been brutal, but here, lying in his coffin, Sir William Laroche looked at peace, his hands intertwined atop his black suit, his high-collared shirt neatly pressed. Lina unveiled her face and leaned forward. "I miss you." She gave him a final kiss, the coolness of his skin lingering on her lips—proof that his comforting words and warm embrace were now but a memory. She then heard the heart-wrenching words whispered by someone in attendance, "Orphan children."

Seven years ago, a heart attack claimed Sofia Laroche's life, leaving a bereaved family and Lina who, at thirteen years old, became a woman. Lina had promptly taken charge of caring for her baby brother, Mateo, as her mother had done. The task presented many challenges, but the boy, now eight, thrived academically and socially. Satisfied with Mateo's place in society and inspired by her post at the local library, Lina had applied for and been accepted to Oxford. She loved the idea of a career in mathematics. There was no room for mistakes in math. It was reliable, constant, so unlike the world in general. And, at times, she felt ill-prepared to confront that world—a world where death played an integral part.

Rumors of a world war circulated through the country, whispers and half-spoken thoughts gathering on the periphery like a far-off storm that had not yet overtaken the sunlight. Before her father's untimely death, she'd feared that when the lightning struck, not only would her father be taken but so would life as every Briton knew it. As a diplomat, William had been aware of the rising menace. Even more so of late, his meetings and telephone calls had multiplied. Lina's thoughts traveled back to the call that stood apart from the others.

Her father had been restless all morning. When the phone rang in his study, he dashed to answer it, neglecting to close the door. The stress in his voice made his words loud and clear. Lina could see him through the dim light of the hallway. He stood near his desk, his back to her, his shoulders slumped as if carrying an invisible weight.

"Nonsense. I refuse to believe that. The man is many things, but not that," William refuted into the receiver. And after a brief pause, he assured, "All right, all right. I will go there and settle this at once."

Lina hadn't thought much of the conversation. But now she wondered if that call was the first of death's plotting. Her gaze returned to her father's rigid body, and her fingers tightened on the edge of the silk-lined coffin. Was this the last time she would ever see him? Lina vaguely remembered the teachings of her youth about life beyond the grave—a topic she had never seriously considered. Moreover, she was convinced that paranormal accounts were fictitious, designed to instigate hope in an afterlife that didn't exist. But now, bereft of both her parents, she felt despondent and would have dearly loved a confirmation that death was not the end. The rawness of daily living, the regrets and disheartenments, and the tremendous responsibility of caring for her brother all seemed too much to bear. And with the assassin still at large, her despair threatened to consume her, trampling any hope that might have been born.

She took a stabilizing breath, repositioned the black veil over her face, and stepped away from the corpse to face the people awaiting the service. Dressed in respectful attire to pay homage to the solemnity of the event, they spoke in hushed voices while staring at the casket. Though many loved William, at least one person hated him enough to take him forever from his children. Lina scanned the chapel and found her brother huddled on a chair in the side aisle, twisting his hands. Her grief multiplied with each step she took toward him. How could she alleviate her own grief, let alone Mateo's?

"Lina, when are we going home?"

"Soon, darling, soon." She knelt in front of him, taking his hands into hers.

"I don't like it here. These people are scary."

"Oh, no, they are dressed in black to show their respect for Father, that's all."

Mateo shook his head. "No, not them."

"Who, then?"

"Him." Mateo pointed to the window at the end of the hallway.

Although the drapes swayed as if someone had brushed past them, Lina couldn't see anyone.

"I think he is very upset," Mateo remarked, shrinking in the chair.

"Well, don't you worry about him," she soothed, attributing his distress to their circumstances. As if losing their mother hadn't been enough, the boy was now fatherless at an age when he needed fatherly support and guidance most.

"I don't want him to look at me anymore."

"It's all right." Lina glanced at the hallway again, but still couldn't see anyone. "I'm right here with you." She slipped onto the seat beside the boy and pulled him close.

"I want to go home." Mateo buried his face in her arm.

"We will soon," Lina said, aware that what they called home was about to change. Today they faced the funeral; tomorrow another trouble awaited.

At William's passing, his brother, Bartholomew Laroche, had become the children's legal guardian and the manager of their estate. Of course, William hadn't anticipated his own sudden death, or he would have taken measures to remove Bartholomew as executor of the family trust.

Their relationship had deteriorated in recent years as Bartholomew's alcohol addiction had morphed him into a violent, unreasonable man. Stating health issues, Bartholomew hadn't bothered coming to the funeral. Instead, he'd busied himself with complicating the siblings' lives by demanding they leave their flat in London and move to Blackwater, the primary residence of the Laroche family for generations.

Preferring London, Lina's father had granted Bartholomew and his wife, Eleonor, charge over the manor. Lina considered a summer or two plenty of time to enjoy the countryside. And since she had spent several there already, she couldn't imagine it as a permanent home. It was too far removed from what she was accustomed to. Nonetheless, there would be no freedom until she turned twenty-one and the law permitted her to manage her inheritance and gain custody of her brother.

The more she thought of it, the angrier she became. Her uncle was robbing them of their home, friends, and even trusted house staff, having made it clear that the personnel would not be relocating with them. He'd also stolen her dream to attend Oxford, at least for now. Though Bartholomew hadn't brought up the subject, there was no way under heaven that Lina would let Mateo face Blackwater alone. They were all that was left of their little family, and she was determined to protect him.

William's agitated telephone call replayed in her mind. Had he been speaking of Bartholomew? If so, what had her uncle done? Did he have something to do with her father's death? After all, William had been en-route to visit the man when he met death as he'd stepped off the train. True, Bartholomew was a scoundrel who took to the bottle to solve his problems, but a murderer? It seemed farfetched, yet possible.

Now, more than ever, she felt vulnerable, powerless, and at the mercy of a man she hardly knew. He'd always been like a shadow lurking at the edge of her life, easy to ignore when her parents were alive. Now, the shadow would become the center of their lives.

Dark clouds hung low over King's Cross Railway Station, threatening to unleash a downpour. The siblings hurried into the building, scurrying past the other travelers. Covertly, Lina searched their faces. Perhaps with a miracle, her father would appear among them, but from his last destination, no one returned.

"Whoa!" Mateo exclaimed, staring at the train as they emerged from the train station onto the platform.

Grand and impressive, the Admiral Sutherland locomotive sat on the tracks. No doubt it had traveled far and wide, its passengers enjoying many adventures. Yet Lina wished she and her brother would never set foot on it. An incoming train rolled in just on the other side of the Admiral, clouds of smoke billowing into the sky. Lina's gaze was lost in the gray fumes, her thoughts returning to her father.

Why had he made this very trip? William had spoken of removing Bartholomew from Blackwater for his bad management, but Lina didn't think it would ever happen. In fact, she was almost certain it wasn't the reason her father had traveled there. *Why did you have to die? What's to become of us?*

Along with the unanswered questions, the feeling that they should not go to Blackwater plagued her again. Ever since the family solicitor announced Bartholomew's decision, Lina had wrestled with a sense of foreboding about living under her uncle's purview. However, legally, she had no options. Running away was tempting, but she would not put Mateo in jeopardy. The small amount of money stashed in her pocket would run out within days, and they would be homeless. She could get a post somewhere, but she had no one to care for the boy. Besides, Bartholomew would soon find them, and their end might be worse than their beginning. At least, for now, she still had a chance to appeal to his sympathy.

Mateo pulled on her sleeve, and her attention returned to the present. "What are you thinking about, Lina?"

"The countryside," she answered, concealing her low spirits. "Getting out of London's gloom will be nice."

"Why do we have to go?"

"Because Uncle Bartholomew is our only family." She adjusted his hat on his black hair, and his brown eyes found her blue ones. His resemblance to their mother was a painful reminder of Sofia and how much Lina missed her. And now her own fair complexion would conjure memories of her father every time she looked in the mirror.

"I don't want to leave my friends," Mateo complained.

"I know. I know." Lina understood him well. She would miss her friends, Irene and Sherley, and their discussions at the library about their latest reads during coffee breaks.

"Will I ever see them again?"

"Of course, you will. We'll be back before you know it." Although she feared they would be forced to stay at Blackwater a whole year, she couldn't bring herself to tell him.

"But I don't like the manor. It's scary."

"Scary? Nonsense."

"Yes, it is. It's gigantic, and there are lots of strange noises." Mateo had a remarkable memory. Even though it had been a while since their last visit, he still remembered. The manor's towering walls and obscure passages did make it quite menacing.

"Listen, there is nothing to fret." Lina's gaze found his. "I'll be with you every second of the day."

"That might be a bit too much," he said.

Lina laughed at the sincerity in his remark.

His attention jumped to a group of soldiers who'd stepped onto the platform, a common sight nowadays. Their loud voices and heavy boots drew notice. Mateo pointed "Look, Lina, look! Soldiers!"

"I see, I see." With a graceful move, she guided his hand back down to his side, wondering what kept the train attendant from inviting them aboard.

"Good morning, miss," a short, chubby soldier greeted her.

She nodded in acknowledgment. Mateo waved, enthusiasm present in the motion.

"Good morning, indeed!" another soldier emphasized, winking at her.

Lina produced a faint smile, not wanting to encourage them, for it was apparent they'd be traveling on the same train. Nonetheless, she felt a surge of pity. Some of them looked younger than her twenty years. And if the rumors of war became reality, the country's fate would rest on the shoulders of young lads like these. She looked down at her little brother. Thankfully he was years from military age, for she shuddered to think of him marching off to war.

The siblings were among the first to turn in their tickets when the train attendant finally summoned the passengers aboard. Lina purposely chose one of the first compartments. Since people tended to move farther down the aisle, she hoped no one would intrude on their space. The events of the past few days had left her starving for solitude and too weary for polite conversation.

"Give me your gloves," Lina instructed Mateo, taking off her own. "And your hat. We don't want to lose them." He did as he was told, and she placed the items inside their small suitcase. At least Bartholomew had sent for most of their belongings ahead of time. She secured the case on the overhead shelf and settled in beside her brother. "There, now we can relax."

Relaxing didn't seem to appeal to Mateo, who slid his body back and forth between his sister and the window. "What are we going to do at Blackwater? Will I go to school?"

"That, or a teacher will come to the house." Mateo's questions intensified her awareness of their precarious circumstances and what might await them at Blackwater.

The rhythmic chugging of the wheels grew louder as the train inched forward.

Lina's stomach churned with uncertainty, the distance between her and the world she had known increasing with each passing second.

"And what else?" Mateo wondered. His inquisitive mind seemingly sought answers to appease his anxiety.

"I think we shall ride horses, and if you are on your best behavior, you might get to have your own," Lina responded, knowing of his love for animals.

"My own horse?" Excitement filled him, but then a new thought occurred. "What if Uncle Bartholomew doesn't let me have a horse?"

Lina frowned. He must've heard more than he should have about their uncle from the house staff. Unhappy with Bartholomew's determination to relocate the siblings, they had openly expressed their opinions on the matter. "In that case, we'll find one in the stables we can call yours—it will be our secret."

Satisfied with her answer and probably musing about horses, Mateo leaned on her and finally sat still. Her blonde hair cascaded down her shoulder and brushed against his face. With a giggle, he tugged on a strand. Lina smiled and tucked him under her arm, feeling the tension in his body dissipate. It wasn't long until he was fast asleep, and when the train rolled into the next station, he snored softly. Some passengers disembarked, and new ones boarded, Mateo oblivious to it all. Lina leaned her head back against the seat as the locomotive pushed on, its steel wheels shrieking on the tracks.

"Come on, chap, come on! We haven't got all day!" The attendant's shouting startled Lina, and she peered through the window for an explanation.

With one hand, the attendant held onto the sidebar while motioning with the other for a late passenger to make haste. Lina's gaze drew to the color of the man's military uniform—blue instead of the usual brown—as he ran along the platform. *Hmm, a higher rank. Yet irresponsible not being on time.* It was a sentiment she'd gotten from her father, who was punctual to a fault, always on schedule. Her free-spirited mother was more relaxed about her relationship with the clock, which Lina had never picked up despite sharing many of her other traits.

As the train accelerated, Lina came to terms with the fact that sleep had escaped her. With a sigh, she dug into her handbag for the novel she had stashed before leaving their flat, and once she had it in hand, the title mocked her. *I Will Remember You Until the Day I Die.*

"Oh, how cheerful," she muttered. "I should have paid more attention." That morning had been nothing but stress-filled as she made sure Mateo had all he needed. Consequently, she found a new appreciation for her parents and regretted some of the things she had so easily censured them for.

"Excuse me, miss. Is this seat taken?" The soldier in the blue uniform pointed to the bench opposite her.

"No, it's not." *And I would like to keep it that way.* And to Mateo, who had briefly awoken, she said, "Go back to sleep," patting his arm.

The boy leaned against the window, brought his legs up on the seat, and was soon comfortably back to dreaming. The soldier installed himself straight across from Lina, dropping his military bag beside him. She anticipated the conversation that surely would ensue. By sad experience, she had learned that some men were tediously dull when in the presence of women, as if their brains quit working. That morning's brief interaction with the soldiers had reaffirmed her feelings on the matter.

She detested flattering words and shallow conversations. Why could they not hold sincere, well-constructed discussions? At times, she dreamed of finding someone more interested in her as a human being than in her looks and of having a romance as special as her parents shared. But after some disappointment, she doubted she would. Besides, she could no longer afford to dream of it. For now, she had Mateo to look after.

Her first move was to avoid eye contact, hoping that time would be merciful, and they'd soon reach Lydney. From there, Bartholomew's chauffeur would take them to Coleford. She lowered her chin, pretending to be engrossed in the print in front of her. When the soldier drew a deep breath and stretched his long legs into her space, she responded by tucking hers closer to her seat.

The train continued its trajectory with a mind-numbing slowness. Now and then, from the corner of her eye, Lina caught glimpses of rolling hills and small villages. Momentarily, her thoughts wandered back to her plight, her mind working diligently to find a solution that didn't involve staying at Blackwater.

When her focus returned to the book, she found it difficult to concentrate. Though her fellow traveler hadn't said a word, she felt his presence. Perhaps speaking to him would have been easier to manage. With a few superficial exchanges, she could've started and promptly ended a conversation, thus mitigating the awkwardness in the compartment. Yes, she should've done just that, and when the soldier coughed, softly, as if calling for her attention, she seized the opportunity.

She lowered the book to her lap but was stunned to find his head tilted, his eyes closed, his features showing no signs of awareness—he slept. Whatever interest she had anticipated from him was nothing more than a product of her imagination. She was chagrined at first, but then smiled inwardly at her foolishness.

She let her gaze linger on him. Probably in his mid-twenties, he had fair skin with softly defined facial features and slightly wavy brown hair. The fit of his uniform indicated a well-shaped figure. Whether a sign of self-discipline or a strenuous life, Lina couldn't say. Yet, despite his pleasant appearance, what captivated her most was the serenity he emanated, a serenity that seemed to come from deep within. He slept as if nothing in the world mattered, as if he were an angel instead of a soldier, devoid of grief and concern. A wave of nostalgia swept over Lina for days that were planned and orderly—balanced. When parenthood didn't weigh upon her shoulders—when she had been the child who needed care.

The soldier made a slight movement, and Lina glanced away, feeling guilty for her perusal. She had condemned the very conduct she now displayed. Nevertheless, her gaze found its way back to him.

"What are you staring at?" Mateo's voice cut through the stillness of the compartment.

"Shh. Hush," Lina whispered, fearing that her uninvited assessment would be exposed. "We mustn't disturb him."

"But why were you staring at him?" Mateo sat up, rubbing his eyes.

Lina wasn't sure, but even though the soldier remained still, she thought she glimpsed an expression of amusement. "I wasn't," she lied, while the heat in her face confirmed that she was blushing.

"Is he a good or bad soldier?" On the topic of the atrocities committed by soldiers in other countries, the house staff also hadn't withheld their opinion. And Mateo hadn't missed a chance to listen, but at his age, it could be challenging to arrange things properly.

"Good. He is good." Her gaze returned to the man, and this time she saw his lips curl softly, as if suppressing a smile. She was now positive he was awake.

"Are you sure?" Mateo's eyebrows knitted together.

"Of course, I'm sure."

"Why isn't he wearing a brown uniform?"

"Sometimes they wear blue." She placed her finger on her lips, signaling for him to be silent.

"I'm bored." Mateo had had enough of quiet. "How much longer do we have to sit for? It's stuffy in here."

Lina didn't know whether to cry or laugh. Once Mateo got into a questioning mood, no power under heaven could make him stop. "We are almost there. I believe Lydney is the next stop."

"But I'm bored, Lina."

"Where is your car? The one you were looking for before we left the flat."

"Oh, I forgot about it." He fumbled in his pocket. "Got it." He waved the red metal car in the air as if it were an airplane.

"Oh, thank heaven," Lina muttered.

The toy entertained Mateo while his sister did her best not to look at the soldier again. He sat ever so still. Not long after, the final whistle shrieked like a banshee, and the locomotive slowed in preparation for its arrival. While Lina stowed the book in her handbag, she realized that even though she had wanted solitude, she was disappointed to have found herself ignored by the soldier.

The train came to a stop, and, letting out a tired yawn, the soldier adjusted himself on the seat. Lina grabbed her bag and sprang to her feet faster than intended, pulling Mateo up by his hand.

"Ouch, Lina!" Mateo wriggled his hand to loosen her grip. "You almost made me drop the car."

She seized the doorknob, the soldier stood, and the compartment suddenly became too crowded. He was more attractive than she had allowed herself to admit, which made her uncomfortable for a reason she didn't fully understand.

"Don't forget this." Reaching over Lina's head, the soldier brought her suitcase down from the rack.

"Thank you." Lina let go of Mateo to retrieve the suitcase while her other hand lingered on the doorknob.

Before she knew it, the soldier had wrapped his fingers around hers and finished sliding the door open. As she stepped into the aisle, he spoke again. "Have a wonderful rest of your day."

Lina turned, and his hazel eyes burned into hers, giving her the impression that they held an unsaid message. "The same to you, sir."

In response, he smiled and nodded.

Ugh. I'm as daft as a brush. I should have said something more intelligent.

Hand in hand, the siblings descended the train. And while they traversed the platform, the sorrow of the place overshadowed Lina with the unbidden image of her father collapsed on the station floor, his life slipping away. Her anguish was as tangible as the coward's bullet that had taken their father from them. Anxious for the day they would return to London, she turned to glance at the Admiral Southerland locomotive one last time.

"I don't think he got off here," observed Mateo, hurrying to keep up with her long strides.

"Who?"

"The soldier."

Lina said nothing. It didn't matter what the soldier's destination was. She would probably never see him again. And the long ride had given her time to solidify the purpose of her immediate future: to protect her brother and discover the truth about her father's death.

CHAPTER 2
BLACKWATER

Mr. Walton, a middle-aged Irishman, fetched them from the railway station in Bartholomew's blue Alvis Silver Eagle. As they rode to Coleford, Lina surmised the chauffeur was a quiet fellow who liked to perform his duties without much chatter, which suited her just fine. She shifted closer to the window. Through a gap in the trees, she spotted Blackwater, named after the several dark pools scattered across the region. The sprawling two-story country manor loomed in the distant reach of the woods.

A kaleidoscope of memories flooded her mind. She remembered herself as a little girl being taught by her father to ride a pony, the sensation of butterflies in her stomach as the pony's steps turned into a trot. She thought of sitting on the south lawn, enjoying the sunshine with her mother and baby brother. Then there was the sycamore tree. Tea was served beneath its shade every afternoon at five o'clock. Her heart yearned for the emotional and physical security of those days—for the inner strength her parents' affection had given her. Now more than ever she needed to draw courage from their memory, for deep within, she feared her losses might break her.

"I don't like this place," Mateo said, interrupting Lina's reverie. Sliding closer, he concealed his face between the back of the seat and her arm.

"As long as we are together, we'll be all right," she whispered, hoping to exclude the chauffeur from her words.

Mateo's insistence about his dislike for the place brought a vague memory to Lina of their past visits. There had been sleepless nights with Mateo pointing into the darkness as he cried out in terror. Lina had been quick to flip on the lights, only to find nothing out of the ordinary. The nightmares had continued until they returned to London.

Just before the last stretch to their destination, Lina caught a movement at the edge of the woods. "Look, Mateo—horses." She lifted him onto her lap so he could see better.

"There are three of them," Mateo noted. "A black one and two brown ones."

While the siblings admired the animals, the car entered the courtyard —a large circular driveway of red pavers.

"Here we are." The chauffeur stated the obvious. "Please, go ahead. I'll park the car and bring in your luggage."

"Thank you, Mr. Walton." Lina exited the Eagle and the first thing she noticed was the bitter cold and thick silence, a stark contrast to her warm memories of happier days. Though the sun was high, faint clouds obscured its radiance. She shivered, and, eager to get inside, she turned to Mateo, who still sat in the car. "Come on. Let's go."

He slid a few inches closer to the edge of the seat but not any farther.

"Mr. Walton has to put the car away. Come on." She reached for Mateo's hand and helped him out.

They climbed the four steps to the entrance, and, out of habit, she reached for the door knocker, the heavy metal collapsing against the wood like a mallet against a gong. Realizing this was now their home and with the sound still reverberating through the soaring ceilings, the siblings slipped into the foyer—a square area with a monstrous staircase straight ahead and several passages shooting off in all directions.

A housemaid with a childlike face, plump cheeks, and soft eyes popped into sight. "You must be Lady Catalina and little Master Mateo! Welcome. Welcome."

"Please, call me Lina."

"I'm Annie, Mrs. Lester's right-hand maid and the go-to person should you need anything." Lina's father had hired Mrs. Lester, the housekeeper, not long ago. Other than that, Lina didn't know much about the woman who was Annie's boss. "It's a pleasure to meet you both."

"The pleasure is mine." Taking an immediate liking to Annie, Lina clasped her hand in a firm shake. Annie could most definitely be an ally and friend.

Annie smiled at Mateo.

His face lit up, and he said, "Hello, Annie."

Annie hung their coats on the rack and then led them down the corridor to their left. Though hours separated them from the night, the farther they went, the darker the house became. Mateo's hesitancy was well-placed. Blackwater was dim and frigid—and indifferent to its inhabitants. Lina glanced at the boy, whose previous joviality was gone. His eyes were alert, his steps mechanical, as if his body had lost its fluidity.

"I think we are going to the library," Lina said, hoping to distract him from the gloominess. "Am I right, Annie?"

"Yes, miss—the library, indeed."

"You'll love how many books are there," Lina told Mateo as she thought of her post at the library in London. Though she had meant to cheer her brother, sadness gripped her heart. She longed for her job, her friends, and their old life. She sighed. The list of people and things she loved and missed kept growing but were far from reach now.

"Is that where," Mateo's voice dropped almost to a whisper, "Mama used to read to me?" Their father had kept their mother's memory alive by frequently rehearsing his memories of Sofia.

"Yes, she read to us there."

Almost at the end of the passage, Annie halted near the French doors, then stepped to the side to let the siblings in. The room was bright, courtesy of the west-facing windows, though the brick fireplace and the bookcases lining the walls retained a subtle darkness. The crystal chandelier drew Lina's gaze. It hung from the ceiling like a gigantic tarantula, its legs extended above the floral armchairs, two sofas, and a gray settee. On the wall opposite the windows, Lina saw the Spanish credenza that had been one of her mother's favorite pieces and, at the far end of the room, a mirror with a grotesque wooden frame.

"What's that smell?" Mateo scratched his nose and sneezed a few times.

Lina recognized the musty smell from the older sections of Chetham's Library. "It's coming from the bookcases. I think some of the books need to be aired out."

"Is that why they smell so bad?" Mateo asked.

"That, along with some other factors." Lina thought of the effect of the humidity on the structure and furniture, but that was a discussion for another day.

"Please, have a seat." Annie pointed at the red sofa facing the fireplace.

The siblings neared the sofa, and Lina felt as if the house had swallowed her into its depths. She'd forgotten how enormous everything was. Her heart ached for the simplicity and coziness of their London flat. One year—it felt like a life sentence.

"I'm afraid Sir Bartholomew and the missus have taken the dogs for a stroll, but I'll fetch Mrs. Lester," Annie said. "She has been quite anxious for your arrival."

Lina found Annie's remark a bit odd. Was Mrs. Lester worried about the extra work their presence could cause? Thankfully, the siblings were used to caring for themselves, and Lina did not intend to change that. "Thank you, Annie."

Mateo's anxious gaze followed the maid as she disappeared into the hallway. Then he exclaimed, "Look, Lina! It's Papa and Mama!" pointing to a large portrait of their parents semi-hidden in a niche between two bookshelves.

"It's still here..."

Something else caught the boy's curiosity, and he scampered about the library, but Lina remained captivated by the painting. Growing up, she'd never paid it much attention, but now it seemed to radiate magnetic energy, as if she gazed at her parents through a window they might fling open at any moment.

Sofia's Spanish complexion radiated light. Her long black hair and chocolate eyes contrasted with her blonde, blue-eyed husband's features. Their eyes seemed to come alive as their daughter studied them. They looked much younger and joyous than she remembered. The pain of their absence welled up in her heart, and she moved on to the mirror in an attempt to distract herself. In its reflective surface she saw her image surrounded by walls and furniture, a frozen moment in time. And at that moment, even when it was obvious that it was just her and Mateo there, she had an inexplicable sensation that someone else watched her. She sensed other eyes, curious and malevolent. Eyes that drew a striking contrast to those of her parents.

She then heard the click-clack of shoes coming from the corridor. Expecting to meet Mrs. Lester, she turned toward the entrance. The noise grew louder as someone walked past, yet her hearing painted a picture that wasn't there. The corridor stood empty. The steps faded into the distance, and Lina glanced at Mateo. It was impossible for anyone to pass the library without being seen. But Mateo seemed unaware of the footsteps. Awestruck by the many volumes on the shelves, his little fingers traced the spines of those within reach.

Another set of footsteps approached—lighter, softer. Determined to discover who they belonged to this time, Lina moved to the doorway. At the same time, a middle-aged woman with short gray hair, a stern face, and square shoulders rushed in, almost crashing into her.

Coming to an abrupt halt, the woman took Lina's hand and shook it. "Miss Laroche, welcome! I'm so relieved you are here. I'm Mrs. Lester."

Lina noticed Mrs. Lester's attire. She sported a delicate brown tweed dress Lina was sure she had seen in the windows of Regent Street. An interesting choice for someone on the salary of a housekeeper. "It's a pleasure to meet you. Please, call me Lina."

Mrs. Lester nodded in acquiescence. "Sir Bartholomew and Eleonor should be back any moment now."

With a book in hand, Mateo joined them.

"Oh, and you must be Mateo." Mrs. Lester extended her hand to him.

He stared at her with a frozen look. True, Mrs. Lester was pleasant enough, but not as jovial or youthful as Annie.

"It's all right," Lina encouraged.

Hesitantly, he grasped Mrs. Lester's hand.

"You will love it here," Mrs. Lester assured him, as if willing it to be true. "There is plenty of room to play in the gardens."

Mateo produced no visible emotion as he broke their grip.

"He is still adjusting," Lina excused.

"There is a great deal of adjusting in store for us all," Mrs. Lester said. "And I imagine the changes must be taxing you, but don't you worry about anything. Annie and I will take good care of you."

Lina wondered at Mrs. Lester's failure to mention her aunt and uncle, but perhaps the housekeeper spoke only on behalf of the house staff. "We are much obliged to you and to Annie. She made us feel most welcome."

"Ah, Annie. She is a splendid girl and a hard worker—qualities not easily found nowadays. I stole her from my previous post."

"That was a good move," Lina commended.

"Can we please read this?" Mateo waved the book in front of his sister.

"We shall a little later. All right?"

"All right." With disappointment in his eyes, Mateo strolled to the window just as loud barking came from the courtyard. He placed his hands on the casement to get a better look outside, and his shoulders tensed.

The housekeeper joined him and informed, "Sir Bartholomew and Mrs. Eleonor have returned."

Lina's heart lurched as the front door opened, then closed. She reminded herself not to conjecture falsehoods about Bartholomew without proof. True, she disliked him for uprooting them from their home in London, but that did not mean he was a murderer; in fact, he might mean well.

All eyes fixed on the threshold when a petite woman with brown hair neatly arranged behind her ears ambled in.

"Welcome home, Lina! You are even more beautiful than when I last saw you."

"Thank you, Aunt Eleonor. It's good to see you again."

Eleonor embraced her niece with a natural, effortless familiarity. The woman's sweet perfume permeated Lina's nostrils, awakening fond childhood memories. For a fraction of a second, Lina felt truly welcomed and wanted, a fleeting sentiment she quickly stored in her heart for her times of need.

"Oh!" exclaimed Eleonor, throwing her arms in the air with delight. "Mateo, you have grown so much. And what a handsome young man you are."

The boy remained by the window, silent.

Eleonor seized his hands before he could hide them. "I see you have found a book." She motioned to the volume sitting on the casement. "I love books, especially the ones about dragons and knights." With those words and a bright smile, she'd captured his enthusiasm. "What is that one about?"

Mateo retrieved the book and handed it to the small-framed woman. The golden letters on the green cover jumped out. *One Thousand and One Nights.*

"Wonderful choice! There is a fascinating story in here about two brothers and forty thieves."

Mateo's eyes lit up. "Ali Baba and Cassim," he muttered, proud to know their names.

"Wonderful, you know the story." Eleonor lowered her voice a bit and added, "If Cassim hadn't been easily persuaded by greed, they could have been a happy family."

"My friend Johnny told me all about it, but I haven't read it," Mateo clarified.

"Is that so?" Eleonor exclaimed. "We must correct that. Let's read it together after supper. Would you like that?"

"Yes, madam."

"Oh, you are such a dear." She laughed. "Call me Aunt Eleonor."

"Yes, Aunt Eleonor."

"Very well, then, we have a date." She returned the book to him. "Until then, keep it with you."

Lina was relieved that Eleonor had so masterfully cut through Mateo's shell. More than anything, she hoped he could enjoy his childhood. Facing their father's death, the sudden separation from his friends, and the relocation to the countryside had pretty much completely overturned his life. Amid all the change, he had grown more attached to Lina, withdrawing from others as if afraid and distrustful. He needed time to work things out, to feel safe again, and people like Eleonor would help speed the process.

"Your uncle will be in shortly. He's gone to feed the dogs." Eleonor guided Mateo to the sofa, where they sat next to each other.

"What breed are they?" Lina asked. Ever since a Doberman Pinscher had attacked her in London, she had been terrified of large breeds. The dog had sunk its teeth into her arm, its owner having forced the beast to let go only before it cut into her bones. She escaped with a few stitches, permanent scars, and a dreadful terror of large dogs.

"Rhodesian Ridgebacks, darling. They are marvelous beasts. You'll love them."

Lina swallowed hard. Hunting dogs, the Ridgebacks were known for their strength and speed. She would not like them.

"Oh my, there is rain on the horizon," Mrs. Lester noted, peering through the window at the sky. "I must remind Annie of the laundry still hanging on the line. Do excuse me." With a stiff nod, she was off.

"Last it rained, Annie forgot about the laundry," explained Eleonor, and just as she finished speaking, a thick, harsh voice roared from the foyer. "Here he comes now."

In a heartbeat, Mateo jumped up from the sofa and hid behind Lina, who stood still. Dressed in a black trench coat and high boots worn by hunters, Bartholomew appeared in the doorway, occupying almost all the space. His figure cast a long shadow into the library. Another little detail Lina had forgotten. Bartholomew was immense, his height and girth unnerving. His walrus mustache must take considerable time to maintain, and, unlike her father, Bartholomew bore a dark complexion with nut-brown hair and eyes. But that wasn't all that separated the brothers. There was the intense, menacing look in Bartholomew's eyes. Now, more than ever, his niece found it difficult to believe he was related to her father.

"I see you found your way here." This was Uncle Bartholomew. There would be no friendly greetings or the slightest commiseration for their misfortune.

"Why wouldn't we?" Lina muttered to herself.

"Come, come, dear," Eleonor encouraged her husband. "Have a seat."

The floor shook under his heavy footsteps as he walked across the library.

"Don't let him intimidate you. He'll warm up soon enough," Eleonor mumbled to her nephew.

Observing Bartholomew's harsh movements, Lina wondered if he had had an early encounter with the bottle. She remembered an incident where her father had pleaded with his younger brother to quit drinking. Though the memory was faint, Bartholomew's reaction—cursing at William for counseling him—remained vivid in her mind. Mateo's hand tightened on her skirt as he peeked out from behind her. Sensing the boy's fear, Lina reminded herself of the promise she'd made when her uncle had ordered them to the manor—he could control her fortune and freedom, but he would not bully them. With that in mind, she figured it wouldn't hurt to be cordial.

"It's nice to see you again." Lina squared her shoulders and extended her hand to him. "How are you, sir?"

Bartholomew bent over her, his foul breath confirming her suspicions about his drinking. He clasped her hand, which disappeared into his gigantic one, his grip seeming to test her pain tolerance. Forcing herself not to flinch, she yanked her hand away.

"I'll be better once the day is over," he growled, then took hold of Lina's arm in a flash. With a single tug, he pulled her aside, exposing Mateo. "Why are you hiding like a frightened creature?"

"Now, dear, let's not overwhelm the child." The speed with which Eleonor moved from the sofa to Mateo's side was remarkable. Safeguarding the boy, she tucked him under her arm.

Yet Eleonor's actions didn't stop Bartholomew from scrutinizing his nephew for an uncomfortable moment, as if his thoughts had taken him to days long gone. A smile was about to warm his features, just before he frowned, and snapping from his trance, he asked, "Now, little fellow, do you like to hunt?"

Eleonor and Lina looked at each other in surprise. Bartholomew's question was unexpected, and in Lina's case, unwelcome. Acid built in her stomach at the idea of Mateo killing animals. She had no intention of introducing her brother to such an activity. Her parents had never been fond of it, and neither was she. Mateo didn't respond.

"What's the matter? Cat got your tongue?" Bartholomew mocked.

"No, I still have my tongue, see?" As if gaining courage from the women, Mateo backed his words by sticking out his tongue.

"Ah, you are quick-witted, just like your old man was." Bartholomew chuckled. "Well then, answer my question. Have you ever been hunting?"

"No, I haven't."

Eleonor was swift to guide Mateo back to the sofa, removing him from Bartholomew's scrutiny. Aunt and nephew sat down together with no space between them. Lina felt stronger staying on her feet.

"Never been hunting, huh? That's unacceptable. It's an important skill for a man and a requirement in this household. I will take you."

Lina looked at her aunt in alarm. Lina might be prepared to deal with her uncle's thoughtless, gruff manner, but she could not handle Mateo spending time with the man, especially considering the proposed activity.

"Well, that's a thought for another day. They must be exhausted after the long trip." Reading the cry for help in her niece's eyes, Eleonor ended the discussion. "Lina, darling, would you ring for Mrs. Lester? She'll help you settle in."

Lina pulled the service cord hanging alongside the fireplace, thinking she liked her aunt more with each passing second. Though Eleonor wasn't a mother, her strong protective instincts were hard to miss.

Bartholomew shed his overcoat, discarding it on an armchair, and stomped to the credenza, where he pulled out a matchbox and two cigar tins. He tapped his fingers on them, deciding which one to light.

Not that one. Lina had never been able to stomach the Abdulla cigars.

As if mocking her silent plea, he selected the very one. And almost instantly, he was puffing like a chimney. "Have you gone through the schedule with them?" he asked Eleonor.

"No, as I said, we must not overwhelm them," she reiterated, beginning to look strained. "They've only just arrived."

Disregarding his wife's opinion, he informed, "Dinner is served at seven and breakfast at eight. I expect everyone to be in their seats on time." Lowering himself onto a settee that barely accommodated his figure, he let out another plume of smoke. "Teatime is at five, but since I'm not fond of the habit, do as you please."

Teatime, one of Lina's favorite memories of being here, was the tradition he disregarded. She was glad if that meant he would not be joining them.

"We'll do our best to be punctual, Uncle," Lina said diplomatically, but there was an undercurrent of insubordination in her remark. He had done nothing to deserve her respect, and his stringent commands made her want to disobey them all.

"Uncle!" He laughed hard, choking on the smoke.

Lina was confused. Why was he so amused?

No sooner had Bartholomew recovered from his self-inflicted discomfort than he growled, "You shall never call me Uncle, nor Bartholomew. Or, heaven forbid, both combined."

"Goodness gracious, Bartholomew!" sputtered Eleonor. "You can't mean that."

"Goodness gracious, woman!" Bartholomew sputtered back with a deadly glance. "I set the rules in this house, not you."

Why the big fuss? What was she supposed to call him? Lina thought of a few names that would suit him just fine. However, since Eleonor seemed on the verge of tears, Lina subdued her emotions and spoke in an effort to de-escalate the situation. "I'm at a loss. What shall we call you, then?"

"Sir. You shall call me sir."

Lina was relieved. After all, addressing him as Uncle bespoke a connection between them, one Lina wished to ignore.

"And before I forget," he added, "no one is allowed to leave their bedroom at night. Am I clear?"

"Crystal." Lina gave him a fake smile.

CHAPTER 3
UNCERTAINTY

The siblings' quarters were both equipped with four-poster Victorian beds, hefty wool rugs that Sofia had acquired during a trip to India, and fireplaces to tame the bitter winters. But best of all, the bedrooms were interconnected by a tunnel-like passage which brought the rooms together but maintained privacy.

Lina ambled to the window, the click-clack of shoes outside the library still echoing in her head. The day had grown gray, with thick clouds and drizzling rain. Fog hovered over the damp land but revealed the edge of the pond tucked back in the trees. Unlike their airy flat, darkness plagued the manor both inside and out, making Lina feel as if a changeling had replaced the joyful spirit of her childhood home. If not for a few lingering memories of happier times, she would think she'd stumbled into a gothic tale complete with a gloomy, foreboding keep. Back then, she'd had her parents, her safe harbor, especially during the daunting hours of the night. Now, she was the parent, soothing Mateo's fears—a task for which she felt inadequate.

It's just one year. We can survive it. Then, we'll move back to London and regain control of our lives. In her mind, it sounded easy. In practice it would be anything but.

Lina was startled from her worries when a disharmonious sound like clanging metal traveled the hallway just outside her bedroom. It came again, dancing at the edge of her discernment, elusive and haunting. It rang one more time, and at last, she recognized it.

The bloody clock. The eighteenth-century longcase, heavily carved with mystical creatures, had been passed down through generations of Laroches. Lina's mother had despised it, feeling the clock was better suited for a Transylvania castle than a country manor. Now that Lina thought about it, she was almost sure the clock had something to do with Mateo's history of waking at night while at Blackwater manor.

The pendulum within the clock struck again. With a sigh, Lina returned to gazing at the outside world, and a movement among the trees caught her eye. Drawing closer to the foggy pane, she watched a shape move to the water's edge, blending so well with its surroundings that had it been still, she would have missed it entirely.

The clock chimed a fifth time, and, at once, the shape headed toward the house. The mist swirled around the figure, seeming to pull it into its folds. Moving rapidly, it covered several yards, placing itself on higher ground where the fog was thinner. Lina took hold of the casement and leaned closer in curiosity. It now became obvious that it was a woman, but the way she moved…There was something peculiar about her, but Lina couldn't tell what it was.

Someone rapped on the door, distracting Lina from the window. When her gaze found the lawn again, the figure had vanished.

Another knock was followed by Mrs. Lester entering the bedroom with a stack of towels. As her eyes connected with Lina's, she said, "Excuse me, miss. I didn't think you were here."

"It's all right. Please, come in."

The housekeeper went straight to the armoire. "I'll store these on the top shelf. The bedding is fresh. We changed it yesterday."

"Thank you."

Mrs. Lester arranged the towels neatly on the armoire's top shelf and turned to examine the bedroom. "I presume Mateo is in his room?"

"He was asleep last I checked." Lina's voice was colorless.

A light of curiosity crossed Mrs. Lester's semblance. "Whatever is the matter? You look unsettled. Are you ill?"

"I'm afraid the journey from London wore me out." Her answer was partial. She omitted being unsettled by the unexpected chiming of the clock and the strange woman in the yard.

The housekeeper touched Lina's hand. "Oh my, you are dreadfully cold. Come, now. Sit by the fire."

Lina settled into the old leather chair, a relic handed down for generations. It creaked under her weight, but despite its complaining, it held.

Adding a few logs to the fireplace and picking up the poker, Mrs. Lester prodded the pile, dislocating and relocating smaller pieces of burnt wood and ashes, fanning it with a newspaper, and repeating the process. "Ah, there you are," she exclaimed when blazing tongues of flame shot up. "That will do."

"That feels very nice. Thank you." Lina edged closer to the grate, extending her hands to warm them.

"Your color has returned," the housekeeper observed, pleased. "Is there anything else I can do for you?"

"You have done enough."

"Very well, then."

Lina closed her eyes, and the image of the woman hurrying through the fog flashed through her mind. Was she one of the staff? "Mrs. Lester, wait."

"Yes?" The housekeeper stepped back into the room.

"Who else works in the house?"

Mrs. Lester's face contorted in a curious manner as if her question was out of place.

Lina hurried to explain, "It's been a while since I've been here, and I imagine things have changed."

"I don't think they have changed that much," Mrs. Lester responded. "As you may remember, apart from Annie and me, there are four others. The twin sisters—Dollie the cook, and her sister, Maggie—work in the kitchen. I understand they have worked here for quite some time."

"Yes, they have." Lina had almost forgotten about them, and for good reason. Tall and slim as candlesticks with long, pale faces, the nearly identical pair kept to themselves. Their presence had frightened Lina as a child, and she'd avoided them and the kitchen altogether. They reminded her of the witches she read about, and her young imagination had gone as far as to convince her that someday the sisters would throw her into a cauldron of boiling water. Of course, she could laugh at the idea now, but their presence was still a bit unsettling.

Mrs. Lester continued, "There is also the groundskeeper, Mr. Krammer. After his sons settled in London and his wife passed away, he permanently moved to Blackwater to avoid the daily journey from town." Lina had a vague recollection of him—a sturdy man with dark hair and an aquiline nose, always moving about the yard with purpose. "He also oversees the stable, though Fred, a young man from the neighboring farm, comes twice daily to care for the horses. And last, but not least, the chauffeur, Mr. Walton. Since his services are required a few times a week, he lives in town."

"That's all the help?"

"I'm afraid so."

Before Lina could ask another question, the housekeeper withdrew, shutting the door behind her. The logs shifted as the flames spread, and as Lina watched the fire dancing in the grate, her thoughts returned to the mysterious woman. There was no reason to disbelieve Mrs. Lester. There was no other maid apart from Annie. And the cook and her sister never abandoned their domain. Even if they did, Lina would have recognized them.

Who in the world had she seen? Was it the same woman who'd walked past the library? Was she hiding in the house? Not likely, but possible. The manor had plenty of rooms and corridors no one ever visited. No, she was not hiding—she moved about freely. But if that was the case, either Mrs. Lester had lied to her, or her imagination was overacting from all the stress.

Lina located the monstrous clock in one of the passages near her dormitory. The carved figures stared at her with mocking eyes. One of the figures was a faun with spiral horns and a curly beard that she had always referred to as the devil. Her father had read bedtime stories about the fauns and how they played music and chased the goddess nymphs. Lina had never noticed it, but she now saw it clearly—a reed pipe in the faun's hands. She could picture Mateo watching the clock in terror. Perhaps it was the mystical creature piping out the devilish tune of each hour that had given her brother nightmares whenever they visited Blackwater. The figure looked so real it was mesmerizing to watch. Lina stood there for the longest time, waiting for it to move. But she knew the faun was only wood and the clock lay dormant, the pendulum still, the device broken.

But how? She had heard it. Bewildered, she headed back to her bedroom, recalling another oddity—the candelabrums. After supper, Lina watched Mrs. Lester carry out the tedious task of lighting candles throughout the main areas, including the hallway just outside the siblings' quarters. Understandably, the electricity would be off to conserve energy, but why the need for any light source? To light whose way? After all, Bartholomew had prohibited them from roaming the house at night.

Ugh, Bartholomew. Lina thanked Providence he had drunk himself to sleep before dinner, relieving her of the discomfort of his presence. She entered her bedroom, then traversed the short passage to Mateo's. He sat on his bed reading "Aladdin and the Wonderful Lamp."

"What took you so long?" he complained.

"Long?" Lina dropped beside him. "It's been only minutes."

"Did you find the clock?"

"I did."

"And?"

"It's broken I think."

"Since you don't like it, that's good." His innocent eyes found hers. "Isn't it?"

"Yes, I suppose it is." She tickled his ribs, and, in between giggles, Mateo wrestled to return the gesture. As their laughs collided, the worries in Lina's heart faded for a moment. Mateo was her only joy in this world. Without him, life would have no purpose, no light.

Lina tickled him harder, and he snorted with laughter. He then rolled out of her reach and wheezed, "Stop it, Lina. It's my turn."

"I'll give you thirty seconds," she conceded and lowered her arms.

Mateo jumped on her and went straight for her ribs. She laughed, wriggled, and turned. When he was satisfied with his revenge, exhausted, he sat beside her and picked up the book. "Do you want to read?"

"Yes."

They started where Mateo had left off, and he fell asleep muttering something about finding a magic lamp. His breathing turned soft but deep. All worries had left him for now. Lina tucked the blankets around his shoulders and kissed his cheek.

She tiptoed to the door that led to the outside hallway and secured the lock before returning to her bedroom through the connecting passage. A flash of lightning illuminated the sky, spilling light through the window. Thunder followed in its wake, and soon, rain pelted the house. *So much for a peaceful night.* Yearning for rest, she slipped between the silk sheets, but the fabric was an instant reminder of death; her father's coffin had been lined with the same material. She pushed the memory away and closed her eyes, trapping the tears inside. *Don't think of anything. Just go to sleep.* Seconds turned into minutes and minutes into hours until she finally drifted into a restless slumber.

Lina stood amid the blinding fog. "Lina, Lina," her father called. She followed his voice, but he was so distant, so unreachable. She waited for him to call again, but instead of his familiar voice, she heard the wild screaming of a terrified woman.

"Run, run, run!" Lina commanded herself, but her legs refused to obey. The mist grew thicker, heavier. A cold hand traveled down her arm, accompanied by the sound of a slamming door.

Lina bolted upright. Was it the intensity of the dream that awoke her or something else? She listened. The storm had abated. The outside world was quiet, holding its breath, just as she was. She glanced at the fireplace, where the fire struggled to remain alive. What was left of the glowing embers only amplified the layers of shadow crossing the room.

The floorboards creaked. The noise was too quick to determine if it was the natural contraction and expansion of the wood or some external force being applied to it. She squinted into the darkest patches in the corners for movement, but there was no motion of any kind. There. The creaking again. Then again. She had no doubts now, someone crept about, but whether in the corridor or somewhere closer she couldn't tell. A clunking noise came next. The lock had turned, and the door groaned on its hinges as it parted just enough to let in a sliver of light from the candelabrum in the hallway.

Fearing that whoever was about to enter had ill intentions, she slid out of bed, and took a defensive stance. Her instincts told her to find something to use as a weapon, but she couldn't think of anything. With fisted hands, she watched the door swing inward, inch by inch. There was now sufficient clarity to see that it had not been unlocked from the outside, but from inside her room. No one was coming in, but someone was going out. In disbelief, Lina exclaimed, "Mateo! Where are you going?"

Silent as the grave, the small figure exited the bedroom. He had never done this. She shouldn't have let him take such a long nap, but it was too late for regrets. Guided by the glow of the candelabrums, she hurried after him. At the end of the corridor, she saw Mateo descending the staircase. Afraid to lose sight of him, she hit the light switch, but there was no response. Brilliant. The storm must have cut the power.

"Mateo, stop. Stop." Her voice chased him down the steps and echoed throughout the foyer below, but he was moving fast, undeterred by her pleas. "Mateo, stop right there. Right now!"

Mateo neither flinched nor looked back.

She took the steps two at a time to catch him, her nightgown tangling around her legs.

He fast approached the front entrance.

"Mateo!" her voice boomed, and then she remembered how her uncle had ordered them to stay in their rooms at night. If he caught them, heaven only knew how they might suffer. She threw a look over her shoulder as she landed at the bottom of the staircase. Hopefully no one had heard her yell. Her focus returned to the foyer. Mateo was nowhere in sight, but she noticed the candelabrum on the side table had been extinguished, though only recently, for smoke still rose from the blackened wicks. She examined the front door. Locked and bolted. He was still inside.

The rain started again, highlighted by intermittent lightning. Thunder followed, and mingled with the rumbling, Lina heard a musical little laugh. With the menace of her uncle at the forefront of her thoughts, she whispered as loud as she dared. "Mateo, show yourself this instant."

The laugh came again, this time in the form of a prolonged, irritating sound, like the notes of an untuned piano. Lina spun toward the north passage. Lightning illuminated the high windows, and just before the bend, she saw a small figure in the vestiges of light. She started after him, feeling her way until she stood before the three doors at the end. Which one?

As if answering her question, a banging came from the kitchen, further rattling her nerves. As she crossed the threshold, another bang shook the air, and a wave of cold air hit her. Her gaze darted to the back door, which stood wide open, welcoming the gusts of wind. Again, the door slammed against the wall with a boom, rebounding halfway. *No, no, no!* He'd gone outside.

Lina rushed across the kitchen and out into the storm, flinching at the heavy droplets that beat against her. Raising her hand to shield her eyes, she instantly noticed something out of place in the landscape, near the pond. Though it was too dark and too far for her to be sure, she couldn't afford to ignore it. She waded through the saturated grounds with determination, but with each step she took, the pond seemed to move farther away.

She pressed on until she reached the spot, drenched and miserable— only to be disappointed. Instead of her brother, she found an evergreen. The dread of losing him filled her—this was madness, and she was under its control. "Mateo, where are you? Please answer me."

There was no response from the boy, but as a mercy from heaven, the rain lightened. Lina drew a calming breath and ran her hand across her face to push the water away. Her gaze then darted to a sudden flash that came from the house. A light appeared, then disappeared, rapidly skipping from window to window. Was Mateo back inside? Again, she observed the restless light jumping from one windowpane to another as if taunting her. However, before venturing back, she needed to make sure he wasn't out here. While the rain morphed into a mere drizzle, she hurried along the edge of the pond. Though visibility was low, she could tell there was nothing around that resembled the boy.

The light now hovered at one window. She retraced her steps, fighting the weight of her sodden nightgown. One yard, two yards, and she heard a rustle from somewhere among the shrubs. Lina stopped in her tracks. "Mateo?" The noise grew louder, and something moved. Then she saw two sets of glowing eyes through the obscurity. The dogs. Knowing she was no match for the Ridgebacks, she bolted. Their vicious barking grew louder as she closed the distance to the door. The dogs seemed determined to enforce their master's rule not to wander Blackwater at night.

It's too far. Too far. Strands of wet hair clung to her face. Her vision blurred, but she kept moving. To her right, a dog growled, and she felt it brush against her leg. The other dog caught up to her, and now they flanked her on either side. Lightning illuminated the yard. She glanced at them. Their ears lay flat, and their upper lips were curled back, their sharp teeth bared. This was it—the end of her. Her jaw clenched as she waited for them to tackle her to the ground.

A clap of thunder boomed across the sky—the loudest yet. Immediately, the animals halted, tilted their heads, and began to howl. Those brief seconds of pause awarded Lina the finish line. She slammed the door behind her and secured the lock, panting. Hands on her knees and bent over, she drew short breaths to stabilize her heartbeat. There was no way she should have been able to outrun them.

As the howling subsided somewhere in the yard, a light pierced the kitchen from the corridor, blinding her. "Lina, is that you?" Mrs. Lester asked.

"Yes, Mrs. Lester. It's me." Lina raised her hand, shielding her eyes, as she realized that the housekeeper had been the prowler with the light. Mateo might be outside after all.

"Good gracious." Mrs. Lester pointed the torch, a small battery-operated device, to the pool of water around Lina's feet. "You went out in the storm? What possessed you to do such a thing?"

"Mateo is missing," Lina choked out, a million horrifying scenarios playing through her head. "I followed him outside, but he is gone."

"Nonsense," Mrs. Lester sputtered.

"Please, help me find him." Lina's fortitude failed her, and she broke down sobbing.

"Now, now, get a grip on yourself. He is sound asleep in his bed." Mrs. Lester unwrapped the shawl from her shoulders and placed it around Lina's. "Come now, let's get you into some dry clothes before you catch a cold."

"No, I have to find Mateo."

"Believe me—you'll find him in his bedroom. I was just there. The wind must have woken me, and I thought to check on you both. He is where he should be, but your door was open. You were the one missing," Mrs. Lester said with a hint of reproach. "Come. Let's go." Not giving Lina a choice, the housekeeper guided her out of the kitchen, down the corridor, and up the stairs.

"The torch is more efficient than candles," Lina remarked as they passed by a candelabrum on a side table. "Don't you think?"

"It is for short term use." Mrs. Lester extended the torch to Lina as they entered the bedroom. "Here, take this. Hopefully, the power will be back on soon, but it's not likely."

Lina hurried to Mateo's room through the connecting passage. She aimed the light at the bed and found her brother tucked under the heavy blanket, peacefully asleep. She lifted the covers and touched his clothes —dry as a bone. She ran her fingers through his hair—also dry. She felt his hand, and it was warm.

"Please, Lina," whispered Mrs. Lester from the passage. "You must change quickly."

Her shivering drove her to heed the housekeeper's words, and she hastened back to her room, a pounding headache coming on. Mrs. Lester handed her a nightgown from the armoire. Lina stepped out of her wet one, swiftly dried off with a towel, and threw on the dry one. She then slipped into bed just as a distant cockerel crowed, welcoming the new day.

Vivid images of the boy scurrying down the corridors danced around and around in Lina's head. The image of the dogs came next, their vicious growling and sharp teeth making her cringe. But then a more ominous thought surfaced—Uncle Bartholomew. He couldn't find out she'd disobeyed his rule.

"Mrs. Lester, please don't mention this to my aunt and uncle."

Mrs. Lester prodded the fire for what Lina thought was a long time before turning from the grate. A trace of reserve, of wariness, veiled her countenance. It was only now that Lina recognized the weight of what she had asked—to betray her employers' trust by keeping information from them. Certainly, Bartholomew would appreciate the news.

"I'll do as you ask just this once," Mrs. Lester agreed.

Lina drew in a long breath, then exhaled in relief.

"Just this once," the housekeeper repeated.

"Don't worry. I'm not planning to make a habit out of it."

Mrs. Lester retrieved the coverlet from the chair and spread it over the already heavy bedding. "There. You should be warm in no time."

"Mrs. Lester, I'm not insane. I saw Mateo leave. Maybe he circled back without me noticing."

"Get some rest," the housekeeper advised. "It was just a dream. Just a dream." She collected the wet clothes and reached for the doorknob.

The door closed, and Lina was left to her thoughts. In her despair to make sense of the night's events, she recalled that Blackwater had been built with secret passages. But she also knew that after the Great War, they had been closed off—along with their hidden vents and viewpoints. Nevertheless, even without the concealed passages, the house was a labyrinth, and Mateo could have somehow crept back, for someone had blown out the candles in the foyer. He also could have unlocked the kitchen door and, faced with the rain, not gone outside. At the pond, she had simply mistaken him for the evergreen. It was dark and rainy, after all. And while it was easy to rationalize it away, Lina was sure it was not a dream.

CHAPTER 4
ILLUSIONS

Lina took a stroll in the gardens. The storm had left a chill in the air, but the rising sun was gaining strength, making the temperature pleasant. Last night's events now seemed distant, the details already slipping from Lina's mind. Mateo had left the bedroom; she'd heard his laugh and followed him through the house. Again, she thought of the possibility that instead of going outside he had slipped back into his room unnoticed. When Mateo crawled into her bed this morning, she had asked him about the incident.

"Last night? I didn't get out of bed," he asserted.

"Are you certain?" she pressed cautiously so as not to alarm him.

He nodded emphatically.

"Not even to use the toilet?"

"I told you already, Lina. I didn't get up. I didn't even have any dreams."

She shook her head in dismay, inclined to believe that if Mateo remembered anything from the previous night, he wouldn't be able to keep quiet about it. If it had been him, he must have been in a profound sleep—but he had never had a problem with sleepwalking.

Was it just a restless night overpowered by a clamorous storm and deep shadows—nothing after all? Well, that nothing could have gotten her eaten by the dogs. *They* were quite real. At breakfast, Mrs. Lester confirmed that the animals freely patrolled the grounds after dusk. During the day, if not with Bartholomew, they were in the doghouse—a fenced-in log structure at the north side of the property. Lina made a mental note to never go near there.

Cutting through the geranium garden, she thanked Providence that Mrs. Lester had kept the night's activities confidential. Bartholomew and Eleonor's quarters were in the opposite wing, away from the back lawn. And muffled by the torrential downpour, they had not heard the racket. The last thing Lina needed was for Bartholomew to make her life worse than it already was.

Mateo skipped through the front entrance, struggling to put on his coat. "Lina, Lina!"

"Hello, young man!" Lina smiled and knelt on the pebble path, ready to embrace him.

His short legs picked up speed. "I missed you," he said, falling into her arms.

"No. You couldn't have." She ruffled his hair. "It hasn't been that long."

"I did."

"Well, you should've come with me on my walk through the gardens."

"I told you, I like short walks, and you take long ones."

"It's good exercise."

"Tell that to Sir. He needs it." Mateo was so observant.

Lina laughed hard. However, she advised, "Even though that is true, don't repeat it, all right?"

"Why?"

"Because it will stir Uncle Bartholomew's temper."

Mateo's shoulders drooped. "Oh."

"How was the house tour?" Lina asked, trying to steer his thoughts in a different direction. "Did Mrs. Lester show you everything?"

"Well..." He wrapped Lina's hair around his fingers. "No."

"No?"

"She only showed me the painting gallery. Aunt Eleonor showed me the rest."

"Did she?"

"Yep. I know where everything is now."

"Splendid." Just as she said the word, she became aware that it might not be a splendid thing after all. If Mateo wandered the house, he could play a never-ending game of hide-and-seek. Choosing to preempt the opportunity to discover where those secret places might be, she proposed, "You'll have to show me your favorite spots."

He giggled, clearly pleased with her proposition.

"Would you like to do that now?"

"No," he answered. "I want to show you something I found."

"What is it?"

"I'm not telling." He swayed on his feet. "You have to see it. It's in the conservatory."

"Let's go, then. I'll race you to the front door." She broke into a run before he could react.

"That's not fair. You're cheating!" He ran to catch up.

Lina slowed a few paces from the finish line, allowing him to pass her.

"I won! I won!"

Seeing Mateo's surprised but prideful countenance was a joy. That, coupled with his warming up to the household, brought her comfort. He was adjusting better than she had anticipated.

"Indeed, you did." She laughed. "I must be growing old and feeble."

"Nuh-uh, I'm just getting faster."

They came into the foyer and quickly shed their coats.

"C'mon, Lina. Hurry up."

She almost had to break into a trot to keep up with Mateo as he hurried ahead. Mixed with their voices, the sound of their shoes against the tile floor echoed off the long passageway. And just like the day they had arrived at Blackwater, the uncanny sensation that unseen eyes watched them came over her. It was a strange feeling, as if she were blindfolded yet she knew there was someone else in the corridor. But that, of course, was illogical; apart from Mateo and her, no one else was here. She turned her thoughts to their destination.

The conservatory had been her mother's pride and joy. Sofia had loved sitting in the sunlight of the greenhouse. Adding exotic plants now and then, she had turned it into a masterpiece, a garden neatly trimmed with sculpted shrubs and beautiful borders. The siblings took the final turn and halted in front of the glass doors, and, for a second or two, Lina wondered where they were. She opened her mouth to say something, but nothing came out.

"C'mon," Mateo urged. When she didn't respond, he shook her arm. "Lina, what's wrong?"

"I..." Her gaze slowly fell to Mateo. "It's so different." Through the grimy glass, she could see that the vegetation grew tangled and unrestrained, an Amazonian jungle in the west part of Gloucestershire. Lina's heart sank to her stomach; her mother's favorite place was a frightful mess, Lina's hopes of reviving good memories annihilated.

Mateo pressed his shoulder against the door. With the plants on the other side pressing against it, it was heavy.

"Here, let me." Lina pushed it open, and they slipped inside.

The muggy air surrounded them as they fought their way through the overgrowth to move about. *Oh my.* Lina's eyes followed the thick vines that crawled up the soiled glass walls. All sorts of slithery things filled her imagination, some of them hidden behind the stems, ready to strike. Conversely, the environment didn't bother Mateo as he was fascinated with insects and all related things.

"This way," Mateo encouraged, maneuvering through the tight space with ease and purpose.

The faster they got this done and left, the better. Lina hurried to keep up, fighting the intrusive reach of the branches.

"Almost there," Mateo announced, disappearing behind the ageratina that had grown wild since Lina saw it last. It was one of the only plants she remembered well, her mother having made a big fuss about it when it arrived from America. She'd even made a solo trip to Blackwater to introduce the compact, medium-sized evergreen shrub to the greenhouse. Sofia had been fascinated by its opposite leaves and small tubular flowers.

"What in the world?" Lina cried out as Eleonor stepped into the path.

The petite woman had been hidden by the statue of a cherubic figure with wings unfurled.

"Dear me. I didn't mean to startle you," Eleonor promptly apologized.

"I didn't expect to see anyone, that is all," Lina answered, her voice a bit shaky.

"I should have told you. I spend a lot of time here." Eleonor wiped her brow with an earth-stained hand. "I just finished adding soil to the mandevillas."

"I see." Lina's gaze swept over the freshly potted plants. Why in the world would anyone want to add to this chaos? She knew her aunt loved nature, but not the confined type. Never had she anticipated the delicate woman to enjoy the greenhouse, especially in its current condition. She envisioned Eleonor in a large straw hat, working on the flower borders around the house—perhaps that was a childhood memory.

"I love letting them grow." Eleonor must have read Lina's expression of disbelief, for she further explained, "It's part of life's natural cycle, and cutting them down would be a crime. I couldn't bear it, for they have a soul of their own."

The crime was to not trim them back. This was a total disaster. Lina managed a smile that hurt from the inside.

Mateo, who had momentarily skipped ahead, reappeared. "Hello, Aunt Eleonor."

"Hello, darling." Eleonor glanced at her shiny wristwatch. "Oh, dear, I've lost track of time. I'm afraid I must return to the kitchen. Mrs. Lester has been pestering me about tonight's menu, and I've finally decided. How does a steak-and-kidney pie sound?"

"Yuck," Mateo said.

"I'm afraid he is not fond of kidneys," Lina excused, hoping their aunt didn't take offense. Eleonor smiled, but behind the smile lay a sentiment Lina couldn't place.

"Right, then. I'll ask Dollie to fix something else for you," their aunt decided.

"I hope it's not too much trouble." The last thing Lina wanted was to burden Dollie with more work. "He can have leftovers."

Mateo looked at his sister sideways. He wasn't fond of leftovers either.

"Nonsense. It's no trouble at all," Eleonor assured her and took her leave.

Lina stood brooding for an instant, watching where Eleonor had disappeared through a curtain of greenery. If last night's journey in the storm didn't feel real, neither did this place, though they were both very much a reality. Mateo grasped Lina's hand and guided her to the other side of the evergreens where they emerged in a clean, square space. Here, the plants were meticulously kept, the floor well swept. The order was shocking in the sea of chaos, an island with a round metal table and two chairs at its center. A sudden idea occurred to Lina, and it felt right —this could very well be Eleonor's haven away from Bartholomew. Indeed, he would never visit the place. Maybe she preferred the disorder as it tendered a hidden refuge.

"Here it is." Mateo tapped his fingers on an aged tin with rough edges that was resting on the table.

"Fancy indeed," observed Lina. "What's in it?"

"Sit down. I'll show you." He spoke with enough enthusiasm to pique Lina's curiosity.

She thoroughly inspected the chair before sitting down. "Good, no critters."

Mateo stood next to her, and his tiny fingers pried the box open, a grin stretching across his face as he extracted a wooden train. Clearly enchanted by it, he aligned the four-piece toy in front of his sister and, pointing at each one, described them. "This one is the locomotive. This one is a boxcar—they can carry anything. This is called a cattle car—they move animals from one farm to another. And this one is the caboose."

"They are beautiful." Lina wrapped her arm around his waist, bringing him closer. "May I?"

"You may."

With her free hand, she picked up the caboose. It was a work of art, its lines and markings revealing a precision learned through years of woodcarving. She flipped it over and found the letters *TJ* discreetly engraved near the bottom. Under the inscription, there was a small stamp depicting a buzzard inside a circle. Mateo opened his mouth to say something but must have thought better of it because he closed it again.

"What were you going to say?"

"Nothing, nothing." Mateo took the caboose and put it back in the line. "Do you like it, Lina?"

"I like it very much. Where did you find it?"

"It was over there," he nodded toward the maze behind them, "inside a pot."

"Inside a pot?"

"Uh-huh."

"I wonder whose it was." Lina was certain she hadn't seen it before.

Mateo shrugged.

"Shall we wash up for luncheon?"

"Do we have to?"

"We do."

"Fine." Mateo stored the train inside its box.

They stepped away from the table, and Lina noticed that he'd left the toy behind. "Aren't you going to bring it with us?"

"No."

"Don't you want to play with it?"

"Yes, but it has to stay here."

"Why?" Lina's eyebrows furrowed with curiosity.

"Just because."

"All right, but I don't want you coming here too often. It's gloomy."

Mateo shrugged again but didn't respond.

Since he was in good spirits, she didn't press him. They left the conservatory and the train behind.

Later, when Bartholomew summoned Lina to his office, she dragged her feet down the corridor, wishing Eleonor were present. The latter was good at keeping the beast on a short leash. The man had a volatile temper, and Lina detested confrontation. Yet, like with the dogs, exposing her fear would only serve to make her more vulnerable. She searched her mind for something to fortify her courage, with thoughts of Mateo's education coming to her rescue. This was her opportunity to bring it up. She could teach him a few subjects, but he needed proper instruction. Besides, there was nothing better than being around other children to ease Mateo's transition into his new life. School was the perfect place for him to make new friends.

His office came into view, and she hesitated. How could a person's unpredictable temper inflict so much uneasiness on others? Lina reminded herself that everyone had a humane side, even if minuscule. If she could successfully appeal to that part of Bartholomew, maybe he would allow them to return to London. Nonetheless, her hand trembled as she tapped the door.

"Yes, yes! Come in, all right," her uncle barked from inside.

With the turn of the knob, she let herself in and was greeted by a wall of smoke. She waved her hands to push back the cloud, and somewhere in the haze, she found several sets of animal eyes peering down at her from their eternal places on the wall. Lina couldn't help but feel commiseration for the beautiful creatures. Her father had not been a hunter and would never have allowed such a display at Blackwater. The deer skulls must have been hung here quite recently.

Choking on the smoke, Lina let out a wheezing sound. Bartholomew left his shabby chair, the permanence of his bulk imprinted on the leather. He stomped over to the window, unlatched the glass, and heaved it open. A wave of fresh air swept over the office, banishing the oppressive atmosphere.

"There, that should help," he grumbled.

"Thank you." Lina choked again, then swallowed hard to stop the intense itching at the back of her throat.

"Come closer," he invited, wasting no time in retaking his seat.

As Lina tentatively stepped forward, a deep growl came from behind her uncle, and last night's assailants emerged beside their master's throne. She wasn't sure, but the dogs, with their muscular frames, beautiful brown coats, and hallmark stripe of backward-growing hair indicative of their breed, seemed taller than they should be. Their glossy eyes fixed upon Lina, and they flashed sharp, long teeth. She remembered those teeth quite vividly, along with the terror she had experienced last night. The animals lowered their heads as they inched closer, and without warning, the gurgling in their throats transformed into an ear-piercing bark. Lina jerked, and though the natural impulse to run seized her, she was too terrified to move.

"Enough. Back down!" Bartholomew ordered, and the dogs retreated. While never losing sight of the visitor, they sat on their haunches alongside the man they obeyed. "Don't just stand there. Sit down," he said to Lina.

She had read once that dogs identified with their owners, not just in temperament but also in appearance. Lina couldn't deny there was a measure of truth in that. She looked at Bartholomew, then at the Rhodesian Ridgebacks, then back at the man, with a certain distrust. "I prefer to stand." She halted behind the high-back Louis XVI chair, shielding herself from the dogs as well as from the man.

"Suit yourself," Bartholomew grumbled as his piercing eyes fixated on her.

There was an awkward pause while Lina wondered if she was supposed to say something but considered it best not to.

"How are you adjusting to country life?" Bartholomew finally spoke.

Lina didn't know what to make of his question. Caring about others' feelings was out of character for him. "I'm not sure yet," she responded cautiously. "It's too soon to say."

"With time, you'll find us quite pleasant to be around." He produced a crooked smile.

Was he making fun of her? Bartholomew's friendly mood was somewhat disturbing. However, Lina was aware that such a favorable moment wouldn't come around often. Before she lost her wits, she said, "Sir, when will Mateo be enrolled in the local school?"

"They are out for the season." Bartholomew ran a finger through his mustache. "But for the time being, I'll check other options and let you know."

Had he looked into it already? She was intrigued but questioning him would be foolish. "Thank you."

Bartholomew readjusted his weight, the seat protesting with a mixture of loose screws and splintering wood. He cleared his throat and started, "The reason I wanted to see you is simple. Eleonor's nephew will visit us shortly."

How odd. Why had he bothered to convey the news? No doubt, Eleonor or Mrs. Lester could have done the same.

"His name is Bray Hamilton, heir of the Hamiltons of Cornwall," he rambled on. "The poor chap has recently returned from active duty in Palestine and needs a break from the buzz of London."

Lina didn't recall the Hamilton surname being spoken at home. But why would she? Eleonor's parents had passed away soon after she married into the Laroche family—though she did remember her parents mentioning Eleonor's sister, Beatrice, who was fifteen years older. Lina wondered, "Is Mr. Hamilton Beatrice's son?"

"That's right," Bartholomew said. "Now, anyone who risks their life serving their country deserves the highest respect. Bray is to be treated as nobility. I won't tolerate any indifference toward him."

"I've been raised to mind my manners," she reminded Bartholomew, unable to stop herself.

"Properly?" He laughed cynically, his walrus mustache bouncing off his fat lip. "Let me make this clear—if Bray wants something, he is to have it."

Lina shifted from one leg to the other, her fingers tightened on the back of the Louis XVI chair, her exasperation rising. His words could mean a million different things. And she wasn't about to sell her soul to the devil by agreeing to something she would never do. Seconds of silence passed while she struggled to determine how to respond.

Bartholomew's expression changed from semibearable to menacing. "Is that understood?" He smashed his open hand on the desk, the Ridgebacks jumped to their feet.

"*My conduct will be irreproachable and worthy of all praise,*" the unmistakable voice of a woman coached. Lina glanced over her shoulder, and her heart faltered when she saw no one. But the dogs heard it. A low guttural sound rose in their throat, their gazes directed to the spot just beyond her.

"Jasper, Ruppert, enough!" Bartholomew commanded, but instead of obeying their master, their growling exploded. "Bloody dogs! What's gotten into you? Shut up!" When the animals refused to be silent, he retrieved a wooden cane with a handle shaped like a king cobra's head.

Lina held her breath.

Two long strides brought Bartholomew to the dogs. He hit the end of the cane on the floor three times. "Enough! Get back!" Thankfully that was sufficient for the Ridgebacks to return to their spots by Bartholomew's chair. Had he struck them in the past? Was that the reason they obeyed when the cane came out?

Lina's gaze fell on the weapon in his hand. Would he hit her? Unpredictable, ill-tempered—the list went on. What chance did she stand against a man like him?

"Now, you haven't given me an answer," Bartholomew pressed, waving the cane in the air like a wand.

"I assure you my conduct will be irreproachable and worthy of all praise." Instinctively, she repeated what the mysterious voice had said.

Bartholomew observed her as if processing the statement. Finally, he threatened, "There will be severe repercussions for disobedience." He punctuated his words by pointing the weapon at Lina. "You may leave now."

Before he uttered the last syllable, she was on her way out. What a hideous, wretched man. If there was a humane side to him, it was so well hidden that it would never be found. She closed the door a little harder than intended. *If he ever touches Mateo or me...*She walked briskly down the corridor and didn't stop until she reached the foyer.

The brightness filtering in through the door's sidelight was inviting. She stood before it, the courtyard—the entryway to her dungeon—beckoned just on the other side of the glass. One year! How would she ever make it? She lowered her chin, closed her eyes, and allowed her emotions to subside. Her uncle's behavior and Mr. Hamilton's upcoming visit, she would process later. Right now, she would focus on the mysterious voice she'd heard.

There had been a woman in the room, but how was it even possible? Unless... It was an absurd idea. Lina reminded herself that she didn't believe in the otherworldly, but she couldn't stop her mind from going there. No. There must be a logical explanation—there always was. Blackwater's secret passages? What if someone had reopened them? But who, and for what purpose?

She hadn't recognized the voice, but whoever it was had known just how to appease the beast in her uncle and protect Lina's integrity. The words Lina had repeated had been perfectly thought out. The more she contemplated, the more muddled she became. *Ugh. I must control my mind, or I'll find myself in an asylum.* She opened her eyes and found the daylight diminishing, bringing with it a sense of foreboding; Blackwater wasn't safe during the long hours of the night.

Preying on her fears, a noise like the rustling of silk startled her. She whirled around and drew near the south passage, where she saw the figure of a woman at the far end. The first thing that struck Lina was how the woman's black hair was arranged in circular layers, almost like a crown. The hem of her dark dress hung almost to the floor, the edges of a white apron peeking from the sides as she vanished around the bend.

A maid? Was this the same woman Lina had seen crossing the grounds? And perhaps the woman who had just spoken to her in the office? Lina's heartbeat accelerated in anticipation of discovering the woman's identity as she dashed after her down the hallway and around the corner. There she saw the woman climb the service stairs the staff used for quick access to the second floor. Lina propelled herself up the steps just in time to see the woman veering into the east corridor, moving with incredible speed. Lina pressed on, afraid to lose sight of her quarry, but, to her delight, the woman took the short passage that ended with the staircase to the attic—the only access in and out of it. Good. There was no way to elude her now.

With the day well-advanced and little illumination in the corridor, the attic steps were hardly visible. Lina placed a foot on the bottom step but then hesitated. Something felt terribly wrong. A chill ran up her arms, and her stomach knotted. Still, her curiosity urged her forward.

A grating sound called her attention to the top of the staircase, where the door parted an inch or two. Her instincts begged her to turn back, but even as the knot in her stomach tightened, her legs pushed her upward. She climbed one step, then another. The door protested on its hinges again as someone pulled it open. Lina froze midway up the steps. A woman in a gray dress emerged from the shadows above. Her pale face cut through the obscurity, a lifeless candlestick raised in her right hand.

At the sight of Lina, the woman's face turned a shade whiter, if that were even possible. "Are you looking for something, miss?" she asked Lina, her tone seemed to imply that the latter shouldn't be there.

"Maggie...I..." Lina paused. Never would she have imagined one of the twins here. Maggie hardly left her assigned area of the mansion. Furthermore, the attic housed only decommissioned furniture and other heirlooms accumulated over the generations of Laroches. The house staff had little or no reason to visit the space.

"Miss, may I help you?" Maggie's fingers tightened around the metal candleholder.

The rising tension confirmed to Lina that something was out of place. Was Maggie hiding the mysterious maid in the attic? If she was, there must be a good explanation. At any rate, since Mrs. Lester had denied the existence of the maid, Lina didn't feel safe bringing it up. And when the intensity in Maggie's gaze demanded an answer, a guarded lie rescued Lina. "I'm looking for Annie. I just saw her go up the steps."

Maggie must have suspected that Lina was hot on the woman's trail, but the mention of Annie brought a look of surprise from Maggie. "Annie? You are mistaken. No one is up here apart from me and a bunch of old things." The door shrieked as Maggie shut it behind her with a force that said it would stay shut. She started her descent.

"Could you have missed her?" Lina pressed.

"No." Maggie towered over Lina, blocking her path and her view of the attic entrance. "Why would anybody be up here?"

Again, Lina felt Maggie's words were directed at her, and she wanted to say, *That's precisely what I would like to ask you*, but Maggie's imposing personality made her think better of it. In any case, it was apparent that the twin wasn't going to disclose the truth.

"I see..." Lina muttered, but the only thing she saw was the candlestick in Maggie's hand. The attic had an electrical connection. True, it was a single bulb, but her father had spared no expense to be among the privileged country folk who enjoyed electricity. Besides, a torch would be more efficient if Maggie were searching for something. What was so unique about candles that the staff preferred them over modern convenience? Perhaps, the answer was as simple as Mrs. Lester had implied; they were a good light source for more extended periods. Lina took another look at the candleholder. It had a broad base and a spike in the middle, the candle burned to its last possible moment. The only thing left was the wax that had leaked to the bottom. Nodding at it, Lina asked, "Is the light out?"

"No. But at my age, a little extra help doesn't hurt. Now, if you don't mind." Maggie motioned to the landing below.

Lina sensed that Maggie wouldn't let her through unless she insisted, and insisting would say she thought Maggie was a liar. Since Lina didn't need more enemies, for now, she abandoned her quest, quietly descending the steps. Uninvited, Maggie accompanied her to the west wing, planting herself at the intersection of the passage leading to Lina's bedroom until the latter entered and secured the door.

CHAPTER 5
NONSENSE

Lina spent the rest of the evening unsuccessfully searching for hidden passages. She didn't even find traces of the ones sealed by her ancestors. Flustered by her failure, she turned in for the night. A fire burned brightly in the hearth; the bedroom filled with a soothing warmth. As Lina's head touched the pillow, the soldier from the train sprang unbidden to her mind. She hadn't given him another thought since that day, and now, here he was, claiming her attention. She remembered how he'd slept on the seat across from hers, so peaceful and seemingly unconcerned with the world around him. She then thought of how he'd stood beside her, his hand over hers on the door handle. The memory of his hazel eyes burning into hers was so strong that for a moment she envisioned being back in the compartment. There had been something in his eyes, something different from the other men she'd interacted with— something good.

Regrettably, she didn't even know his name. Lina groaned, wishing she had spoken to him, but she had missed the opportunity—an opportunity that would almost certainly never present itself again. As she forced herself to quit thinking of the handsome stranger, the stranger her uncle had mentioned, Bray Hamilton, popped into her mind. "*If Bray wants something, he is to have it,*" Bartholomew had said. She did not know why her uncle was so concerned with pampering him. But whoever he was, she wouldn't compromise her character to please his whims.

Casting aside thoughts of this Hamilton, she found herself contemplating her father's assassination, and her grief stirred anew. She dearly missed his comforting embrace and advice. But most of all, she longed for the sense of belonging and stability he provided. The thought of not seeing him again was too much to bear. She couldn't dwell on it, for it would drive her mad. And though there was nothing she could do to bring her father back, if she unmasked and brought his killer to justice, there would be peace and closure in that. Why had his life been taken? Why so suddenly? Money was a powerful motive for murder, but she couldn't shake off the presentiment that there was more to it.

She thought of her visit to Uncle Bartholomew's office—of his violent movements, harsh words, and the power of his cane. Though he hadn't hurt the dogs with it, its mere presence had been enough to control them. Undoubtedly, Bartholomew was a man of great strength who had no qualms enforcing his will upon others. But would he resort to violence to do so? If yes, would he have gone so far as to kill his brother? Although he might be capable, there was still doubt in her heart. Taking someone's life was hard enough to fathom, let alone the idea of killing one's own kin. Still, someone had killed her father, and she was determined to unmask them and bring them to justice. How to do this, she wasn't sure yet.

Lina turned roughly to her other side and punched the pillow a few times to soften it before lying back down. Why was human nature so conflicting? Why was it so easy to take our loved ones for granted when they were with us? Why did it take tragedy to bring into focus what truly mattered in life? Now that all she had left was Mateo, everything else that had seemed so important before took less prominence—her dreams of a life on campus, meeting new people, and even a career—could wait indefinitely. Her priority was to protect Mateo and help him be happy. He was the most important person in her life, and she couldn't imagine being without him. The notion was so painful she banished it from her thoughts, forcing them to quiet down. As time ticked by, she fell into a serene slumber.

Lina's eyes snapped open. Something had catapulted her from deep sleep into heightened alertness. She sat up. The glow from the hearth barely extended into the room. She studied the faint traces of light, trying to separate them from the shadows. It wasn't long until every shape and contour made sense, justifying its presence. With the reassurance that there was no one else in her room, she listened. This was an old house after all, plagued by strange noises—a rattling pipe, a drift of air finding its way indoors, a bird stuck in the chimney—the possibilities were many.

The gentle yet distinctive sound of floorboards creaking and popping came to her ears. Where was it coming from? She squeezed her eyes shut, concentrating on the noise. But it was no use, for it seemed to come from every direction. The sudden confusion brought back to her mind the night before. *No, Mateo. Not again.* If indeed he roamed the house, she had to prevent him from escaping at all costs. She flung her legs over the edge of the bed and placed her feet on the floor. Just then, as fast as it had come, the noise was replaced by a deathly silence. She stared at the passage leading to Mateo's room. The distance suddenly felt like miles.

Lina took one hesitant step and froze. A distinct hum cut through the stillness. It was an alluring, mind-numbing sound, like a violin note indefinitely held. Her head tilted upward. There was someone in the attic. The humming grew louder, and Lina's heart hammered against her ribcage. She glimpsed at the window. Dawn was still far away. The low steady hum stopped, giving way to the groan of the floorboards again. This time, Lina knew that footsteps traveled the floor above.

The footfalls paced restlessly back and forth. Who would be up at this hour? And why were they up there? Maggie? Yesterday, Lina's presence on the stairway had bothered the twin as if one of the two shouldn't be there. Maggie's defensive demeanor could have meant only one thing: she had hidden something or someone in the attic. And that someone, no doubt, was the maid Lina had seen. So perhaps it wasn't Maggie, but the maid moving about restlessly.

Quietly but swiftly, Lina walked into Mateo's bedroom. The fire in his hearth had fared better than hers and cast a warm radiance over his bed.

He slept peacefully, his covers tucked around his sides as Lina had left them. She checked his door. It was locked.

Lina shuffled back to her room and halted by her bed, listening. It was eerily quiet. She was just sliding under the covers when the planks overhead complained again. The footsteps grew heavy, angry. Then she heard a thump, as if someone had jumped off a chair. Realizing that sleep wouldn't come until the noises ceased, she put on her shoes and went to the door.

This is not a good idea. Her better judgment screamed for her to go back to bed. Mrs. Lester wouldn't cover for her again. Lina winced when the key produced a sharp sound as she turned it in the lock of her door. She stepped into the corridor, and at once, was startled by a bone-chilling shriek. The grandfather clock. It struck three times, even though she knew it wasn't working. Every strike carried a malevolent, haunting energy that prickled Lina's body like a cascading current of electricity. There was no logical explanation for its resurrecting episodes, just the absolute sense that something was amiss with the device.

Instinctively, she looked at the light switch, but Bartholomew's warning not to wander made her reconsider, and she seized the candelabrum from the side table instead. Holding the candles high enough to guide her, she started down the passage. Tonight, Mrs. Lester had lit fewer candles, and Lina suspected it might have something to do with the full moon, which cast a blue hue through the high windows.

The irrepressible voice in her head warned her to turn back before Bartholomew caught her, but she didn't heed it. *"Fools rush in where angels fear to tread,"* her father had once said. She was about to prove him right. It wasn't until she faced the attic stairway that the magnitude of her actions hit her. She looked up at the obscure door and lingered, undecided. Whoever was here would not take her presence kindly. It dawned on her that if there was a stranger concealed at Blackwater, that might be the reason why Bartholomew didn't want her out after bedtime. All the more reason to find out the truth. Lina climbed the steps, cringing every time one of the old boards broadcasted her approach. She ascended yet one more step, and a thought jolted her. What if she had been lured here and someone was lying in wait for her? She halted. The hair on the back of her neck stood on end, and she threw a look at the gloom below. In her mind's eyes she saw her body tumbling down the rigid steps and lying lifeless on the landing.

"Never turn your back on the enemy," her father had also said.

Lina took a long, slow breath and refocused. Finding the planks quieter at the edges, she resumed her ascent on the side of the steps. Blackwater was her house. She had the right to be wherever she pleased, she told herself. But her pitiful attempt at comfort did nothing but solidify what she already knew—she shouldn't be here.

She grasped the doorknob and turned it. The latch whined, then clicked open, and as she pushed the door inward a cold draft hit her. Her hand shook a little, and the candle flickered. Now that there was no turning back, she hit the wall switch. The single bulb buzzed, threatening to go out, but stayed on. Maggie was fully justified in bringing a candle up here. Even with two light sources, it was quite dark. The area, filled with furniture and odd items, expanded over several of the bedrooms below. Beams ran horizontally across the ceiling, extending as far back as Lina could see. At the end of the timbers, the roof slanted to join the walls.

Lina strained her hearing to pick up even the slightest sound, but there was no humming, no footsteps. The silence was alarming, as if the attic held its breath due to some evil within. Lina opted for the left side, aware that the light was sufficient to guide her but not enough to dispel the shadows living among the clutter. A person could easily crouch behind the furniture. She gripped the candelabrum a bit tighter, thinking it would make for an excellent weapon. One hard blow would put anyone to sleep for a while.

She weaved her way farther into the maze, checking around the sides of the tallest pieces as she passed them. She then saw some wooden crates stacked three high against the wall. She ran her fingers along one of them, a cloud of dust rising into the air. Squinting, she examined everything within sight. As far as she could tell, nothing had been spared from the years of neglect. Her gaze found the ceiling, where cobwebs hung from the beams. Now that she had seen them, they multiplied everywhere she looked.

Nothing appeared disturbed. Maggie had said that a little extra light didn't hurt, but for what? Raising the candle higher, she peered around a gigantic mirror covered with a sheet. Behind it, she saw a table around which a few feet of space had been cleared. *How very odd*. The attic had been arranged to maximize use of every square inch, and this generous space stuck out sorely.

Lina set the candlestick on the table and was surprised that there was no dust on it. She then spotted something smooth and shiny on its surface—melted wax. It lay in clumps on the tabletop and, as she bent down, she saw it on the floor as well. It had not come from one candle but many. Had Maggie lit them all? Had the maid? If this was where she hid, it made sense.

A thump just like the one Lina had heard in her bedroom made her stand up straight, a scream trapped in her throat. The beam above her shook, and the thump came again. Distracted by the noise, she watched the ceiling intently, momentarily losing awareness of her surroundings. The beam shook again, and something pulled on her nightgown. The scream tore from her throat, echoing from every direction it amplified her horror.

"What are you doing here?" a little voice asked.

"Mateo, for goodness' sake!"

"Why are you here?" he insisted, rubbing his eyes.

"Me? What are *you* doing here?" She placed a hand over her heart to stop it from beating so wildly. "You scared me stiff."

"Sorry."

"You should be in bed," she said reproachfully.

"So should you. I went to your bedroom, and you weren't there."

Lina grabbed the candlestick, trying not to let her emotions get the best of her. There was no need to be harsh. "How did you know where to find me?"

"I followed the maid."

"What maid?"

He shrugged. "I don't know who she is."

"You must know," Lina said, alarmed. "Was it Annie, Dollie, or Maggie? Or maybe Mrs. Lester?"

Mateo shook his head decisively. "No, it was someone else."

"Why did you follow her?"

"I don't know." He shrugged again. "She was out in the corridor, and I just followed."

There was no doubt now. This woman lived at Blackwater, and no one would admit it. Who was she, and what was she up to? Lina suddenly felt desperate to flee the attic. Desperate to get Mateo to safety. "Come on, let's go back to bed."

She turned and looked at the beam before they exited the attic.

The garden sun warmed Lina's body while her thoughts went around and around, trying to explain last night's disturbances, but they only succeeded in confusing her further. The first thing she had done today was check on the grandfather clock. After a thorough inspection, Lina discarded the possibility that it might go off on its own occasionally. It had been silent as the grave, dead. Thus, someone must have tampered with it during the night.

She had been foolish to leave Mateo alone. Not only had the unknown woman lured her to the attic, but she had also led Mateo there. Complicating matters, she didn't trust anyone enough to ask them about the mysterious woman—indeed, the household appeared to be in on the secret. And if that were the case, there had to be a compelling reason behind it—one connected to the odd things taking place at Blackwater. Things that challenged Lina to think beyond the explainable, and she wasn't good at that. She was good at managing her world with rationality. The mismatch between her expectations and her present situation disrupted the natural order of life. Furthermore, Lina wasn't prolific at following her inner warnings, but she was determined to heed this one: she would tell no one about the maid or last night until she had solid proof of her existence.

"Lina, come with us to town," Eleonor invited, stepping into the garden through the French doors of the drawing room.

Mateo followed his aunt outside. "You must come, Lina. It will be fun."

"When are you leaving?"

"As soon as Mr. Walton brings the car up front," Eleonor informed.

"I'll grab my coat." Lina seized the opportunity to escape the house with the hope that a change of scenery would help her to think clearly.

Eleonor tasked Annie with purchasing her medicine, then disappeared into one of the oldest shops in town, a Victorian-looking ladies' outfitter and draper. Two mannequins dressed in high-end clothing, well-adorned hats, and fashionable bags stood in the center of the display window. To the side, a third mannequin with a red wig modeled the latest fashion for women's riding clothes—a fitted dark jacket with brass buttons, light-colored jodhpurs, and tall black leather boots.

As Lina and Mateo waited for Annie to come out of the chemist shop, they watched the happy patrons entering and exiting the stores on the main road. Among the shops were a dispensary, a confectionery, a shoe store, and an herbalist who advertised all sorts of teas and medicinal herbs.

"Thank heaven they had Mrs. Eleonor's sleeping draught. She can't sleep without it," Annie exclaimed, surging onto the pavement with a brown sack in hand. "And I don't want to come back tomorrow. Coming to town is such a dreadful chore."

"How often do you come?" Lina was curious.

"More than I'd like. Mrs. Eleonor goes through her medicine faster than Mrs. Lester downs her Woolworths Buttered Brazils—and that is saying something."

"You don't say." Lina laughed at Annie's frankness.

"Oh, yes. Mrs. Lester threw a fit when she learned the candy was not sold in the area. Whenever her stash is depleted, she goes as far as making the painful journey to London to get it."

Lina understood her aunt somewhat. *If I were married to Bartholomew, I would most likely require a full bottle of sleeping medicine every night.* But Mrs. Lester's addiction to sweets came as a surprise. The woman didn't strike Lina as one with character flaws. Lester's weakness was Woolworths Buttered Brazils. Who would have thought?

"London is quite the trip just to satisfy a sweet tooth. Surely, you could find something at the local confectioner," Lina reasoned. But then she remembered her father's love for a specific brand of cigars, and giving Mrs. Lester the benefit of the doubt, she added, "Though one can become fixed on a brand."

"Oh, she's obsessed with Woolworths, all right. I prefer Cadbury. But now that I think about it," Annie paused, her eyebrows contracting thoughtfully, "I don't recall her mentioning Buttered Brazils in our previous post."

"Hmm." There was something about the whole candy affair that didn't sit well with Lina. "Where did you and Mrs. Lester work before coming to Blackwater?"

"We were at a house in Camberley until the owners relocated to America and had us pack and shut up the place like a museum." Annie sighed at the memory. "You should have seen the furniture, smothered with white cloth. By the time we were done, it looked like a house of ghosts."

They strolled past a small shop showcasing a variety of wooden toys. Mateo let go of his sister's hand and ran back to admire the merchandise through the glass. Lina and Annie backtracked to join him. The board above the entrance read Bert's Shop in large block letters and had a unique logo with a buzzard inside a double circle. It reminded Lina of the train back in the greenhouse. The logo was the same one she saw on the stamp, but the letters *TJ* were missing here. Perhaps the shop had changed its name.

Lina addressed Mateo. "Go on. Go look inside." She fished around in her pocket, producing a few coins. "We'll wait right here."

Had he discovered a trunk of gold, his face could not have shown greater delight. "Thank you, Lina!" He took the money and skipped into the toy shop.

Lina seized the chance to prod Annie for information. Not only was Annie approachable, but she also didn't strike Lina as one to keep secrets. Folding her arms across her chest, she asked casually, "Annie, may I ask you something?"

"Well, of course."

"The night my father was shot, you were at Blackwater, yes?"

"I was," Annie responded promptly. Though, from the anxiety in her eyes, it was obvious Lina's question had caught her off guard.

"Tell me about it. What happened at the house?"

"I..."

"Please, I would like to know." Appealing to Annie's sympathy, Lina reminded her, "My father lost his life that night, leaving Mateo and me orphans."

Annie drew a short, decisive breath. "Please don't tell Mrs. Lester. She disapproves of exposing household affairs."

"This conversation dies with us. You have my word."

"All right, then." Annie's gaze traveled down the cobblestone street as she recalled, "It was Mrs. Lester's day off. She left for town early that morning. Well, I suppose she did."

"You're not sure?"

"She took off in the wrong direction. I found it odd, that's all. But perhaps she had another stop." Annie nervously unfolded and folded the edge of the medicine sack.

"What then?"

"Business went on as usual that day. After supper, Sir Bartholomew announced that he would fetch his brother from the railway station. Mrs. Eleonor retired to her quarters soon after he left. Although..." Annie glanced at Lina sheepishly "...I overheard a quarrel at the dinner table."

"Go on." Lina placed a reassuring hand on Annie's arm. "What was the quarrel about?"

Annie's cheeks colored as she went on in a flurry of words. "Mrs. Eleonor was disappointed in her husband's behavior. She called him a fool of a man. She said they would have to leave Blackwater in shame and penniless because of him. She said Sir William would remove him from the estate and disaffiliate him from the family civil duties in town."

So, her father had been coming to remove Bartholomew from the house, after all? And Bartholomew penniless? True, he spent a fortune on drinking, but he still should be well off. Upon her grandfather's death, William and Bartholomew had received large sums of money, land, and stocks, but William inherited the estate. If Bartholomew was indeed broke, he would most definitely benefit from her father's death. Their solicitor hadn't yet disclosed the contents of William's will due to the regulations of premature death. It was likely William had left some of the family assets to his brother and the rest to his children. But for now, Bartholomew would temporarily oversee the siblings' fortune.

Annie interrupted Lina's silent analysis. "Sir Bartholomew was enraged, cursing and threatening poor Mrs. Eleonor. He even shattered a wine bottle against the wall. Mrs. Eleonor fled the room, crying hysterically."

"That's horrid." The thought of her aunt fleeing the vicious wolf like a helpless rabbit made Lina furious.

"Horrid indeed."

"Do they argue a lot?"

"More so lately, but that night was particularly trying for me because Mrs. Lester wasn't around."

"I can imagine," Lina sympathized but swiftly steered the conversation back to the facts. "And after the quarrel, my uncle left to fetch my father?"

"Yes. Mr. Walton drove Sir Bartholomew to the station. But they had car troubles on the way, and when Sir Bartholomew arrived, the police were already there. He called to speak to Mrs. Eleonor, but she had taken an extra dose of sleeping powder and was quite drowsy. He relayed to me that Sir William had been shot and that he, Bartholomew, would most likely remain at the police station the rest of the night."

"And Mr. Walton stayed with him?"

"No, he remained at a nearby farm with the car, waiting for the mechanic. The farmer drove Sir Bartholomew to town."

"Hmm." Lina didn't like the chain of events. The car breaking down and Bartholomew getting to the station without Walton was a perfect alibi. Bartholomew could have distorted the timeline, getting to the station just in time to kill her father and hide in town to then reappear after the police arrived.

"It was a terrible night. When Mrs. Eleonor was awake enough to hear the news, she became inconsolable," Annie continued. "The shock took a while to set in for all of us. Oh, I wish Mrs. Lester had been there. She would have handled the situation much better."

"I'm sure you did just fine." Lina reassured Annie with a warm smile. The poor girl seemed traumatized by the events.

"Lina, Lina, look what I got!" Mateo burst out of the shop with a wooden toy.

"Oh, he is lovely!"

"I named him Sam."

"That's a fine name," Lina said, admiring the wooden dog in Mateo's hand.

The trio started toward the general store, with Mateo skipping a few paces ahead. Lina walked in silence, her thoughts returning to Annie's story. Something about the events the night of her father's death nudged at her. Apart from the sudden breakdown of her uncle's car—there was something that, for the time being, eluded her.

Mateo made a sharp turn at the corner and collided with a man carrying a box; the impact sent the boy to the ground and onto his backside. The box fell from the stranger's hands, its contents scattering across the pavement.

With a demeanor that spoke of self-mastery and maturity, the man spoke, "Sorry, little fellow. Here, let me help you," and extended his hand to Mateo.

The boy took the helping hand and stood at once.

"Are you all right?" the newcomer asked him.

Mateo nodded, and his eyes widened with recognition. "Oh, it's you —the soldier from the train."

Lina's gaze flew to the man. In the frenzy of the moment, and still processing Annie's account of the night her father died, she had failed to recognize him. Yes, it was the soldier with the beautiful hazel eyes. She couldn't help but notice how well his white button-up shirt and dark trousers suited him.

"Oh yes. We shared the compartment from London." The man

extended his hand to Mateo again, this time to introduce himself. "I'm Max."

"I'm Mateo."

"Miss, it's a pleasure to see you again."

"Catalina Laroche." Lina shook his hand, her cheeks growing warm as she stared into his eyes. Not in a million years did she think they'd meet again. *Max.* She wouldn't have to guess his name any longer.

It was Annie's turn to greet the newcomer, and she did so with a brief introduction and several giggles, after which Max kneeled to collect his items. Mateo was swift to help. A bottle of lighter fluid, a box of matches, a package of candles, a newspaper, and a couple of comic books completed his assemblage.

"I'm sorry about the trouble," Lina offered for the sake of propriety as Max rose with the box secured in his arms.

"It's no trouble at all." Max smiled.

"Do you come to town often?" Annie asked Max. "I don't recall seeing you before."

"No, not very often," Max answered, glancing at Lina.

"We mustn't keep you," Lina said, though she wouldn't mind a longer visit. "We have taken enough of your time."

Annie frowned, clearly displeased that their conversation with the handsome man might be curtailed.

"Actually, I've done what I needed to, so I'm in no real hurry," Max said.

"Where do you live?" Mateo asked him.

"Mateo, that's an intrusive question," reprimanded his sister, and to Max, she said, "I'm afraid Mateo is a bit overexcited today."

"I don't mind it. Curiosity can be a good thing." Max patted Mateo on the head. "I live just at the edge of town."

At the edge of town? Lina was puzzled. Max hadn't descended the train in Lydney, or had he? In her eagerness to leave the station, she must have missed him.

"That's not too far, is it?" Mateo wondered.

"Not far at all," Max responded.

"There you are!" Eleonor came striding around the corner. Several shopping bags hung from her wrists. "I thought I'd lost you."

"Allow me to help," Annie offered, lightening her load.

"I see you have made a friend already," Eleonor observed, smiling at Max.

"Umm, no, well." Lina couldn't precisely define what Max was. A fellow traveler on the train? An acquaintance? A stranger?

Max shook Eleonor's hand firmly. "I'm Max, a clumsy bloke who bumped into this young man." His gaze jumped to Mateo before returning his attention to Eleonor. "And you are?"

"Eleonor Laroche."

"It's a pleasure to make your acquaintance, ma'am." Max turned to Lina. "You have a beautiful mother."

"Oh no. This is my aunt, married to my uncle Bartholomew," Lina explained.

"Is that so?" Max's gaze darted back at Eleonor.

"There is but a small step from aunt to mother. She is like a daughter to me," Eleonor said, with an edge of pride in her voice.

"Well, it was very nice to meet you all. Please enjoy the rest of your day," Max wished.

"You too, sir," Lina replied.

With a nod, Max resumed his journey as if he had forgotten to do something important.

"Bye." Quickly moving on from his interest in the soldier, Mateo produced Sam from his pocket.

"We'll see you around, then." Annie watched Max disappear behind a shop. Lina suspected that Annie wouldn't mind coming to town so much anymore.

The group moved again. Eleonor caught up with Mateo, inquiring about the toy. Losing no time, he launched into a thorough description of his new, four-legged wooden friend. Eleonor listened with motherly patience until he was done. Then she patted the side of her shopping bag, which Lina noticed had a gorgeous black horse printed on it, and said, "Guess what I bought for you?"

"What is it?" Mateo asked with excitement.

"Riding clothes. You like horses, don't you?"

Mateo nodded, and his face lit up. "Thank you. Thank you!"

"You are most welcome."

"When can we ride?" He was eager to know.

"Tomorrow morning. Say, nine o'clock sharp?"

"Oh! I can't wait." Mateo laced his arm through hers.

A look of satisfaction filled Eleonor's eyes.

Lina and Annie fell several yards behind the joyful pair.

"My aunt has grown fond of Mateo, and Mateo feels the same way," Lina noted. "I'm grateful for that. It makes Blackwater easier to handle."

"Yes, yes…" Annie answered absentmindedly. "What a striking man. Indeed, you don't come across those very often. Oh, my, and so well-proportioned—"

Lina's eyes widened, and her cheeks colored at Annie's statement.

Glancing sideways at Lina, Annie quickly apologized, sounding mortified. "Oh, do forgive me. I don't know what came over me."

Lina had a pretty good idea what had come over Annie, for she silently agreed. Max was handsome, indeed. She now realized his looks had been the destabilizing force during the train ride. That, added to the graceful way he carried himself, made him difficult to miss. Had he been a flirtatious man, ready to jump at the first romantic opportunity that came his way, Lina would have forgotten him already. In her mind, men like that weren't worth dating—for they could be found by the dozens in each town, ready to move on to the next girl.

Mateo skipped ahead again, crossing the street rather carelessly. Compared to the streets in London, Coleford was a ghost town, but there still were plenty of vehicles. At once, Eleonor trotted after him. Annie and Lina reached the intersection seconds behind and waited for a truck to pass before crossing.

The driver waved at the women, and suddenly Lina recalled Bray. "My uncle mentioned that Bray Hamilton is coming to visit."

"Is he?" Annie's face fell, her jolly mood having fled. "When?"

"He didn't say. Why? What's the matter?"

"Bray Hamilton is a dishonorable man. A scoundrel!" The passion with which Annie spoke startled Lina.

"Annie, you can't be serious."

"Oh, I'm very serious." Annie went on with an edge of anger. "He is devilishly attractive, not to mention extremely wealthy. On his last visit, he enticed one of the young housemaids, Mary, who I liked very much. Well, at least up to that point. They disappeared together for three days, and Mrs. Lester dismissed her when they returned. Though Sir Bartholomew asked Mary to stay until Hamilton left."

"So Bray could have his toy readily available," Lina sputtered. Ugh, one more philanderer.

"Exactly, but the shocking thing was," Annie pointed out, "that although Mary consented to Sir Bartholomew's request, she left before Hamilton, not even bothering to collect her final salary."

"Did she say why?"

"No. She just up and left. In fact, no one saw her leave," Annie said.

"Hmm. That is rather odd."

"Extremely, but one can never know what goes through someone's mind."

"She might have been too embarrassed to stay or even say her goodbyes," Lina proposed.

"No, she wasn't one to care about opinions," Annie stated. "I did write to her parents' address shortly after but never got a response."

"What did she look like?" A fleeting idea sprang to life. Could Mary be the mysterious woman hiding in the house? No. If she had stayed, she wouldn't be hiding. Would she?

"Dark hair, tall, very sure of herself, but nothing special, you know." The description matched the woman Lina had seen, but it also matched lots of women.

"Tell me, Annie, apart from Mary, have other maids worked at Blackwater recently?"

"Not since I've been here. After the fiasco with Mary, knowing that Hamilton will visit again, Mrs. Lester refuses to take such a risk. And I don't blame her. Hamilton even made advances toward me. I became so paranoid that Mrs. Lester allowed me to sleep in her quarters until he left. At which time, Sir Bartholomew called the staff and unleashed a torrent of reproofs and reminders about the house's reputation and so on, as if Hamilton's behavior was our fault."

"The typical hypocrite—blaming others for his sins," Lina sputtered. "Tell me, Annie, what did my aunt say about all this?"

Annie's face showed disappointment. "I could be wrong, but I believe Mrs. Eleonor regards Bray as the child she never had. One of those mothers, you know, whose child can never do anything wrong. Frankly, I think she is blind to his dark side."

Bartholomew's words pounded through Lina's head: *"If Bray wants something, he is to have it."*

CHAPTER 6
BRAY

The next day, Lina took another long walk through the gardens. Though Lina's feet ached, the fresh air calmed her nerves. She approached the house and saw Eleonor on horseback in the south clearing. Eleonor maneuvered the black horse with remarkable dexterity, leaving no doubt who was master. Another horse appeared, galloping after hers. Lina didn't recognize the man riding it, but Mateo was seated in front of him. She lingered on the path as the animals neared.

"Would you like to join the fun?" Eleonor asked Lina, dismounting. "Take my horse."

"Since I'm already in trousers, I don't see why not." Lina mounted, and before she could ask Eleonor who the man was, the latter hurried up the path to the house. Lina turned toward the other riders.

"Hello, Lina." Mateo waved enthusiastically. "Do you like my hat? Aunt Eleonor got it for me." The black, sturdy hat looked like a war helmet.

"It's lovely."

"Good morning," Mateo's companion greeted.

"Good morning." Lina naturally assessed Mateo's companion—a slender man in his late twenties with dark hair and a fair complexion. Dressed in a three-piece, checkered suit, his good looks were impossible to miss.

"Bray Hamilton. It's a pleasure to meet you," he introduced himself.

She should have known. "Catalina Laroche." Annie's tales about him had her instantly on guard.

"But everyone calls you Lina?"

"That's correct." Their gaze connected, and she saw that his green eyes were calculating and portrayed a hint of arrogance.

"Please, call me Bray."

She assented with a soft nod.

"What do you say, Lina? Race to the edge of the woods and back?"

Looking at her brother, Lina hesitated. More concerned about Mateo's safety than Bray losing the race, she said, "I'm afraid you'll be at a disadvantage."

"Ah, the suit doesn't bother me." He looked down at his clothing. "Besides, it's too much trouble to change."

"No, I meant Mateo—the extra weight."

"I hardly weigh anything," Mateo protested.

"I'm afraid she might be right," Bray told Mateo.

"All right...I have to use the bog anyway," Mateo said with a frown.

"The toilet," Lina corrected.

Mateo frowned again.

"I'll drop him off." Bray swiftly veered his horse to the main path.

As Lina awaited his return, her competitive side kicked in, and she prepared for the challenge. "We are going to win this," she whispered to the horse, patting his head. She sunk a bit deeper into the saddle and adjusted her feet in the stirrups, holding the reins softly.

Bray came back with a bright smile across his face. Clearly, he expected to win. "Are you ready?"

"Ready."

"On the count of three." He counted, "One, two, three."

The horses took off like cannonballs, their hooves thundering across the open field. Bray's horse was rapidly gaining the lead. Lina struggled to catch up until they came to the tree line. The turn slowed him as his animal negotiated the weight it carried. She took advantage of her ability to swiftly halt her horse and turned him to gallop back.

"Come on, come on!" she encouraged the horse, pressing her heels against its flanks to capitalize on her advantage. "We can win this."

The black horse crossed the finish line seconds ahead of the brown, giving Lina the win. Concealing her delight, she dismounted near the house.

"I must say I'm impressed," Bray confessed. "I wasn't expecting to lose twice in a row. You're just as good as Eleonor." He jumped off the horse.

"I doubt that."

"It must be the suit, then," he joked.

"They deserve a treat." Lina gently patted the horse's forehead. "Don't you think?"

"Yours maybe. Mine, I'm not so sure," Bray joked again. "He's bent on humiliating me today."

Lina laughed.

They were halfway across the lawn when Bray spotted Mr. Krammer. "Hey, old chap," he called as if he had known the gardener all his life. "Take the horses to the stable and give them a treat, would you?"

"Of course, sir," Mr. Krammer responded, but Lina saw a trace of annoyance in his eyes. Bray's lack of manners didn't sit well with the gardener—or her.

"Thank you, Mr. Krammer," Lina emphasized. "We appreciate your help."

As soon as Mr. Krammer took her horse, Lina headed to the house, not waiting for Bray. He hustled after her, but she made sure to stay ahead, bothered by the casual if not insolent way he had treated the gardener.

Once inside, they joined Eleonor in the library.

"I'm so glad you came to visit," Eleonor said to Bray. "I couldn't imagine living in London. It becomes dreadfully dull after a while."

Bray opened the credenza drawer and took a cigar from the Capstan tin box. Lina noticed the ease with which he carried himself at Blackwater. "Though the countryside is a welcome change, I must disagree with you, Aunt. London can never be a bore to me." From his pocket, he produced a lighter and lit his cigar. "There are endless activities for the gentry."

"Endless, I'm sure," Lina murmured, for even when she loved the city, she doubted Bray enjoyed the same things she did. With the memory of Annie's warning about the man, she settled on the sofa. So far, there wasn't anything alarming, but just in case, she would maintain her distance.

"I wonder what is keeping Bartholomew," Eleonor remarked. "Lester should have fetched him already."

"Agreed," Bray responded swiftly. "The old man is taking rather long, and I have urgent matters to discuss with him." He raised an eyebrow at his aunt.

"I shall retrieve him myself." Catching his hint, Eleonor withdrew.

Bray sat on the armchair across from Lina, enjoying his cigar. For a fleeting moment, she saw a younger Bartholomew in Bray. The older man seemed strangely protective of Eleonor's nephew, obviously willing to overlook the other's faults and supposed moral misconduct. The only explanation Lina could imagine for such a relationship was that Bartholomew also saw himself in Bray. Yes, though not blood-related, these men were very much alike.

"I'm very sorry for your loss," Bray said unexpectedly. "I didn't know your father, but I heard wonderful things about him."

Lina pursed her lips and nodded, acknowledging his sympathy.

"Moving out here must be a difficult adjustment for you and your brother," Bray continued. "I'd hate living in the country. A week or two, you know—it's all I can handle."

"Yes, I'm afraid I miss London terribly," Lina confessed. "Not so much the city but my home and friends."

"I understand. I went through something similar when I was sent to Palestine. Besides dealing with the issues of war, I was quite homesick—but time makes it easier. You get into a routine and find new things to keep you from thinking about the past."

"I hope that's the case," Lina said wishfully, for the year ahead seemed like a hundred.

"Eleonor mentioned that you were accepted to Oxford."

"That's correct." Lina was a bit surprised by his interest in her life, and she wondered if he wasn't as detestable as Annie thought.

"You must be brilliant, then," he praised. "I don't think I would ever be admitted to Oxford—I mean, I'm not dimwitted, but neither am I extremely clever." He was so serious that Lina had to contain a laugh.

"Surely you exaggerate," she said politely.

"No, but it's all right. Now that the military is behind me, I'll determine what route I'd like to take."

"You aren't on leave?"

"No, I was honorably discharged."

"Oh." She noticed how he'd emphasized *honorably*.

"My convoy was ambushed. It was a nasty encounter that killed several men and wounded others." He tugged his shirt to the side to reveal a considerable scar on his shoulder. "They sent me back to get surgery."

"It looks painful."

"It's not bad, but I can't fire a rifle anymore."

"I'm sorry—what a horrid experience to go through."

"It's all right. The past is the past. There is no use crying over it. I must focus on the future." He sent another puff of smoke into the air.

"That's wise." Could the war's unfortunate events have reshaped his character and placed him on a better path? It was too early to tell.

Bray left the chair in search of an ashtray.

Lina rose to her feet. "I promised my brother I'd read with him. I hope my uncle joins you soon."

With ashtray in hand, Bray stood before Lina. She looked up at him and found his gaze. There was something devilishly attractive about his eyes, something that made her want to keep looking at him.

"It was nice chatting with you," he said.

Lina smiled and left his company with a less decisive opinion about him.

Lina climbed the staircase but halted when she heard arguing in the east wing. The heated voices were too tangled to break apart, and Lina couldn't resist the impulse to figure out what the quarrel was about. Not giving it another thought, she tiptoed down the passage and stopped before she rounded the corner.

"What else do you want from me, woman?" Bartholomew shouted.

"Love and respect at the very least!" Eleonor shouted back.

"You are a wretched creature, impossible to please," Bartholomew sputtered.

Lina inched closer to the bend to peek at them. The couple stood not far from their bedrooms.

"Who wouldn't be, married to a man like you?" Eleonor snapped.

"Ugh. Have it your way." Bartholomew made a motion of dismissal with his hand and turned toward his dormitory, ready to end the fight.

"You know what you are, Bartholomew Laroche?" Eleonor blurted, not willing to let him have the last word. "You are a murderer. That's what you are!"

In response to this, his gigantic frame spun, and the back of his hand struck Eleonor's face, the impact sending her to the floor.

Lina gasped, and her knees wobbled. He was inclined to inflict physical pain upon others, after all. In this case, Eleonor suffered his wrath for having said too much. Lina wanted to help, but the man's brutality paralyzed her. If she could muster enough courage to step into the open, she could yell to try to stop him. But in her mind's eyes, she saw Bartholomew striking her to the ground.

Eleonor scrambled to her feet, whimpering.

"Say that again!" Bartholomew challenged and, grabbing Eleonor by the arms, slammed her against the wall.

Lina stepped toward the corridor junction, but a hand descended on her shoulder, detaining her.

"Let me," Bray said. So submerged had she been in the ordeal that she had failed to hear his approach. "It's better that you don't interfere. It would only enrage Bartholomew more." Not waiting for a response, Bray dashed in the couple's direction.

Lina's heartbeat hammered in her ears as she watched Bray approach them. Poor Annie. Lina now understood how she must feel witnessing her employers' quarrels, and her hesitancy to speak about it.

"Come on, you two, break it up," Bray commanded.

His sudden appearance startled Bartholomew, who let go of Eleonor. She burst into a hysterical cry, and Bray embraced her. Bartholomew cursed under his breath, entered his bedroom, and slammed the door.

"It's all right," Bray soothed Eleonor. "It's all right."

"He can be such a brute," Eleonor sobbed.

"Are you hurt?"

"No. I'm fine."

"Come on, let's get you some tea," Bray suggested, seemingly not convinced at her response.

"No. I don't want anyone to see me like this," Eleonor decided. "I just need to lie down."

"Are you sure?"

"I'm sure." Eleonor wiped the tears from her face. "Thank you, Bray."

"Right, then—I'll be downstairs if you need me."

"Bray," she called as he attempted to retrace his steps down the corridor. "I would be frightfully mortified if anyone hears about this."

"I won't say a word."

Eleonor disappeared inside her bedroom, three doors past Bartholomew's.

Lina leaned against the wall. Eleonor had called Bartholomew a murderer. Had she meant it, or had she said it to infuriate him? Lina found it difficult to believe that Eleonor would accuse him of murder without reason. What did she know?

"You are pale," Bray remarked, returning to Lina.

"That was quite nasty."

"It's over now."

"Thank you for helping her," Lina said.

"She was quite shaken."

"And rightly so. Bartholomew was beside himself. You could have received a blow or two yourself."

"No, the old man wouldn't lay a finger on me."

"I wouldn't be so sure," Lina countered.

"Come on, let's get some tea," Bray proposed and grabbed her hand to guide her to the staircase. "And don't say no. I already got turned down once."

She held on tight. After the brutality she had witnessed, Bray's touch felt good. They descended the steps, and she glanced at him as they came to the library. Not only was he an attractive man, but he had a courageous side to him. One that she hadn't expected.

"You stay here." Bray walked her to the sofa. "I'll get the tea."

Lina closed her eyes while Bray's footsteps faded in the distance. She felt like she was stuck in a malfunctioning roundabout that continued to increase speed, and she couldn't get off. The quarrel, the couple's accusations, Bray's closeness—it was all so overwhelming. She softly inhaled and exhaled, calming her nerves, but traces of her distress remained.

Minutes later, Bray came in with a serving tray. He handed Lina a cup of tea and settled in an armchair to drink his.

"This is perfect," Lina observed. "Thank you."

"Dollie made it extra strong."

"Thank goodness." Lina took another sip. "I did not expect the day to turn out this way."

"What do you mean? Today turned out much better than I'd anticipated." Bray's eyes swept over her as if he were ready for a lot more than holding hands. Though the contact had been comforting, she didn't expect a repeat.

"You appraise me like merchandise on a shelf. Do you find me to your liking?" Lina said impulsively.

"Fancy that." Bray let out a short laugh. "Let me assure you that whatever delusion you entertain is just that, a delusion. But I must confess that you have spirit, and I like that."

The certainty in his words nullified her assessment, and she felt ashamed for being so blunt—after all, maybe he hadn't looked at her the way she thought he had.

"Do forgive me. I'm still on edge. I'll see you at dinner." She placed the teacup on the tray and left before she made things worse.

Lina endured an agonizing supper under Bartholomew's iron fist. With the memory of what happened still on her mind, she participated in a dozen inane topics, producing more fake smiles in that single setting than in her entire life. After the meal, Annie graciously took charge of Mateo, while Lina was herded into the drawing room, where socialization continued.

Eleonor, Bartholomew, Bray, and Lina sat around the game table. Lina's heart sank every time she looked at Eleonor's bruised face. Though Eleonor had sponged a considerable amount of makeup on it, it was painfully visible. Earlier, Lina had attempted to inquire about the bruising, but Eleonor had dismissed it at once. And since Eleonor wasn't aware of her niece's eavesdropping, Lina deemed it best not to push it any further. Even so, more startling was the amicable way her uncle and aunt treated each other. In a matter of hours, they had gone from hate and blows to calm words and laughter. Acknowledging how volatile their relationship was made Lina extremely uncomfortable, and she was impatient for the evening to end.

She looked forward to the comfort of her bed and the disconnect from reality sleep provided—assuming the maid didn't reappear. The thought of her made Lina's stomach turn. For even though she wanted to know who she was and why no one admitted her existence, she couldn't risk leaving Mateo exposed. She would search for the woman in the safety of daylight. No matter what happened tonight, she'd lock the door and stay in bed.

"That's enough of bridge," Bray decided. Bartholomew and he had won again. "Let's play something else."

"Very well," Bartholomew assented.

"Limericks, word-making, quotations, perhaps?" Eleonor proposed.

A short debate followed, and cards prevailed. They introduced Lina to a host of games she hadn't heard of. And while she never felt the satisfaction of winning, the newness of the games challenged her intellect, and she did her best.

"Hey, old man, let's make a trip to Venice this summer." Bray's voice was lively after another prideful win. "What do you say? I hear their casinos are spectacular, not to mention their wom..." His eyes snapped from Lina to Eleonor, and he didn't finish his sentence.

A large puff of smoke rose from Bartholomew's mouth as he lowered the cigar. Lina angled her body away from him and held her breath until the cloud passed.

"If it weren't for the bloody long trip, I would consider it," Bartholomew responded with a chuckle.

"Ah, a few drinks here and there on the way makes the travel bearable," Bray affirmed. "But meanwhile, London and Paris are always good options." He addressed Lina. "Tell me something—do you prefer daytime or evening affairs?" There was a strange edge of malice in his question.

"That depends on one's company," Lina responded uncompromisingly, her patience wearing thin. Annie's painting of Bray started to take shape. His advances throughout the night had been slow but constant and not in a good way. He hadn't missed a chance to casually touch her hand, lean too close, or briefly put his arm around her shoulders. She had had enough, and it was time to clarify her stance. For she was now convinced that earlier, Bray had indeed appraised her like merchandise on a shelf. Most alarming yet was the notion that he had a skill for making others doubt their instincts.

"Let's say that I was your companion." He smiled. "Which one would you prefer?"

"Neither."

"Ah, you do have spirit." Bray laughed. "Yes, you do." Clasping his glass, he left the table in search of more wine. If Lina had counted accurately, this would be his fifth refill.

"Oh." Eleonor giggled, lifting her empty glass. "I suppose I need a drink myself." She followed Bray to the liquor table.

Lina shot a glance at Bartholomew, who shuffled the deck of cards while letting out a string of slurred words. He hadn't drunk as much as Bray, but his glass had been filled with gin and whiskey throughout the evening.

"Sir, are you all right?" Lina asked as the cards fell from his hands and onto the table and floor.

"Of course, I am," he barked, but his eyes danced about the room.

He would collapse any moment now. Lina abandoned the drunken man and ambled to the window. The bright moonlight made the lawn somewhat visible. At the edge of her vision, something drifted near the darkest part of the pond. Lina squinted, trying to make out the form.

Mr. Krammer? There was no need for him to be out this late. Perhaps the dogs? They loved to prowl the grounds at night. *Keep coming. Keep coming.* The shape emerged from the lowest parts of the terrain into the middle of the lawn, where the moonlight further illuminated it. Its height and silhouette weren't those of a man or animal, and not a woman either. *Just a few more steps...Come on...*

"If it weren't so cold, I'd take you for a stroll." Bray stepped between Lina and the window, blocking her view.

"What am I? A dog that needs walking?" She stepped around Bray, searching for the figure, but it was gone.

"Don't be absurd. Dogs are more obedient," he said arrogantly. "And I have a feeling you aren't easily tamed."

Tamed? Lina faced the brazen man. Clearly, he was ignoring her lack of interest in him. "Please don't waste your time with any ideas other than friendship between us."

Discontent momentarily flooded his features, but he disguised it by throwing his head back and laughing. Lina retreated to the center of the room, painfully aware of how different Bray was from Max. Unlike Bray, Max was mindful not to overstep personal boundaries.

"You two look adorable together," Eleonor opined while tapping her husband's shoulder to rouse him. Bartholomew had dropped on the table, his arms stretched over his head. "I suspected you would get along well."

How could she not see Lina's blatant indifference toward the brute? As Annie had mentioned, Eleonor was inclined to overplease her nephew, seemingly blind to Lina's dislike for him and even more blind to his questionable morality. Although, compared to her husband, Bray could be considered quite civil.

"Get along well? Who?" Bartholomew barked, roused from his sleep. Clearly disoriented, he ran the back of his hand over his mouth.

"Bray and Lina, of course," his wife answered.

Bartholomew managed to find and hold his niece's gaze and affirmed, "Of course, Bray is one of the most coveted bachelors in England. A very good catch, Lina."

Lina's head was now spinning. The whole situation was preposterous. He wasn't a good catch; he was a lost cause—with money.

"Well, folks, thank you for the pleasant evening." Bray read the time on his wristwatch. "It is well past time to retire."

Lina breathed a sigh of relief. She had survived the evening.

"If you permit, I'll escort Lina to her quarters," he added.

Bray's audacity caught her off guard, a sense of desperation replacing her previous hope of a reprieve. After Annie's tales, his constant encroaching, and all the drinking, Lina could only imagine what his intentions might be.

"That won't be necessary." The words exploded from Lina's mouth. "I'll keep Aunt Eleonor company a little longer." She would stay up all night inventing topics for discussion if needed.

"I'm afraid I'm getting weary as well, dear," Eleonor said. "I must get to bed."

Bartholomew stumbled from his chair with a nod to Bray's request. "Accompany Lina upstairs, then. Good night, you two."

Lina's body tensed, but her mind accelerated. Bray seemed impulsive and careless, but from what Annie had told her, he hadn't forced Mary into anything; he had persuaded her. At this point, her uncle was beyond reason, though she doubted much would change were he sober. As for Bray, she had managed thus far and would continue to do so. She would challenge one devil instead of both, as their gaming abilities vastly improved when they played together. But while the bridge table had not suited her talents, this was a game she would not lose.

"Good night." Lina moved to the doorway with Bray at her heels, but not before throwing another pleading look at Eleonor. Eleonor's countenance had fallen. She looked haggard and worn out, her attention on her inebriated husband. It was clear she hadn't the energy to spare for helping others, hardly having enough to deal with her own problems.

With a sigh of disappointment at the caliber of men that surrounded her, Lina walked briskly ahead of her companion. As they crossed the foyer, climbed the staircase, and headed to her quarters, she was busy concocting a plan. She would distance herself from him, say good night, dash into her bedroom, and lock the door before he had time to do anything other than retreat. When her thoughts switched gears and she wondered what Bray was thinking, she forced herself not to go there.

To her dismay, at the last possible minute, Bray picked up his pace and beat her to her door. It was painfully evident that he knew quite well where she slept. She stopped at a safe distance, watching him carefully. Since he hadn't done anything to provoke her yet, maybe he would simply leave after she bid him good night.

"Thank you, Bray. I'll see you at breakfast."

"Why the rush?" He leaned against the wall. He wasn't going to leave quietly.

"It's been a long day, and I'm worn out."

"You are too young to be tired."

"Well, I am."

"Nonsense. Let's get to know each other a little better."

His persistence angered her. Clearly, he had no regard for what she wanted. Besides, thus far she didn't want to know him better. She glanced at the door and had the strong feeling he would try to detain her if she got too close to him. Physically she was at a disadvantage, so she had to outsmart him.

"I'm sorry, but I must say good night." Instead of moving forward, she quickly backed up and slipped through Mateo's door into his bedroom. She was even quicker to turn the key.

She flipped on the light. Mateo wasn't in his bed.

"Mateo?"

She dashed through the connecting passage to her quarters. She had to find him. To her great relief, through the light coming from his room, she could see that Mateo lay asleep on her bed. She secured the lock, changed into her nightgown, and slipped in beside him. It wasn't long until she drifted off to sleep.

A jolt of intense awareness surged through Lina. The tranquil atmosphere vanished as she opened her eyes and saw Mateo leaving the bedroom. *Oh, no, you don't.* Without a second thought, she jumped off the bed and went after him—each stride driven by an unwavering resolve—to catch him before he slipped away. She ran past the candlestick stationed in the corridor. Its light flickered at the rushed motion, sending long shadows dancing across the walls. Within the penumbras, the tiny figure marched toward the staircase.

"Mateo, stop—stop."

He continued, unmoved by her call.

"Mateo, stop right there!" Her voice boomed in the space.

To her surprise, he lingered by the banister.

She came to him and placed her hands on his shoulders. "Where are you going?"

"To get a drink," he responded with a languished tone.

"Did you forget there is a glass of water on your night table?"

He shook his head, but it was apparent that he had.

"Come on. I'll show you." She grasped his hand and guided him back into the security of their quarters. Once inside, a sigh of relief escaped her lips, and the tension that had knotted her muscles released. Mateo was safe.

Lina tucked her crochet project, a green scarf for Mateo, in the willow basket and shifted to the French doors leading to the garden. The morning had brought with it the first snow of the year. A thin, white blanket now covered the ground. Last night could have been disastrous, Lina thought, if she hadn't caught Mateo on time. For even when her resolution to find the strange maid remained unaltered, she had no idea what her purpose was or what she might be capable of. Hence, wandering the house at night was a foolish idea.

Through the glass, she observed Mr. Krammer, aided by Mateo, hurrying to rearrange some Victorian pots. Evidently, the groundskeeper wanted to group those requiring shelter from the frost. The sight warmed her heart. Mateo could use a good male figure in his life, and Mr. Krammer was the image of a wise, morally upright man.

Lina left the drawing room with a smile on her lips and headed to the kitchen. If luck favored her, she might be able to steal a slice of Dollie's French bread. Topped with homemade raspberry jam, it was heavenly. She emerged into the main hallway and heard animated voices coming from Bartholomew's office. She slowed as she recognized the self-assured voice of Bray speaking to her uncle. Their tone was serious, but their words weren't clear enough to tell them apart. Her curiosity urged her to draw near. Her logic told her that if she got caught, apart from the humiliation, Bartholomew would punish her. Was it worth the risk? They were probably discussing rubbish about hunting or the latest liquor on the market anyway. But what if their conversation shed light on her father's assassination or maybe even on the mysterious woman?

She crept closer, her pulse increasing with every step. She pressed her ear to the door, hardly believing her audacity.

"I've exhausted all my resources." Bartholomew's voice sounded paranoid.

"Same. I invested most of my savings and yearly allowance in that terrible business."

"But it was fun," the older man laughed a bitter laugh, "while it lasted."

"Not for me. I wish one of those useless horses had won a bloody race," lamented Bray.

Horse races?

"Well, my lad, there is no use crying over spilt milk."

"If my parents find out about the money I've lost, they'll disown me. I've got to do something before they realize it's gone."

"This new enterprise from India sounds promising," Bartholomew said. "If it works out, it will save us from ruin."

"We can't let it slip through our fingers," Bray stated. "The tea business is booming."

"The only inconvenience is that without her money, my hands are tied. I wasn't expecting the trust to have restrictions. I can't touch the money—at least not large sums, nor can she until she comes of age or gets married."

"That's where I fit in most perfectly." Bray laughed.

"It's a win-win. Besides, she is a beautiful woman, and I trust you can make her happy."

"I'd surely try. Beauty and money are the perfect combination in a wife," answered Bray.

Lina emitted a sudden exclamation of disbelief. It was loud. Too loud. She covered her mouth with her hand. Holding her breath, she listened, hoping they hadn't heard.

"Well, my boy. We mustn't dawdle. The clock is ticking," said Bartholomew enthusiastically.

She released the breath. They were not aware of her intrusion.

"You can say that again," Bray agreed.

"At least we got the main obstacle out of the way," Bartholomew said.

The main obstacle? Did they speak of her father? The possibility made Lina tremble with rage, but nothing was certain. Hopefully, knowing their plan placed her ahead of the game.

"Yes, but I have the feeling she'll not be easily convinced," Bray admitted, and Lina imagined him frowning. "You need to persuade her."

"Persuade, you say? It won't work, at least not coming from me," Bartholomew assured. "She is as stubborn as her mother was. I think she'll respond better to you. Perhaps you can be a bit more aggressive. Women like that."

"I can go further if you'd like, but I tell you, it might backfire," Bray warned.

Footsteps neared from inside. Lina considered retreating, but soon, the footsteps headed in the other direction. Bray was pacing.

"I have an ace up my sleeve if everything else fails," Bartholomew informed.

"I wouldn't expect any less of you."

Footfalls now echoed from somewhere down the passage. *No, no, no. Why now?* Lina couldn't believe her luck. She wanted to learn more from the discussion, but she couldn't risk anyone seeing her here. She hurried away from the office, and, despite her rattled nerves, managed a steady pace. Annie soon emerged from around the bend ahead, tea tray in hand. Lina smiled and nodded as they passed each other. The men would never know she had listened to their cunning plan.

Bray was here to save his skin by marrying her. Lina knew she could never be happy with him, nor could she make him happy. She hardly knew the man, and from what she had seen, she didn't want to. Bartholomew, of course, was the facilitator and, as such, would benefit from the arrangement. It was apparent that what Annie overheard was true. Bartholomew was financially broke, which explained the shortage of house staff. Her uncle and Bray needed her money, but they would never have it. That much she was sure of.

"We got the main obstacle out of the way," Bartholomew had said matter-of-factly. And Eleonor had called him a murderer. If he was the killer, Lina had to prove it. But how? Like a ray of light cutting through an obscure tunnel, Lina recalled the police visit to her flat after her father's death. The shock of the news and the unanticipated changes that followed had caused her to forget about it; as the detective had spoken of the assassination and what they had gathered, she had sat on the sofa, petrified. Of the things he'd related, she now remembered one. *"We suspect he was killed with a .38 caliber revolver."* How and why they believed that escaped her memory, but if she found one at Blackwater, it might incriminate Bartholomew. And at this point, Lina clung to even the faintest of hopes.

And Bray? Was he an accomplice? Nothing seemed unlikely anymore. Although Bartholomew could have been referring to bringing the siblings to the countryside to exploit them. Thankfully, her father had the foresight to enforce the trust with strict rules. She hoped her uncle would never find the loophole he so desperately sought.

"I have an ace up my sleeve if everything else fails." Bartholomew's words circled endlessly through Lina's head, their meaning currently beyond her imagination.

CHAPTER 7
LOST

"Where have you been?" Lina asked Mateo as he came into the library.

"Nowhere." He avoided her gaze.

"That's not true. You came from somewhere." Lina then noticed the patches of fresh soil on his pants. "You were in the conservatory. Weren't you?"

Mateo pursed his lips and swayed on his feet.

"I told you—I don't want you in there."

"I just wanted to play with the train," he responded sheepishly.

"Bring the train with you then."

"No."

"Why not? No one would mind if you did."

"I don't want to," Mateo said.

Lina recognized the stubbornness in his tone and knew that no matter what she said he wouldn't budge. She contemplated him for a minute or two. Mateo had been acting a bit peculiar lately, and she couldn't shake off the presentiment that he concealed something from her. There was no doubt that Blackwater was full of deceit, and she feared that harm would soon find him.

With that in mind, and not having discarded the idea of Mateo using secret passages to move about, she dropped the subject of the toy and asked, "Do you remember when Aunt Eleonor gave you a tour of the house?"

Mateo nodded.

"Would you show me your favorite spots?"

"Yes, come on," he agreed, more excited than Lina anticipated. "I'll show you."

She followed him to the art gallery, where the walls were adorned with paintings of all sizes and marble sculptures sat on large tables scattered about the room. Mateo headed to a large oil replica of one of England's kings.

"Pull on the right corner," he instructed.

"What do you mean?"

"Like this." Mateo grabbed the edge of the portrait and pulled. Like a window, the painting opened, revealing a niche. Resting in it was a shoe box, the perfect size for hiding a small item.

"What's in the box?" Lina was astounded; she'd had no knowledge of the niche.

"Nothing. I already checked."

Lina peeked inside.

"I told you," Mateo said.

"I know, but I had to see for myself." Why would anyone have left an empty box in here? "Did Aunt Eleonor say why it's in here?"

"No." Mateo pushed the painting shut. "Come on. Follow me."

His little feet pattered down the hallway to Bartholomew's office. Lina's heartbeat accelerated as Mateo pressed his ear to the door. Though she had recently done the very thing, she couldn't imagine Mateo picking up the habit of eavesdropping.

"What are you doing?" Lina whispered.

"Shh!" Mateo put a finger to his lips.

"This is not a good idea." Lina reached for his hand, but Mateo dodged her.

"He isn't here, and you have to see this."

"How do you know he isn't?" Lina imagined the man sitting behind his desk, running his finger through his mustache, eagerly waiting for them to cross his boundaries.

"Because I don't hear him making weird noises," Mateo answered. True, Bartholomew was always grunting, shifting nervously on his chair, and speaking to himself. Almost imperceptibly, the boy scurried inside the room.

Lina followed, hardly believing his audacity, though she wasn't much different. If their uncle caught them, she would have to invent a reason for their being there—a reason to want to speak to him.

Mateo went to the wooden panels covering the east wall and pressed one of the vertical moldings with his finger. To Lina's amazement, a large piece of the wall moved slightly outward. Just like he had done with the niche in the painting gallery, Mateo opened it, and a short tunnel stretched in front of them, ending in a brick barricade.

"Aunt Eleonor said this used to be a hidden passage leading into the woods, but they closed it. It would be so fun if we could still use it," Mateo said.

Of course, when Lina had searched for hidden tunnels, her fear had kept her from even considering Bartholomew's office. But even if she had, she doubted she would have discovered this. She studied the space. It was wide and deep enough to conceal a person. In fact, the woman she'd heard a while ago could have been hiding in there—although Lina was almost certain the voice had come from somewhere behind her.

Mateo secured the panel back in place.

Lina faced the room and had a sudden idea. "Mateo, would you stand in the hallway and keep watch for a minute?"

"Why? You want to sneak around?"

Lina suppressed a laugh. Yes, sneaking was exactly what she had in mind. "Papa's favorite book is not in the library. Sir might have it in a drawer, and I want it back."

Thankfully, Mateo was innocent, or perhaps, mischievous enough not to question her. "I'll let you know if I hear him coming." The man's heavy footsteps were so loud that it was easy to hear his approach.

As soon as Mateo went out to the hallway, Lina rushed to search the desk and everything around it. All the while, she felt the curious, saddened eyes from the mounts on the walls, watching her every move. Surely, if the animals could speak, they would warn her that, if caught, she would end up like them. As if confirming her thoughts, she observed a couple of rifles on the floor behind the desk, but no small firearms. She revisited one of the drawers. It was deep and filled with stacks of documents. She dug to the bottom but only felt paper.

"Lina, Lina!" Mateo called in distress. "He is coming."

In a frenzy, she slammed the drawer closed, but it rebounded halfway as she hurried to leave. No use, she had no time to correct it. She stepped into the hallway and grabbed Mateo's hand.

"Pretend we are just walking by," she instructed.

The thundering footsteps met them at the bend in the corridor. Bartholomew gave them a strange look and then grunted. Mateo smiled. Lina was too scared to hold the man's gaze. She looked straight ahead, silently pleading he wouldn't notice anything amiss in his office.

After the office, Mateo showed her other curious spots in Blackwater. However, she found no revolvers, no open tunnels. The only other place she could think any evidence might be was Bartholomew's bedroom. She would have to find the perfect time to make a visit there.

"Lina." Eleonor caught up with her niece in the courtyard. "Are you going to town with Mr. Walton?"

"Yes. I want to buy some wool to finish my project."

"May I bother you to drop off my watch at the jewelry store for me? It's not keeping time as it should."

"Certainly," Lina said. "If it's a minor issue, they might be able to fix it while I'm there."

"Oh, no. I'm sending this one to ensure they order the same brand but in the latest model," Eleonor announced, handing the watch to Lina. "Their supply comes from London, and I hate mistakes and delays."

Lina rotated the watch in her hands. Eleonor had a taste for expensive things, which didn't make sense considering their financial state. But everyone had their quirks when coping with life's stresses.

"I'll head back on this road once I'm done with the errands," Mr. Walton said.

"Very well. I'll keep an eye out for you." Lina exited the car in front of the jewelry store.

She hurried to drop off Eleonor's watch and went across the street to buy green wool and a smaller weaving needle than the one she already had. After completing the transaction, she strode down the pavement. There was no sign of Mr. Walton. She halted at the bookstore's display window. Memories of her days working at the London library were swift to come. She missed inspecting and cataloging new arrivals, helping patrons find and select titles, the tranquil spirit that possessed its aisles—she missed it all.

"Catalina Laroche, isn't it?" A voice startled her.

Lina whirled and was pleasantly surprised to see that it was Max who had addressed her.

"Good morning," she greeted. "Please, call me Lina."

"Are you contemplating buying a book, Lina?" He secured his hands inside his pockets as if prepared to visit for a while.

"Oh, no, just browsing. There are plenty of books at Blackwater—the manor where I live."

"Ah, I imagine it's one of those prehistoric houses equipped with a gigantic library and a dungeon?" He smiled and though she knew better than to equate charm with character, she still found herself captivated.

"I suppose you can say that." She smiled back. "How about you? Are you shopping?"

"More or less. The tailor is designing a couple of shirts for me. She took my measurements, but I couldn't decide what colors I wanted. I'll have to come back, I guess." Max pulled out four fabric samples from his pocket. "Which one do you like?"

Flattered that Max had asked for her opinion. She studied the swatches one by one against the collar of his shirt. Her fingers brushed against his neck—the warmth of his skin sent a current through her body. "I like this one and this one." Lina separated the dark burgundy and the navy-blue fabric from the rest. All the while, she hoped he didn't notice how nervous he made her feel.

"You make it so easy. Too bad you weren't there with me."

Yes, too bad.

A car approaching the curb drew Lina's attention. Mr. Walton's return bothered Lina more than she would have anticipated.

"That's my ride. It was a pleasure to see you again, Max."

"The pleasure was all mine."

Lina couldn't stop thinking of Max the entire trip back to Blackwater. He was a very attractive man. Not just in appearance but in character as well. He seemed like an intelligent, collected fellow. So unlike Bray. He was overbearing, and she feared he hadn't shown his true colors yet.

The conversation between Bray and Bartholomew that Lina had overheard had amplified her dislike for the men. Bray is so unlike Max, Lina lamented, the encounter with Max fresh in her memory and heart. But for the time being, since she had to deal with Bray, she pushed thoughts of Max to the back of her mind. She resolved to keep a cool head even as Bray's undesirable advances grew in audacity and a game of hide-and-seek began—a game that deviated from the rules in one particular—Lina would hide but never seek.

Annie brought a fresh pot of coffee to the drawing room, where the family gathered. Lina cast Bray a sideways glance as he pulled a chair closer and sat down. How could he be so handsome and so horrible at the same time?

"Nothing better to start the morning than hot coffee," Bartholomew observed, sniffing the steam rising from his cup.

"Oh my." Eleonor stared at the newspaper's front page with horror. "Another rally has gone sour in Bethnal Green."

"Nothing to fret about, Aunt," Bray said. "I attended one of them to see what the fuss was about."

"And?" Bartholomew inquired.

"I can only say that these demonstrations are a sign of the political division tearing us apart. On one side, you have those sounding the alarm against this new figure rising in Germany—"

"Oh, yes. Hitler, I presume?" Eleonor said.

"That's correct," Bray responded. "On the other side, groups are surfacing in support of the man and his ideals."

"Everyone should be allowed to express their concerns. The problem is lack of civil discourse." Eleonor pointed to the picture of the brawl under the headline.

Lina made out a few details: people swinging punches at each other under a veil of smoke, black flags trampled underfoot, a lorry topped with loudspeakers vandalized—all in all, a mass of violence.

"What do you think of the matter?" Bartholomew asked Lina. "Coming from London, you must have an idea of what is brewing on the horizon."

"I don't know much about it," she answered truthfully. "I've never been to a demonstration."

"I find it hard to believe you wouldn't have an opinion," Bartholomew challenged. "You don't have to take to the streets to form one. William held a high government position, allowing him firsthand information. What was his position on Hitler's rise to power? Was he concerned with anything in particular?"

Lina found Bartholomew's line of inquiry odd. Why would he care about what her father thought?

"My father," Lina started, suppressing the suspicion in her voice, "was a reserved man. He never said more than necessary. And, certainly, he never divulged anything about his work." She wasn't exaggerating. William was even more cautious with what he recorded on paper. In a way, she lamented that was the case—after his death, Lina had gone through his belongings searching for clues that might lead her to the assassin but found nothing.

"William must have said something." Bartholomew seemed determined to retrieve information from his niece. "It's not a secret that he worked arduously to safeguard Britain's security. Hitler must have rattled his cage pretty good."

"I'm sorry. I don't recall anything at all," Lina stated. "And I haven't studied the problem enough to have an opinion, at least not an educated one." She felt a bit ashamed that this was the case.

"You are clever indeed, darling," Eleonor praised. "Too many people, poorly informed, I'm afraid, go about inflicting their erroneous beliefs upon others." She flipped the page of the paper, swiftly moving on from the subject. "Let's discuss something more cheerful."

Lina raised her cup to her lips. When Bray shifted closer and put his hand on her knee under the table, her cup clattered onto her saucer, and her body stiffened. His hand slid up her inner thigh, and she sprung from the chair like a cat on hot bricks, her coffee spilling on him and the cup crashing to the floor.

"Bloody!" Bray shot to his feet and looked in disbelief at the black stain on his cream vest and trousers.

"Oh my, what's happened?" Eleonor's eyes widened, a flare of sudden surprise crossing them.

Thankfully, Bartholomew had been engaged in lighting a cigar and missed the incident. He stared at Bray with a puzzled look.

Shocked by Bray's impertinence, Lina stood brooding for a moment. She could expose him, but she knew her uncle would laugh at Bray's actions and punish Lina for hers. And Eleonor would probably explain it away as a misunderstanding. It would do no good to say anything, and she had to think of what was best for Mateo.

"Forgive me. How clumsy of me," Lina said but glared at Bray. Then she walked out of the room, irritated by not having been able to speak her mind but content with having ruined his suit.

Lina successfully evaded Bray until nightfall. Eleonor had taken Mateo horseback riding, giving Lina time alone, which she spent sorting recipes from her mother's cookbook, an enormous handwritten volume Lina brought with her from London. The day would come when she would run the household, and she was determined to preserve her mother's famous dishes, including one of Lina's favorites, paella. The dish was a mix of rice, vegetables, and meats from Sofia's place of birth in Valencia, Spain. Lina cherished the memory of watching her mother making the savory dish. Even now, she could almost taste the saffron her mother always added.

When Mateo came inside, he was exhausted, and after an early meal, he fell asleep on the sofa. Lina carried him to his bed and returned to the dining room. She was purposely the last one to arrive, sitting as far away from Bray as possible. There would be no further physical contact between them.

"You are five minutes late," Bartholomew reproached.

"I'm sorry, sir," she replied curtly, tired of the oppression.

"Oh, come on, old man. Don't be so unbending," Bray defended. "It's not good for your health."

Lina flung a fierce glance at Bray. She neither needed nor wanted his help.

Bartholomew responded with a disapproving grunt.

"Mateo truly enjoyed riding today," Eleonor noted. "He learns incredibly fast."

"Thanks to you," Lina said to her aunt.

"I won't take all the credit," Eleonor responded. "He is quite clever, and, if I may say so, curious and eager to learn. He goes from one thing to another. As soon as we were done riding, he went in search of Krammer. He's quite interested in gardening."

"I'm thrilled that's the case. As comfortable as our flat was, we didn't have the luxury of a garden," Lina regretted. "Although, in this cold weather I imagine there is not much to do out there."

"Oh, you'd be surprised. There is always work to be done on such a large property," Eleonor affirmed. "If I'm not mistaken, Mateo helped Krammer to secure the covering over the cabbage garden. Krammer is determined to keep it from the snow."

They went on discussing the outdoors, and soon the men were talking about the upcoming hunting season. Bartholomew related in detail his preferred methods of tracking down and catching the animals. Bray, well-informed on the latest gadgets, advised the older man on which to acquire to become a more prolific hunter. Lina blocked out most of their conversation by engaging her aunt in a discussion about horses and Eleonor's glory days competing in Bristol.

"Those were the days," Eleonor said dreamily, then launched into an extensive recollection of the best race of her life.

While Lina listened, the evening passed surprisingly well, though she planned to leave early to prevent Bray from following her. Just then, Annie walked in with a tray of Lina's favorite dessert, Strawberry Fool. Nothing was better than the pulp of cooked fruit with cream and sugar. Lina so badly wanted some, but the risk wasn't worth it. She would sneak into the kitchen later, looking for leftovers.

Apparently exhausted from telling her stories, Eleonor unexpectedly announced, "I have the most dreadful headache. Do forgive me, but I must retire." She pushed back her chair with a grating sound. "Annie, whenever you are done here, please help me prepare for the night." Rubbing her temples, she strode to the door.

Lina sighed. Her aunt had beaten her to the punch. Now, any excuse would sound contrived.

"Yes, Mrs. Eleonor. I'll be up shortly." Annie prepared to serve the tempting treat.

"I'll not be having any," Bartholomew said. "I prefer a drink." He retreated to the side table, where a variety of alcoholic drinks awaited.

"Same here." Bray followed the older man.

Annie looked at Lina, who shook her head, declining dessert and instead helping the maid clear the table, her urge to escape escalating.

"Lina, please don't bother," Annie protested.

"It's no trouble at all." Lina collected the last fork, preparing to withdraw with Annie.

The men refilled their glasses, then huddled at the room's far end like two cunning crows. Their voices grew quiet, their countenances dark. The women strategically arranged the dishes on the trays to make only one trip and soon left the dining room. Lina's body relaxed; her breathing eased as she left Bray behind.

"Thank you for warning me about Bray," Lina said sincerely.

"Has he been pestering you?"

"Nothing I can't handle." Lina thought it best not to disclose too much.

"I avoid him like the plague."

"Thank goodness he's leaving the day after tomorrow."

"That can be a long time to deal with him," Annie lamented. "You mustn't lower your guard."

"I won't."

Lina had only to reach the safety of her bedroom and she would have conquered another day—but she still had to face the night. The ongoing need to protect herself and Mateo was putting an unbearable physical and mental strain on her. Would the deceptive maid be silent tonight? Or would she once more disrupt Lina's rest? Worse yet, would Mateo be restless and leave his room? Always at the back of her mind, those thoughts caused her to shiver, the dishes on the tray rattling.

"You feel that chilly patch of air too?" Annie asked, mistaking Lina's discomfort.

"I must have."

"It's this last stretch of the passage that gets particularly cold," observed Annie casually. "I'm not sure where the draft comes from, but it's strongest at night."

They stepped into the kitchen, where Dollie and Maggie took over their delivery. The twins looked ready to call it a day.

"May I help with the washing?" Lina offered.

"Certainly not," answered Maggie. "We have an efficient routine."

In other words, "Get out of our way." Lina got the message, the chance for a friendly chat out of the question.

"It's been a long day," muttered Dollie, extending her arms and stretching her back.

"I'll sweep the floor." Annie seized the broom.

"Where is Mrs. Lester?" Lina reached for some of the dessert. As expected, it was heavenly.

"She was just here but left to prepare the house for the night," Dollie answered.

Lina made a quick mental calculation. Lighting the candles alone would take Mrs. Lester a considerable amount of time. She swallowed the last bite of Strawberry Fool and, before Maggie could detain her, washed the glass bowl and put it back in the cupboard. "Is there anything at all I can do to help?" Lina insisted, disheartened that the women were overworked and most likely underpaid but wouldn't accept any help.

"Don't worry about us. We are almost done. Go on. Go get some rest," Annie suggested.

"Have a good night," Maggie said, dismissing Lina.

"Good night." Lina was defeated. She had no idea how to win over Maggie and her sister, a disappointment because she needed every ally she could find. Lina left the kitchen on the lookout for Bray, cautiously peering down the corridors before venturing into the open. Watching over her shoulder, she rushed up the staircase and along the west wing. She was sure she would later laugh at her behavior, but the man was menacing. He was probably drinking joyfully with Bartholomew, but she couldn't relax until she was locked in the safety of her bedroom.

She made the final turn and inhaled sharply. Halfway up the passage, Bray stood outside her quarters. She racked her brain for what to do but couldn't think of anything other than dismissing him as civilly as possible. Yet, something warned her that she faced danger on a grander scale.

"Why are you here?" Lina asked flatly.

"I wanted to see you." He blocked the entrance to her room, making it impossible for her to squeeze past him.

"It's late," she stated. "Let's talk in the morning."

"Don't be such a bore." He stepped suffocatingly close, his hot breath on her. It was immediately apparent that he was drunk. "Come on, spare me a few minutes."

"Please leave." Lina stepped backward to take the same escape route she had taken the other night, but before she could reach Mateo's doorknob, Bray seized her arm and pulled her back.

"I'm a fast learner," he said. "Come on. Invite me in."

"Not a chance." Lina pressed a warning hand to his chest, realizing too late that she was trapped—she wouldn't succeed in pushing him out of the way or in running to the stairs. In either case, Bray would overpower her. She tried to wrestle out of his grip, but he held her in place. She wanted to scream, but Mateo might hear, and it would only trouble him. "Let go of me this instant!"

Instead of letting her free, he dug his fingers into her skin with a force she hadn't anticipated. "Let's have a little fun."

"Have you lost your senses? Let me go."

Bray stretched his hand out and, with a single turn of the knob, managed to back Lina into her bedroom. He then used his foot to shut the door, pushing her farther into the isolation of the chamber. The space was semi-lit by the lively flames dancing in the fireplace. He pulled her into him, and terror filled her with the realization that she might have underestimated what Bray was capable of.

"And if I don't? What are you going to do? Run to Bartholomew? He won't care."

He spoke the truth, but still she argued, "I'm his niece! He must care!"

Like a cold snake, his lips slithered down her neck as he taunted, "Actually, running to him is not a bad idea. He'll force you to be with me."

"I'll die first." She wriggled with all her might, but there was no use.

"Dying would be less fun." Bray forcefully pressed his lips on hers.

His breath, reeking of alcohol, filled her nostrils. She was going to be sick. She threw her head back, pulling away.

He tucked his arm around her back, restraining both of hers while using his free hand to undo his belt. "Don't be nervous." He stepped out of his slacks.

Lina could see no way out of this hell. She was no match for him, not physically. Even if she lost everything else, she must stay in control. Summoning a surreal inner strength, she relaxed her muscles, and her lips found his. Though every cell in her body screamed in disgust, she gained dominion over Bray. The ardency of her kiss subdued his urgency, and he lowered his guard just enough for her to free one arm.

"May I?" she whispered, pointing at her clothing.

Bray's eyes brimmed with lust. "You may."

In a calculated movement, Lina slowly unfastened her blouse. The golden hue of the fire illuminated her fair skin, and Bray smiled. She carefully pulled back the arm still in his grip, and, to her surprise, he let go. In one heartbeat, she dashed to the hearth and grabbed the poker from the fire. Its handle was hot but not enough to stop her. Without a thought, she lunged at Bray, but he was too quick and caught the poker by the hotter end. With a wail and a curse, he dropped it as it seared his flesh.

Suddenly, the light was on, and Mrs. Lester stood in the doorway with wide eyes. "What's going on here?"

Lina stepped sideways and kicked Bray's trousers toward the door. "Mrs. Lester, I'm afraid Mr. Hamilton had a bit too much to drink and has lost his way. Would you mind showing him and his trousers to their room?"

No one said a word as Bray picked up his clothes and pressed them to his injured hand. He then walked away, trying to maintain his dignity as best he could.

"My dear, are you all right?" Mrs. Lester glanced at Lina's unbuttoned blouse.

"Yes, but I'm afraid he got burned and might need some ointment."

"I'll see to it." The housekeeper's gaze fell on the fire poker lying on the floor, out of place.

"Please don't tell anyone," Lina pleaded. Bray would most definitely tell Bartholomew, but there was no need for anyone else to know. Even if it wasn't her fault, she would be dreadfully ashamed.

"I shall not."

"Thank you."

Lina secured the door after the housekeeper and hurried to Mateo's room to lock his. With trembling fingers, she turned the key and looked at the small figure huddled under the covers. Any other time she would have sat on the edge of his bed and watched him sleep for a moment or two. Not tonight. She felt filthy and unwell. So she returned to her bedroom and retrieved the poker from the floor.

The feat of undressing after what had just occurred seemed almost impossible. Fully dressed and feeling like a ruffled hen having escaped a ravenous fox, she crawled into bed, the fire poker next to her. She didn't want to cry, but the shock set in, forcing her to deal with badly shaken nerves. He had been about to hurt her...and not just physically...He must have burnt his hand quite badly. What was Bartholomew going to say about this? *Oh, heaven, please help me.* Hot tears betrayed her, streaming down her cheeks until sleep rescued her.

A playful little laugh filled Lina's ears, raising an alarm in her subconsciousness. She fought against the call to wake up as exhaustion enveloped her and she welcomed the disconnection from her troubles. *Let me sleep just a while longer.* The giggling persisted, and she felt something pull on the blanket. Was Mateo in her bed? Lina extended her arm, feeling for her brother but grasped nothing but the covers. *Mateo?*

The door drifted open as if it had never been locked—no sound came from the knob or hinges. The dim light from the candelabrum in the hallway spilled into the bedroom. Lina raised her head from the pillow, squinting to adjust her vision. From within the shadows at the edges of the passage, a short figure stared back at her.

"Mateo? Is that you?"

More giggling.

She pushed the blanket aside and left the bed. Still trying to shake off the lethargy, she peered into the gloom. The boy darted down the hall toward the staircase.

Why was this happening again? It must be this wretched house.

She hustled down the hallway, and when a piercing sound, like a nail scratching metal, sent a chill up her spine, she stopped abruptly. When the sound came again, she released the breath stuck in her chest. The clock chimed four more times. That bloody clock. Someone was meddling with it again. And that someone wasn't Mateo, for he had gone opposite to where the clock slept. Who could it be? And for what reason? It couldn't just be to annoy her, could it?

Lina clung to the banister and looked at the foyer below. This time, she would not lose her brother. Thanks to Bray, when morning came, she'd be in trouble anyway, so she flipped the light switch, and the gigantic chandelier at eye level came to life, sending sparks throughout the entryway below. Aided by the light, she leaned over the railing just in time to see Mateo squeeze through the front door.

Taking the steps two at a time, she descended the staircase, grateful that she wasn't wearing her nightgown. The thickness of her blouse and skirt would keep her a bit warmer. Nevertheless, at the threshold, she remembered another threat. The memory of the Ridgebacks curdled her blood. Escaping them once had been a miracle that surely wouldn't repeat itself. Instinctively, she pressed her hand to the scar on her arm—the Doberman Pinscher's vicious attack in London still gave her nightmares. Nonetheless, what choice did she have? The desire to keep Mateo safe overpowered her fears, and she stepped into the frigid, starlit night.

She heard more laughter—a playful yet somewhat hysterical sound. With rising panic, she followed his giggles around the structure and to the back lawn.

"Mateo, where are you? Answer me."

"Come play with me," the voice reverberated through the frosty air.

"Stop this nonsense and show yourself at once," Lina demanded.

The moon hung near the trees that encircled the pond, casting a soft glow over the murky water. She squinted, hunting amongst the patches of vegetation for movement. To her horror she made out two sets of glowing eyes watching her from the tree line. The dogs.

The boy laughed again. Lina's gaze darted to the sound, and up ahead, she saw the tiny figure quickly heading to the pond.

"Mateo, stop!" Lina choked out, bolting after him. "Please, stop!" To her utter disbelief, Mateo entered the water. She pushed her legs to move faster, but the boy, showing no signs of distress, waded farther in. *Come on, come on. I'm almost there.* The bark of the Ridgebacks boomed in her ears. They were at her heels.

Lina rushed into the pond, gasping as the icy water stung her body. She looked back at the dogs, drawing another lungful of cold air. Their barks converted into angry growls while they paced on the bank as if daring her to come out. She turned from them and waded through the hydrilla plants, struggling against the pull of the mud under her feet. "Mateo, where are you?" She batted down the vegetation that blocked her view, and among a cluster of reeds, she spotted a silhouette deeper into the pond. The moonlight formed a soft halo around it, making it easier for her to follow. "Mateo, turn around. Look at me."

The figure didn't move.

A few more steps, and he was finally within arm's reach. Lina threw her arms around him but plunged into the water—for there was nothing but a bunch of slimy plants within her reach. She broke the surface, took a breath, and went back under. She gyrated in the water, stretching her arms in every direction, hoping to find Mateo. She came back up for air, and once again, dived under, this time going farther in. He wasn't here, but that was impossible. She had seen him in the pond. Hadn't she?

She emerged with a gasp, but the shifting mud gave way beneath her, causing her to go under yet again. She frantically kicked her legs and paddled her arms until her head was above the surface, but she still couldn't touch the bottom. "Don't stop moving," she ordered herself. If she did, she would never leave the pond.

Suddenly, the Ridgebacks emitted a blood-curdling howl and fled into the shadows. Lina struggled to stay afloat, but the thought of Mateo kept her moving. Her heart ached for him. If she drowned, he would be at the mercy of Bartholomew. Instead of adventure and laughter, his childhood would be full of fear and violence. She envisioned Mateo standing beside Bartholomew and Bray, surrounded by their addictions. That couldn't happen. She had to live for him.

She focused on the bank. Although her limbs were almost frozen and wouldn't move as fast as she told them to, she had to reach it. The moon must have moved, for it now shone brightly on a narrow spot where the grass met the pond. There, motionless, a woman watched Lina. The sight fueled Lina with hope. "Please help me!" she cried, but the newcomer appeared unmoved. On second glance, Lina recognized the dark dress, white apron, and unmistakable cone-shaped hair. The maid. Instant hateful energy emanated from the woman. It was as if an ice ball had been forced into Lina's heart—it hurt and weighed her down more than the freezing water did.

It took all Lina had to keep her chin above water. In between her wild splashing, she saw the maid's eyes glow red. Lina screamed in terror, her voice traveled through the openness and died somewhere among the trees. The woman vanished, and Lina lost all sensation in her body, succumbing to the pull of the underworld.

She was slipping into nothingness, too exhausted to fight. Before she knew what was happening, she felt pressure against her torso and found herself being propelled upward. She choked, trading muddy liquid for oxygen. Her throat, lungs, and entire being were racked with painful numbing. Her eyes struggled to focus, but she knew she floated toward the edge; something or someone was saving her life.

Whatever it was, it released her on the bank just as the first light of dawn crossed the sky. She crawled to higher ground and collapsed on the grass, breathing in sharp bursts. After a moment, she pushed herself up on her hands and saw the Ridgebacks shaking water off their fur nearby. If Mateo not being here didn't make sense, neither did the dogs plunging into the pond to save her. Just minutes before, they had chased her across the yard, and the other night, she'd barely escaped them. No, they had let her go both times. Of that, she was now sure. She took another look at them. One was rubbing his eyes with his paw. The other was still shaking off the weight of the water from his body. The dogs were her saviors, but her ordeal wasn't over yet.

She looked at the house. It was so far away. She had to move, but how, it wasn't clear. Her body trembled uncontrollably, and she felt pain in every breath. The Ridgebacks approached and nosed at her, encouraging her to get up. Lina got to her knees and, with much effort, stood on trembling legs. The dogs stayed at her side as she slowly made her way across the lawn. "Thank you," she said faintly.

The sight of the kitchen entrance was a miracle. As she crossed the threshold, the dogs retreated in the doghouse's direction. Maggie and Dollie spun on their heels and gasped at the appearance of the mud-covered woman. Lina fell into a chair, and everything went black.

"This cursed house." Eleonor's mournful voice brought her niece to awareness.

Lina tried to open her eyes, but her eyelids felt so heavy. She groaned and turned her head from side to side, but she couldn't shake off the exhaustion.

"It's all right, dear. Go back to sleep." Eleonor laid a hand on Lina's shoulder.

The sound of the door opening was followed by footsteps advancing into the room. "How is she doing?" Annie's voice inquired.

"Remarkably well, considering. Things could have been much worse." The sadness in Eleonor's tone pricked Lina's conscience. Though her thoughts were jumbled, she knew she had caused their grief.

"She must have been sleepwalking," Annie surmised.

"She must have been, for I can't fathom what would possess her to do such a thing," Eleonor remarked. "This must never happen again."

Eleonor ran a hand across Lina's forehead, the warmth and tenderness of the action making Lina long for her deceased mother. But Sofia's love and gentleness had gone with her to the grave.

Her aunt spoke again. "Annie do not leave this room until Mrs. Lester, or I, return. We are lucky she hasn't developed a fever, and we must keep it that way. The doctor won't be back in town for days. As it is, we were lucky to get ahold of him by telephone."

They'd called the doctor. Bartholomew must know.

"Yes, Mrs. Eleonor."

Lina felt a lovely, comforting heat against her sides—Mrs. Lester's hot water bottles. The room grew still, and Lina's exhaustion pulled her under completely.

Lina searched through the gloom for Mateo and found him facing the pond. He faced her, his eyes glowing red. He raised his hands; they were covered in blood.

Lina sat upright with a shriek, disoriented.

"Lina, are you all right?" Annie hustled in from the connecting passage.

"Where's Mateo?" Lina brought a shaky hand to her sore throat. "Where is he?" The events of last night flooded her mind. She wanted to yell for her little brother, but her voice failed her.

"Now, now, don't fret. He is safe and sound." Annie coaxed Lina to lie back down.

"I followed him to the pond. I saw him go in, but then he wasn't there..." The absurdity of what she had just said struck her—but it was true.

"You were probably sleepy and confused him with something else."

"I was awake," Lina defended. "His clothing must be wet."

"No, nothing of the sort." Annie sat on the chair Eleonor must have previously occupied.

"Annie, please. Are you sure?"

"Completely sure."

"Where is he now?"

"Dollie was teaching him to knead bread last I saw."

If Mateo wasn't out there, who was?

"Come now." Annie patted Lina's arm. "You must relax."

"How can I when nothing makes sense?" Lina let out a groan of exasperation and instantly regretted it when her throat contracted in pain.

"Well," Annie started, "I'm guessing that with the stress of these past weeks, it's your dreams troubling you, maybe even causing you to sleepwalk."

It was impossible. She had been fully awake. What she didn't know with certainty was what she had seen.

Annie continued in a mournful tone. "In the olden days, people would tie the sleepwalker to their bed to prevent them from being harmed."

That was a cheerful thought. Bray would love that. Lina closed her eyes, and Annie's voice faded into the background as she went on to painstakingly describe the process of securing sleepwalkers and the types of cords used. The implication in Annie's words about nightwalkers had Lina searching furiously for a solution that didn't involve being restrained to her bed.

Her trip to the pond swirled through her mind in fragments. The images of the maid came—she stood by the water's edge, watching Lina drown, her eyes red like fire. Moreover, she had contributed to Lina's misfortune through her negative energy. An energy that had pulled Lina under more than the water had.

She's a ghost. The notion came as serene and irrefutable as the dawn of day. Even so, it was a dreadful proposition, one that had been nudging her all this time, one she had thoroughly dismissed. Even now, after all she had been through, it was hard to consider the supernatural. She did not believe in such a thing—therein lay the problem. Denying the existence of the otherworldly had kept her from the truth. If ghosts did exist, then everything would make sense—the clock, the attic, the voices, the maid. And since Lina had also seen the woman in broad daylight when she had no doubt been awake, she was either going mad or being tormented by the supernatural. Just as she refused to believe she was a sleepwalker, she refused to believe she was mad. Hence, there was only one explanation, even as far-fetched as it might seem. Ghosts did exist and did not need secret passages to move about.

The small figure she had chased through the yard and into the pond appeared in her mind. Her heart sunk into her stomach. What if there was more than one ghost at Blackwater? What if she had been chasing the ghost of a child? Just as the idea formed, she rejected it. As far as she knew, no child had died at the manor. In fact, very few had even lived here.

She recalled a story she had read in the newspaper long ago. Legend had it that the ghost of a baroness roamed the grounds of Kensal Green Cemetery, seeking revenge for her three sons, who were murdered in a riot outside London. In her rage, she supposedly followed the cemetery's visitors home to drive them mad. Rumor had it that she even had the power to appear as someone significant to the victims, torturing them with an alternate reality until they took their own lives.

Maybe, just maybe, there was some truth in the tale. *The maid's ghost must be playing tricks on my mind, making me see things that aren't real, luring me out of my bedroom to cause harm. No, there is no other ghost. She wants me to believe Mateo is out there when he isn't. That's why she was at the pond. But then, why would she help me to handle Bartholomew that day in his office? For it must have been her.*

Annie walked to the hearth and threw in a couple more logs. Using the iron poker Lina had used to threaten Bray, Annie stirred the new wood in with the old to help them catch faster.

Heaven, have mercy on me. Bartholomew is going to wring my neck.

She had brazenly disobeyed two of her uncle's orders. By now, he was surely aware of it. First, she'd refused to give his protégée anything he had wanted. Second, she had left her room during the night. And as if that wasn't enough, she had dived into the frozen pond. Lina adjusted the hot water bottles under her arm and instantly remembered how Jasper and Ruppert had come to her rescue—an unexpected miracle for which she was profoundly grateful. But her uncle must never find out about it. It would only add to his wrath if he learned they had gone into the water thanks to her.

With a satisfied nod of approval at her work, Annie returned to the chair by Lina's bedside. Annie's thoughts must have been stirred along with the fire because she commented, "What an interesting night."

"Did something else happen?" Had Bray disclosed how he had burned his hand to the entire household?

"Well, yes. Mr. Hamilton took his things and left."

"Did he say why?" Lina held her breath, dreading the answer.

"Not that I know of. He hardly spoke to anyone."

Lina released the air stuck in her chest. Perhaps Bray was more respectable than she had thought and had kept the incident from Bartholomew, sparing her a confrontation. On the other hand, he might have been too humiliated by her rejection to let anyone know, especially Bartholomew. Suddenly, Lina thought of Mary, the maid that Bray had seduced during one of his visits, and how she had left without a trace. Could the maid's ghost be Mary? If that were the case, Mary was dead. It would explain her sudden disappearance. But how and why had Bray's lover died?

CHAPTER 8
UNFATHOMABLE

Lina sat at the kitchen table with a cup of coffee, wrestling with the implications of her new theory. Ghosts? They belonged in horror books, not in the mortal realm. Lina shook her head as if the action would organize her thoughts into something that made sense. Who was the ghost? What was she after? Though she couldn't answer those questions, the more she pondered it, the more convinced she became that the ghost was playing with her sanity, making her chase mirages. But how could she fight a menace that she knew nothing about?

Maggie and Dollie popped in through the back door, their arms filled with freshly cut fennel.

"Miss Lina, you are still here." Dollie stated the obvious, reminding Lina she had lost track of time. And to Maggie, she instructed, "Keep the scraps for the bunnies," as they neared the sink.

"You haven't finished your coffee." Maggie looked at the cup in Lina's hand. "Is there something wrong with it?"

"No, not at all." If anyone knew the ghost's identity, it had to be these sisters who had worked at Blackwater the longest. After all, it was apparent that Maggie and the mystery maid were both acquainted with the attic. It now dawned on Lina that Maggie had told the truth the day she'd followed the ghost. No one had actually gone into the attic. And if, indeed, the ghost was Mary, the sisters might know more about her sudden departure. Lina would have to tread lightly. "I went to the attic looking for one of my mother's paintings," she lied, having decided to clear the mystery of the wax first. "I was surprised to see a table covered with candle wax. Do you know who lit them and why?"

The sisters' gaze darted at each other.

"Well, that's hard to say. We go up there now and then, and after years it accumulates," Maggie said matter-of-factly.

"We should clean that up soon," Dollie added.

"It seems quite fresh to me..." Lina argued.

Dollie cleared her throat and, turning from Lina, opened the tap. The water descended on the vegetables in the sink.

"Well," Maggie said, "If you must know, our budget has been drastically reduced. So, often, we find ourselves in the attic looking for kitchen gadgets to replace the ones that break."

"Oh, yes, yes," Dollie giggled. "I don't mind it. They don't make things the way they used to anymore."

"That's right," Maggie agreed. "Old artifacts last longer than new ones nowadays."

Lina didn't believe them. Judging by the amount of wax left in the attic, the kitchen should have been filled with ancient gadgets, and it wasn't. Besides, the candles wouldn't have been stationary when most boxes weren't near the table.

"We must hurry," Maggie told Dollie, joining her in washing the fennel. "The day is flying by."

Lina dropped the topic of the candles. It would only reinforce the twins' position in the matter and cast suspicions about her interest in a seemingly insignificant detail. She downed the rest of the now-cold coffee.

"On another note," Lina spoke as casually as she could, "I've been thinking about the many helpers who have worked for us through the years."

"Too many to remember," Maggie responded wearily, as if the mere thought tired her.

"Thank goodness for Sir William," Dollie interjected. "May his soul rest in peace. For a while the staff became quite depleted. That is, until

Sir William brought Mrs. Lester to lift the burden off our shoulders. And thankfully she brought Annie." She shook off the water from the fennel and placed it on the counter.

"I keep thinking of one of the maids. I'm curious to know what became of her." Fishing for the truth, Lina lied again. "I don't recall her name, but she was tall, in her mid-thirties, and she had the most beautiful black hair. She always wore it in a high bun, like a wizard's hat. Perhaps that's why she stood out to me."

Dollie shot an alarmed glance at her, then looked away, the knife dropping from her hand onto the cutting board. "I must bring this to the bunnies before I forget." She collected the scraps and marched out of the kitchen without another word.

"Well," Lina pressed Maggie, "you know who I'm speaking of, don't you?"

"I'm afraid I don't." The expression on Maggie's face belied her words. Her eyes dropped to her wristwatch, and she exclaimed, "Oh my, it's midmorning and we don't have a green light on the luncheon menu. I must find Mrs. Lester." With exaggerated urgency, Maggie withdrew.

Lina let out a sigh of frustration. Whatever the twins knew, they would not disclose it.

Everyone in this house seemed to be hiding something. Guilt pricked at Lina, reminding her that she also had secrets. Seeing a ghost and eavesdropping on Bartholomew and Bray topped the list. Mary or not Mary, Maggie and Dollie knew who the maid was. Why wouldn't they speak about her?

Heavy footsteps approached the library. In a moment, Bartholomew's large frame filled the doorway, and Lina's heart stuttered. She had anticipated this moment—but now that it was upon her, she shrank at what it could mean. Was he going to scold her for her dip in the pond, or, heaven forbid, had he gotten wind of her rejection of Bray and was ready to crush her like a cockroach?

"Come to my office," Bartholomew ordered. "I would like a word with you."

Lina followed, feeling the floor tremble in his wake, his imposing stature minuscule compared to the violent spirit she sensed in him. How could he possibly be her father's brother? The memory of her gentle father, with his loving gaze and soft voice, did nothing to alleviate the fight-or-flight emotions that arose in her when around Bartholomew.

The curtains in the office were drawn, keeping daylight out. The lamp on the desk cast a faint glow, trying to fight off the gloom of the dark wall panels. Lina searched the shadows for the Ridgebacks in vain. The Ridgebacks. She would have drowned in the pond if it weren't for them. Their behavior, so different from what Lina had expected, still amazed her. They imposed their dominance and gained respect by inflicting fear through their ill temperament. However, their instincts were inclined to protect and save.

Bartholomew sank into his chair behind the desk, wasting no time in lighting a cigar. Lina dragged her chair a few inches back. The farther from her uncle, the better. Before he commanded her to do so, she sat down, feeling nauseated.

Silence and large puffs of smoke filled the air. Lina's eyes started to sting, and her nose burned from the fumes. Yet she didn't flinch, aware that some violent emotion brewed behind Bartholomew's casual demeanor.

However, when he spoke, his voice was eerily serene. "As your legal guardian, I'm responsible for overseeing your well-being, physically and financially. Your parents left you a good inheritance, but we live in hard times. Investments aren't bringing the returns they used to, and many are failing altogether."

Investments such as horse races? Perhaps he was in the wrong business. Though her thoughts roamed freely, Lina clenched her jaw, trapping her tongue.

"I feel a great responsibility to preserve what has been entrusted to me. My late brother would've expected as much. And, most certainly, he would have me protect the Laroche name and legacy at all costs."

Liar. He never cared for her father.

"With that in mind and considering the episode at the pond, I have made a difficult decision," he announced. Lina was somewhat relieved. He did not know about Bray. "It is evident that losing your father and the responsibility of caring for your brother has impacted you in a negative, even life-threatening way."

Was he insinuating that she was mad? Arguing would only make matters worse. And one mention of the word *ghost* would put her in the asylum for sure. She forced her voice to come out calm and steady. "The pond was an accident that will not repeat itself."

"I'm not taking any chances. You need an anchor in your life." He smashed the end of the cigar on the ashtray. "Bray has asked for your hand in marriage, and I have consented."

She couldn't breathe. The absurdity of what he had said was just that, absurd. He had no moral, or legal right for that matter, to select a husband on her behalf. The men had plotted for Bray to convince her to marry him. Ironically, judging by his actions, he knew nothing about courting—not that it would have made any difference. However, she had not anticipated that her uncle would force her into an unwanted marriage. For a split instant, she considered letting Bartholomew know of Bray's attack the other night, but she thought better of it— Bartholomew might have been the one to send him to her room.

Lina sprang to her feet. The bruises on Eleonor's face crossed her mind, and her knees weakened as she looked at Bartholomew's beefy hands. Even still, she said, "I will do no such thing," though in a softer voice than she'd have liked.

Bartholomew rubbed his neck with a ferocity that worried her. Was he thinking of wringing hers? "I wouldn't be so hasty to turn down the opportunity. You must think of your brother's welfare."

Mateo? The mention of him strengthened her resolve. "I will not be forced into an arranged marriage. You'll have to drag my dead body to the altar."

Like the flip of a switch, Bartholomew's wrath erupted, propelling him to stand. He shot around the desk, lunging toward his prey, his lamp crashing to the ground as he barreled past it. "Listen carefully," he spat in her face.

Perhaps it was foolish, but she would not back down. She would not allow him to intimidate her like he did Eleonor. If he touched her, she would go to the authorities. They might not help much, but at least he would think twice before striking her again. Conversely, her silence would only encourage his abuse.

"I'm listening." The look in Lina's eyes matched the intensity in his.

"If you don't cooperate, you'll force me to—" He stopped mid-sentence, and she realized she was slightly shaking. But soon enough, whatever had stopped him vanished, and he unleashed the fulness of his malice but in a calmer voice. "If you accept Bray, you'll be better suited to care for your brother. If not, it's in his best interest that we separate him from you. In your state of mind, you might drown him alongside you one of these days."

This she had not anticipated. Her sense of bewilderment made her chest tighten, suffocating her. She couldn't imagine a life without Mateo. But neither could she imagine life with Bray, especially after he'd violated her boundaries. Her gaze fell from her uncle to the ground as she contained her anger, but it burned through her entire being.

"You have until Sunday to make a decision," Bartholomew announced, shaking his finger in warning.

"And if I still refuse?"

"The boy will be placed in boarding school, far from your influence."

***

Faced with Bartholomew's threat to send Mateo away, the night with its haunting ghost seemed minuscule in comparison. Lina tossed and turned, unable to sleep, her chest searing with anger. Time passed by faster when one didn't want it to. Though Bartholomew had given her a few days to respond, it felt like hours. Hours when her mind worked nonstop to find a solution. He was Mateo's legal guardian until she became of age and, as such, had the power to put her brother in boarding school. For all she knew, he could send the boy to America. Just as she had before coming here, she considered running away with Mateo. But to where? They had no means and no other close relatives.

Bartholomew would hunt them down and lock her in a mental institution.

Her uncle's endgame was to get the siblings' money no matter how he did it. If he found a way to get rid of Lina, he might find a way to manipulate the trust and access their inheritance until Mateo was old enough—so many years from now. Then, of course, there was Bray, one more pawn in her uncle's game. Bartholomew would win if she married the man, but at least she would have Mateo.

The whole picture became clear. No matter which road she chose, these men were determined to herd her into the slaughterhouse. The anguish in her chest increased until her body turned the pain into numbness to protect her from a breakdown, and, mercifully, she slept.

A subtle sound, faint but constant, awoke her. She turned onto her back and pulled the covers down, straining her ears. The noise continued.

Rmm-rmm, rmmmmm.

It stopped for a moment or two, then started again, and the cycle went on. She listened more intently. It sounded like something rolling across the floor. She pushed the blanket aside and sat up.

There it was again.

Lina slid off the bed. The fire in the hearth still burned strong, the night young. She scanned what she could see of her surroundings but found nothing out of the ordinary.

A little laugh reached her through the darkness, pinpricking her every nerve.

It wasn't Mateo's laugh. Was it? She wouldn't be fooled again, but she had to be certain. She hurried through the connecting passage. Mateo's sheets were pulled back, his bed empty. Her attention jumped to the sliver of light coming from his slightly open door.

Rmm-rmm-rmmmm.

Soft giggling followed the noise from the corridor.

Doing her best to avoid the squeaky floorboards, she tiptoed to the door and peered through the gap. The hallway lay desolate except for the candelabrum, which sat on the floor instead of on the side table. Lina pulled on the doorknob, widening her view.

A marble rolled into the swath of light created by the candles, then was swallowed by the gloom a little farther down the corridor. After a brief silence, the marble returned.

Who was playing with the marble? Lina stepped out of the bedroom. To her right, Mateo sat on the floor, crossed-legged. To her left was only the marble—which abruptly rolled back toward her brother, seemingly on its own. She flipped the switch on the wall, and light flooded the space. Apart from her brother, there was no one.

"Mateo, what are you doing?" Just as she said that a sense of danger washed over her. She couldn't explain it, but she knew they weren't alone. Some unseen spirit accompanied them, their gaze weighing heavily upon Lina. "Mateo?"

He looked up at her with the dazed look of one not fully awake.

"Mateo? Can you hear me? Answer me. What are you doing?"

He didn't respond.

With a hiss of exasperation, Lina restored the candelabrum to its rightful spot on the table and turned off the light. "Come on. Let's go back to bed." She extended her hand, and he took it. Rising from the floor, he deposited the marble in his pocket. Conflicting emotions filled Lina. Should she interrogate or reprimand him? Or let it wait until morning? She locked the door behind them, and as they approached his bed, she thought better of it. "Come to my room."

Mateo jumped into her bed with a mischievous smile. Lina snuggled beside him. The boy was instantly asleep, as if he had just returned from a long, exhausting journey. This time, indeed, Mateo had been out of bed. She couldn't let her guard down, especially now, for she had a feeling that her life, along with everything she believed to be true, was about to change more than it already had, and that was hard to fathom.

Another ominous thought formed. The marble. Unless the floor was terribly uneven, an unseen force had sent the marble back toward Mateo. Lina shrunk at the image her mind conjured of the maid with her quick steps and malevolent eyes. Had she been out there with Mateo? Was she luring him out of bed? Just the other night, he had followed her to the attic. But why?

CHAPTER 9
COLLIDING

Winter was quietly settling in, and Lina's bedroom was frostier than usual. So far, the snow had been sporadic and fast dissipating, but that was bound to change. She left the bed and placed more firewood on the fire. Soon the crackling of wood increased along with its heat. She lay back down as daylight streamed in around the edges of the curtains. The sight of Mateo sleeping peacefully beside her warmed her heart. But that feeling quickly faded when she thought about Bartholomew sending him away. If she refused to marry Bray, how could she function without Mateo? How would Mateo take the separation? No, it was too awful to dwell on it.

Another unwelcome thought came—the past hours' eerie happenings. She slipped her hand into Mateo's pocket and retrieved the marble. Making as little noise as possible, she snuck through the passage to his room and went out to the hallway. Then she positioned herself where Mateo had been and rolled the marble across the floor. The ball rolled as far as her force had pushed it, then stopped. There *had* been someone else with Mateo. The maid? But why hadn't Lina been able to see her?

Lina headed back to bed with more unanswered questions. At least the grandfather clock hadn't gone off last night—though she didn't know if that was good or bad. She snuggled under the covers. Mateo woke up and faced her.

"Good morning, Lina," he said between yawns.

"Good morning. How did you sleep?"

"Fine."

"Last night, in the hallway, who were you playing marbles with?" she asked, unable to quell her curiosity.

"Me? I didn't—" His eyes grew large. "I wasn't playing with anyone."

"Yes, you were. I brought you back to bed, remember?"

He shook his head and reached for Lina's hand. "I don't." He opened her fingers and saw the marble. "Why do you have my marble?" He seized it at once.

"It was on the bed," she lied.

"Oh, it probably fell out of my pocket."

How convenient. He remembers where he put the marble but not the rest of his nocturnal activities.

Mateo raised the marble to eye level. It was a shiny white sphere with golden swirls.

"Where did you find it?" Lina inquired.

"I don't know. I don't remember."

Mateo avoided her gaze. Was he lying?

"You must remember something."

"I already told you. I don't," he answered stubbornly.

Clearly, Lina wasn't going to get a straight answer from him. She would have to help Mateo reach the point where he felt safe sharing whatever he knew.

"Mateo ..."

"Yes?"

"Don't forget that I love you all the way to the moon and back."

"I know. I know." He smiled. "Can we go downstairs now?"

Standing at the head of the table, Bartholomew towered over the seated group. He slammed his fist down, the silverware jumping and liquids dancing in their glasses. "If someone has taken it, they'll pay dearly!"

The man was in a rare temper over some misplaced document, his daylong search ending without success, his patience wearing thin. Lina couldn't comprehend his desperation—unless it was a matter of life or death.

"Sooner or later, I'll discover who took it." His eyes found Lina's.

Did he think she had? Oh, heaven, did he know she'd gone through his things? Her guilty conscience ate at her confidence, and along with Bartholomew's aggressive behavior, strangled her appetite. Mateo lowered his chin and reached for his sister's hand, his small frame quivering. She squeezed his hand to soothe him, but he continued to involuntarily shake.

"Come now, dear. Settle down," Eleonor said, rising from her seat to stand next to her husband.

Lina stared at her aunt in amazement. How did she have the courage to approach him in the state he was in? Maybe she trusted he wouldn't smack her in front of others, but Lina wasn't so sure.

"No one would take anything from you. It's probably buried at the bottom of a drawer somewhere. It'll turn up soon enough," Eleonor said.

Bartholomew grunted and stepped backward, knocking his chair to the floor. "Don't speak to me as if I were a child!" He stomped out of the room, his behavior contradicting his statement. He was much like the spoiled boy who pouted when things didn't go his way.

Eleonor moved to the vacant chair next to her nephew and brought him into a motherly embrace. "Don't worry about the old man. He is just having a rough evening. He'll be in a better mood in the morning."

Mateo returned the hug before heading to the serving table for another piece of lemon cake. Lina sat back and let out a long breath, the tension in her body releasing.

"I'm sorry, Lina. For everyone's sake, I hope he finds that document soon." The moisture in Eleonor's eyes revealed how thinly she was stretched.

"What is he looking for?" Lina's interest was piqued by the man's distress.

"Oh, some deed for the northern properties. They are barren lands, not worth anything. I'm not sure why he wants it just now."

To pay a gambling debt? Collectors knocking at his door?

"I better make sure he made it to the bedroom," Eleonor decided. "He was a little unstable, if you know what I mean."

Lina gave her a sympathetic smile, but she did not know what to think of Eleonor's concern for the man when he treated her so poorly. Eleonor withdrew, and Lina neared the window. She watched the sky darken as daylight faded. The night was here, bringing with it the dilemma of the dead. There truly was evil in this house—and not just the ghostly kind. Ever so present in her mind was Bartholomew's deadline for an answer about marrying Bray. Time was running out. And whatever she chose to do, she couldn't imagine the repercussions it would bring.

With an inward sigh, Lina joined Mateo by the table.

He swallowed the last bite of cake and wiped his mouth with his sleeve.

"Mateo, that's not good manners."

The boy shrugged.

"See these?" Lina pointed to the napkins on the table. "They are meant to wipe your mouth. Understood?"

"Yes, yes."

"Right, then—use them next time." Lina smiled.

"I'm going to bed," Mateo announced, with no trace of his previous fright.

"Since when do you go to sleep this early?" Her eyebrows knitted in curiosity as she observed an intriguing look in his eyes. Never had he seemed so willing to turn in for the night.

"My hands are tired from kneading bread. Dollie had me help with three loaves today. And my tail end is sore from riding the horse."

"Is that so?" Mateo's frankness was endearing and funny, but Lina refrained from laughing. The women in the house knew how to exhaust his energy.

"Good night, Lina." He wrapped his arms around her neck and kissed her cheek.

"I love you." She held on to him, wishing the hug would last forever. For a moment, her uncle's ultimatum to send the boy away threatened to undo her.

"I love you too." He wriggled in her arms. "Now, let me go."

"All right, all right." Out of habit, she ruffled his hair. "I'll be up to tuck you in soon."

"You don't have to."

"I'd like to."

"Annie said she would do it."

"Did she?"

With a small nod he walked away, and Lina saw him pull something from his pocket.

The marble. Lina's heart skipped a beat. She opened her mouth to say something but decided against it as Mateo disappeared into the hallway. Perhaps it was nothing, but she couldn't shake the feeling that he was hiding something from her. Whatever it was, it could harm him. She waited a few minutes before starting after him, and, turning harshly around the corner, she bumped into Annie.

"Oh, goodness. Forgive me," Annie said.

"It's my fault." Lina's gaze fell to the stack of sheets cradled in Annie's arms. "Where are these going?"

"To the linen cabinet." Annie's voice was weary. "I've been working on the laundry all day."

"It's a monstrous task," Lina sympathized. If Annie would only accept her help, but she had turned down the offer twice. Lina suspected that it had something to do with Mrs. Lester's Victorian ways of propriety.

"Indeed."

"Tell me, Annie, did Mateo say anything about going to bed early?"

"No, he didn't say anything to me."

"He's been acting a little odd today." And lying. "He headed upstairs a few minutes ago."

"He must be exhausted after playing outside most of the day," Annie offered. "I'll check on him as soon as I put these away."

"Don't worry about it. You have enough to do as it is." Lina patted Annie's shoulder. The poor girl looked spent. "I'll take care of Mateo, and you get to bed as soon as possible."

"I'll try." With a smile and renewed energy, Annie resumed her journey.

Lina trotted up the staircase. In her rush, the passages came and went in a blur, and Mateo's door appeared in the dim light of the corridor. She pushed it open just enough to peek inside. Though the bedroom was obscure, she could see the empty bed and hear chattering. She listened.

"I told you already. I'll get in trouble if I go outside at night," Mateo whispered.

Lina's stomach sank. Who was he speaking to?

Lina instantly recognized the sudden rumbling. A marble rolled across the floor.

"No, don't worry. I won't tell," Mateo whispered again.

Won't tell what?

Unable to contain herself, Lina slipped in and flipped on the light. "Mateo, where are you?"

"Here." At once, her brother popped out from underneath the bed.

"What are you doing?"

"Just playing."

"Playing with who?"

"No one." He jumped onto the bed.

A multitude of childhood horrors—monsters and evil men hiding under beds and in closets—filled her mind. She found herself doing exactly what she would have done twelve years ago. She knelt next to the bed and looked under it, only to see a few marbles scattered across the floorboards. She next went to the colossal armoire and flung its doors open. Satisfied that they were alone, she dropped next to Mateo. Though she had resolved to be patient with him, her body stiffened with irritation, and she couldn't stop herself from asking, "I heard you speaking to someone. Who was it?" This time her tone required an answer.

"I already told you. No one."

"That's not true, and I want to know the truth."

Mateo paused. She could see the wheels turning in his head. "I was speaking to myself—just playing, you know?"

"Why are you lying to me?"

"Lina, I'm not lying." His brown eyes grew sad.

Lina reminded herself that coercion might not do any good. She had no idea what powers she fought against or how to defeat them. Only one thing was apparent—the ghost had befriended Mateo. Exerting a great amount of willpower, she cooled her emotions. "Very well, then." She might have lost the battle, but she didn't intend to lose the war. "Would you like to take a bath?"

"May I bring the marbles?"

"By all means, bring the blessed marbles."

He leaped off the bed and crawled underneath to retrieve the balls.

As they walked to the washroom, Mateo's words cut through Lina's mind like a sharp blade, "*I told you already. I'll get into trouble if I go outside.*"

Anger such as Lina had never felt before, seized her. The woman's ghost would drive her insane. It seemed that the mind tricks weren't enough. She wanted to bring Mateo out to the grounds. How long would it be until Mateo did her bidding? An even more baleful notion surged— what if she was manifesting herself to Mateo in the form of a child? This had to be stopped—but how? There was one place that Lina associated the woman with. The attic. The ghost lingered there. Lina decided to wait until the household was asleep to pay a visit to the ghost's domain, breaking the rules one more time.

Not taking any chances, Lina had Mateo sleep in her bed. As she traced his hair with the tips of her fingers, he murmured softly and turned to the other side. He was so innocent and filled with excitement for life. In contrast, Bartholomew's demeanor at supper shook her. The fear she'd seen in Mateo's eyes at their uncle's angry threats stabbed at her heart.

Then, she had almost lost her patience with him when she found him *talking to himself* under the bed. The poor boy. No doubt he was going through a lot. But right now, the imminent danger was the woman's ghost.

Lina had to discover who she was and what she was after. There must be some way to make her leave them alone. Lina couldn't believe how she had gone from rejecting the otherworldly to accepting its existence, and from there to wanting to step into it. And although she was determined, now that the moment was here, her courage wavered.

Do not go there. It's her territory, and she'll be waiting for you, the voice in her head warned. She left Mateo's side as quietly as she could, making sure she didn't wake him up. One, two, three steps—her heart pounded against her ribs, screaming that what she was about to do was a terrible idea. She reached the door and froze when a noise came from the bed. She waited, listening over the pounding of her heart. After a few moments, when Mateo didn't move again, she tiptoed away.

Lina sought reassurance in logic. This time would be different, she told herself. She was doing this of her own free will, not because she'd been tricked to leave her bedroom. But her pitiful rationale did nothing to help her anxiety. Her nightgown slapped against her legs like nails clawing at her skin as she navigated the passages, guided by the candelabrum she'd picked up outside her door. She noticed each light switch as she passed by them. The notion that she could always reach for them was somewhat comforting, but she wanted to avoid waking the household. Bartholomew didn't need more ammunition against her. He had already insinuated that she might be mad, and she didn't want to think about what he could and would do given another excuse. His ultimatum for her to marry Bray or say goodbye to Mateo was already more than she could handle.

All too soon, the stairwell to the attic loomed before her. Now that she was here, she realized she wasn't sure what to do next. What would she say to the ghost? Would the ghost even be aware of her presence? The way she had held Lina's gaze at the pond attested that she might be. Lina again recalled the red eyes. It would not be a friendly encounter. Her father's favorite line was, "A wise man gets more use from his enemies than a fool from his friends." Well, she was about to put that to the test. Though, a wise person might not have placed themselves in this situation. She lifted the candelabrum a little higher and placed her foot on the first step. The candles' glow didn't extend far, but she could make out the boards. She forced her legs to move upward, remembering to keep to the edges, where the wood was quieter.

She reached the top with a pounding heart that shouted for her to turn back. Instead, she turned the knob. The door swung inward, and a gust of air came through the opening, extinguishing the candles. The ghost was here. Lina's grip tightened around the candlestick until her fingers hurt, though it would be useless against a specter. She took three steps into the gloom, and the warning voice resurfaced. *Leave while you still can.*

The door was less than an arm's length away. There was still time to retreat—but she couldn't, not when she was already here. What she could do, now that she was far from sight, was risk turning on the light. Stretching her hand out, she swept it up and down, feeling along the wall. Where was the switch? After a few failed attempts to locate it, she hesitantly moved deeper into the clutter. Blinking several times to adjust her vision, she became aware of faint moonlight shining through the window ahead. The light became her anchor. And just as she determined to follow it, a subtle, raspy noise came from behind her. She whirled, and with horror observed the door's outline slowly moving as if someone had pushed it. Then it clicked shut.

Lina was left with no one but herself to blame for her folly. Through the heaps of items that hemmed her in from all directions, she made it to the center of the space when yet another noise like splintering wood came from above her. The main beam supporting the high-pitched roof groaned again as if under unexpected pressure. The wind against the roof? No, that couldn't be it. She went closer to the far end and saw slivers of light through the curtains.

She sat the candelabrum on the floor, amazed it wasn't permanently fused to her hand, and pulled the drapes apart. A bright moon hung in the sky, illuminating the grounds and instantly bathing the attic in light. The outside world was still. There was no sign of the faintest breeze. In the distance, the pond's surface glittered like a fallen star backed by a host of giant trees.

A whooshing sound hissed through the attic, and something brushed the back of Lina's neck. Shivers raced across her skin as she spun on her heels. With heightened alertness, she scanned the space. Though the moonlight was strong, it didn't fully reach the edges where the shadows were the thickest. In this dimness, details became elusive, and familiar objects took on unfamiliar forms, blurring the line between reality and imagination. In her mind's eyes, she could see a thousand demons watching her, ready to pounce. And among them, the woman's ghost, eager yet patiently waiting to make her move.

Lina controlled her panic and forced her vision to go farther until she could make out most shapes and contours. Crates, the table up ahead, and other familiar objects took form. Her mind settled a bit upon recognizing them, but there in the farthest corner was the outline of something she didn't remember. She squinted at the dark shape. Cold beads of sweat formed on her forehead as two red eyes, fixed on her, glowed in the darkness. Almost imperceptibly, they moved closer. She thought of the candlestick on the floor—even if she couldn't hurt the ghost, it would give Lina a sense of security. If nothing else, she could swing it in the air to try to keep the menace at a safe distance. She wanted to reach for it, but her legs refused to move.

The silhouette traveled to where the moonlight revealed the black dress and white apron, the woman's colorless face a striking contrast to the rest of her.

"Who are you?" Lina croaked, fighting the tightness in her throat.

The ghost remained immobile, silent.

"Tell me." Lina raised her trembling voice a bit. "What do you want?"

Almost imperceptibly, the ghost moved again. The same destructive energy Lina felt at the pond struck her now. But this time, it was as if a fireball had been forced into her heart, burning her from the inside out. Instinctively, Lina stepped backward, unintentionally trapping herself between the window and the specter. The red eyes bore into Lina as she backed up against the casing. She would be pushed through the window and fall two stories to her death.

"You can't keep him from me." The ghost's voice reverberated through the attic.

"Who?" Lina asked.

"You can't keep him from me," the ghost repeated.

"Are you speaking of Mateo?" The scorching in her chest intensified, and Lina looked down, sure she was bleeding.

"He is mine."

"No, he isn't. He's mine," Lina cried, attempting to step sideways.

The ghost wailed, then launched at Lina with arms outstretched, her white hands tossing Lina to the dusty floor. The next thing she knew, the ghost was on top of her. Lina couldn't feel the ghost's hands or its body straddling her, but a powerful force pinned her to the ground. Meanwhile, the heat within her intensified.

"He's mine!" the ghost howled.

The resoluteness behind the specter's words awoke something in Lina—an absolute determination to safeguard Mateo. With body and mind, she pushed against the force restraining her. In a heartbeat the ghost was thrown back from her victim. With a painful groan, Lina rolled to her knees and rose. Then she scrambled through the maze, shoving at anything in her path.

She thrust the door open and rushed down the staircase to the corridor below. Panting, she looked over her shoulder, almost certain the ghost would be upon her, but the blazing eyes were gone.

"Why are you out of bed?" A barely audible voice came from down the passage, jolting her.

"Mateo?" Lina couldn't bring herself out of the nightmare. "Is that you?" She hurried after the voice, desperate to find the boy.

The only response was the laughter she'd heard the night she almost drowned. A piercing, short laugh that made her skin crawl. A sudden thought struck her, bringing her to a halt. What if the woman was playing tricks on her again? Lina couldn't take the risk—or could she? After all, Mateo had left his room at night before. It was madness.

The impulse to turn on the lights seized her, but unlike in the attic, she feared causing distress to the household. She then fought an even more compelling urge—to shout after the boy, to order, threaten, do whatever it took to get him to come to her. But fear of Bartholomew subdued the urge. She should have stayed in bed with Mateo.

As Lina came to the next intersection, the glow from Mrs. Lester's candles lightened her spirit. She followed the light and neared the top of the main stairs, where she looked down. The foyer was semi-lit by the large candelabrum on the entrance table. Out of the corner of her eye, Lina spotted a shadow scurrying along the edges. Should she check her bedroom or hurry downstairs? If Mateo wasn't in the room, she would lose precious minutes in finding him, and she was already at a disadvantage.

With her decision made, she rushed down the steps. Three more steps, two, one. She landed at the bottom, and someone blew the candles out. The darkness swallowed her.

A little laugh echoed from where the shadow had disappeared. Using her hands to feel her way, she followed the sound. Soon she reached the conservatory. Of all the places in the house, he had to pick this one. She stared at the grimy door, imagining a thousand creeping things lying in wait. She just had to get Mateo and go back to her room—if he was even here.

The mischievous laugh sounded closer.

As Lina slipped through the door of the greenhouse, she became aware of two things. The moonlight came in through the walls of windows, softening the obscurity, and she felt a drop in temperature—a cruel icy-cold air that lodged to her skin. Lina assessed her surroundings, her imagination betraying her. Images of the ghost, with her fiery eyes and white fingers, bursting out of the jungle to cause harm, shook her. With difficulty she forced the images away, replacing them with the urgency to find her brother.

"Mateo," she called softly. "Are you in here?"

A faint sound was followed by a disturbance in the tangled vegetation.

"Mateo?" She wrestled the overgrowth, unconcerned if she made a mess of it. Regardless of Eleonor's opinion, they needed trimming.

A thumping sounded in the distance, whether from inside the house or outside, she couldn't tell. Whatever it was, she had to get the boy and get out of there. The noise grew closer, but she still couldn't place it.

Then she saw a shadow break through the greenery into the sitting space. But when she reached the table, there were no signs of Mateo. However, the toy train, each wooden piece perfectly aligned, sat on the floor beside her feet. Suddenly, the little locomotive flipped onto its side as if someone had kicked it. Lina gave a startled jump. The thumping sound came again, louder this time. Something was coming through the plants toward her.

CHAPTER 10
CONSEQUENCES

Plants bent and branches snapped. Lina held her breath as a brutish figure emerged.

"What the devil are you doing here?" Bartholomew roared.

Lina stared at him wordlessly. She had done all she could to avoid this very moment, and it had come anyway.

"Answer me!" Bartholomew placed a meaty hand on her shoulder and shook her a little.

The ghost, Lina thought as if the man's presence had broken the spell. She must be playing with Lina's mind. Mateo had never left his bed. She'd been chasing an illusion—again. An image of the red eyes swirled mockingly through her head. She glanced at the toy train on the ground. Had the ghost caused it to flip over?

"Ugh, foolish girl, intent on making mischief," Bartholomew hissed. "Looking for things to incriminate me, aren't you?" He seized her arm and dragged her out of the greenhouse.

Helplessly, Lina half-walked, half-trotted alongside the man. Bartholomew hit the switches in their path. Light flooded the passageways, further dissipating any ghostly illusions.

"Even if I have to tie you to your bed, this is the last time you wander the house at night," he threatened.

Annie's remark about imprisoning sleepwalkers might indeed

become a reality. Lina felt ill. She would be strapped to her bed while the ghost lured Mateo out for real. Surely Aunt Eleonor wouldn't allow her husband to go that far. Just in case, Lina said, "I'm sorry. I came down to fetch some water and heard noises."

"From the greenhouse? It's a long way from the kitchen, don't you think?" His fingers tightened on her skin, prompting her to walk faster. "But even if I were to believe you, why would you go poking about in the dark? What do you expect to find other than trouble?"

He had a point.

"Sir, I promise I meant no harm." Lina hated the sound of her voice, for it reminded her of Eleonor's, vibrating with trepidation.

"No." He let out a mirthless laugh. "You are a troublemaker, indeed."

Lina bit her tongue to keep from saying something she might regret. As far as trouble went, however, she couldn't deny she'd brought it upon herself. Furthermore, since she had poked about in the past for something to incriminate him, his accusation had some substance. But evidently, something bothered him, and that something seemed to be associated with her. Was it related to her father's death or something entirely different?

Bartholomew whistled. "Ruppert, Jasper, come here, boys." The dogs surged from behind the stairwell.

Were the dogs loose inside the house? After they had rescued Lina from the pond, she saw them in a different light. They weren't enemies, but she wouldn't consider them friends either, for they were still under their master's control.

Bartholomew and Lina climbed the steps, followed by the Rhodesian Ridgebacks. All the while, he continued to rant. "If I don't have a positive answer about marrying Bray by noon, I'll take the necessary measures to end your games."

By noon? The compressed timeline stunned her. Games? If she refused to marry Bray, would her uncle play the insanity card? It might not be as terrible as being chained to the bed every night, but he'd separate her from Mateo.

When they reached the top of the steps, Bartholomew said, "Sit and guard." The dogs obediently settled next to the banister. "If you leave your bedroom again, I will know. You will stay there until breakfast." With a harsh motion, he released her arm.

As Lina marched down the passage, like a deadly summons from the other world, the grandfather clock banged four times, reverberating until she reached her bedchamber and shut the door. Blasted clock. Why must it taunt her? In the warm light coming from the fire, she saw Mateo asleep just as she had left him, curled comfortably under the thick covers, not having moved an inch. Thank goodness. Cautious not to wake him, she slipped into the bed, hardly believing what had occurred. She now had two dangerous enemies in the house. She recalled the scene from the attic. The ghost was powerful and could inflict harm, and, apparently, she could speak but only on her own terms.

"*He is mine,*" she had said.

Lina realized the woman was infatuated with Mateo, wanting him all to herself, but for that, she needed Lina out of the way. How could Lina protect Mateo from the woman when she had no idea what the ghost could or would do? She'd been lucky to escape tonight, and she wasn't even sure how she had. Recalling the anguish she suffered under the woman's influence, tears of anger built behind her eyes. Was she losing her marbles? *Ugh. Marbles.*

Mateo pushed the covers down and turned onto his back. Lina gazed at his angelic face and again resolved to protect him from the ghost and Bartholomew at all costs. Bartholomew wasn't bluffing. As dawn inched its way into the room, Lina knew that noon would come too soon, and she would have to respond to his ultimatum.

Like a caged animal, Lina paced the library, her hands hot and sweaty. She was being forced to make a life-altering decision that she might regret forever. Mateo was her entire world; his happiness and safety were at the forefront of her decision. He had suffered enough; the loss of their parents having affected him in ways she feared might leave long-lasting scars. Despite that, being together had given them enough strength to push on. And now that their connection was in jeopardy, turning twenty-one seemed unreachable. Until then, battling both the mortal and immortal worlds as she was, she had no option but to give in to one of her enemies. She gazed at the small clock on top of the credenza. Exactly when her uncle had said he wanted an answer, his heavy feet thundered down the corridor.

Dressed in his long overcoat and high boots, Bartholomew swept into the library with the Rhodesian Ridgebacks trailing behind. "What's it going to be?"

Though her heart withered, Lina squared her shoulders and looked him in the eyes. "I will not marry Hamilton."

Bartholomew's haughty demeanor faltered momentarily, the color in his face draining. "What did you say?"

"I will not marry Bray."

Bartholomew's gaze turned angry. Lina's breathing became shallow, and for a fleeting moment, she imagined him striking her as he had Eleonor.

"Well then, you can say your goodbyes to Mateo. I'll see that he is sent to boarding school at once," he said with a calmness that scared her more than if he had blown up. "Come, come. It's a nice day for a stroll." His pets followed him out.

The sound of his footfall died in the distance, and she collapsed onto the sofa. The accumulated emotions surged like a tempest, overwhelming her entirely. Heavy tears flowed down her cheeks as if they would never stop. If she didn't know any better, she would swear that her heart had been yanked from her chest, an empty hole in its place. How could she have done what she just did? Seeking reassurance, she went over the reasons for her decision.

Bartholomew was a sadistic man with a gambling addiction, along with all its dubious implications, and was on the verge of bankruptcy. Surely a scandal loomed over the family's reputation—one he seemed intent on avoiding by acquiring the funds he needed regardless of how he did it. On top of that, he most likely wanted to continue his habits, and for that, he needed money.

If she gave in, Bartholomew would not only squander their fortune, but he might still send Mateo away. More importantly, her self-worth would plummet if she married against her will. She hardly knew Bray, and what she did know of him, she disliked intensely. He treated women as objects, and, like her uncle, was up to his neck in debt. His interest in her was based on only two things: money and sex. If she had anything to say about it, he would get neither from her.

In the end, her independence was her most precious possession, and she would protect it at all costs. She would endure a year without Mateo. After all, it would be safer for him to be away from the manor and the spiteful ghost haunting its grounds. He would also benefit from new friends, living ones. And not having Mateo around might also help Lina, as the ghost wouldn't be able to use him to deceive her. How her heart would handle the separation, especially if Bartholomew didn't allow her to visit, she didn't know. She would count down the days until she turned twenty-one while trying to expose her father's killer—and perchance discover the ghost's identity and why it lingered at Blackwater.

A faint ray of hope touched her soul; maybe, just maybe, she could wake up from the nightmare before a year passed.

The sun finally came out after a dreary winter day. Its rays embraced the towering walls of Blackwater manor, but it was too late in the season to provide any lasting warmth. Lina wrapped a scarf around her neck and stuffed her hands into her pockets as she took the south path bordering the house. Eleonor came into view dressed as if prepared for a visit to Antarctica. She wore a brown fur coat to her ankles, a matching hat, and high boots. Lina smiled. Petite Eleonor hardly had any meat on her bones to protect her from the bitter temperatures, but her love for the outdoors was such that the weather couldn't deter her from being outside.

"How are you feeling, dear?" Eleonor trembled a little despite her heavy attire.

"Cold, very cold," Lina answered, referring not only to the weather but to her heart.

"Let's get you inside."

"My heart will still be frozen indoors." In a quivering voice, Lina added, "Did I make the correct choice about Mateo?"

"Oh, darling, I think you have. I think you have."

"I'm not so sure." The pain of the upcoming separation ate at her, and she couldn't help but wonder if agreeing to Bartholomew's terms would be better.

"As much as I adore Bray, I don't blame you for not wanting to marry him. One must be truly in love to make such a commitment. For once you are in it, only love can overcome the difficulties of marriage."

Lina supposed Eleonor knew what she spoke of. However, in considering Bartholomew and Eleonor's relationship, an idea occurred to her. True love was doing one's best to safeguard the well-being of others while not compromising one's own self in the process. The words from her mother's journal made sense now: "If we fall with those who fall, how can we raise them up?" It seemed to Lina that her aunt had fallen into a cycle of abuse with no idea how to get out. Her silent rationalization brought her a measure of sadness for Eleonor and a measure of reassurance that she had done the right thing to send Mateo away no matter how much it hurt.

"Speaking of Bray," Eleonor said. "He left in such haste I didn't have the chance to say goodbye."

"Why did he leave?" Lina asked casually, hoping Eleonor did not know the truth, which Lina assumed was a result of her defensive attack against Bray.

"I don't know, but he comes and goes as he pleases, and it won't be long until he returns. He loves it out here."

Please heaven, have mercy on me and keep him in London. As if Bray wasn't overbearing enough, how could she face him after what happened? Ironically, though he deserved what he got, she felt like she owed him for not telling on her. While she contemplated her standing with the handsome scoundrel, a moment passed when the only sound was their feet on the soft snow covering the cobblestones.

Eleonor must have taken her niece's silence as a sign of sadness, for she soothed, "I know how overwhelming the circumstances are. I'm sorry I couldn't convince Bartholomew to send Mateo to the local school." She intertwined her arm in Lina's as they traversed the east path. "But for now, remember that it might be best for Mateo. Blackwater isn't the best fit for a child, and he is excited about making friends his age. He never complains, but he must get dreadfully bored here. And with all the energy he has, even his infatuation with the horses will soon fade."

"You are right. I hope he'll like the school, that's all. One hears horror stories and—"

"Now, dear, don't allow yourself to go there. You'll go mad if you do."

Too late for that.

"Even if it's the last thing I do, I'll ensure he lands in the best school possible," Eleonor promised.

"I'm indebted to you. Thank you."

How Bartholomew so quickly arranged Mateo's departure, Lina couldn't say. All she knew was that her brother was enrolled in a boarding school in London. Aunt Eleonor had been assigned to drop him off. Lina's gaze followed each movement Mateo made as he ran about the courtyard, unaware of her sadness. She sat on the chilly front steps, wishing the moment would last forever, hoping to engrave every detail of him in her memory.

The chauffeur brought the car up to the house. Whistling softly under his breath, he got out. "Good day, miss."

"Hello, Mr. Walton."

"The little fellow's belongings..." Mr. Walton paused when he looked into Lina's eyes.

"In the foyer."

With a sympathetic nod, he went around her and into the house.

"Look, Lina! Look what I found!" Mateo showed her a glossy, orange-colored stone. "It's pretty, isn't it?"

"Indeed, it is."

"Why are you sad, Lina?" Mateo caressed her cheek.

"I'm not." She avoided his searching gaze.

"Yes, you are. Tell me—why are you sad? I'll stay with you if you don't want me to go."

If he only knew there was no choice, it would tear his tender heart apart. At least informing him about boarding school had been handled civilly. Aunt Eleonor had introduced the idea, building his excitement with the promise of friends and thrilling activities.

Lina could no longer hold back the tears. She brought him into her arms and held him tight. "Don't be silly. I want you to go. You'll have a lovely time learning new things and making new friends."

"Then why are you crying?"

"Because I will miss you."

"I will miss you too." As was his habit, he wrapped his fingers in her hair. "But you'll come to see me, won't you?"

"As soon as the school allows," she lied. "But until then, you'll think of me every time you see your scarf, yes?" She fastened the green scarf she had made for him around his neck.

"Yes, I will." Reaching into his pocket, he produced the wooden locomotive. "Here, I forgot to put this back. Can you do it for me?"

The sight of the toy caused her stomach to lurch. She recalled how it had flipped over without a visible explanation. "Oh, you finally took it from the conservatory."

"Just this piece."

"Why don't you take it with you?"

He shook his head decisively. "No, put it back."

"Are you sure?"

"Yes. I promised I would put it back." His eyes followed the toy as she placed it in her pocket.

"You promised who?"

"Uh...no one." He looked beyond Lina as if he had made eye contact with someone, but she saw only a large terracotta pot there.

Cradling her face in his hand, he said, "Please, Lina, make sure you align it with the rest of the cars. Do you remember the order I showed you?"

He'd grown too fond of it. Was the toy a way for the ghost to secure Mateo's trust?

"I do."

"Oh, good." But just in case, he explained, "The locomotive goes first, then the boxcar, then the cattle car, and the caboose is last."

"I will align them in that order." She smiled warmly and ran her fingers through his hair. Oh, how she would miss his beautiful, messy mane.

Mrs. Lester, Aunt Eleonor, and Mr. Walton emerged from the house, bringing Lina to her feet and her conversation with Mateo to an end. Mr. Walton secured the boy's luggage in the boot while Mrs. Lester came over to Mateo. She inspected the boy's attire, fixed his hair with a comb she produced from her pocket, and launched into a quick lesson on good behavior at school. Lina took a step away from them, brushing at her tears.

"Don't worry, darling," Eleonor consoled. "I'll ensure everything is in order before leaving him."

"You are wonderfully kind." Lina owed her aunt for the smooth transition and her constant support. Eleonor had not only helped Mateo with the sudden change, but she had also convinced her husband to keep the boy in England. "I'm not sure how you managed to have him stay close, but I'm indebted to you," Lina whispered away from Mateo.

"I took it from the reputation angle," Eleonor whispered back. "It wouldn't reflect well on your uncle if he sent his orphan nephew so precipitously out of the country."

"That was brilliant of you." Lina touched the locomotive in her pocket and reflexively pulled it out, just enough for Eleonor to see it. "Do you know who this belongs to?"

Eleonor's eyes widened. "I...where did you find it?"

"Mateo found it in the greenhouse. Whose was it?"

"Yours, from your childhood?"

"I don't remember having anything like it."

"Well, I wouldn't worry about it. It's just a toy." With a swing of her hand, she dismissed the subject and settled into the back seat of the car.

Mrs. Lester hugged Mateo. He soon escaped her tight embrace and skipped around the courtyard one final time before coming to his sister. "Here, you keep it." He handed Lina the orange stone he'd found.

"Thank you. I'll take good care of it."

"I love you, Lina." He hugged her tightly.

"I love you too, young man. Be good." She kissed his cheek, and he returned the gesture.

"I will."

Mateo jumped into the car next to their aunt. As Mr. Walton drove away, Mateo waved at Lina from the back window until they were out of view, taking her heart with him.

CHAPTER 11
SURFACING

Lina watched the twilight steadily descend through the window from the comfort of her bed. Evenings at the manor were a striking contrast to what they had been back in London, especially without Mateo. From their flat, she had enjoyed the beautiful refraction of sunlight over the city just before dusk. Sitting with her father by the hearth to discuss the day's events and future dreams was a treasured memory. "Grandchildren?" he once had said with joy in his eyes. "They will be the crown jewel of my life, but I must finish raising you two first." Lina felt an almost unbearable yearning for him, for their connection. For the first time in her life, she felt alone, dispirited, and like she fought a war impossible to win.

Before coming to Blackwater, she didn't believe in life beyond the mortal realm, but now she could no longer deny it, the ghost's existence attested to some form of life after death—different, devoid of flesh and bones, but a continuation of the essence of who one was. If that was the case, why was this woman so violent, so full of rage? Thoughts of the unknown brought Lina to her most intimate hurts and desires. Would she be with her parents again someday? Though it still seemed implausible, part of her wanted to believe it.

Before long, the windowpane grew black as night fell. Hopefully Mateo's absence would keep the ghost away. Lina closed her eyes, and it wasn't long until slumber found her. A clutter of dreams came and went, among them, images of a building with large windows, followed by Mateo signaling to her from one of them. Was he happy at school? Did he like the other boys? Would he fit in? The desire to answer those questions gnawed at the fringes of her subconsciousness.

"Why did you send him away?" The voice broke through her sleep.

Lina bolted upright, a wave of frosty air chilling her. The door was partially opened. She scrambled to her feet, dispelling the sleepy haze, and saw a short figure at the threshold. *No, no, no.* This shouldn't be happening.

"Why did you send him away?" The accusation cut to her very core.

The visitor backed into the hallway, and Lina followed. If nothing else, she needed to relock the door, even when it would do little to keep the ghost out. Under the dim glow of the corridor's candles, Lina saw clearly, and her breath stopped short. Time stood still as everything she had conjectured unraveled. His presence, his energy, was almost palpable. The boy staring at Lina couldn't be more than eight or nine years old. He wore blue-striped pajamas, and his arms hung limply at his sides. His large, sunken eyes looked back at her from a phantom-white face surrounded by a mane of disheveled blonde hair. Unlike the adult ghost, the boy exuded a semitransparent light.

Lina had been wrong all along. Indeed, he was an independent entity. This was another thing she couldn't explain, but speaking to him was like meeting a mortal person; there was no doubt of their existence. Not one but two ghosts haunted Blackwater. All this time, Lina had pursued the ghost of a child, not Mateo or a mind trick fabricated by the female ghost.

"Who are you?" Lina choked out.

The boy ignored her question. "Is he coming back?"

He was looking for Mateo. An even more shocking notion came— Mateo had not only been able to see the boy's ghost but had interacted with him. This was Mateo's playmate.

"Is he coming back?" the ghost asked yet again, and it was then that Lina saw the forlornness in his gaze. He had been in the courtyard when Mateo left. He missed him.

She opened her mouth to answer, but his loneliness penetrated deep into her soul, and she couldn't bring herself to tell him the truth. Mateo could be gone for quite some time. The ghost seemed to perceive her hesitation, and his countenance filled with a new sentiment. Was it disappointment or anger? He looked at the candelabrum, pursed his lips, and blew a breath of air that turned into tiny ice crystals as it crossed the hallway, prickling Lina's entire body. The candles flickered, their flames fighting to stay alive.

"Tell me your name," Lina pleaded.

The boy blew harder this time, and the candles went out.

"Wait—" It was too late. His shadow had slipped down the darkened passage. She took a few steps after him but stopped. Bartholomew would display her head on his wall if he caught her out and about again. With Mateo now safe at school, the risk of going after the ghost wasn't worth taking. At least not tonight.

Dawn brought with it more clarity to Lina's mind. She turned the locomotive in her hands, not believing how easily she had been fooled. The female ghost wasn't after Mateo. She must have been seeking the ghost of the boy. And when Lina had pursued his ghost, she must have perceived Lina as a threat. They must be connected somehow. Lina pondered. She had never seen them together. Indeed, the boy always fled to the outside world while the woman seemed to prefer the house. Lina turned these thoughts over and over in her mind. She recalled the sad eyes of the young ghost. Who was he? Had he lived at the manor? If he hadn't, then her previous assumption that ghosts lingered where they lived in mortality was wrong. And if he had, then it must have been long ago, otherwise she would surely have heard about him. Where, how, and why had he died at such a tender age? Then it hit Lina. Aunt Eleonor's reaction when she had shown her the toy was recognition. She knew who it belonged to. But why all the secrecy? At this point, she could solely focus on discovering her father's killer, but something told her that the specters played a vital part in her quest to do so. Besides, she was now too curious about the boy's ghost. She couldn't shake off his wretched appearance, the loneliness she saw in his eyes.

The idea came as an epiphany. Tired of being lied to, Lina would seek help outside Blackwater. If she couldn't find out who the female ghost was, perhaps she would have better luck identifying the boy.

The walk into town was tiresome. The cold breeze bit her face, and she arrived at Bert's shop weary and windblown. Before entering, she took a minute to fix her hair and adjust her coat. First impressions were important. She patted her pocket, making sure the locomotive, notepaper, and pencil were still there. If the shop had made the toy, they might remember something about it. Any information could help.

The bell attached to the door rang softly as Lina entered and headed to the counter. She moved quickly through the aisle stocked with merchandise, noting that the first few shelves were filled with intricately carved jungle animals, followed by wooden houses and trains. Younger than she'd expected, the clerk was lanky and sported a large nose and a set of eyes too small for his face. He watched her approach with a look of annoyance as if she had interrupted something important. Though he didn't appear to be doing much other than flipping through the pages of a catalog.

"Good afternoon, sir," Lina greeted, noticing the curtain of beads behind him that led to the back of the building.

"Miss." His fingers drummed on the counter.

Lina took the train out of her pocket. "I'm hoping you can tell me the history of this fine toy. I believe it was made in this shop."

The man took the locomotive from her and rotated it in his hands. "It has seen better days, hasn't it? See this here?" He tapped on the logo at the bottom. "We changed it six years ago to two circles. I can't tell you anything about it other than it's at least that old."

"What about these letters?" she pointed to the inscribed *TJ*. "Can you tell me anything about them?"

"I'd guess they are the initials of its owner. People often request a name to be carved or printed on a toy, especially if it's a gift."

Prodding wasn't in her nature, but she had hit a dead end at every turn. Hoping to jog his memory, she said, "Well, this locomotive was part of a set with a boxcar, cattle car, and caboose. Do you have any idea, even remotely, who it was made for?"

"I don't. We sell to the entire region. As you can imagine, there is no way to know where an item will end up."

Lina tried a more direct approach. "I found it at Blackwater Manor. Perhaps you have a record of its purchase?"

Now his gaze held an intense curiosity, reminding Lina that her interest in the toy seemed rather excessive. She gave him a faint smile.

"Our records only go back five years." He handed the locomotive to her. "I'm sorry I can't help you." The finality in his tone assured her she had annoyed him all right.

"Thank you." Lina turned, and through the display window, she saw a man walk past the shop. Her heart stuttered, instantly recognizing Max, the man who wandered through her dreams now and then. The impulse to run to the pavement and "accidentally" bump into him was strong. She imagined looking into his eyes, speaking to him, hearing his voice.

The beads rattled, and Lina whirled around to see a hunched, white-haired man slowly walk in through the curtain. His thick spectacles reminded her of the bottom of a wine bottle. Pulling herself together, she banished her thoughts of Max.

"Did I hear something about Blackwater?" the aged man asked in a crystal-clear voice.

"Mr. Snow," exclaimed the clerk in surprise. "I didn't know you were coming in today."

"Well, Paul, here I am." Mr. Snow adjusted his spectacles on the bridge of his nose and looked at Lina. "You must be William's daughter."

His observation took her aback, and she furrowed her brow.

"It's a small town," Mr. Snow explained. At once, she perceived that though his body lacked the agility of youth, his brain was sharp. There was keen awareness in his eyes.

"I'm sorry, yes." She extended her hand to him. "I'm Catalina Laroche."

Mr. Snow shook her hand slowly but firmly. "I'm Bert Snow, owner of this shop. Your father was an exceptional gentleman. The news of his passing was a shock to us all."

"I appreciate your kindness. We miss him dearly."

His attention drifted to the toy in Lina's hand. "May I see that?" Mr. Snow made approving and disapproving sounds as he examined the piece. When his gaze landed on the stamp and letters on it, it became distant, as if his thoughts had taken him to days long gone.

"It's part of a set." Lina said. "Is there anything you can tell me about it?"

"Paul, why don't you start working on the new merchandise that's just arrived?" Mr. Snow said.

"Very well." With a frown at the sudden dismissal, Paul retreated through the beads.

"Miss Laroche, I made this toy myself, so yes, I can tell you a few things about it."

She felt like clapping in delight but instead said, "I'd appreciate that very much."

"But first, may I ask why the interest?" With the experience of years backing him, he'd efficiently turned the tables on her.

Not having thought about an answer to such a question, she stared at him blankly. *Well...there is the ghost of a child at Blackwater making my life difficult. I want to know who he is, and since I believe this is his, maybe you can tell me his name and what caused his premature death.*

Surprisingly, an alternative truth came to her lips. "My little brother found it at the manor, and since his birthday is coming up, I wish to commission a few more pieces. Along with that, I'd like to order a storage box for the train—something he can treasure for years to come."

His eyes narrowed. "How old is your brother?"

"Eight."

"Are you planning to stay in Blackwater for a while?"

"For a year or so, but my brother just left for boarding school."

"Good. Good for him." His demeanor changed. Was it relief that passed his eyes?

"He should be home for the holidays, though. That's when I hope to give him the additional pieces."

"I see..." Mr. Snow continued to examine the locomotive with his long, bony fingers. "If I recall, I made this toy more than ten years ago. It was a wonderful project."

That was a long time ago. "Who ordered it?"

"I believe it was your uncle, Bartholomew Laroche."

"My uncle?" Lina was dumbfounded. Bartholomew didn't come across as a man who would consider or bestow such a delicate gift. "Who was it meant for?"

"That, I don't know."

"You don't know who TJ is?" She pointed at the initials.

"Hmm...nothing comes to mind."

"Are you certain?" She couldn't help but feel he withheld something from her. After all, Mr. Snow had been around for a while, and even if he hadn't personally known Bartholomew, he must have heard rumors about him and Blackwater.

"At my age, miss, of course, I'm not certain. And although I'm retired, I'll be happy to work on a few additions to the train if you'd like." He said this as if he would be honored.

"Thank you, Mr. Snow. My brother will be thrilled with the gift. I'm afraid he's grown fond of the toy."

"Interesting." Mr. Snow pulled a booklet and pencil from a drawer. "What pieces would you like to add to the original five?"

"Five?" She had only seen four.

"Well, yes," he answered matter-of-factly. "That, I remember clearly. I made the locomotive, a passenger, a boxcar, and a cattle car, along with a caboose."

"I'm afraid we have lost the passenger car."

"Right, then," Mr. Snow promptly decided, "let's start with a replacement piece."

They finalized the details, and Lina left the shop with her thoughts in a blur. She felt the train was somehow an essential part of Blackwater's mystery. She just had no idea where it fit. Why would her uncle order a toy train? As she traveled east on the pavement, she couldn't help but wonder if Max was still in town. She wouldn't admit it, but she purposely lingered at a large display window in case he popped out of one of the shops or simply turned the corner and came in her direction. While keeping an eye on the street in the reflection, she perused the large selection of artifacts on the other side of the glass. She then read the store board: Coleford Antiques.

Lina had been enthralled with history from a young age. Setting her inquietudes momentarily aside, she observed a pair of bronze candelabrums. The ones at Blackwater were dated, but not like this. These, bestowed with a thick base and seven arms, were taller than two feet. Most likely, they had come from a castle or mansion, and Lina imagined that carrying them around was quite an exercise.

Her gaze darted to a group of iron lanterns, and she wondered if perhaps they had belonged to Hurst Castle—the artillery fortress built by Henry VIII down south. Their square frames were painted dark red, and their handles were designed so they could be carried long distances.

Try as she might, her reverie wasn't to last. Her gaze was drawn to the item she had avoided since standing before the window—the marble carving depicting a cluster of winged angelic beings with large eyes that seemed to glow with unnatural human vitality. Where had they come from? A church? No. The answer sent a chill through her spine. A cemetery. Naturally, she thought of the dead boy at the manor. He might be buried in the cemetery. A tombstone could provide the information she sought. Giving up on seeing Max, she headed toward the graveyard. Block after block, she grew more anxious about her destination. Would she find something useful or just waste her time?

Her question was about to be answered as she came to the tombs scattered behind the white church. The first thing she noticed was the absence of sound. No birds shifted in the trees, no breeze, no voices. And though she didn't see anything unusual, she feared the stillness concealed the unseen company she felt, as if the owners of the graves watched her closely, curiously, perhaps angry at her intrusion. Her newfound sense of the otherworldly started to feel like a curse.

"Feeling," Lina told herself, "is worse than seeing." At least the latter forewarns us of what to expect.

She turned up the collar of her coat and ordered her mind to stay on task. Propelled by the desire to spend as little time as possible in the graveyard, she hurried past the large tombs, looking for smaller ones. It wasn't long before she found the first, and at once, she knew it wasn't the right one. This grave belonged to a child that died a year ago, at age two. She went on, finding three other tombs with a similar result. Either the initials didn't match, or they were too recent or too old.

With a sigh of disappointment, Lina retraced her steps toward the entrance, noticing the gigantic trees at the south edge. Through their bare branches, she could see the steeple of the ancient chapel. The records of the deceased were housed there. It was promising, but she couldn't bring herself to approach the chapel. Her uncle had significant influence in town, and, sooner or later, he would discover she had been inquiring about the dead without a logical reason to do so. For the time being, she could only hope he didn't find out she had been prowling around the cemetery.

Almost to the exit, she swerved between two white marble graves and caught sight of the tomb of a child she had missed. Could this be the boy's ghost resting place? It lay secluded in a corner, just beyond a giant sequoia tree. She dropped to her knees beside it, her heartbeat accelerating.

At first look, her hopes were crushed. There was no inscription on the upright stone, but from underneath a thick cover of decaying leaves, she saw the edge of a carving on the slab on the ground. She quickly brushed the leaves away.

Tacie___ Jan_____
19__ t __9

It was a girl. Lina wondered if she was chasing a mirage. Then, it occurred to her that Tacie could be short for Stacie, which was also a boy's name. Still, it was a far-fetched idea. The name Stacie wasn't popular, especially as a given name, and, worse yet, she couldn't make out the dates. Just like with everything else she had unearthed, though possible, it wasn't certain.

Feeling like screaming with exasperation, Lina made her way back to Blackwater and lingered on the grounds. Even when the cold breeze pecked at her skin, she couldn't bring herself to go inside. She was restless, her thoughts running like wildfire. Bartholomew had bought the train for someone. Up to this point, she had directly correlated the toy with the young ghost. What if it had nothing to do with him? But then again, it made sense that it was his.

Lina sat on a bench and, from her pocket, extracted the notepaper and pencil she had taken to town. She constructed a detailed list of the facts, going from her father's telephone conversation, to his death, to Bartholomew's gambling problems and involvement with Bray, to the ghosts inhabiting the manor. The inkling that all of it was somehow connected grew stronger. She studied the list for the longest while but, in the end, was no closer to solving her conundrum.

With a heavy feeling of defeat, Lina left the bench and strolled alongside the northwest edge of the house. Her body was as cold as she felt inside. The uncertainty of the unknown, coupled with Mateo's absence, had turned her world hostile and frigid. What wouldn't she give to see him, even if for a few minutes? No matter how terrible she had felt, his zeal for life had always cheered her up—always brightened her path. From Eleonor, she'd learned that Mateo was at High Point Boarding School in the heart of London. The school was considered one of England's best. She'd also learned that the school wouldn't allow anyone to visit the boy without Bartholomew's written consent.

Mr. Krammer came into view, laboriously removing several shrubs that had expired after a long life.

"Morning, miss." The gardener rested his hands on the handle of the shovel.

"Mr. Krammer, how are you?"

"I'll be better once these little beasts are removed and I can get back to it in the spring, when my hands aren't threatening to fall off." The gardener rubbed his gloved hands together to heat them.

"What will you plant here?"

"Some type of groundcover that doesn't grow too high, you know." He motioned with his head to the house. "We don't need any more shade."

"Indeed." On impulse, Lina asked, "Do you remember anyone by the name of Tacie or Stacie, or maybe TJ who might have lived here?"

"Tacie?"

"Or Stacie."

"Hmm..." The groundskeeper paused pensively. "It's been years, and I could be mistaken, but..."

"What?" Lina was all ears.

"There was a youth who came to the house often. Dollie bought fresh eggs from him. I think his name was Stacie. Although," Mr. Krammer admitted, "it could have been Stanley—yes, yes, it could have."

"Did the boy live in town or on a farm?"

"In town I think, but I'm not sure. Like I said, it's been years, and I never saw him again after he stopped coming." Lina was about to inquire a bit more to jog his memory when the gardener's gaze traveled past her shoulder and he stated, "We have company."

Lina turned, and her heart stopped.

Bray came briskly down the path.

For heaven's sake. Not again. "Mr. Krammer," she whispered, "whatever happens, please don't go too far."

There was no need to say anything else. The gardener's eyes showed understanding, and he assented with a slight nod.

"Good morning," greeted Bray.

"Good morning, sir," answered Mr. Krammer.

"Mr. Hamilton, I didn't expect you to be back so soon," Lina said in a grave tone, putting up a barrier of propriety by using his surname.

"Trust me, it wasn't an easy decision." Bray produced a half smile; to Lina's dismay, it was a penitent one. "May I have a word with you?"

As a matter of course, Mr. Krammer resumed his work.

Knowing the gardener had her back, she acquiesced. "Let's move to the sunshine."

They headed to a patch of grass that was out of earshot of the gardener but still in sight. Meanwhile, Lina struggled to process Bray's presence and what it could mean. Was he here to blackmail her? Mateo's departure and the ghost dilemma had consumed her thoughts and energy, and she hadn't stopped to consider the possibility of this very moment. Bray folded his arms across his chest. Lina stood a few steps away, biting her lip.

"I didn't know you had taken up gardening," he remarked playfully, breaking the ice that separated them.

"If you call chatting with Mr. Krammer while he works, gardening, then, yes, I'm remarkably good at it," she responded, half playfully, half sardonically.

Bray smiled and looked down as if he did not know how to say what he wanted to say. Under the pleasant sunlight, Lina couldn't help but notice how attractive the man was, though his attractiveness was more sensual than endearing. Still, his presence was not only strongly felt but commanding of attention.

"Listen, I want you to know I'm ashamed of my behavior the other night. I was beyond drunk and almost did something I'd have kicked myself for the rest of my life over. For that, I sincerely apologize."

A brief silence ensued as she digested his words. The last thing she expected was an apology.

"Please forgive me," he pleaded.

Lina searched her heart, assessing her options. Did she trust him? No, but she wasn't about to start a quarrel when, even if temporarily, what happened between them could be left in the past—far from her uncle's knowledge. After all, Bray had been drunk, and everyone made mistakes. Just this once, and since she would have to deal with him while he stayed at Blackwater, she would give him the benefit of the doubt. Still, if need be, she could ask Annie to sleep in her bedroom to keep safe from the man. "All right. Apology accepted."

"Thank you."

Lina produced a faint smile.

"Does that mean you'll call me Bray again? Mr. Hamilton sounds like I'm an old crow."

"I can do that. And...I am sorry about your hand."

"Me too." Bray looked at it. "I have a permanent mark, and it hurts now and then, but what can I say? It's a good reminder of my stupidity."

"We all have our scars, don't we?"

"Indeed, we do." He sighed. "But listen, your lips are turning blue. Let's go inside."

Lina smiled reassuringly at Mr. Krammer as they passed him on their way to the house, and Bray waved in a friendly manner. Seeing Bray's humble demeanor, she wondered if she should ask him about Mary. If Mary was the female ghost, he might know something about her passing. He might also have some knowledge of the boy.

She opened her mouth to speak, but then reconsidered. He had apologized, but he was far from trustworthy. For all she knew, he could have been involved in Mary's disappearance. Yes, it was best she didn't bring it up. They climbed the front steps. Lina was anxious to get out of the cold. That was before they entered the foyer and heard Bartholomew shouting.

CHAPTER 12
POSSIBILITIES

With worried expressions, the staff streamed into the main corridor.

In passing, Lina heard Maggie ask Dollie, "Did you let Mr. Krammer know?"

"Yes, but in case he forgot, I just signaled him to come in," Dollie responded.

Annie hurried to catch up with the twins as they hustled to Bartholomew's office, the echo of their shoes sounding in the wake of the man's tirade.

"What has happened?" Lina asked Mrs. Lester, who hurried from the drawing room.

"Sir Bartholomew has summoned us."

"Sounds like an emergency," Bray observed.

"We shall soon find out." With quick steps, Mrs. Lester resumed her march.

"Hmm. I wonder what Bartholomew has up his sleeve," Bray said.

"I'm not sure I want to know," Lina muttered.

"The more you know your enemy, the better prepared you are to combat him." Bray winked at Lina. "Though I think the old man is all mouth and no trousers."

An unexpected smile formed on Lina's lips. Where had this Bray come from? This side of him was unforeseen but pleasant. Perhaps now that she had seen his arrogant, ugly, and finally his penitent side, he had nothing else to hide, and they could become friends.

Mr. Krammer burst into the house with an unhappy expression. Lina surmised he did not like being yanked from the outside world as he stomped down the corridor in his muddy boots. Undoubtedly, Mrs. Lester would have a word with him.

"It must be really serious if even Mr. Krammer has been called," Lina said.

"Let's find out." Not waiting for an answer, Bray grasped Lina's hand and pulled her after him.

They slipped into the office. To her right, Mrs. Lester stood near Mr. Krammer, frowning at his footwear, but his attention was on Bartholomew, who sat on his chair like a king waiting to torture his subjects. As if wanting to minimize her presence, Annie stood a step behind the twin sisters. Dollie fidgeted with the side of her apron, while Maggie wore her usual impassive facade. She would excel at cards.

Bartholomew's eyes widened as he watched the latest arrivals. "How marvelous," sarcasm laced each syllable, "it is to witness your change of heart."

A bit disconcerted by his words, Lina followed the direction of his gaze and found her hand still in Bray's. She pulled it away.

"Well, old man, what's the commotion about?" Bray asked, striking a pose as if he were modeling tailcoats in London. "Don't keep us waiting." He drew everyone's eyes, including Bartholomew's, sparing Lina her uncle's glare.

"Meddling young people. Don't know how to mind their own business," Bartholomew retorted. "Don't you have anything better to do?"

"Not at the moment." Bray smirked.

"Ugh." Bartholomew snorted and turned to the staff. "I've misplaced some documents."

"Surprise, surprise," mumbled Bray.

Bartholomew threw him a condescending look.

Lina placed a hand on Bray's shoulder, pulling his head toward hers. "Do let him speak."

"Don't do that again," Bray said.

She mouthed the words, "Do what?"

"Whisper in my ear. It drives me mad." He winked playfully, but Lina feared he was serious.

"Actually, misplaced is not quite right. Someone stole them from this very drawer." Bartholomew rose from his chair with impetuous authority. He slammed the drawer shut; the very drawer Lina had inspected. "And we are going to find and punish the thief."

Lina's brow furrowed. Why would anyone steal them? His urgency to find them told her they had nothing to do with land deeds as Eleonor had said before. Lina's focus to find the gun in Bartholomew's office had blinded her to the possibility of other incriminating material—related or not to her father's death, she would take whatever she could to remove herself from beneath her uncle's iron fist.

"You are to search the entire house," Bartholomew ordered. "The bedrooms will be thoroughly inspected by someone other than their occupants." The room grew so quiet a pin could have been heard dropping to the floor. "I want every nook and cranny, including the outbuildings—all of it, searched."

The outbuildings? Lina found it an unusual order.

"They were inside a brown envelope. But bring me anything resembling an official document with or without an envelope. Understood?"

A collective "Yes, sir" was followed by Mrs. Lester dismissing the personnel. The staff filed out of the office, accompanied by an almost tangible cloud of anxiety. If one of them had betrayed their master, they would be discharged at once.

"I'll say, Uncle! These papers of yours must be quite important to put the entire household through such a hassle," Bray exclaimed.

"They are." The older man sank back into his seat.

"Perhaps we can help," Bray offered. "Any particular place you suspect they might be?"

"We have sufficient help, lad. You keep working on your projects," Bartholomew teased with a sly look.

Lina had a feeling Bartholomew didn't want her or Bray near those papers, which only piqued her interest more. And since it was apparent Bray hadn't a clue as to their nature, they might not be related to her uncle's gambling addiction. With an idea already forming, Lina withdrew, Bray following.

"Where are you going?" he asked as he caught up.

"To help with the search."

"I'll join you."

In the kitchen, they found Mrs. Lester assigning the staff search areas with the requirement that anything found was to go through her before reaching Bartholomew. Lina found it peculiar since he had explicitly told them to bring the papers to him directly. Perhaps she had misunderstood or simply wanted to reaffirm her position among the others.

"Annie will go through Lina's and Mateo's quarters," Mrs. Lester decided.

Lina sighed inwardly. Annie's familiarity with the siblings' bedroom minimized the intrusion. "I'd like to help. Where should I start?" Lina asked, hoping Bartholomew hadn't already prohibited her aid.

Mrs. Lester took a moment to consider.

Annie quickly intervened. "The attic and Mrs. Lester's room haven't been assigned."

The mention of the attic chilled Lina, her encounter with the ghost still vivid in her mind.

"We can do those," Bray offered.

We. Lina hesitated. Though some of her panic toward him had subsided, she still needed to be cautious. Being alone with Bray in the attic might prove unwise, but searching it by herself at present..."May I do Mrs. Lester's room, and Bray take the attic?" she counter-offered.

"Let's do them together," Bray insisted. "It will be faster and less daunting."

The sudden notion that she hadn't yet inspected the attic for the gun drove her to accept the offer. Besides, if Bray were faking his repentance, sooner or later, he would find a way to get to her. Keeping him close might be best, and the staff moving about the house would hear her scream. "Very well," Lina acquiesced.

As if reading Lina's mind, Mrs. Lester said, "Should you need anything, I'll be nearby," and threw a warning look at Bray.

Annie's gaze dashed to Lina. How Lina had gone from disliking Bray to willingly allowing him to be her partner would be difficult to explain to Annie. Feeling Annie's stare burning into her back, Lina left the kitchen with Bray. They swiftly made their way to the housekeeper's quarters.

"This is it." Lina let herself in.

"There is a first time for everything, but this is something else," Bray noted. "It's an awful breach of privacy."

Coming from a man who hadn't needed an invitation to her bedroom, his words struck her as ironic. "Let's do this quickly." In Lina's view, less time meant less intrusion.

"Agreed, but let's be thorough." Bray's tone told Lina he was deeply interested in finding the documents.

She briefly looked at him—he was so devilishly handsome. Sadly, not all that glitters is gold. Although, adversity made strange bedfellows. Again, Lina wondered if Bray could go from foe to friend. With his knowledge of Bartholomew's clandestine activities, he could make a powerful ally—but only time would tell.

With a sigh, Lina refocused. Mrs. Lester's bedroom was furnished with a large bed, a night table, an armoire, and a wooden rocking chair that sat beneath an oversized window. Lina imagined the housekeeper sitting in the chair and staring out into the yard. Upon further inspection, she noted that the rockers were well-worn. What occupied Mrs. Lester's mind while she rocked back and forth day after day?

Bray went to work, and as he fumbled through the armoire drawers, the neatness of the space struck Lina. Too clean. True, Mrs. Lester was efficiency itself, but the room had the feel of an uninhabited one.

"Are you going to help?" Bray called, kneeling to look under the armoire. "You said it yourself, the sooner we get this over with, the better."

"Yes, of course." Putting an end to her musings, she turned to the adjacent dressing room.

Order reigned there as well. Lina inspected the washbasin storage, the medicine cabinet, and the shelves along the far wall. There was nothing out of the ordinary. She was about to retreat when her eyes fell on a chair tucked in the darkest corner. On the chair rested a large suitcase. She unzipped it and found it packed with the housekeeper's belongings. She turned to look at the basin to find only a few items there. It was as if Mrs. Lester was ready to flee at a moment's notice. Lina dug through the items in the suitcase, and seeing nothing to match Bartholomew's request, she returned to the bedroom.

"All done," Bray announced. "She is clean."

"Did you go through all the drawers?"

"All of them."

"I'll say, that was fast."

"There is barely anything in them," Bray observed. "She must wear the same dress every day."

Most of her clothes were in the ready-to-go suitcase.

"Oh, wait." Bray stood on his toes and ran his hand across the top of the armoire. "There is something here." He pushed the chair over. "Hold on to it, would you?"

Lina kept it from rocking while Bray brought down a box. He placed it on the bed, and Lina's heart lurched. *Webley* was stamped on the lid.

"I'll say! It's a gun box," Bray exclaimed.

"What would Mrs. Lester be doing with a gun?"

Bray flung the box open, and buttons of all sizes and colors mocked them from within.

"Buttons?" Lina was sincerely surprised.

"Older ladies and their habits." Bray laughed. "They don't waste a perfectly good box when it can be put to good use."

"You don't think she owns a gun?"

"No. If she did, why not keep it in the box? She probably got it from one of her employers." Bray returned it to its place.

"You are probably right." Indeed, the box could have belonged to Bartholomew.

"Shall we take on the garret?" Bray was eager to move on.

Before stepping out of the housekeeper's domain, Lina scanned it one last time, her gaze falling upon a yellow jar on the night table. "Hold on."

She untwisted its lid, and found it filled to the brim with Woolworths Buttered Brazils. "Hmm."

"What is it?" Bray neared her.

"Just candy." She tipped the jar so he could see inside.

"Let's go, then."

They traveled the long distance to the attic without a word—very unlike Bray. On the other hand, Lina had a good excuse for her silence. Her mind was preoccupied with Mrs. Lester's candy jar and gun box. Annie had said that Mrs. Lester had thrown a fit when she found out the candy was not sold around here and that when her stash was depleted, she'd made the painful journey to London to replenish it. The problem was that Mrs. Lester hadn't been to London for quite some time and her stash sat untouched. If she loved the sweets so much, why wasn't she eating them?

The mystery surrounding Mrs. Lester evaporated from Lina's mind as she climbed the attic steps, replaced by an image of the ghastly woman ready to strike. She drew a long breath as she followed Bray inside. Faint daylight penetrated the space through the window at the far side, but it wasn't enough to see clearly. Bray wasted no time in reaching for the light controller. The single lightbulb came to life with a few disgruntled sounds.

"Oh," Lina muttered, staring at the switch adjacent to the doorframe.

"What?"

"Nothing." When Lina was last here, she had failed to find it as if it had moved on its own.

"Nothing is an understatement. Don't you think?" His eyes widened as he looked over the mountain of items facing them. "This is going to be painful."

"Much of it is furniture," Lina said, trying to cheer herself up more than comfort Bray.

"All right." Bray was swift to take charge. "You start here, and I'll search the back."

Wonderful. Staying close to the exit, far from where she had last seen the ghost, was most welcomed. Lina couldn't deny that working with Bray was better than she'd expected. Unencumbered by the manor's secrets or the paranormal, his focus was clear, his actions efficient. Soon he was out of sight, concealed by the piles separating them. Lina went through the easy items first, such as furniture and other things that required only a superficial check. The crates came next. Inside them, she found old kitchen gadgets, lamps, and frames—the usual stuff families accumulated over the years.

Lina energetically sorted through them, fighting against the wave of dust that filled the air. But the tiny particles lodged deep in her nose and stung her eyes. She sneezed several times and blinked in an effort to stop the irritation in her eyes. Why had nothing been disturbed when Maggie had claimed to have been looking for something?

"Holy smokes!" exclaimed Bray from across the room.

"What's the matter? Did you find something?"

"Something indeed—a table of burnt offerings."

"Oh, yes. That table has seen too many candles," Lina said with a sigh.

"You have seen it before?" Bray sounded intrigued. "Don't tell me you are into the dark arts."

Lina laughed. "I saw it while looking for an old painting," she lied.

"Well, someone has spent lots of time up here, but who in their right mind would do such a thing? And why the candles? I mean, I prefer electricity."

Lina sighed again. She wanted to know the same things. She opened a crate full of glassless frames. Not bothering to empty the box, she thrust her hand into it, feeling around the edges for different textures. At the very bottom, she felt paper. Digging underneath it, she grasped it and pulled it out. A newspaper. Probably used for packing. Shunning the ordeal of pushing it back down, she left it on top of the frames and replaced the lid.

The noises Bray made as he rummaged through things had stopped. In fact, Lina suddenly realized, the silence was minutes old. For a moment or two, she listened to the stillness, and then she began to worry.

"Bray?"

A feeling of uneasiness rose in her, and instinctively she glanced at the open door. She could flee if needed, but what in the world was Bray doing? Had he seen the ghost and fainted? She wouldn't be surprised. Then she heard a noise like a soft shuffling, too quick and indistinct for her to be sure. She waited, but it didn't repeat itself.

"Bray! Answer me. Where are you?" Goose bumps prickled her body. She didn't have to turn to know someone stood behind her. Something touched her back, and a piercing scream erupted from her.

"It's just me." Bray chuckled.

"For goodness' sake, Bray! What an idiot you are!" The harsh words came out sooner than she could process them, considering that Bray knew nothing of the ghosts and her constant edginess. "You scared me stiff."

"I'm sorry. I'm sorry." He raised his hands as if protecting himself from her fury. "I was just having a little fun."

"I wouldn't call that fun." She shook her head in disappointment, and reclaiming composure, asked, "Did you find anything?"

"No, there is nothing here. Well, nothing interesting anyway."

If he only knew. "I'm afraid I haven't found anything either."

"Shall we call it good?" Bray stood on the threshold. "Let's find something to eat."

Lina hated defeat. Finding whatever Bartholomew so frantically wanted could answer some questions, but they were done with their task, and her brain needed a break—a disconnection from reality. "I'd like that."

The card game was lengthy but fun. Her playful side was in full swing, and, for once, she was thoroughly enjoying spending time with Bray. The latter had depicted unprecedented temperance, seemingly content with his opponent's delight, even when it came at the cost of losing to her.

"I'll say, you are doing quite well. Have you considered playing for money?"

"Me?" Lina laughed. "No, that's not in my nature."

"It's an acquired taste."

"Not for me." Lina left the table. "If you'll excuse me. It's been a long day. I better get some sleep."

Bray looked at his wristwatch. "It's early, and you don't have the little fellow to worry about."

At the mention of Mateo, a wall of longing descended on Lina. He wasn't here to read a story to or to kiss good night. Her cheerful demeanor dropped, her raw feelings exposed.

"You must forgive me," Bray quickly apologized. "I shouldn't have said anything."

"It's all right."

Bray's eyes left her and settled on the lively fire in the grate.

"Good night, Bray."

"Wait. I have an idea." He spoke eagerly, jumping up from his seat. "Wait here for a few minutes."

"Wait for what? Where are you going?"

"To speak to Eleonor. Just wait for me." He hastened away.

Eleonor?

Lina paced the drawing room, her troubled thoughts returning with a vengeance. Was Mateo happy at school? Why were the lost papers so important to Bartholomew? Was the box in Lester's room truly used just for buttons? Would the woman's ghost wreak havoc tonight? Even worse, would the boy's ghost enter her room and scare the living daylights out of her? She rubbed her temples, hoping to stop the growing pressure. Thankfully, Bray reappeared rather fast.

"Come on." He brought her to the telephone and extended a piece of paper with a number written on it. "Ring the operator."

"Whose number is this?"

"The little fellow's."

"Mateo?"

Bray nodded enthusiastically.

"Eleonor? She gave it to you?"

He nodded again. "Go on. Ring it."

Lina picked up the receiver. "Wait, they won't let me speak to him without Bartholomew's approval."

Bray placed a hand on her shoulder, his eyes locked on hers. "Don't fret. If they ask, tell them that Eleonor gave permission."

Not believing her luck, Lina gave the number to the operator and was connected to High Point Boarding School. A woman with a delicate, elderly voice received the call and had Mateo on the line soon thereafter. Bray sat on the oversized chair by the fireplace, giving Lina privacy.

"Hello," Mateo said.

Lina felt extraordinary happiness, her heart burning at the sound of his sweet voice. "Mateo! It's me, Lina!"

"Lina! Lina! I knew you'd call!"

"How are you?"

"I'm fine. When are you coming to see me? I drew some pictures for you. Did you get the three I sent with Max?" His words were a torrent of excitement.

"Max?" He was the last person she would have expected Mateo to speak of.

"The soldier from the train. Remember? We saw him in town."

"Wait, he visited you?" Of course, she remembered Max. But what was he doing at Mateo's school?

"Yes. Well, no."

"Did he or did he not?"

"He came to visit another boy, and I said hello."

"Oh, and then you sent him on an errand to bring me your drawings? That's quite brazen, young man."

"No, he said he was going back to the forest and could bring them to you."

"Well, I haven't seen him yet." The prospect of a visit from Max added to her elation. "But tell me, do you like school?"

"I think so. I've already made lots of friends, and we get time to play in the afternoon."

"That's wonderful. And your teachers—do you like them?"

"I guess so. Well, except for Mr. Cook. I don't like him."

Lina smiled. As usual, Mateo was brutally honest. "You don't? Why not?"

"He is my penmanship teacher and says my handwriting is atrocious. He makes me write loads of practice sheets."

"Your handwriting is good, but there is always room for improvement."

"He says that too."

"Who is your favorite teacher?"

"Mrs. Rogers. She teaches French."

"I didn't know you liked French."

"I don't, but she doesn't give us too much homework. I would like to visit the Eiffel Tower sometime. Mrs. Rogers lived near it before coming to England, and she speaks about it nonstop."

"Does she, now?" Lina smiled again.

"Uh-huh."

"We'll have to visit France in the future then." Though it hadn't been long since Mateo had left, he already sounded much older. "But for now, do your very best at school."

"I will, but, Lina, you haven't told me when you are coming to see me."

"If I could, I'd come tomorrow, but it's a bit complicated." She paused, torn between reality and Mateo's hopes. She might not see him for a while. "I need you to be patient. Can you do that for me?"

"Why can't you just come?"

"I'll come as soon as I can. I promise."

The woman who had received the call spoke in the background. "It's time to get ready for bed. Say your goodbyes."

"I have to go, Lina."

"I love you."

"I love you too."

The line went dead. She replaced the receiver in the cradle and walked over to where Bray sat. "Thank you. I needed to hear his voice."

"Don't mention it. I owed you. How is he doing?"

"Surprisingly well."

"Listen, I was thinking..." Bray started.

"Yes?"

"Would you like to see the little fellow?"

CHAPTER 13
BITTERSWEET

What a daft question. "You know I would."

"Come with me to London, then," Bray proposed.

"What do you mean?"

"I can get you into the school to see Mateo."

"My uncle will not agree to it." A telephone call was one thing, a visit another.

"You underestimate me." Bray smiled brightly.

After hearing Mateo's voice, she missed him even more. Her heart screamed for her to accept Bray's offer, but she knew she walked on thin ice. Bray's sudden civility was suspicious, and he might require payment for his good deeds.

"If you say yes, I'll work on it right away," he persisted.

"Listen, arranging the call was frightfully generous of you, and seeing Mateo would be a dream come true, but I don't want to send the wrong message."

"What are you fussing about?" Bray left the chair and stood before her.

She made her stance crystal clear. "You are a handsome man, but I'm not attracted to you that way. Besides, I am not ready for anything of that sort right now." She twisted her fingers nervously. "In fact, I won't be for a long time."

"Whoa, whoa," Bray exclaimed. "Hold it right there. True, I have something in mind in exchange for my generosity."

Here it comes.

"But it's not what you are thinking."

"What, then?" Seeing the fire poker near the grate, Lina blushed. She did not want to be forced to use it again.

"I've been invited to a social gathering at Count Easton's place."

"And?"

"If it's not too much to ask, I'd like you to accompany me. Important people will be there, and a good impression will go a long way." He cleared his throat, and with pride in his voice, announced, "I'm considering a run for Parliament."

"Parliament?" Lina stared at him, trying her best not to show her lack of faith in his leadership skills. "That's a lofty goal."

"Trust me, I know. It's not something that will happen in a day. It will take time to build connections. So, will you accompany me? We could visit Mateo before the party."

She was about to suggest that any of his female friends would be better suited for the task when her father's political standings came to mind. Connections. Bray was asking for validation and an endorsement based on her deceased father's reputation. Fear that Bray could irremediably smear her father's name made her vacillate. However, the idea of abandoning the manor with Bartholomew and its ghosts, coupled with fulfilling her promise to visit Mateo, was irresistible. In the end, society could work up its own opinion of Bray Hamilton.

"We have a deal," Lina assented, but she needed more security. "If Mrs. Lester comes with me, that is."

"I'll arrange it."

Lina headed to the kitchen. She could hardly believe she would soon escape the manor's unpleasant inhabitants, both living and dead for a few days. Returning to London, even if temporary, made her feel like she had won a battle with Bartholomew. Surely, Bartholomew had allowed the trip in the hopes of bringing her closer to Bray and aiding his ambitions, but she and Bray would never be anything other than friends.

"I'm just doing my job," Mr. Krammer said to Dollie, pouring himself a cup of coffee.

"Good morning," Lina greeted, looking at the fresh dough on the counter.

"Morning." Mr. Krammer sat comfortably at the table.

"Good morning." Dollie wrestled with the oven to turn it on.

"Don't mind me," Lina said. "I just need a drink." She filled a glass with tap water and, seizing the newspaper from the counter, sat down opposite the gardener. She flipped through the pages, feigning interest.

"What are you going to do?" Dollie asked the gardener, resuming their discussion.

"Wait until they make up their mind," he replied.

"Being caught in a household dispute is terribly awkward," Dollie offered.

"The worst is that I had already torn out a few pieces when Sir Bartholomew told me to stop," he said. "I hope they reach an agreement soon. It can't stay like this."

"What's the matter?" Lina inquired.

"Mrs. Eleonor asked me to remove the south terrace floor. She wants to bring in some Italian stones, but Sir Bartholomew doesn't agree," Mr. Krammer answered.

"It's not that old, is it?" Lina recalled her mother mentioning the terrace's beauty a few times.

"Well, Sir Bartholomew had me build it about fourteen or so years ago."

"It's still in good condition, then?" Lina was curious. Considering that money was tight, why destroy something that didn't need repair?

"It's in excellent condition," the gardener assured.

"Mrs. Eleonor has never liked it," Dollie opined. "She preferred another tile and detested the fact that she wasn't involved in the project."

"She wasn't?" Lina wondered if Maggie's absence had loosened

Dollie's tongue. She had never spoken this much before, at least not about the household.

"Sir Bartholomew commissioned it on a whim, surprising everyone. In fact, we learned of it the day the materials arrived," Dollie explained. "Mr. Krammer had to drop everything to work on the terrace."

"Is that so?" Lina addressed the gardener.

"That's right. It was a bit hectic, but it turned out quite well. Sir Bartholomew even helped prepare the ground to place the stones, so I understand if he doesn't want to replace it. One can get attached to one's work, you know." Mr. Krammer swallowed the last of his coffee. "Well, I ought to get back to work."

"Allow me." Dollie took the empty cup from him, and the groundskeeper left. "Poor Krammer. I think he's overwhelmed by the amount of work."

"Indeed, it's a lot for one person to take on," Lina sympathized.

"And he's been faithfully doing it for years."

"Speaking of time," Lina casually said. "The other day, he told me there was a boy named Stacie who used to come to Blackwater."

"Stacie?" Dollie looked at Lina with a blank expression. "I don't remember anyone by that name."

"He mentioned that the boy used to sell eggs to you."

"Oh," Dollie exclaimed with growing awareness. "It's not Stacie, it's Stanley. He brought me the most beautiful colored eggs. He came with his father, George, the milkman. But that was years ago."

"What happened to them?" Lina inquired, to conceal her disappointment. Stanley did not match the name in the graveyard.

"Well ..." Dollie glanced at the doors as if making sure no one was listening. "The thing is that George was a widower, and Maggie got involved with him."

"Involved? As in a romantic relationship?"

"Yes."

"Oh." Lina was astounded. She would have never guessed that romance was on Maggie's radar. George must have been a unique man to like her detached personality.

Dollie hurriedly continued. "To this day, I'm not sure why they stopped seeing each other. Maggie won't talk about it, but I suspect it might have had something to do with Stanley. Maggie wasn't too fond of the boy. He missed his mother and never wasted a chance to express his opinion about having a stepmother. He abhorred it. Whatever it was, Maggie can't stand their names being mentioned, so please don't repeat any of this."

"I wouldn't dare," Lina stated truthfully, frightened by Maggie's enigmatic personality as it was.

"After that, whenever George and Stanley dropped by, it was quite uncomfortable. Then, one day, they simply stopped coming. I can't tell you how much I missed Stanley's happy face. He was a curious, free-spirited boy."

"You never saw them again?"

"No." Dollie shook her head. "Well, there you have it. A lot more information than you probably wanted."

"It's too bad it didn't work out for Maggie and George."

"Indeed, it is."

Maggie had secrets like everyone else. Lina wondered why she and George parted and what became of Stanley.

"The entrance hall was quite dusty." Annie popped into the kitchen, carrying a pail of dirty water.

"It always is, isn't it?" Dollie lamented.

"The sad reality." Annie left the pail near the back door. "Do you need a hand with the bread?"

"Oh, my—" Dollie dashed to the dough on the counter. "I forgot to put it in the oven, but I can manage."

"When would you like me to help you pack?" Annie turned to Lina, always thinking of the next task.

"Later this afternoon? But if you have other things to do, I'll be fine."

"It's all right. I'll give you a hand." Annie settled on a chair beside Lina.

"It won't take long. I won't be bringing much."

"Yes, it's only a few days..." Annie muttered, and Lina noted an edginess in her tone. Since Lina had told her about the trip to London with Bray, Annie had been a little more tense than usual.

Lina whispered so Dollie wouldn't overhear. "Don't you worry. There is nothing going on between Bray and me. I just want to see Mateo, and Mrs. Lester will be there the entire time."

Annie placed her hand on Lina's arm as if reinforcing what she was about to say. "A wolf can change his coat but not his character. Promise me you'll be extremely vigilant."

For an instant, the fervor in Annie's words made Lina second-guess her plans. However, the trip was already set in motion, and changing her mind now could have repercussions. Bartholomew might decide not to allow her to see or speak to Mateo for a very long time. "I promise." Lina felt a pang of guilt to have concealed Bray's attack from Annie. Yet, for Annie's sake, it was best to keep it that way. Annie seriously did not like the man.

"Oh, speaking of Hamilton," Annie said. "I received a letter from Mary this morning."

"You did?"

"Yes, she said she has taken a post as a lady's companion in the south of France. She didn't elaborate, but she sounds quite happy."

"I'm glad to hear it." Lina was sincerely relieved Mary hadn't suffered a terrible fate.

"Can you imagine wintering on the French Riviera?" Annie said with a dreamy look in her eyes. "Although, my life has such a dreadful sameness that I would be just as content with Bournemouth or the Isle of Wight."

"Yes, yes—sounds marvelous," Lina answered absentmindedly. If Mary wasn't the woman's ghost, who was?

Bray had secured train passage for Lina and himself, accompanied by Mrs. Lester. Upon arriving at King's Cross Station in London, he hailed a cab to take Lina and Mrs. Lester to her family's flat, while he headed off to his mother's terraced house to get situated. Returning to the city was refreshing. In contrast to the countryside, Lina was now surrounded by the busyness of the city, with familiar places to visit and activities to enjoy. But what she truly loved was returning to her flat. Although her parents and brother weren't here, and Bartholomew had dismissed the staff, it was still home. Her most profound connections in life had been forged and nurtured here. Many happy memories had been created within these walls, along with long-lasting lessons learned through the good and not-so-good times. She missed it all.

"I'll run to the market for a few groceries," Mrs. Lester informed. "I'll be back soon."

"Don't forget to buy some Woolworths Buttered Brazils," Lina said.

"Anything else you'd like?"

"No, not for me. The candies are for you."

Mrs. Lester observed Lina as if she hadn't ever heard about the candy.

"You like them, don't you?"

"Oh, well, of course." Mrs. Lester laughed. "There are just too many things in my head at the moment—but yes, of course, I'll make sure to grab some."

The housekeeper left, and Lina ambled to her father's office.

It was quiet. She inhaled, taking in the spicy smell of his aftershave cologne that still lingered in the room. His notebook, ink pen, and a couple of volumes on international relations sat on his desk just as he had left them. She settled on his chair, her heart yearning for him. Sitting in his office, Lina allowed herself to pretend she was back in happier days; that her father might walk through the door any time. But after a few minutes, she stood and left the office. Those happy days were long gone, never to return.

―――――――――――

Lina sat beside Bray in the cab. Unfortunately, her uncle had given her only three days of freedom, and she would be accompanied by Bray most of that time. Bray had a dangerously appealing side; he embraced the enjoyment of the moment, the superficial satisfaction of the spontaneous. Lina couldn't deny that a little fun in life was a must, but when it became the center of existence—annulling responsibility and self-respect—it was a destructive force. His gambling addiction and fascination with women came to the forefront of her thoughts. She shook her head a fraction of an inch to each side in disappointment.

"The next intersection will do, chap," Bray said to the driver.

"Very well, sir."

The cab halted, the engine idling as the passengers descended. Bray handed the driver a few bills, and the three moved quickly up the pavement toward a red three-story building. The sign above the double doors read High Point Boarding School. Lina's stomach did a somersault with each step closer to Mateo.

Bray tapped the iron knocker against the wood. When an older man with a round face answered, Bray explained their business in a casual, relaxed manner. Lina was glad she didn't have to do it, for even though she had Bartholomew's permission, she couldn't help feeling that she was not allowed to be here.

The man introduced himself as Mr. Floyd, the school's caretaker, and instructed them to follow him. They strolled to the inner courtyard—a beautiful garden populated with stone benches and a gigantic water fountain at the center.

"Wait here," Mr. Floyd requested. "I will advise the secretary to fetch Mateo from class."

Lina sat at the edge of the cold bench, nervously picking at her nails. Bray, hands in his pockets, sauntered about, whistling to himself. Thankfully, Lina didn't have to wait long.

"Lina! Lina!" shouted Mateo, bursting into the garden from a side door.

She kneeled to embrace him. "Oh, my boy! I have missed you so much!"

"You came! You came!" He wrapped his fingers around her hair and kissed her cheek.

"I told you I would." Exhilaration, unlike anything she had ever experienced, filled her soul, and she thanked heaven for bestowing her this moment.

"Here, this is for you." She handed Mateo a package.

His little fingers couldn't unwrap it fast enough. "Gloves! Thank you, Lina. I love them."

"I finally finished them. I'm still working on a pair of socks."

"You can bring them next time you come," he said happily.

"I shall."

After saying hello to Mateo, Bray left to attend to some business. Lina was thrilled to stay. Time flew by as she met the school staff and played games with some of Mateo's friends. She was pleased to find him quite content and surrounded by good people. More importantly, he was safe and away from the dangers of Blackwater.

"This is the art classroom," Mateo announced.

"It's impressive." Lina took in the colorful walls plastered with students' drawings.

"Let's draw something before class starts again," Mateo proposed, placing a blank piece of paper on a student's desk.

Lina squeezed in beside him on the bench, and together they drew a picture of London Bridge.

A short woman with black hair emerged into the room. "Ah, I see the love of art runs in the family," she noted. "I'm Mrs. Cooper, Mateo's art teacher."

"It's a pleasure to meet you." Lina rose and shook her hand. "I'm Mateo's sister, Catalina Laroche."

"I must say I'm delighted to have Mateo in my class. He is a deep thinker, and, as such, expresses himself through his drawings in a most remarkable manner. I find layers of meaning in his work."

"You are most kind. Thank you." Lina had never thought about it that way but was elated to hear Mrs. Cooper's assessment of Mateo's talent.

The first bell rang, summoning the students from recess. Mrs. Cooper excused herself to prepare for class, then retreated to her desk at the back of the room.

Mateo signed his name at the edge of the paper. "Your turn. Sign here." He handed Lina a pencil, then watched with interest as she wrote her name.

"There," Lina said. "It's our official masterpiece now."

Clearly pleased, Mateo taped their drawing on the wall among the others. "I have art class next, so I'll show it to my friends."

Lina looked at her wristwatch and was sure its hands conspired against her. The end of her visit was almost here. The uncertainty of not knowing when she'd see Mateo again was painful. Holding hands, they made their way back to the courtyard.

"Did you put the locomotive back in the greenhouse?" Mateo suddenly asked.

"Yes." Of all the things he could ask about, why this? "Why is it so important that it went back there?"

"No reason." Mateo avoided her gaze.

She pulled him to a bench and sat him down, then squatted in front of him. "Mateo, look at me." His large eyes sheepishly focused on hers. "Why did you want the locomotive back in the conservatory? Tell me the truth." She suspected the answer, but she had to be sure.

"I promised him I would put it back."

Her stomach heaved. "Who?"

Mateo's little feet swung back and forth above the ground. "The boy who lives in the manor. It's his train." He'd confirmed Lina's suspicions. Mateo had interacted with the boy, but did he realize the boy was a ghost? Lina decided not to mention it. If Mateo didn't know, there was no point in scaring him. Children had a unique, innocent way of perceiving the world—of not questioning their surroundings like adults did.

"Do you know his name?"

"Tommy." Mateo quickly responded.

Tommy? The letter *T* was carved on the wooden toy. "Do you know his surname?"

"What's a surname?"

"It's the family name—ours is Laroche."

"No, I don't."

"Why didn't you tell me about him before?"

"He told me not to tell anybody."

"Why not?"

"He said he might get in trouble if they find out, and he didn't want to stop playing with me."

"Who are *they*?" Chills ran down Lina's arms.

Mateo shrugged. "I don't know." He seemed sincere. "The marbles are his too. They were in the box in the niche."

"In the painting gallery?"

"Yes. He said I could play with them."

The sound of the knocker came from the entrance hall, its tap, tap, tap echoing through the garden, upsetting Lina. Bray was back. Just when Mateo had lowered the wall of secrecy, her time had run out.

Mr. Floyd strolled across the garden to answer the call. And too soon, Bray surfaced.

"I'm afraid I must go," Lina said disappointed.

Mateo jumped off the bench and hugged her. "I miss you already."

"I love you very much and am thrilled with your school. It's fabulous."

"I like it too." His arms tightened around her neck. "I love you, Lina."

"I love you more."

He giggled and ran off to the art classroom.

———

Lina looked down at her fancy dress, displeased. "Wear your best," Bray had advised. Her best would attract unwanted attention from him, which was the last thing she needed. Nonetheless, a plain dress would be disrespectful to the host. Her blue gown featured a three-quarter sleeve, round neck, and full skirt that hung an inch above the floor. Completing the ensemble, Mrs. Lester arranged Lina's hair in a crown braid, which Lina insisted she keep to one layer, not wanting to resemble the ghost.

The doorbell rang, and the housekeeper heeded its call.

Lina read the time on the clock on the wall. "Unnecessarily early."

"Please come in, Mr. Hamilton," Mrs. Lester invited, and Bray crossed the threshold dressed in a dark vested suit and white shirt.

"Good evening." Lina hadn't seen him dressed this well before, and though she loathed to admit it, he cut a dashing figure.

"Good evening, indeed. You look ravishing." Not bothering to hide his assessment of her appearance, his eyes swept over her with thorough approval.

She ignored his compliment. "Let me grab my coat."

Soon, the three were on their way to the mansion of Count Easton in a highly distinguished area of London. With Bray behind the wheel, the half-hour drive felt life-threatening. He pressed too hard on the gas pedal, his eyes on Lina instead of the road.

"Now, now," Mrs. Lester said from the back seat. "Mr. Hamilton, if you could please read the names of the intersections for me, I would be much obliged. Sadly, my vision is not what it used to be, and I would like to know where we are."

Lina suspected that Mrs. Lester's request had two brilliant purposes. First, if he were to read the signs, he had to slow down. Second, he would have to keep his eyes on the road.

"I'll do my best." For the next while, Bray dutifully read the names of the streets and added some comments about them, boasting of his knowledge of the city. However, his attention soon returned to Lina.

"Watch the light!" Mrs. Lester exclaimed.

When Bray reacted, it was too late to hit the brakes, so he ran the red light.

Mrs. Lester mumbled something that sounded like a prayer for help, while Lina urged, "For goodness' sake, Bray, watch where we're going."

Seemingly unconcerned, Bray smiled, his eyes telling all—he was thoroughly enchanted with his companion. Lina glanced at the housekeeper, grateful for her company, for she was now convinced Mrs. Lester's presence influenced his behavior, keeping any inappropriate comments in check.

Lina breathed a little easier when they arrived at the count's property.

"It's a full house." Bray noted the obvious. Cars were parked bumper to bumper down the long driveway. Bray circled twice and, seeing the valet busy with other guests, ended up finding a spot a block away.

Having made their way to the house on foot, the trio entered the grand hall, where Mrs. Lester left them in the butler's company. "If you'll excuse me, I'll make myself useful." Holding Lina's gaze, she added, "I'll be in the kitchen."

The butler, a large man whose sweaty forehead spoke of an already hectic evening, said to Mrs. Lester, "That's kind of you, madam," and, despite his apparent distress, fulfilled his duties with admirable precision. In a matter of minutes, he'd gathered their coats, informed the newcomers of the most prominent figures in attendance, and highlighted the excellent refreshments.

Lina and Bray thanked him, then joined the lively crowd. Lina scanned the vast room for any familiar faces. Apart from a few older men she vaguely remembered from another gathering with her father, she didn't recognize anyone.

"Listen to the orchestra. They are so talented," exclaimed a blonde woman who rushed past Lina.

"The count knows how to throw a party," added her companion, a short man with a well-trimmed mustache.

"Let's get a drink," Bray proposed, and they squeezed their way through the crowd to the refreshment table.

Lina picked up a glass and took a sip. "Wow, it's strong."

"French champagne." As Bray tasted his, his eyes were drawn to a group of men marching into the great hall. "Would you look at that? General McAllister in the flesh!"

The general was a middle-aged man with graying hair and sharp blue eyes. He sported a dark uniform decorated with a solid line of metals and ribbons across the pockets. In addition to his extensive history, his large stature and perfect posture demanded respect. Lina's father had spoken highly of him. As a young man, McAllister had led some of the most important battles during the Great War. Frustrated by the poor planning and rash decisions of others, his priority had been to protect the lives of his men by carefully developing and executing his attacks—and with much success. His expertise and wisdom remained a great asset to the country. A month rarely passed without him making news, always engaged in improving the nation and its military relationships worldwide. Reverently, all eyes fell on him, and people graciously stepped out of his path.

"I cannot believe my luck," Bray reflected. "I would have never thought he would be here."

"And why is that?"

"You haven't heard, have you?"

"Heard what?"

"The Secret Service learned of an assassination plot against him," Bray said in a hushed tone. "And with the increasing instability in Europe, he went underground."

"Perhaps things have settled." Lina remembered reading something about Manchuria and the fear of Germany invading Czechoslovakia.

"Maybe so."

The men passed into the adjacent room where the dancing was to take place. A younger fellow in a blue uniform who had fallen behind McAllister's group hustled after them. Lina recognized his brown hair, hazel eyes, and broad shoulders. Max. He seemed to be everywhere—the train, Coleford town, Mateo's school. Her heart skipped a beat just as it had when she had spotted him through the window of the toy shop. At last, another chance to interact with him.

Like a dog after a bone, Bray started after the group.

"Bray? Where are you going?"

"Just give me a moment."

Still thinking about Max, Lina did a lap around the dessert table and tried the carrot cake. Finding the treat nicely flavored with a pinch of nutmeg, she took another piece. Perhaps her appetite was induced by anxiety, but she also tried the chocolate cake and a portion of fig pudding. She then finished her champagne and placed the empty glass on a waiter's tray just as the orchestra announced the start of the dance. Where is Bray? Just then, she felt a hand on her shoulder.

"Come on. I'll introduce you to the general." Bray laced his arm through Lina's and led her to the ballroom.

General McAllister stood with the group he came in with, which included Max.

"This is Miss Catalina Laroche," Bray introduced.

"Miss Laroche, it's a pleasure to make your acquaintance," the general said politely.

"My pleasure, General."

Taking her hands into his, he added, "Please accept my deepest condolences. Your father is sorely missed." His eyes teared up, taking her aback. Given his reputation for possessing an iron character, she was surprised by his emotion.

"Thank you, General."

McAllister released her hands and introduced the rest of the men. Their names came and went, the only one to stick was that of Lieutenant Maxwell LeBlanc. Max nodded a greeting. She nodded back; there was no need to advise the rest of their previous encounters.

With the introductions complete, Bray planted himself next to the powerful man and launched into a political discussion. The change in the mood was palpable. Embarrassed for Bray, Lina felt her palms start to sweat. As if already the Head of Parliament, he spoke passionately of the country's weaknesses. The general indulged Bray, but Lina saw the irritation in his eyes.

Two of the men quietly separated themselves from the company. Lina fidgeted with her bracelet, wanting to flee but not knowing how to do so discreetly. Adding to her anxiety, Max glanced at her now and then but didn't speak. She racked her brain for something to say without showing too much interest in him. She couldn't produce anything fast enough, but to her delight, Max inched closer.

"May I?" He offered his hand.

The answer was a resounding yes. She didn't care about the nasty look Bray threw her. He was behaving like a fool, and the general would put him in his place soon enough. She jumped at the chance to escape the shameful episode.

Max placed a hand on Lina's back, she reached for his shoulder, and their free hands clasped as they moved to the music. He pulled her into him and said, "It's nice to see you again. I must say I did not expect you to be here."

"I could say the same."

"I move about a lot."

"Speaking of which…I understand you visited my brother at his school."

His eyebrows contracted.

Had Mateo mistaken him for another soldier? Impossible. The boy was good at remembering people. Lina clarified, "Mateo, my brother. He's at High Point Boarding School here in London."

"Oh, yes. Forgive me. It's been a long week. Yes, I did see him there." He smiled, and for the third time since they started dancing, his eyes darted to the general and lingered there for a moment.

"Who do you know at High Point?" Lina did her best not to misstep as she glanced at Bray. He still spoke to the general, his hand gestures punctuating his words.

"Who do I know at High Point?" Max repeated in a soft voice.

"That's what I asked." His apparent disconnection annoyed her, and she asked point blank, "Do you have a son there?"

The mention of a son brought Max to full alertness, and he chuckled. "No. No! Nothing of the sort. I happened to be there on an official errand, and your brother recognized me. I wasn't expecting to find him there. I assumed he would be at school in the forest."

"It was a last-minute decision."

"Ah, well, he seemed happy." He threw another look in his superior's direction. "Oh, before I forget—Mateo commissioned me to deliver some drawings to you."

Did he? She could have sworn Mateo said the soldier had volunteered. Moreover, Mateo was under the impression Max was there visiting another boy. "And when were you planning to deliver them?"

"I'll be in London a little longer, but as soon as I return to Coleford. He said you are at Blackwater. Is that right?"

"That's correct."

Max drew Lina closer as the orchestra played a slow melody, his closeness making Lina's pulse quicken. His skin against hers felt like a magnet; she didn't want to let go. Though the emotions startled her, she kept them hidden under a mask of coolness.

"How do you know Hamilton?" Max asked.

"He is my aunt's nephew."

"No blood connection, then?"

"Absolutely not," she responded.

"How long are you staying in London?"

"I'm heading back to Coleford in the morning."

"I envy you. It's peaceful there."

You have no idea. Lina looked up at Max. He was much taller than she recalled. She also realized she had no clue what his job was. He had been introduced as a lieutenant, but that didn't tell her much. "What exactly is it that you do in the army?"

"Whatever the general commands." His answer was evasive.

"Such as?"

"You seriously want to know, don't you?" A smile crossed his eyes.

"I wouldn't ask if I didn't." Lina's face grew hot at her bluntness. "Not every day do I meet someone so close to the general."

"Let's just say I do a variety of things. However, to satisfy your curiosity, tonight, I'm with the security detail."

"A bodyguard?"

"More or less."

"I see." Not wanting to come across as someone adept at prying into others' affairs, she feigned satisfaction with his vague explanation.

Once again, Max looked in his superior's direction. Lina followed suit. General McAllister took his hands out of his pockets and, shaking a finger at Bray, said something and walked away. Bray remained on the spot, staring after the man, his jaw visibly clenched. Max's body tensed. Lina sensed he wanted to go to the general, but he held back, though never losing sight of him. When the song ended, Lina expected Max to leave, but to her delight, he reached for her hand as the next song began. Two more songs came and went, and it wasn't until Bray stomped toward them that their closeness ended.

"It was a pleasure," Max said as he stepped away, giving her to Bray.

The pleasure was mine. As Lina watched him disappear among the crowd, Bray seized her hand for a dance. In contrast to Max's warmth, the physical contact felt like ice. And after her encounter with the pond, she hated ice. Furthermore, his breath spoke of too much drink. It was only obvious that he had spent the last two songs drinking—and quite aggressively. The scent reminded her of their past altercation, and Bray's silence was alarming. His eyes were distant and filled with a dark emotion. What could the general have said to radically change his mood?

Finally, what seemed like a never-ending melody faded, and determined to end the awkward situation, Lina asked, "Are you all right?"

"Why wouldn't I be?"

"You seem upset."

"It's nothing," he responded. "Other than the outright dreadful luck I have. Just hours ago, I thought the door to success lay wide open."

"And that's no longer the case?"

"The only door open right now is the one to hell." He laughed sardonically.

"Goodness gracious, Bray. What did McAllister say to you?"

"Forget it," he fumed. "I'm ready to leave whenever you are."

She had no objections. After all, she had only come as a favor to him. "Let me fetch Mrs. Lester."

"Let's get the car first and bring it out front. It might save her a chill."

"That's considerate of you."

On their way out, Bray paused to enjoy one last drink. Lina pulled him to the exit, where the butler retrieved their coats.

"Do me a favor, chap, and let Mrs. Lester know I'll bring the car to the front," Bray tasked the butler.

"Right away, sir."

Bray grasped Lina's hand, and they stepped into the frosty night. "Let's cut through the grounds." Bray moved as if escaping something, and before Lina knew it, he had pulled her deep into the property, out of view and out of earshot. She looked at the moonless sky, trying to gain a sense of direction. She was sure they had parked the car on the other side of the house, which was now behind them.

"We are going in the wrong direction." She halted.

"I hate to disagree." He kept going, dragging her along.

Try as she might, she couldn't break free. And just like on that wretched night not long ago, Lina felt the same panic. "Stop, Bray! I want to go back!"

"Must you go on fussing?"

"I will go on until you listen."

He let go of her hand and seized her wrist.

"You are hurting me. Stop! I want to go back!"

"Too late for that."

CHAPTER 14
BEGUILED

His ambition for statesmanship left behind, Bray continued to yank Lina across the grounds, her dread intensifying the farther they went. Each step made it more evident that he had thought this through. He knew where he was taking her. At some point during their march, she quit resisting so as to avoid a broken wrist and save energy for the upcoming fight.

All too soon they came to a brick-paved pavilion. At its heart, a dormant fountain watched their approach, guarded by a winged statue and a lamppost emitting a faint, flickering light. Lina inhaled as Bray finally slowed down. She had no fire poker to protect herself, and she doubted her knuckles would do the trick, but she had to try. "Take a firm stance. Make a proper fist to avoid injuries. Punching power comes from the lower, not upper, body," her father taught her years ago. She fisted her free hand, placing her thumb over her index and middle fingers as he had also taught her.

Bray turned, seizing her free hand as if he'd guessed her plan. "I know you want nothing to do with marrying me, and I can accept that—"

"Let's forget about this and find the car."

"Let me finish," he demanded. "I know you're attracted to me. Perhaps not in a romantic way, like how half-witted girls fall in love. No, you are sexually attracted to me. So, stop the farce, and let's have some fun. No one will ever know about this." He brought her into him. "Surely you are in for something."

The fallacy in his reasoning shocked her more than his aggression. He was truly convinced she would give in to his desires. "I'm in for nothing. You have a dreadful fascination with women and a terrible problem accepting defeat." His face contorted at her words, and it dawned on her that, pushed by this evening's failures, he sought an outlet to feed his hurt ego.

"Defeat, you say? No one defeats me. Sooner or later, I get what I want." He grabbed her by the hair and forced his lips on hers.

Trying to gain control, she dug her nails into his hand. Though he briefly let her go, it only infuriated him. With a sneer, he pulled her behind the wall of evergreens.

"Bray, no, no!"

"Scream all you want. No one will hear you, and I like when women scream."

He wrestled her to the frozen ground. Lina thrashed, twisted, and tried to kick free, but she was no match for his strength. They rolled over one final time, and he straddled her, pinning her in place.

"You are revolting. I can't believe I trusted you!" Lina spat.

"You won't think the same when I'm done."

Lina's world was coming to an end. She had been beyond foolish to lower her guard, and now there was nothing she could do but suffer the consequences. Bray reached for the bottom of her dress, and Lina's hand flew at his face, trying to scratch his eyes. If she had to, she would dig them out. A scream caught in her throat as he took a swing at her. She jerked her head, hoping to miss the blow, when something smacked Bray from behind, sending him unconscious to the grass.

"Well, that wraps up the night," Mrs. Lester said. She dropped the weapon in her hands and gathered Lina in her arms, helping her to her feet.

Lina stood on badly shaking legs, her nerves not faring much better as she tried to process what had happened. He'd intended to harm her in a most despicable manner, and the housekeeper had proficiently knocked him out.

"Lina, are you hurt?"

Aware of her impossibly fast breathing, Lina tried to control it, but her lungs were in overdrive. She stared at Mrs. Lester, speechless.

"It's all right—it's all right." Mrs. Lester brought Lina into the light of the lamppost to inspect her. "Take a few deep breaths."

Lina followed Mrs. Lester's advice, and after a moment, the thumping in her chest finally subsided. She adjusted her coat and gathered her thoughts. Though she was physically uninjured, her pride had suffered a severe blow. She should have known better. After the night he'd forced his way into her room, drunk or not, she should have cut him off entirely.

"No permanent damage has been done." Mrs. Lester finished brushing the debris from Lina's clothing. "Am I correct?"

"Yes, thanks to you. A few minutes later, and I—"

"Don't dwell on it. It's over now."

Bray groaned from the other side of the shrubs. Lina wanted to pound him. Instinctively, her gaze traveled to where the weapon had fallen. "What did you hit him with?"

"A metal pipe I found in a pile of rubbish behind the house," Mrs. Lester responded casually. "Come on, dear. Let's go before he resurrects and forces me to send him to his grave once and for all." She wrapped her arm around Lina's shoulder in a motherly fashion, and they walked back to the house.

With her appreciation for the housekeeper expanding exponentially, Lina asked, "Mrs. Lester, where did you learn to hit like that?"

"When you have been a single woman for as long as I have, you learn a lot of things, especially smelling scoundrels from miles away. I suspected he was up to no good tonight. Thankfully, I was in the yard having a puff when I saw you two crossing the grounds."

She smoked? Lina didn't recall seeing any cigarettes in her quarters. "Thank you again. I'm indebted to you."

"Nonsense. Sir William wouldn't have expected any less. Now, that nasty Hamilton—heaven forbid he show his face at Blackwater again."

"I should have kept the pipe," Lina said, half joking, half serious, doubting that he would stay away for long.

Mrs. Lester let out an unexpected laugh. "There are plenty of pipes at Blackwater."

"Though I'm afraid I wouldn't be as efficient with them," Lina observed. "In my case, a gun would be more beneficial." A gun. She remembered the box in the housekeepers' quarters.

"I'm not so sure. A firearm can cause unintended harm."

"Do you own one?"

"Heaven's no."

Lina and Mrs. Lester traveled back to Blackwater alone. Lina was grateful Bray had remained in London and prayed he would stay there. The entire trip back, she had struggled to forgive herself for having trusted the man. Condemnation for what Bray had done would never be forthcoming from her aunt and uncle, so there was no point in bringing it up. All she could do was learn from her mistake and move on. Safely in her bedroom, she closed her eyes. And with a little of Eleonor's sleeping powder, intercepted by Annie, she was fast asleep in no time.

"Nonsense. I refuse to believe that. The man is many things, but not that," her father said into the receiver. *"All right, all right. I will go there myself and settle this at once."* That her father spoke of Bartholomew, Lina had no doubt. *What atrocious deed had Bartholomew committed? Until now, she had considered money the driving force behind her father's assassination, but what if one murder covered another? What if William had discovered his brother was a murderer? But who would Bartholomew have killed?*

Lina suddenly found herself watching Bray as he spoke passionately to General McAllister. The latter grew impatient yet indulged Bray longer than expected. What was he discussing with the general? What did Bray know?

Next, Mrs. Lester came to her aid. The housekeeper's quick thinking and agility struck Lina as surreal, and then another memory surfaced. The female ghost, enshrouded in darkness, moved about agitated, determined to inflict her sorrow upon others. Her image was replaced by the ghost of the boy creeping down the passages and bringing terror to Lina's nights. The spirit halted, his sunken eyes finding hers. "Why did you send him away? Why? Why? Why?" *His accusatory voice thundered through her head.*

Lina tossed her head from side to side on the pillow, pushing herself to wake up and shake off the vision of those eyes, but the nightmare persisted.

The ghost of the boy vanished among the shadows, and a profound emptiness filled Lina—the same kind of emptiness she'd experienced in the days following her father's death. The boy was lost, alone, and friendless. Then she saw the crates in the attic tumbling onto their sides, spilling their contents, old frames, candlesticks, and odd things rolling onto the floor. Lina tried to secure the items, but they flew up and down, escaping her grasp. Amidst the chaos, she caught sight of the newspaper, and when she tried to grab it, its edge cut her finger and blood dripped onto the floor.

With a gasp Lina came fully awake. Blackwater lay eerily silent. The light of dawn came in through the drapes. She had slept through the night. Either the ghosts had been dormant, or the sleeping aid had prevented them from waking her. She hadn't dreamed much lately, and this dream seemed peculiar. She replayed the collage of recollections in her mind.

The newspaper.

Lina jumped out of bed. The urgency of discovering something helpful banished her fears. Ghosts or no ghosts, she rushed to the attic. The door creaked open, and immediately she felt the drop in temperature. She hit the light switch, begging it to work. After a few flickering attempts, it came to life. Quickly finding the crate where she had last seen the paper, she pushed the lid off, feeling the pressure of the pulse in her neck. A stack of wooden frames mocked her.

No, no, no! It had to be here. She was sure she had placed the newspaper on top. She dumped the contents, the items scattering on the floor like in her dream. No paper. Her chest constricted in exasperation, almost bringing her to tears. Wait…She turned to the crates behind her. There were two boxes of frames. She removed another cover, and the first thing she saw was the newspaper. "There!"

Her hands trembled as she made her way to the window, seeking more light. Thankfully, the newspaper was still in fairly good condition. *"Gloucestershire News*, March 1924." She scanned the headlines: "Financial Instability Worldwide Continues to Build"..."South Floods Still Rising"..."Commoners Centuries-old Grazing Rights Being Challenged."

Dropping to her knees, she spread the newspaper across the floorboards, then methodically flipped through the pages, trying to find something of interest. The title on page seven spoke for itself. *"Tragedy Strikes Blackwater Yet Again."* The throbbing in her neck was so strong now she pressed her fingers to it as she began to read the article.

"Constable Holmes confirmed that death visited Blackwater manor this past week. The victim was identified as thirty-five-year-old Ruby Jones, a house staff member. Early reports indicate that Mrs. Jones hung herself in the house."

A creaking came from the highest beam above Lina, a nerve-racking noise like that of splintering wood under mounting pressure. That noise again. She had heard it when she visited the attic before. Lina gazed at the window, though she knew the noise had nothing to do with the outside world. No wind disturbed the morning.

There it was again.

A cold sweat beaded on Lina's skin, warning her of danger, but as the daylight coming through the glass intensified, she drew courage and returned to the article.

"The Laroche family has made no comments, and no further information is available as to why Mrs. Jones ended her life. Some speculate, however, that the loss of her child eleven months ago is the root of the dreadful outcome."

Lina reread the paragraph, its meaning registering. Ruby Jones had hung herself. She had had a child—the ghost of the boy. Tommy Jones. TJ. But what had happened to him?

Lina gathered the paper and got to her feet. Almost immediately, a shadow spread throughout the room. The sun disappeared, and she stumbled through the clutter.

A banging noise, like a hammer to a nail, now reverberated from the ceiling. Lina turned sharply, and her gaze found the wax-laden table. The piece of timber directly above it was shaking. And then, with a terrifying wail, the woman's ghost appeared, hanging from the beam. Her head slumped to the side; a thick cord wrapped around her neck. Her eyes stared blankly into space from a strikingly white face. Lina screamed, and the image of the dead woman vanished as fast as it had come.

Armed with the newspaper, Lina went in search of her aunt. Eleonor had denied knowing the owner of the train. She had lied. She must have suspected it belonged to Ruby Jones's son. If the boy had lived at the house, it would fit with Bartholomew gifting him the toy.

"Mrs. Lester, have you seen my aunt?" Lina asked, stepping into the drawing room.

"Last I saw her, she was in the library." Mrs. Lester hurried to finish her inspection of the room. Nothing could be out of place under her watch.

Through the French doors, Lina saw Mr. Krammer pushing a wheelbarrow toward the south terrace. "Is he going to dig up the floor after all?"

"Hmm?" The housekeeper followed Lina's gaze to the yard.

"Mr. Krammer," Lina explained. "He was waiting for my uncle's decision on the terrace."

"Oh, yes, yes. They decided to leave it alone for the time being. He must be patching the damaged spot."

"Hopefully my aunt is not too disappointed." Lina wasn't too surprised. Of course, Bartholomew would have won that battle. "Thank you, Mrs. Lester."

In the library, Lina found Eleonor sitting in the armchair by the fire, engrossed in a book. "May I have a word?"

"Well, of course, darling." After dog-earing the page, Eleonor closed the book and placed it on her lap. Pointing at the title, *Cards on the Table*, by Agatha Christie, she said, "I started reading it this morning and can't put it down. It's a mystery novel."

"Seems that mysteries are the order of the day." The words came out naturally, though her aunt understood them in a different light.

"Oh, yes, this author is gaining much success. She is a master at crafting mysteries. But what did you want to talk about?" Eleonor appeared anxious to return to the world of Christie.

"Who is Ruby Jones?"

"Ruby J—" Eleonor's face drained of color as if she had suddenly seen Ruby's ghost.

"Don't tell me you don't know who she is." Not letting Eleonor deny her knowledge of the deceased woman, Lina opened the newspaper to page seven and placed it on Eleonor's lap. "She used to work here. She took her life in this house."

"Where did you find this?" Eleonor asked, her eyes glued to the article.

"In a drawer," Lina lied. "Tell me about her."

"Dear me." She glanced vaguely at the seat beside hers. "Please, darling, sit down."

Lina obeyed, leaning forward in rapt attention.

"The things I'm about to tell you are part of a past I wish never existed. And you must promise me you'll not repeat them, and you must not think evil of anyone," Eleonor insisted in a mournful tone.

Lina nodded, assenting to her aunt's request, though she feared that the extent of Eleonor's petition might interfere with her investigation.

"I'll start from the very beginning. When I married your uncle, we were very much in love. We tried for quite some time to have children, but by the time I was finally expecting, Bartholomew had picked up the habit of excessive drinking. Our marriage grew tense as I tried to keep him from the pub. That and financial problems made him bitter. He came home drunk one night, having lost a substantial amount of money playing cards." Eleonor's eyes clouded with tears. "I was young and didn't have much restraint with words. I accused him of not caring about our unborn child or me. One word led to another, and he lost control and struck me repeatedly. I lost the child."

Lina's hand flew to her mouth, muffling her exclamation of horror.

Eleonor continued. "When Bartholomew found out what he had done, he was inconsolable. He begged for my forgiveness, but the damage was done, and our marriage was never the same."

"Did you bring charges against him?"

"No, as I said, I was young and naïve. Besides, the police wouldn't have done much." A tear rolled down her cheek. She swiftly wiped it away. "I pitied him. He was a prisoner to the bottle, and even after that horrible incident, I hoped he would recover."

"Did my parents know about this?"

"No one did. It was too early in the pregnancy to have shared the news."

Once again, Eleonor's devotion to her husband bothered Lina. However, she had nothing to compare it to. She had never been married or madly in love. Still, in love or not, the physical and emotional abuse her aunt had suffered should never have occurred. Lina reached for her hand. "I'm sorry this happened to you. You would have been a wonderful mother."

"I would like to think so." Eleonor's lips twitched. "After I lost the baby, I never conceived again. As for Ruby, she was a widow with a young child to care for, so I hired her. It was an exception to the norm. As you know, we prefer helpers who have no other responsibilities. And when they do, like in Mr. Krammer's case, they live in town. I just wanted to help Ruby."

"How old was the child?"

"About nine. At first, Bartholomew liked the boy. I couldn't blame him, for so did I. Tommy was such a darling that I loved him as my own, but soon he wanted to spend most of his time with your uncle. But in time, Bartholomew became more and more wearied by the boy and his constant demand for attention. He asked that Tommy be kept in the staff quarters, but Tommy was a typically active little boy, and we couldn't keep him from your uncle. He would sneak into his office, causing Bartholomew to burst into the corridor cursing and calling for someone to retrieve the child. You know, there is a secret niche in there behind a wood panel. Tommy would hide in it and scare your uncle stiff.

I found it funny, but Bartholomew did not." Eleonor paused, and longing filled her eyes. "During one of those incidents, the little rascal went upstairs and occupied himself with the grandfather clock. He didn't mean to break it, but the incident only fueled your uncle's dislike for him."

It dawned on Lina that Tommy was still fiddling with the clock—making it chime when it was broken. It was also evident that no one knew him as TJ.

"Oh, the poor boy. Sometimes I wonder if he was a reminder to Bartholomew of his role in the demise of his unborn child." Eleonor's gaze dropped to her hands.

Bartholomew hadn't seemed too disappointed that she had refused Bray and opted to send Mateo to boarding school instead. Perchance Mateo's absence was a relief to the man's guilty conscience. Just like Tommy, Mateo would be a constant reminder of the child he might have had.

Eleonor interrupted Lina's silent speculations. "Then, one day, the house grew quiet. There was no more yelling from Bartholomew and no more little feet pattering down the corridors. Tommy was simply gone. Ruby and I were on the verge of insanity trying to find him. We didn't eat or sleep for days until exhaustion took over." Eleonor swallowed hard, her emotions at a tipping point. "We never found him."

The excessive amount of sleeping powder her aunt took now made sense. The only way to escape the nightmare of her reality was through sleep, and sleep came only through artificial means.

"What do you think happened to Tommy?"

Eleonor closed her eyes, trying to suppress the tears, but they flowed freely down her face. "We'll probably never know. What I do know is that the day Tommy went missing, your uncle was completely inebriated. He slept the whole day but wrestled with his dreams. Now and then, I caught some of his delirious words, words that alarmed me, and I don't want to come to any conclusions, for I pray I'm wrong."

"What did he say? Tell me."

"It's been a long time, and sparing me from lunacy, my mind has erased many of the memories."

"You must remember something. Please," Lina pleaded, hoping to learn something useful.

Eleonor's eyes narrowed as if intrigued by Lina's insistence, and she paused for a long while as if considering what to share. "One thing he said was, 'Tommy, wake up, wake up.'" She hid her face in her hands and, in between sobs, confessed, "I dread that your uncle might have lost his temper with the boy, just like he did with me long before and so many times since."

"Oh, Aunt Eleonor, that's a horrid thought." The altercation between Bartholomew and Eleonor that Lina had witnessed affirmed that the man was prompt to be quick-tempered and violent. Even when Lina had been a silent spectator, the feelings of helplessness and darkness she had experienced were still hard to process. She didn't want to imagine how Tommy must have felt being Bartholomew's target.

"One that never ceases to haunt me." Eleonor composed herself somewhat. "But in a way, I'm at peace knowing the police did all they could to find Tommy. The entire region joined the search. I've told myself many times that the poor creature got lost and a hunter took him away and raised him as his own. He liked to venture deep into the forest, after all."

If he survived Bartholomew's wrath, it was more likely he had been eaten by wild animals. Lina didn't say it aloud because her aunt was visibly upset, but she knew Tommy was dead.

"Years have passed," Lina reflected. "We have more advanced techniques. Perhaps if the case is reopened, more information will come to light."

"Well..." Eleonor seemed to consider Lina's proposition momentarily. "Your uncle wouldn't allow it. And without his consent, the police can't search the grounds."

"Once I take control of Blackwater, I will spare no expense in finding Tommy," Lina exclaimed with such passion that it left no doubt that she would.

"You have your father's heart, darling." Eleonor smiled sweetly. "Time is flying by. It won't be long now. And Ruby—oh, poor Ruby, she would have been pleased with your kindness. So devastated was she that she took her life. After almost a year, she lost all hope of finding Tommy. She couldn't live with that grief. It was just too much."

"I must say, I'm ashamed not to recall any of it."

"Oh no, you were too little, and your parents wouldn't have spoken of it in your presence. Had they, you'd have hated Blackwater, knowing that a child had disappeared. Besides, those were the years your father was working in India, and you didn't visit then."

"I had almost forgotten about India." Lina thought of the year of the newspaper, 1924. She would have been six years old when Tommy vanished and seven when Ruby died. Eleonor was correct—even if she had heard anything about them, she wouldn't have remembered much, if anything.

"And nowadays, we don't talk about the Joneses because old wounds can be more painful than fresh ones as they've had time to fester," Eleonor reflected, explaining the staff's secrecy.

Lina could understand that. If it weren't that she knew Ruby and Tommy had never left Blackwater, she wouldn't want to speak about them either. Of course, her aunt didn't know that. At the same time, she surmised the Joneses' story brought to Eleonor's mind her own tragedy, becoming too much for her to bear. A new awareness emerged, and Lina said, "Is it because of Ruby that Maggie lights candles in the attic?"

"I'm afraid so. Maggie is a superstitious creature. She believes the dead who suffered such a dreadful fate are restless and return to torment others. She lights the candles to pacify Ruby's soul."

Well, it's not working. "And Mrs. Lester's habit of lighting the corridors at night?"

"With Mrs. Lester, one can never be sure, though she doesn't strike me as the type to fear anything."

Recalling what Mrs. Lester had done to Bray, Lina agreed with her aunt; the housekeeper was fierce in the face of danger.

Eleonor went on, "Besides, she hasn't been around long enough to know about the tragedy. As you've said, I think it's just a habit. I understand she has worked in the remotest parts of the country in homes without modern conveniences. She must have gotten used to using candles at night. I don't mind it. We have a surplus of them."

"Wouldn't oil lamps be more efficient?" Lina couldn't help but wonder.

"I suggested the very thing to Lester, but she isn't fond of them. She mentioned that a relative's house burned down due to an oil lamp."

"I suppose I see her point." Lina left the chair and stood before the window. The gardens stretched in front of her while her thoughts veered to Blackwater's ghosts.

Tommy had asked Mateo not to talk about him. "He might get in trouble if they find out," Mateo had said. Even in death, Tommy was painfully aware of his previous restrictions in moving about the house, which explained why he chose the cover of night to appear. And if his innocent presence had caused Bartholomew to snap and get rid of him, all the more reason to stay hidden.

As everything fell easily into place, Ruby's words echoed in her mind. "I'll find him." She was still looking for Tommy. Lina had never seen the ghosts of the woman and child together. Could the way to appease Ruby and comfort Tommy be to reunite them? If yes, how could Lina accomplish that? Would finding Tommy's body help?

Through the glass, Lina caught a glimpse of Bartholomew, accompanied by the dogs, heading into the woods. How could one man cause so much damage and go about his business so nonchalantly? The last of his long trench coat vanished among the trees, followed by Ruppert and Jasper. Bartholomew must have played a part in Tommy's disappearance. If Tommy had been murdered, perhaps this was why Lina's father had come to Blackwater. Though years had passed, might her father have discovered something?

"Oh, dear. I almost forgot," Eleonor called, signaling to the Spanish credenza. "A letter for you arrived by morning post."

Lina crossed the room and picked up the envelope with curiosity and excitement, momentarily distracting her from thoughts of the murder. Not bothering to find a letter opener, she ran her forefinger along the edge of the back flap and unsealed it. She quickly extracted four sheets of paper. She spread the first three on the credenza and smiled. The first was a drawing of a group of boys. On the back, Mateo had written that they were his school friends, along with their names. The second was a simple image of the Eiffel Tower. Lina turned the paper over and read, "Mrs. Rogers brought a picture of the tower to class, and I drew it for you." Her gaze lingered on the last drawing.

Mateo had drawn a scene depicting Blackwater's grounds: A bright, orange sun rose above the yard. In the background lay the pond, crystal blue instead of murky. The water's edge was surrounded by trees, their green-leafed branches extending over the pond. And at the center of the drawing, a boy in a gray derby hat sat cross-legged in the grass, playing with a train. She instantly knew it wasn't Mateo. She focused on the water. What had Mrs. Cooper said about Mateo's artistic talent? Oh, yes, "I find layers of meaning in his work," she had said.

The realization came naturally: Tommy's body was in the pond. Perhaps Mateo had repeatedly seen him near the water, giving rise to the depiction. That was why Tommy had fled to it and why Bartholomew would never allow a search. And without proof, there was little hope of convincing anyone to reopen the case.

Flustered, Lina turned to the fourth paper. It was a note.

Lina,

I have opted to mail these to you since I will not be coming back to the forest as soon as I had hoped. Meanwhile, please ring the central military office if I can be of any assistance. They know where to find me.

Max LeBlanc

"What is it, darling?" Eleonor joined her niece.

An unexpected wave of disappointment rushed through Lina. She would not be seeing Max anytime soon. With her attention still on the note, she answered, "Mateo sent these."

"He is getting really good at drawing," Eleonor exclaimed, examining the papers. She paid particular attention to the one with the boy. "Oh, how I miss the little one. I'm delighted you got to see him. It was nice of Bray to make it possible, wasn't it?"

"Indeed, it was." Lina hoped her aunt would never learn how that day had ended for Bray.

"Who sent them?" Eleonor looked at the paper in Lina's hand.

Lina extended Max's note.

"Who is Max?"

"Remember the man we bumped into in town?"

"The soldier?"

Lina nodded. "I guess Max visited High Point, and somehow he ended up with these."

"It's a small world, after all," Eleonor said, but she seemed perplexed. "And quite considerate of him to offer his assistance."

"I also ran into Max at the count's house in London. He was escorting General McAllister," Lina further explained.

"General McAllister, dear me! Was he in attendance? I heard he's been flying under the radar."

Lina bit her lip. Not having been aware of the general's recent concealment from the public, she had been the only one not shocked by the man's appearance at the party. "Well, the general was there. And Max said he would bring Mateo's drawings to me, but as you can see, he decided to mail them instead."

"Wait, so he works for McAllister?"

"Apparently so."

CHAPTER 15
REMOVED

Bartholomew would never allow a search for Tommy—of that Lina was sure. But at least she could gauge his reaction. Though she didn't have solid evidence, what she had gathered pointed to the pond being Tommy's tomb. Last night the house and its ghosts had been quiet, but not her thoughts. She had imagined different scenarios about how to proceed until she reached an agreeable one. A scenario that hopefully wouldn't bring out the worst in Bartholomew. But now that she observed his exuberant figure at the end of the table, ferociously cutting the sausage on his plate, her courage wavered. Eleonor, on the other hand, prodded her food with a fork pensively. Lina felt a pang of guilt for what she was about to do—ruin the poor woman's breakfast.

"I think I know why Tommy Jones was never found," Lina announced to her aunt and uncle.

Bartholomew's piercing eyes shot to Lina. His hand shook as he lowered the fork to the table. And for an instant, time seemed to stand still as Lina awaited his response.

"Did your father tell you about the boy?" he asked in an irritated tone.

"My father? No. I read it in an old newspaper."

"I was right. You have been snooping around and causing trouble." A storm brewed, ready to be unleashed.

"I happened to come upon the newspaper by chance," Lina defended, concealing that she had learned about Tommy's fate from Eleonor, "and found it intriguing that the boy was never found."

"Lina, let's leave this for another time, shall we?" Eleonor was noticeably pale.

"I just wanted to share my thoughts."

"There is no need for that," Bartholomew fumed. "The boy is gone, and that's the end of it."

Disturbed by the detached way Bartholomew spoke of Tommy, Lina's words came out before she could stop them. "No, it's not the end of it."

If looks could kill, Bartholomew's would have annihilated Lina. "If I say it is, it is!" He slammed his fist on the table, causing the drinks to splash out of their glasses. "I'll not hear another word of it." He stormed out of the dining room cursing and shouting at the world in general.

"As you can see, he is still traumatized by the past," Eleonor excused, relief spreading over her countenance at the man's departure.

Lina couldn't complain. It had gone better than she had expected, even when he clearly didn't want to hear Tommy's name.

"Now, darling, do tell me. Why did you comment about Tommy?"

"It's just an inkling, really. I'm sure I'm not the first to have thought about it."

"Tell me." Eleonor's eyebrows knitted with curiosity.

"I think Tommy's body is in the pond."

"Hmm." Eleonor took a moment to gather her thoughts.

"It's possible, isn't it?"

"Yes, in fact, I thought the same as you, but the police searched the pond." Eleonor leaned back on the chair.

Lina was stunned. "Did they?"

"I suggested to the authorities that he might have drowned because he couldn't swim, but Ruby wasn't so sure. She argued that Tommy was too fearful of the water to go near it."

Could Tommy's death have been an accident after all? Could he have drowned?

"And they didn't find anything at all?"

"The diver spent days searching, but nothing was to be found."

"He could have simply missed him." Lina was unwilling to give up on the idea.

"He could have, but I think that if he were there, we would have found him. Besides, sooner or later, his body would have surfaced." Eleonor paused thoughtfully. "But, dear, even if we found him now, after these many years, I'm not sure what good it would do. I'd rather remember him alive and well. And maybe even living happily somewhere far from here."

Lina saw the wisdom in her aunt's words. Stirring up the past would undoubtedly cause suffering—and for the first time since embarking on solving the mystery, Lina wondered if it was wise. Even if they found Tommy's body, they wouldn't be able to establish the cause of death. But then her thoughts turned to Ruby's anguish and Tommy's loneliness. They shouldn't have to remain in such a state forever.

"Aunt Eleonor, do you believe in ghosts?"

"Ghosts? What an odd thing to ask."

"I suppose it is."

Eleonor searched Lina's eyes. "Have you seen a ghost, Lina?"

Recalling Bartholomew's mention of her fragile mental state, Lina quickly determined not to speak of the ghosts. "No, but sometimes I'm awakened by noises. It may just be my dreams, but I could almost swear that the old grandfather clock chimes during the middle of the night."

Eleonor's eyes widened. "I'm afraid that that clock has not chimed since the day Tommy broke it. There might be demons at Blackwater, but not ghosts—of that I can assure you."

"I'm so sorry I mentioned Tommy tonight." Hoping she hadn't said too much, Lina left the chair.

"Don't worry. Your uncle will soon be over it."

"I hope so."

On her way out of the dining room, Lina looked at the pond through the window. Across the yard, it was the picture of tranquility. If Tommy's remains were not there—where, then? Like a lightning strike, she recalled Mr. Krammer's discussion about the terrace floor. It had been built around the time Tommy disappeared, and Bartholomew had commissioned it on a whim. He had even helped prepare the ground. Could Tommy be buried under the stones? It could be the reason why Bartholomew hadn't allowed it to be replaced. But then again, his body could be anywhere, and she couldn't dig up the entire property.

Though the path forward was daunting, she had to unlock the secrets of the past to figure out how to put Tommy's spirit to rest and help his mother find him. How to do it, she wasn't sure.

Bartholomew was out walking Jasper and Ruppert and wouldn't be back for at least thirty minutes. Aunt Eleonor was happily seated in the library with a book. It was the perfect opportunity for Lina to visit her uncle's bedroom.

Slipping in through the door, she quickly shut it behind her. Unlike Mrs. Lester's room, this wasn't an unlived-in form of order. On the contrary, it was comfortable and cozy. A burgundy cover was neatly spread over his bed, just as Lina imagined Annie had left it this morning. The hearth was dead, but the heap of ashes and worn armchair before it assured Lina that Bartholomew put it to good use. On the nightstand, she observed a pile of books. One by one, she perused their covers and discovered they were volumes on nature and history. Who would have thought?

Lina opened his armoire, and the pungent smell of naphthalene hit her. No doubt Bartholomew was determined to keep moths away. He didn't own much clothing, and what he did was plain and simple. She patted down the pockets, but other than mothballs, they were empty. She moved to the dressing area, where his hunting clothes hung from pegs on the wall. Across from them stood a tall glass cabinet of firearms. Lina's heart jumped, anticipating a revolver in the mix. She pulled on the knob, and the door rattled but didn't budge.

Oh, please don't shatter.

Lina pulled again, and this time it gave. Quickly, she fumbled through the rifles and shotguns, making sure to search every nook and cranny. But, as if the man despised revolvers and pistols, there were none, which she found suspicious. Before returning to the bedroom, she looked through the weapons again with the same result.

She pattered across to the impressive mahogany dresser and searched the drawers, careful not to disturb the contents too much. With a sigh of defeat, her focus fell on the picture frames on top. Lina picked one up, and a much younger Bartholomew dressed in military uniform stared back at her. Then, he had been a completely different man—young, tall, and handsome. She did not know he had been in the service. It was a shame she didn't know much about her uncle.

She exchanged that frame for another. It took her a second or two to recognize the people in the image. Bartholomew stood in the yard, the pond in the background, with a hand on his brother's shoulder, the two young men smiling at the camera. The joy evident in their eyes spoke of a life of perfect harmony and comfort in each other's company. Warmth flooded Lina's heart, and she felt as if she were there with them and shared the deep bond of love between them. For the first time in her life, Lina thought of her uncle as a lot more than his horrible habits.

Extracting her from the past, Ruppert and Jasper barked from the grounds below. Lina's stomach lurched as she peeked through the window. Bartholomew approached the house with long strides. The stocky frame sporting his black trench coat and high boots looked nothing like the lovely man in the pictures. To avoid making the same mistake she had in the past by leaving a drawer semi-opened, Lina pressed on them one last time. She was almost certain he suspected she had searched his office. But his bedroom was a much higher level of intrusion—one that under any other circumstances she would have avoided. She exited the room wondering what he would do if he found out.

The view from Blackwater's courtyard revealed a gloomy day born of a quiet, snowy night. Again, there had been no nightly disturbances, for which Lina was grateful. Why were the ghosts now silent? Did it have something to do with Mateo's absence? Had Ruby confused him with her son? Or had she felt

Tommy's presence as he'd played with Mateo? Regardless, the ghosts' absence had allowed Lina to catch up on some much-needed sleep.

A sense of foreboding filled her as she took in the dark sky. But after everything she had been through, she figured it was only natural to be on edge. She needed a walk to clear her mind and sort out the information about the dead and the living. Although now that she contemplated the blanket of snow covering the woods, she wished she'd worn additional layers. Her pullover, trousers, boots, and overcoat would have to do.

"Dear me, are you going for a stroll in this weather?" Eleonor appeared on the threshold in a red dress with a white scarf wrapped around her neck.

"I need some fresh air." Lina's fingers, already chilled, struggled to secure the last button on her coat.

"Yes, darling, I understand that, but have you seen the sky?"

"It's just like it was yesterday and the day before," Lina said stubbornly.

"No, it isn't. I've many years of experience, and I tell you, I can sense the change in the weather."

"Don't worry. I won't go far."

Eleonor descended the steps to the courtyard and, taking off her scarf, wrapped it around her niece's neck. "Don't be long." Eleonor wrapped her arms across her torso as if defying the bitter breeze and, remaining where she was, watched Lina walk away from the house.

Lina was acquainted with the east path bordering the woods. She had taken a few leisurely walks there with her father. Since it didn't lead to town, it was mainly deserted except for the occasional hunter or farmer who used it as a shortcut through the trees. She moved briskly, oblivious to her surroundings as her thoughts and steps intertwined in an almost hypnotizing rhythm, lulling her senses. Something poked at the back of her mind, some clue that screamed for her consideration, yet she couldn't figure out what. Had she overlooked someone? Something they had said or done? While the notion escaped her, she inadvertently lengthened her stride.

It wasn't until the snow began to fall that Lina realized how far she had strayed from Blackwater. Seeing that the once-distant clouds now hung low overhead, casting a dark shadow over the woods, she reversed her course. Soon, large snowflakes swirled in the sky, and icy crystals pelted her face.

I should have listened to Eleonor.

The faster she went, the harder it was to see her way. Step after step, she kept moving, and above the wind, she heard a soft, drumming noise. She stopped and brought her hand to her eyes, shielding them from the weather. Visibility was low, but she made out a shadow. A horse? Mr. Krammer, perhaps, sent by Eleonor? As she blinked the moisture from her eyelashes, not one but two horses materialized, galloping in her direction.

She watched as they halted paces from her. The riders wore long leather coats, flat caps, and dark scarves around their faces. Only their eyes were visible. One look at them and Lina surmised they had not come to her rescue.

"Well, what do we have here?" the slender one said.

"Tell us your name, pretty face," the other added.

When she didn't reply, he spurred his horse toward her, making her stumble backward.

"Come on. Don't be shy," he pressed.

Lina didn't think it wise to reveal her name, but fearing that he wouldn't stop until she answered, she said the first name that came to her mind. "Beth."

"Beth, eh? Why don't I believe you, *Beth*?"

"She doesn't look like a Beth to me." The slender one inched his mount closer. "Does she now, Bill?"

Bill. She would never forget that name.

"She surely doesn't," Bill responded.

"Please." Lina's voice was weaker than she would have liked. "I want no trouble. Let me pass."

"Didn't think about trouble before venturing out here alone, did you?" the man mocked.

"No, she did not, but she's a good liar. Aren't you, Miss Laroche?" Bill chuckled.

His words shook Lina, her thoughts becoming frenzied. They were after her. She gazed at the bleak path, and the tearing desire to run seized her—no, no, that would be foolish. Even on foot, they'd overrun her in seconds. "What do you want with me?"

"Go ahead, Bill, answer the pretty girl's question," the slender man encouraged, and Lina pegged him as the leader.

"We'd like to take you for a ride, that's all," Bill said maliciously. "A very short one."

Lina's instinct for self-preservation had her glancing at the trees to her left. They were closely knit—an impediment to the horses. Without thinking, she dashed into them. Foul language and cursing followed her as the two miscreants scrambled to pursue her.

Don't look back. Keep running. Keep moving! she told herself.

The farther she went, the denser the woods became, presenting a significant challenge to her pursuers. Soon the men would have to chase her on foot. With that glimmer of hope, she redoubled her efforts to put as much distance between her and them as possible.

Feeling too heavy, too slow, she pulled on her coat until the buttons loosened, and it was soon left behind, along with Eleonor's scarf, which had snagged on a branch. Sheer dread pushed her to lengthen every stride, but as minutes went by, her body felt the strain. A burning pain shot through her legs, and her breathing became labored as her lungs worked to absorb oxygen, but it never seemed to be enough. She risked a look over her shoulder, and not seeing the men, slowed to a trot.

Had she lost them?

The forest thinned, and Lina found herself in a clearing. The glistening snow, unobstructed by the woods, fell thicker here. Like an endless curtain it kept coming down, gaining strength. In a split-second decision, she turned south, following the line of trees that boarded the clearing, staying under the protection of the forest. At least she hoped it was south. If it was, she would end up at one of the farms skirting town. If not, she would end up farther away from safety.

Mechanically, she took one step after another. Though exhausted, her senses heightened. Her hearing stretched beyond her loud breathing to the sporadic scurrying of animals on the forest floor, to the shifting of the tree branches as the snow weighed them down. When a consecutive snapping disrupted the pattern, Lina stopped, breath held. *Twigs breaking.* Followed by a low, gentle rumbling tune—the whinny of a horse.

Lina crouched against the security of a tree and dared to peer around the trunk. Seconds later, the rider Lina had identified as the leader appeared. With a swift kick to its flanks, he spurred the animal on, urging it to break through the narrow path. Lina raised her hand to her mouth to muffle her breathing and made herself as small as possible, hoping to avoid detection.

The rider hovered nearby, his head turning almost imperceptibly. His eyes, the only visible feature on his hidden face, searched the area meticulously. He was going to see her. The horse snorted and swung its head as if sensing her presence, but, surprisingly, it whirled in the opposite direction. The leader followed the animal's instincts, and they weaved away from her.

Where was the other man? Despite the chilly air, sweat formed on Lina's brow when she realized he could be watching her this very instant. In fact, the leader could have been a distraction so Bill could spot her. She threw a cautious look at her surroundings and stood. Through the bare branches up ahead, she glimpsed a curl of smoke rising into the air across the clearing.

A chimney? It was so close and yet so far. If it was a house, safety lay but yards away. But to cross the open area would put her in plain sight. Conversely, if she continued her march, and *if* her chosen south was south, she was bound to find help eventually. However, she had no idea how deep into the woods she'd wandered. And now that she had another option, she questioned just how far she would have to walk until she reached safety. How much longer would her legs carry her before the men found her?

If not bold, her decision was insane. But things that one might recoil from attempting normally are easily tackled in a moment of desperation. Leaving the security of the trees, she dashed into the clearing—her feet thrashing against the freshly fallen snow, while her body broke through the flurry of flakes that struck her without respite. It wasn't long until Lina heard the uproar from behind—the horses plowed through the whiteness after her, whinnying and snorting, their hooves rapidly gaining speed. The riders yelled at each other to catch her before she reached the other side.

Run faster! Almost there. Come on, come on! She'd almost reached the trees when a noise like breaking glass shot across the open space.

She froze.

"Bill, stop! Stop right there!" the leader yelled. Both horses came to a halt thirty yards or so from their prey.

Lina's eagerness to keep running died with the sudden awareness that she was in the middle of a large circle where the snow was flatter, the surface glossy. *Heaven, have mercy on me.* She stood above a pool of water...on ice.

There was no way to know how deep the water was, but she imagined sinking through the ice, her body going into shock. This would make her incident in the pond look like a walk in the park. She ran the back of her hand across her forehead, wiping away the droplets of snow. Her gaze again found the smoke rising from the trees, beckoning her to keep moving. The trees. She had to reach them, and preferably not by wading through frozen water. In a calculated motion, she sidestepped, holding her breath with each footfall.

The edge seemed so close yet so far. The ice creaked beneath her, and her legs became immobile. The men chuckled, probably hoping the pond would finish the job for them. She glared at them as they neared as much as they dared, ready to trample her if she made it past the ice. Their actions, though intended to intimidate her, fortified her resolve to escape them. She slid one foot forward, then brought her feet together and repeated the motion. Blessedly, the surface held. The men's taunting receded to the back of her mind as she focused on reaching solid ground.

Just two more steps. Lina beheld the men and perceived that from their point of view, they probably couldn't tell where exactly the pool of water ended. If she waited until they circled to the farthest side of her, she could gain precious minutes to run into the trees. Once she merged with the woods, the horses would be forced to slow down, giving her the advantage to reach the source of the smoke—and help. Keeping them in her peripheral vision, she calculated her steps to hit the ground at the right time.

Now. She bolted. *Come on, come on.* Sheer determination to preserve her life fueled her body, and her legs ran faster than ever. *Almost there!*

The hit was sudden and briefly disorienting. Lina crashed against the side of one of the horses. In her frenzied run and, encumbered by the elements, she had failed to see that the rider had finished circling the pond. The impact sent her to the ground, the snow mercifully softening her fall.

"Come on, Bill. Hurry!" the leader called.

His words told Lina this was her last chance. One man she might be able to escape, but not two. She scrambled to her feet and attempted to go around the animal, but her body was slow to obey, and this time, the rider was prepared. He maneuvered the horse, anticipating her movements. When she found his eyes, she saw the desire to smash her under the animal's powerful hooves. Why hadn't he already?

When Bill reached them, the leader dismounted and handed him the reins. "This has taken long enough." He seized Lina and dragged her back to the frozen pool of water.

"Let go of me!" she yelled. Bray's grip had been nothing compared to this man's.

"Stop the fuss! It will be over soon." He moved his foot back and forth, pushing the snow aside. He then stabbed the ice with the spur of his boot until water surged up, creating a hole. Lina shuddered at what he was about to do; he would drown her, making her death appear like an accident—no unnatural wounds, no broken bones. One thing was clear, whoever these men were, they had no right to end her existence. There was much more she wanted and needed to experience in life. But, unarmed, physically, she had no chance to overpower them.

"If you are going to kill me, at least tell me who hired you," she said, in a last effort to gain time.

Her question took the man aback. "You don't know?"

"No." Lina saw the indecision on his face and quickly added, "Please, tell me."

"What's going on?" Bill shouted from the background.

Bill's voice shook the leader from any inclination he might have had to answer her question, for he said, "It's better that you go without knowing." His attention returned to the frozen ground, ready to resume his work.

Lina jerked her arm free, attempting to escape. At once, he struck her face with the back of his hand, the blow sending her sprawling onto the snow. With another quick movement, he pulled her to her knees. She took a breath and closed her eyes as he forced her face into the frozen water.

Don't you dare give up. The words came from the deepest part of her soul, and recognition that they were her father's shot through her. Lina threw herself backward, twisting her body, and launched at the man, clawing at his face. They turned and twisted, fighting for control. Her fingers found their way into his eyes, and the wrap concealing his face came down. He cursed in fury, his retribution swift. He landed on her, his hands holding her arms, his knees pinning her to the ground. She took a long look at him.

He laughed. "The game is over."

Lina spat in his face.

"C'mon. Finish it!" Bill shouted impatiently.

However much they had been paid for the nasty job, Lina would make sure it wasn't enough. She spat on him again.

The leader seized the top of her hair, mercilessly smashing her skull against the ground again and again. With each hit, she felt her strength leaving, and soon she lost all sense of time and direction. Then the man hauled her limp body to the water and shoved her head under. The shock of the icy water revived her, and she summoned all the energy she had left, wrestling against her assailant, but she was spent. Tommy crossed her mind. Had he died like this? Had he felt this helpless and scared? The thought of Mateo came next.

I love you.

The man pressed her deeper into the water. Reaching her breaking point, she took an involuntary breath, her mouth filling with water. Suddenly, her body felt light, her mind at peace. Joyful memories came and went, and Lina embraced them. She saw childhood days filled with laughter and friends, days teaching Mateo to read, and days where the sun shone brightly over Hyde Park. The trees were beautiful, their branches heavy with impossibly green leaves. She found herself walking down a long path, her father and mother waiting just ahead. In a purple gown with her black hair flowing down her shoulders, Sofia was more beautiful than Lina remembered. William, her tall and imposing father, was full of life, his face radiating joy, so unlike when Lina had last seen him. The pair looked at their daughter and smiled, instantly transmitting their love for her.

"How can it be? You are dead." Tears flooded Lina's eyes.

"We are not far, Lina. Take care of Mateo," Sofia said.

"You have our love. Don't give up," her father added.

Lina ran toward them, but the closer she got, the farther they were. "No, don't leave me." The image started to fade—the path, the trees, her parents—consumed by large clouds. All color disappeared, and Lina's mind went blank.

Was she on fire? The oxygen that filled Lina's lungs burned like acid. She gasped and choked, choked and gasped, as her breathing normalized. And for a second or two, she closed her eyes tight to correct the hazy filter obscuring them. Though she still couldn't see the details, she saw the pool of water and instinctively scooted away.

The man had been about to drown her. Despite the pain and bitter cold, she planted her hands in the snow and leaned on them. Her eyes followed the snowflakes to the ground, where they landed in a puddle of red. She touched the ache at the back of her skull and felt a warm, sticky substance.

Nearby, the horses neighed, and she looked their way. She could just make out the shape of three men engaged in a fight. Her head reeled; she couldn't get her bearings on reality. Her body felt too tired to stay awake, and she collapsed to the ground. It was dark, very dark, inside her thoughts.

From somewhere in the distance came a voice. "Don't worry," it comforted. "You're going to be all right." She trusted the voice and let go.

CHAPTER 16
RESCUED

How long had Lina been asleep? It felt like forever, but her aches were fresh, and the slightest movement caused her pain. The memory of her assailants, her desperate flight through the woods, and drowning in the icy water brought her to full awareness. She tried to open her eyes, but something pressed down on them. She instinctively reached up and found cloth there.

"Steady there. Steady," a male voice said.

Terror seized her. Where was she? Who was she with? Her fingers clutched the fabric over her eyes, trying to remove it.

"Don't do that," he warned. She felt a movement on the bed, and then someone gently grabbed her hands and brought her arms to rest alongside her body. "You'll hurt yourself."

Lina knew the voice, but amid the rising confusion, she couldn't place it.

"Listen, you have a nasty wound on your head. If you stop squirming, I'll try to rearrange the dressing so you can see."

"All right." Lina's fear calmed at his words. If he wanted to hurt her, he would have done so already.

"Relax," he advised, still not letting go of her.

Aided by a long breath, Lina relaxed on the mattress. She felt him move closer, and soon he was engaged in unwrapping the blindfold. His hands worked efficiently, but his uneven breathing exposed his uneasiness. He must dread making a move that would leave her screaming. His fears were well founded, for every single touch, even when executed with care, sent her reeling in pain.

"Hang on. I'm almost done," he soothed. "It will take a moment for you to adjust to the light, though there isn't much in the room, just a few candles."

"How long have I been here?"

"Six or seven hours."

It was a long time to be unconscious.

"Are you ready?"

"Yes." As the bandage was fully lifted, the light touched her eyes.

"Easy now."

She blinked until the ceiling stopped swirling and came into focus. Though the candlelight was dim, she could make out wooden beams above her. A cabin? She lowered her gaze to the man who sat beside her. For an instant, she wondered if she was dreaming. Of course, she knew his voice. "Max?" Still, she felt adrift. He was the last person she expected to see. Why was he here?

He smiled reassuringly. "Hello again."

"I didn't think you would return to the forest this soon."

"Neither did I, but here I am."

"What changed?"

He looked at her as if her curiosity was unexpected. "I..." he started, "I'm working on assessing the local military facilities left from the Great War, with a mind to restore them."

It seemed a long stretch from guarding General McAllister to checking out buildings. She didn't believe him, but being in no position to question his duties, she switched angles. "I saw the smoke rising above the trees. Was it coming from here?"

"Smoke?"

"Yes, probably from a chimney. I was trying to get there—to get help."

Recognition crossed his eyes. "There was a cabin near where I found you, but we are much deeper in the woods."

Lina tried to shift to her side, but a flash of pain shot through her skull and seized her spine, making her reconsider. "Oh! That was not a good idea."

"What's the matter? What do you need?"

"Maybe another pillow."

Max left and returned with a well-worn pillow. Gently, he raised her head and placed the extra cushion behind her neck. "How is that?"

"Much better. Thank you." The new height relieved some of the pressure in her head, and she took in her surroundings. The room was tiny, furnished with a bed, chair, and chest of drawers, on top of which sat two candles. Over Max's shoulder, she saw a door that led into another room. Her gaze jumped to the dark window, and her curiosity overpowered her. "What were you doing out in the storm?"

Max took longer than needed to reply. "I was horseback riding."

True, she was a little off, but she wasn't an idiot. "In a blizzard?"

"I didn't think it was going to get this bad."

His answer was reasonable. She had also underestimated the weather when she left Blackwater. Still, having the advantage of a horse, he could have returned indoors quickly.

"It's still coming down quite hard. In fact, we are snowed in, completely cut off," he stated.

Should she panic or be relieved? She opted for the latter. She was probably safer here than at the manor. The notion brought a vivid recollection of the attack, and she shivered. Someone was determined to end her life.

"I don't have any more blankets, but the fire is going." Max misinterpreted her discomfort. "Can you feel the heat coming in?" He made a gesture toward the adjacent space.

"Yes, it's pleasant."

He touched her forehead with the back of his hand. "Good. No signs of fever."

"Who were those men?"

"I was hoping you could tell me that," Max said.

"I have never seen them before."

"A crime of opportunity?"

"No, they knew who I was. They were after me."

"What have you done to put a target on your back?" Max asked playfully, easing the tension.

"I'm not sure." She wasn't ready to navigate the complexity of her situation. By now she was certain her uncle had masterminded the attack. *"It's better that you go without knowing,"* Bill had said, confirming that someone had hired them to take her life. And that someone must have alerted them of her whereabouts. Bartholomew's calmness at her rejection of Bray had been a farce, a decoy to avoid suspicion when she was found dead. There was nothing left of the man she had seen in the pictures in his bedroom. If he was capable of murdering Tommy, she had no doubt whatsoever that he'd also killed her father and would kill her. It had been his plan all along. He'd sent Mateo away to readily accomplish his goal, but how in the world would she prove any of it?

"Well, as soon as the storm lets up, I'll ride to town. I might find them," Max decided, unknowingly answering her inquietude. If the scoundrels disclosed who hired them, she would have a way to send Bartholomew to prison.

"Bill. The heavier of the two—his name is Bill. That's what the other man called him."

"Good. His name and the bruises on his face will make him easier to find." Max folded his arms across his chest and stared pensively at the wall. "I shouldn't have let them go, but I had no choice. You'd have died of hypothermia. Besides, I had no idea how badly hurt you were."

"And how hurt am I?"

"Your head is quite swollen, and it's going to get worse before it gets better."

She remembered the man smashing her against the ground. Marvelous. She probably looked like a hot air balloon.

Max went on. "The gash on the side of your head is not deep, but it's long. You have three stitches."

"Stitches?" She was flabbergasted. "You sewed my head?"

"I did the best I could. I'm no doctor, but I had first-aid training in military school."

"I didn't know stitches were considered first aid," she noted.

"In my profession they are."

"I don't remember any of it." Undoubtedly, she would have felt a needle poking her skull.

"I may have given you a sedative."

"Oh..."

What else had he done as she lay unconscious? The question struck her, and her eyes darted to her torso. She pushed the blanket down and found a large button-up blue shirt covering her.

He must have read the apprehension in her eyes, for he quickly explained, "I had to get you warm. I hung your clothes by the fire. They are almost dry."

"Good." With a growing throbbing in her temples, Lina closed her eyes. There was too much to assimilate at once.

"Are you hungry?" Max got to his feet.

"No."

"I won't force you to eat, but I think you should have at least a few spoonfuls of soup. You don't want to be nauseated."

Knowing that an empty stomach and whatever medicine he had given her might justify his concern, she agreed. "Right, then. Thank you."

"Give me a moment." He turned to leave.

"Max, wait. When can I go back to Blackwater?"

"As soon as the weather allows it, and you can handle the ride."

The faint light of dawn cut through the obscurity of the cabin. Lina wondered if Max had flavored the soup with sedatives, for she had slept through the night. Though she recalled feeling physical discomfort, her mind had been at peace. She hadn't been this serene since her father's death. Losing him had taken away any sense of safety from her life, leaving her in constant fight-or-flight mode. But last night was different. Last night she had rested, knowing someone protected her.

The skittering of a mouse brought her gaze to the corner of the ceiling. Any other time, she would have been distressed over sharing the room with rodents, but there was no use in worrying about them now. The cabin was probably infested, and, compared to ghosts, Lina wasn't going to complain. If she let the mice be, she hoped, they would return the favor. She then picked up the sound of the wind. It howled through the trees, rushing past the bare branches, several of which scratched against the cabin. The hoot of an owl cut through the wind. In her mind, she pictured a robust white bird with black markings and yellow eyes snuggled under the eaves.

Lina rolled onto her side and, pushing on her elbow, sat up. Her muscles and skin hurt more than before, but her mind was lucid. She leaned against the headboard and called, "Max?" She soon heard the scrape of a chair on the floor, followed by footsteps.

Max appeared in the doorway, squinting to shake off his slumber. "Good morning." He still wore dark trousers, but his white shirt was untucked, his hair ruffled.

"Did I wake you?"

"I suppose you did."

"I'm sorry," Lina said. He moved a few steps into the room where the daylight coming through the window was stronger, and she got a good look at his face. There was a bruise near his eye.

"Are you all right?" He ran his fingers through his hair, molding it into its usual place.

"Yes, I think so."

"I'll get us some coffee."

Lina waited until he was out of sight to force her legs over the side of the bed. Her feet touched the floor, and, for an instant, her head felt like a bowl of water that had just been kicked. She waited until the dizziness passed, then took a few slow steps, and as she neared the doorway, she saw her legs were bare. The hem of Max's blue shirt reached only halfway down her thighs. She looked around and spotted a trench coat hanging from the wall in the adjacent room. She went straight to it, ignoring the cramping in her calves.

"I'll say! You shouldn't be out of bed," Max exclaimed.

Lina ignored him, hurrying to put on the coat. She then faced the room. The heat from the stone fireplace to her right felt heavenly. There was a large amount of chopped firewood resting beside it. And beyond a square table, she observed a line of battered cupboards guarded by a window on one side and a narrow door on the other.

"Through there is the toilet." Max signaled to the back door.

Lina headed straight there, and when she returned, the smell of coffee brightened her morning.

"Come sit down." Max pointed to the chairs by the fire.

"It stopped snowing."

"Not for long. We'll get a few more inches before the day is over." He extended a large mug of freshly brewed coffee to her. "Sorry I don't have much for breakfast. I'll head out in a minute. We'll need a few supplies for tonight."

"Tonight? I can't stay here that long. My family is probably sick with worry." She was thinking of her aunt and the house staff.

"You are in no condition to ride. The roads are terrible, and, as I said, it's not done snowing. If I ride alone, I'll be back in a jiffy."

"They've probably informed the police," she reflected. Albeit to cover his tracks, there was a chance that Bartholomew would wait awhile before doing so.

"I'll stop by the constable's and let him know what happened. He can inform your family and start looking for the two brutes." Max settled on the chair beside Lina and took a sip of his coffee.

"They'll appreciate the message." Her uncle wouldn't. He'd get indigestion when he learned she was still alive. However, if the men were found, this ordeal might be worth it. It might be just enough to unravel Bartholomew's lies. The wound in her head started to pulse as if someone was tapping on the delicate skin. Instinctively, she placed her hand on it, applying pressure.

"Still hurts a lot, huh?"

"Yes, but it's better than yesterday."

Max walked to the table and returned with a pill. "Here, take this. It will help."

"Thank you." Lina gulped it down with some coffee.

"I have plenty of those. Let me know when you need another. What I don't have is disinfectant. Hopefully, the chemist's shop will be open. We'll clean the wound when I get back."

"I'm not looking forward to that." The thought of fiddling with the wrap and alcohol touching the raw skin made her shrink.

"I wouldn't either, but it's a necessary evil." Max finished his drink, and after depositing the cup in the basin, he retrieved her folded clothes from the table. Lina had failed to notice them until now. "Trade me for my trench coat, will you?"

"Give me a minute."

"Do you need any help?" Max asked sincerely, and to his credit he colored slightly.

"I'll be all right." Her face heated, knowing he had changed her clothes before.

Setting the empty cup on the table, Lina made her way to the bedroom. Usually, she would've changed in a few minutes. It now took a shameful amount of time, even when she bravely endured the sharp aches that came with stretching and bending her limbs. She returned to Max, dressed in her black slacks and green pullover. He had slipped into his boots and thrown on a sweater and a hat.

"Here." She handed him his coat, and he slipped his arms through the sleeves.

"It's already nice and warm." For an instant, he looked at her with a disarming light in his eyes. "I'd better be on my way."

"How long will you be gone?" She worried at the possibility that the men had followed them. Could they be watching, waiting to finish the job?

"A couple of hours, more or less. Dexter is reliable but doesn't like to be pushed." He wrapped a thick wool scarf around his neck.

"Your horse?"

"Yep."

"Is he out in the snow?"

Max chuckled and reiterated, "He is a horse."

"Still, it's dreadful out there."

"Believe me, the rascal has it good. He's under the covered porch on the side of the cabin and has enough hay to enjoy himself. In fact, I'm expecting him to put up a good fight before I can get him going."

It was Lina's turn to laugh. "Dexter has you well trained."

"Yep, the only things he budges for are apples and carrots."

The fire crackled. Lina glanced at it, and the unsettling feeling of staying alone tugged at her again.

Either Max noticed her unease or had some concerns of his own, but he pointed to a couple of steel crossbars. "See those? I want you to put them on these hooks." There were two iron hooks on either side of the door for the bars to rest on, making it impossible to open from the outside. "And unless it's me, don't let anybody in. Understood?"

Lina nodded. Max contemplated her for an instant, and Lina's heart skipped a beat. The maturity and confidence he possessed, along with his good looks, made her stomach turn and twist. She felt nervous and thrilled all at once. Max walked out, and after securing the bars, Lina retreated to the bedroom, her weariness taking over. She crawled under the blanket and fell asleep, hoping Max wouldn't delay.

CHAPTER 17
AWARE

When Lina woke, the cabin was quiet except for a sporadic plopping sound like snow sliding off the roof and falling to the ground. Lina felt rested, but her muscles longed for motion. She abandoned the bed and paced about, thinking of Max. He had been on the train, in town, in London, and now here in the woods. Who was he? And why did he keep appearing in her life?

At the sound of hoofbeats and with the threat of her attackers still fresh on her mind, she neared the window with rattled nerves. Through the gap between the curtain and the glass, she saw the snow-covered figures of Dexter and Max.

Minutes later there was a soft knock at the door. "Lina, it's Max."

As she lifted the crossbars and pulled the door open, her pulse quickened in anticipation of seeing him. Accompanied by a wave of arctic air, he hurried inside, dropped a large sack onto the ground, and secured the door. "Brrrr. It's freezing out there."

"I can see that. You are as white as a ghost." That last word reminded her of Tommy. The poor creature seemed so lonely and lost. Sending Mateo to school had been the right thing to do, but she felt a bit of remorse for having taken away Tommy's only friend.

"It was bearable until the wind picked up." Max took off his boots, then shed his winter layer. "It's coming down hard again though."

Max crouched in front of the fire, rubbing his hands together. The glow reflected on him, and Lina found herself unable to steer her gaze away. There was something about him that pulled her in. She wasn't a fool. His appearance was enough to attract many a girl, but something deeper captivated her.

"I didn't find any traces of the men," Max said disappointingly, throwing a few more logs in the fire. "But I had a good chat with the constable and cast a few lines in town. Hopefully we'll get a bite."

"There is always someone who knows something."

"Speaking of which, the constable will send one of his men to Blackwater to let your family know you are all right."

"Thank you."

Max grabbed the grocery sack and emptied it onto the table. Tins of soup, a loaf of bread, bandages, and a bottle of iodine rolled across the surface. Holding the disinfectant, he turned to Lina and said, "Have a seat."

"I'd hoped you would forget about it."

"Not a chance."

She settled on the chair in front of the hearth, and Max pulled his up beside hers.

"We just need to make sure it's healing properly." With cautious hands, he proceeded to unwrap the cloth around her head.

Lina closed her eyes and focused on her breathing.

"We are almost to the last piece," he announced sooner than she anticipated.

The fabric pulled on her hair, tugging at the wound. "Ouch."

"Darn. It's sticking to the dry blood."

"Cut it," she swiftly decided.

"I can't without cutting your hair with it. Hold on." He retreated to the cupboards.

Lina touched her head and felt the hardened masses of hair stuck to the wrap. "I think it calcified."

"This will help." He returned with a bowl of water and a cloth, which he used to soak her hair while his fingers delicately loosened the bandage. Momentarily, his closeness distracted her from the discomfort.

His body was just inches from hers, and it made her heartbeat hammer against her flesh.

She hoped he didn't realize the effect he had on her.

"That wasn't too bad, was it?" Max said with a smile.

"Not at all."

"The wound looks better." He sounded satisfied. "I'll clean it, rewrap it, and we are done."

"Thank you, Max, and thanks for saving my life."

"Anytime." His face lit up.

"The bruise on your face is darkening," Lina observed.

"I know. Not pretty, huh?"

She wasn't going to answer that. The more she looked at him, bruised or not, the more attractive he was.

"Ready for some soup?" Max asked as he finished securing the wrap. "Sorry I couldn't find any tin meat."

"Soup would be lovely."

"It will be ready in no time."

"May I help you?"

"No, thank you. I think I can manage a premade soup." He opened one of the tins and poured the liquid into a pot, then placed it on the iron grill above the burning logs in the fireplace. "Canned foods are lifesavers. I'm ashamed to say I've come to rely on them more than I should."

"I don't think there is anything wrong with it. Cooking takes too much time—time we sometimes don't have."

"That's true in my case, but you have a cook, don't you?" Max engaged in cutting a few slices of bread and poured them two glasses of water.

"We do. I must say that, unlike our cook in London, the one at Blackwater would never entertain the idea of sharing her space. Before coming here, my father and I used to cook three or four times a week."

"Ah, it's a good skill to have. I hope my future wife fares well in the kitchen." Max winked at her.

Lina's face grew hot, and she knew it had turned red. If the comment had come from Bray, it would not have caused the same effect. Handling

Bray was surprisingly easier, in part because the connection to him was on a much lower level than what she felt toward Max.

Max tasted the soup and brought it to the table.

"I didn't know soup from a tin could be so tasty," she confessed as they settled in to enjoy the meal.

"You must be hungry." Max looked amused. "It took me a long time to get used to it."

"How often do you stay here?"

"More than I would like to."

"It's a nice place. Whose is it?"

"The military's."

"I thought you said you lived on the edge of town." Lina recalled Max's answer when they'd bumped into him in Coleford.

"I may have exaggerated the distance a bit." He smirked.

"You didn't grow up around here or in London, did you?"

"Liverpool."

"My father loved Liverpool." Lina set her spoon in her bowl. "He used to take me on the ferry to get the best view of The Three Graces." The three breathtaking buildings—the Royal Liver, the Cunard, and the Port of Liverpool—overlooking the River Mersey, had been built as symbols of Liverpool's industry and commerce.

"I used to go for runs along the waterfront. That's proper architecture there."

"Indeed."

"Are you tired?" Max changed the course of their conversation, likely intentionally. His answers had been evasive.

"No, I'm afraid I couldn't sleep if I wanted to. How about you? Did you sleep at all?"

"A little."

"On the chair?" Lina couldn't imagine doing so—too uncomfortable and precarious.

"No, right there." He pointed at the rug in front of the fire.

"On the floor?" Even worse.

He pressed his lips together and nodded.

"Well, I see why you didn't sleep much. It would be frightfully hard on your body."

"I've slept on worse." Max cleared the table. "Are you acquainted with American crossword puzzles?"

"My father brought them home a few times." William had made sure to save the American newspapers that came across his office every so often. Together, father and daughter had become good at solving puzzles. "Do you have some?"

"I do. Would you like to play?"

"Certainly."

Max retrieved several newspaper pages and two pencils from a cupboard. "I only keep the crossword puzzles. The rest I use for kindling." He spread them on the table. "How would you like to go about it?"

"Your choice," she answered.

"We'll read the first clue together, and whoever figures it out keeps going. If not, it'll be the other's turn. Shall we say two minutes to come up with the answer?" He tapped his wristwatch. "We'll go off my watch, and whoever gets the most, wins. Fair enough?"

"I think so." Lina smiled, reaching for a pencil.

Max read aloud. "First one across, four spaces: Such and nothing more."

Lina turned the riddle in her mind and soon had it. "Mere."

"Sounds right. Next, four spaces: What this puzzle is."

"Hard," she said with confidence.

"You are doing well." He tilted his head a little and cleared his throat. "This one has seven." His tone was mocking, as if seven would undo her prowess. "The close of a day."

Lina had solved this one before and remembered it well. She wrinkled her nose but didn't wait to answer. "Evening."

"I'll say! You have done this puzzle before," he accused, and rightly so.

"Maybe I have, maybe I haven't." She smiled.

"Hmm…"

On and on he went, reading the clues, and on and on she went, solving them, giving him no chance to counter. He checked the answers a few times, coughing and mumbling to himself as he did so.

"Well, how did I do?" Lina readjusted her body on the chair, feeling incredibly proud of herself. Meanwhile, Max checked the answers yet again. And before they knew it, silence enveloped them—the silence of being totally at ease with each other. Her gaze rose to meet his, the warmth in his eyes disarming her. He had the power to break down her barriers. It was a thrilling though scary realization. She had never considered that being smitten meant losing part of oneself to another person, for she feared he was slowly taking over her head and heart.

"You got them all right," Max conceded, reaching for another puzzle. "Since I'm the loser, I'll go first this time, and you can't answer until I give up."

"You want an unfair advantage?"

He frowned. "No, just enough time to think."

"Three spaces: Disencumber," she read, and told herself the answer, *rid.*

"Oh, I think I got it. No, it doesn't fit. Oh, darn."

"Would you like help?" She smirked.

"No! I got it, all right. It's rid."

"Splendid!"

"Don't enjoy yourself too much," Max advised. "I'm a bit rusty, that's all. Besides, you make me nervous."

"Of course, blame it on me," she responded playfully.

The game resumed, and Max solved the next one faster.

"Brilliant," Lina said as he guessed another.

"Shh, you are distracting me. Let's see, across four spaces. The third one is an e: regrets."

"It's a tricky one," she observed, unable to figure it out.

He tapped the pencil on the paper as he considered. Lina didn't mind that he was winning them all or taking his time to do it. She didn't want their time together to end.

"I got it. Rues. The answer is 'rues'," Max announced proudly.

Her body was broken, frozen, dead, her once-beautiful hair floating on the surface, becoming an integral part of the ice. The coldness of death burned, and she let out a wail of despair.

"No! I can't be dead. I can't!" Lina awoke screaming, her nightmare rekindling the paralyzing terror she'd felt that day.

"Hey, it's all right. It's just a dream," Max soothed.

"Max?" His voice brought reassurance, and she searched the shadows, extending her trembling arms into the obscurity. "Where are you?"

"I'm here." He reached for her.

"Max." She sobbed, pulling him into her.

"Shh. You are safe." He lay down beside her, taking her into his arms. She held him tightly.

"It was just a nightmare, that's all. A nightmare."

"I saw the men in the clearing, and I was dead."

"They are gone, and you are not dead. You are safe here with me."

Still, the shock of the vivid dream lingered, and Lina pleaded, "Please, don't leave me." Max's voice and the warmth of his embrace gave her a sense of security.

"I won't. Go back to sleep."

She buried her face in his chest. Time went on, her emotions settled, and sleep found her once again. When sunlight poured into the room, she was already awake—and still in Max's arms. She looked up at him. He was asleep. Their faces were close, so close. His soft breathing brushed her cheek, and her heartbeat accelerated. She studied his features, and, like on the train, couldn't take her eyes off him. This stranger was a stranger no longer.

"Good morning," he whispered without opening his eyes.

Lina's blood ran hot. He seemed aware of her intrusion. "Good morning."

"Are you feeling better?"

She wanted to answer, "Much better, indeed." Instead, she said, "Yes, the pain has lessened quite a bit."

"I was afraid you'd hurt yourself last night. You were terrified."

"Oh, the dream. It was awful. I'm sorry I bothered you."

"I'm not. I was thrilled I didn't have to sleep on the floor."

Me too.

"*I Will Remember You Until the Day I Die,*" Max said softly, taking Lina aback.

"I can't believe you remember the name of the book I had on the train."

"Of course, I do. I kept my eyes on it until I fell asleep."

"Why didn't you say anything?" she taunted.

"Did you want me to?"

"You can't answer my question with another question."

"I guess not. But I already know the answer to mine," he bluffed.

"You do? Please tell me."

"You were dying for me to speak to you and were much disappointed when I didn't."

"Is that so?" Now that he had seen through her facade, the impulse to kiss him seized her, but she quickly contained it. "You know what, Max?"

"What?"

"You are full of yourself."

"Me?" He laughed. "I wasn't the one so focused on myself I couldn't even acknowledge the other's existence."

"I was reading a book," she defended. *And mourning my father's death.* "If you wanted to say something, I would have answered."

"If I would have asked how your day was, what would you have said?"

"Fine, thank you."

"And that's it?" He raised an eyebrow.

"Yes, that's it."

"Why didn't you, then?"

"Because you didn't ask but instead decided to take a bloody nap." It came out a little stronger than she intended, revealing that his indifference had indeed annoyed her.

Max thought for a moment and then said, "Catalina?"

"Yes?"

"How is your day?"

"Fine, thank you." She smiled.

"Are we good now?"

"I guess so."

Max tightened his arms around her, bringing her closer. His closeness was overpowering, and the impulse to kiss him seized her again. She raised her head looking for his lips, but before she had the chance, he jumped to his feet.

"I'll prepare some coffee."

The fire died down, and the temperature inside the cabin dropped considerably. Max put on his coat and headed to the covered porch in search of more firewood. Meanwhile, Lina moved about the bedroom, feeling foolish. She had been dying to kiss him, and he'd avoided her. She wrapped her arms around herself to keep from shivering. Having left her coat in the woods, her pullover wasn't enough to keep her warm. She turned to the chest of drawers. Of course, Max wouldn't mind if she borrowed an extra layer. Unfortunately, she found nothing but shirts and trousers. However, as she was about to close the bottom drawer, underneath the clothing, she spotted a bundle of papers.

Without thinking, she pulled it out and removed the string wrapped around it. She flipped through the pages. Her intrusive behavior could be considered a result of wanting to know more about Max and his lack of cooperation, she reasoned. Whatever it was, her heart thumped against her ribs, proof that her actions were detestable if not criminal. The document, written in German, presented a challenge. In exasperation, she turned a few more pages. And then she saw words she understood all too well: "Sir William Laroche—Blackwater Manor, Coleford." Lina stared at the papers, speechless. One thing was clear. While she had been careful not to disclose her plight, Max was apparently well-informed about her family's affairs.

Why German? Was it something Father had been working on? She should have known more about his dealings, but he'd been so tight-lipped. She'd taken for granted the time they had together, and now, just as quickly as she'd lost her father, she'd lost confidence in Max. Was he just using her for information? He couldn't be. She knew less than he did.

Lina felt like the walls were closing in and suffocating her as they had at Blackwater. She had to confront Max. She was certain he would try to lie his way out of this one, having lied all along, but she had to try. More troubling was the fact that whatever had brought her father to Coleford the day he died must be something more than Lina anticipated. Maybe even beyond Bartholomew's involvement.

She came into the kitchen as Max walked in with a load of firewood. He deposited it on the floor and removed his coat and boots.

"Are you all right?" He was perceptive.

"What are these?" She waved the papers, realizing it was going to be a long day if she didn't like his answers.

He leaned against the wall and looked at her for a long, uncomfortable moment. The light in his eyes revealed his effort to formulate a response. But in them, she also saw a mixture of anger and disappointment, whether in Lina or himself, she couldn't tell.

"You went through my stuff?" he finally said in an acid tone.

"I was looking for a coat."

"Inside the drawer?" In a flash, he snatched it from her.

"No, I just..." She couldn't construct a feasible defense. She had invaded his privacy and betrayed his trust. She had to change angles, and fast. "My father was troubled by something significant in the days preceding his death. You were on the train when I was forced to come to Blackwater, and you seem to have been at arm's reach ever since. And now, I find those papers with his name on them."

"Listen, my life is complicated enough as it is. Believe me when I say you should forget about these papers altogether."

"That's not an option."

"That's the only option."

"You must tell me something," she insisted.

"I can't," he replied unflinchingly. "I've already broken protocol more than I should have."

His words made her pause, and she realized she might be an unfortunate coincidence in his life. "I shouldn't be here, should I?"

"No, and I shouldn't like you as much as I do, but here we are."

His admission startled her, but she had to stay focused. "I'm assuming the reason you are in Coleford is related to my father's job or murder, maybe both, and my presence conflicts with it. Am I correct?"

"I'm on a military assignment."

She scoffed. "Yes, to inspect military facilities."

"You know, it's best you believe that, since it's all I'm going to say about it," he responded with finality.

Lina was beyond disappointed. The conversation could remain within those walls, and they could pretend it never happened. But Max's loyalty was to the military, and he wouldn't be moved. Ironically, his commitment to duty reminded her of her father, and her feelings became confused between wanting to know more and trusting Max. She wanted to press him, but since Max was so stubborn, waiting might prove the better path.

"Right, then." She found her words painful as they came out. "Have it your way."

He looked at her as if he hadn't expected her surrender but was quick to say, "I'm glad. Otherwise, you would've had to sleep outside with Dexter."

"The horse might be better company," she snapped.

"I doubt that."

"I don't. As obstinate as horses can be, Dexter might be more reasonable than you are."

"Are you calling me a pigheaded?" Amusement crossed his eyes.

"More or less."

"Well, I'll take it as a compliment."

"You are impossible." Lina frowned.

Max laughed. "You know what?"

"What?"

"You are irresistible when you get upset."

Max came to her so rapidly she had no time to react as he firmly kissed her. His cold lips merged with hers, and her heart burned, as if at last, the world was in perfect harmony. "Since we now understand that some things must remain unsaid, this never took place." Then he kissed her again, easing the frustration in her heart and leaving her wanting more.

The sun shone in splendor upon the woods. Its light reflected off the thick layer of snow and blinded Lina as she stepped outside for the first time since being rescued. A sense of tranquility reigned over the forest— a soothing quietness that brought peace to her heart. She beheld the cabin one last time, not comprehending all the emotions that swept over her. She would miss the little place where she had found safety and a renewed energy to keep fighting for her rights and a brighter future for Mateo.

Lieutenant Maxwell LeBlanc had been a calming force in the storm, both literally and figuratively. If it hadn't been for those blasted papers. For a moment, her heart wavered, but then it steadied. She couldn't fully trust him. His secrets were a barrier between them. And those secrets might hold the answer to her father's death.

"Here, put this on," Max ordered, handing her an overcoat. "It's a long ride. You will freeze if you don't."

"Where did you get it?" She hadn't seen it before.

"From the porch. I cover Dexter with it sometimes. Be careful. He might take it from you."

"I could have used it before."

"I didn't think about it. Besides, if you were comfortable enough, you wouldn't have allowed me to sleep in the bed last night." He winked.

Lina shook her head and slipped into the coat. It had a forest-y scent and smelled like its owner, refreshing and clean. And it reminded her of his kiss. Despite the uncertainty surrounding their friendship, she would never forget his kiss.

Max helped her up onto Dexter, then got on behind her. Dexter started through the snow, his hooves carving deep furrows in the wintry landscape. White trees came and went while the crisp air bit the riders' faces. Lina had no idea where they were, but, clearly, she wouldn't have been able to find her way alone. It was a long distance from Blackwater, and they traveled on back roads and abandoned paths.

"How are you holding up?" he inquired, leaning closer to her.

"Fine."

"Let me know when you need a break."

Dexter went on with remarkable strength and steadiness even in the treacherous stretches of the path—when he sunk a little deeper in the whiteness or stepped on unlevel ground, he was quick to correct his balance.

"This is the hardest patch of the journey." Max wrapped his arms around Lina's waist to keep her from swerving.

She didn't mind it. His gentle closeness revived the feelings she had experienced in the cabin. Regardless of what he concealed: she would miss him.

CHAPTER 18
PROTECTED

Blackwater formed ahead, magnificent against the late-afternoon sun, its appearance momentarily masking the aura of darkness and sorrow within. Fleetingly, Lina wished there was somewhere else she could go. She had temporarily found safety with Max, but she had to be cautious and not lose sight of her mission. Apart from freeing Mateo and herself from their uncle's claws, she had to unmask Blackwater's killer and what had happened to Tommy.

Dexter weaved through a deep pile of snow with powerful grace. Lina wasn't faring as well. Her body ached, and the monotonous march of the last stretch had left her feeling rather queasy. If it weren't for Max keeping her in place, she'd have fallen off long ago. As they approached the house, Lina spotted Mr. Krammer toiling to clear the snow from the front porch. Becoming aware of the newcomers, he dropped the shovel and met them in the courtyard.

"Welcome home, miss. Blackwater has been on pins and needles awaiting your return."

"Mr. Krammer, it's nice to see you." Lina noted how fond she had grown of the gardener.

"Hello." The men shook hands. "I'm Lieutenant LeBlanc."

"A pleasure to meet you, sir."

Max extended his arms to Lina and helped her dismount. Once on the ground, the coolness emanating from the mansion's walls reached her, and the threats of Bartholomew's dangerous character and treacherous ghosts crept into her blood. Despite her resoluteness to solve Blackwater's mysteries, her tenacity wavered. Injured as she was, she feared she would be vulnerable to her enemies. She felt both hunted and haunted in this house.

Mr. Krammer's voice brought Lina out of her thoughts.

"I'll take care of this fine boy." He grabbed Dexter's reins, observing Lina with much concern. "Please, go on inside."

"Thank you, Mr. Krammer." Max patted Dexter on the back and said, "Be good and mind your manners."

As the gardener led Dexter away, the horse flung his head about, snorting playfully as if anticipating a treat.

Max raised Lina's chin and looked into her eyes. "How are you doing?"

"Feeling a bit clumsy."

"Lean on me." Max pulled her tightly to his side.

"I must look dreadful. Mr. Krammer was startled by my appearance." It was obvious to her that while the household might be aware of her getting lost in the storm, they might know nothing about the attack.

"If you want to know," Max mumbled, "you look a little worse for wear, but you could never look dreadful."

"Thank you, Lieutenant, but I look hopelessly hideous, I'm sure," she accepted, but his compliment forced her to smile.

"You just need time and rest. You'll sleep better tonight in a plush bed, surrounded by people to help you."

"I like the helper I have now."

"You may change your mind once you see the stitches," he remarked with a twinkle in his eye.

As they came to the door, her anxiety spiked. "I must warn you. My uncle can be quite barbaric."

"I hope he isn't. I'm not ready for another brawl just yet." He rubbed his jaw.

"Seriously, he is a large man."

"I can handle myself."

They stepped into the foyer, and Mrs. Lester came running to them. "Lina! Oh, my goodness gracious! What happened to you?" Taking a swift appraisal of Lina, the housekeeper's composure faltered, but she was quick to subdue her emotions. Returning to her steady, professional manner, she stated, "Well, there is plenty of time to discuss that, I suppose." She helped Lina out of the coat.

"Thank you, Mrs. Lester. This is Lieutenant LeBlanc."

"Thanks for bringing her home, Lieutenant." Not showing further interest in Max, Mrs. Lester wrapped an arm around Lina's shoulders. "Oh my, you are as cold as ice. Come, come. Let's get you warm."

Max followed the women into the library, where Mrs. Lester installed Lina on the sofa and placed a pillow behind her back. To Max, she said, "Please, Lieutenant, have a seat," and hurried to wrestle with the fireplace to revive its fire.

"Thank you. I prefer to stand."

A rapid footfall came from the hallway. "Oh, my darling, it is you! Thank goodness you are safe!" exclaimed Eleonor, though her voice rapidly turned mournful. Her gaze wandered from the wrap on Lina's face to her bruises and back to the wrap. "We were informed you were at a farm weathering the storm, but..." She slipped onto the sofa and embraced her niece. "What happened?"

"I was attacked in the woods." Lina decided she would share further details, including the stitches in her head, at a future time.

Eleonor uttered a horrified little cry. "Attacked?"

"Mrs. Laroche," Max interjected, "thankfully, I came upon Lina just in time to chase her attackers away. The outcome would have been different otherwise."

Recognition filled Eleonor's eyes. "You are the soldier from town, the one who sent Mateo's drawings."

"That's correct."

"We are indebted to you. Oh, how brutish of me. Please, sit down."

Max shook his head, rejecting the offer a second time.

"Wait, did you say attackers?" Eleonor's face contorted in horror. "More than one?"

"There were two," Max responded.

"Who were they? Are they in custody?"

"No, ma'am. They fled. Do you have any idea who would want to harm your niece?"

"No, of course not," Eleonor answered, but her voice lacked confidence.

A new notion seemed to hit Max, his face hardening in response to it.

Lina pursed her lips. She was sure Eleonor suspected her husband to be the perpetrator, but fearing or pitying the man, she wouldn't dare accuse him. Lina couldn't help but feel heartbroken for her aunt; she now had another crime to add to her husband's violent history.

Mrs. Lester, who stood near the bookshelves with keen awareness, now spoke. "Mrs. Eleonor, shall I bring some tea?"

"Please, Mrs. Lester. That would be most wonderful," Eleonor responded.

"At once." The housekeeper withdrew.

"Are you sure you are fine?" Eleonor asked Lina. "We must call the doctor at once."

"Yes, I'm all right."

Eleonor embraced her niece again.

The library shook under Bartholomew's thundering footsteps as he arrived in his usual blustery manner. "You have proven to be a true Laroche," he barked. "Incredibly resilient." There was no sign of sympathy in his voice.

He might as well do without the hypocrisy and say, "a tough bird to kill."

Bartholomew's comment didn't seem to sit well with Max either. Looking the massive man straight in the eye, he said, "She is lucky to be alive."

"Who the devil are you?" Bartholomew grumbled.

Eleonor neared her husband, scrambling to control the situation. "Now, dear, Lina was attacked in the woods, and if not for the lieutenant's help, she probably wouldn't be here. Please be civil."

"Attacked?" Bartholomew appeared sincerely startled. "The message from the constable didn't mention anything of the sort."

"Since Lina was safe, there was no need to alarm you with all the information." Max addressed Bartholomew in a measured tone that in no way masked his unbending resolve. "And in response to your previous question, my name is Lieutenant Maxwell LeBlanc. I work under the direction of General Peter McAllister." He produced an identification card from his pocket and handed it to Bartholomew.

Bartholomew twisted the card in his hands, the thick veins in his neck bulging as they pumped blood at an alarming velocity. He ran a finger around his shirt collar to relieve the pressure. "How do I know this is legitimate?"

"You are more than welcome to ring headquarters."

"I'm sure there is no need for that," Eleonor assured. "I'm sorry, Lieutenant. I implore you to consider how distraught we have been these past days. Even knowing Lina was safe, we couldn't stop worrying until she returned. Please accept our apologies and do sit down." Eleonor reached for her husband's arm. "Come now, dear, you too have a seat." She helped him to the settee near the fireplace.

Bartholomew laughed, a sound containing a hint of hysteria. "Yes, of course. Lina is back. She is, and that's all that matters." Like the flip of a switch, his demeanor had dramatically changed.

Lina glared at him, conveying what she couldn't say aloud. He didn't care that she had been lost or maybe even killed, not when her death would have solved his financial troubles. Her unexpected survival was the real shocker. That, coupled with her new friend's rank, had shaken Bartholomew. Yet, for a split second, Lina was sure she detected a strange conflict brewing within him, something that contradicted her assumptions.

The change in Bartholomew's mood spread throughout the group, and the atmosphere lightened somewhat. At last, Max settled next to Lina, crossing his legs in a relaxed manner.

"Lieutenant, you must join us for dinner," Eleonor invited.

"Yes, you must," said Bartholomew, but, unlike his wife, there was no excitement in his voice.

"If I didn't have urgent matters to attend to, I would accept the invitation."

Eleonor stood in front of the young couple with an expression of gratitude. "Tea, then? Surely you can spare a minute for tea. Considering what you've done for our niece, we must retain you a little longer," she begged.

"Very well," Max relented, and Lina got the impression he did so to appease her aunt. Having tea would take less time than trying to refuse her.

"Splendid. I shall see what's taking Mrs. Lester this long." Eleonor hurried away.

Bartholomew presented a cool, collected demeanor as he lit a cigar and said, "Don't get me wrong, LeBlanc, I'm grateful you helped Lina, but since there are no soldiers stationed in the forest and you aren't from these parts, I wonder why you are here."

"You are quite observant," Max noted. "You are correct. There are no permanent personnel in these parts. That's why I come and go from Coleford. As you may know, we still have a few facilities in the region, which the military intends to revive."

"Hmm, Europe's instability is rattling the country, isn't it?" Bartholomew said as he blew out a wave of smoke.

Remarkable how quickly the man pivoted from vitriol to avuncular. Lina shifted on the sofa, her nausea exacerbated by the smell of the cigar.

Max didn't elaborate. Instead, he said, "Before I forget, I've relayed the details of Lina's attack to the constable, and since I interacted with the assailants, he'll keep me in the loop. I'd expect him to come by in the morning."

Bartholomew tried to speak, but a coughing fit seized him. He choked and gasped for air until finally his lungs cleared. Meanwhile, Max watched him with much interest.

"Well, I suppose I'll hear the full account of the events, then," Bartholomew stated in a wheezing voice. "The sooner he comes, the better."

"I find it disturbing that two perfect strangers would want to kill me for no reason—for that was their objective. Don't you find that peculiar, sir?" Lina exposed the facts, unable to suppress the subtle accusation in her statement.

"Yes, yes," her uncle answered a bit too eagerly. "But one can never know the devices of people of that sort. If you put up a good fight, which I don't doubt you did, you might have changed their plans."

"Their plan was to kill me," Lina reiterated, unable to contain the anger in her voice. "And I'm convinced someone hired them to do so."

"Hired? That's not likely," Bartholomew exclaimed, smashing the cigar onto the ashtray. "No, not likely. We mustn't forget that there are plenty of thieves in the woods looking for an opportunity to plunder."

Thieves. Lina laughed internally at the man's hypocrisy. The only thief she knew was him.

"Likely or not, we'll soon find out," Max stated. "These types quickly spill the beans before being hanged. Getting details from them should be fairly easy."

"Yes, yes. That's about right." Bartholomew said. "Now, where exactly in the woods were you?"

Max beat her to the answer. "She was at the west end bordering the trees."

Lina was shocked by Max's deliberate lie. He'd found her in the clearing, deep in the forest.

"I see." Bartholomew unbuttoned the top of his shirt and reached for another cigar.

Lina wondered what he saw. "I need some fresh air." She abandoned her seat, unable to tolerate the smell any longer.

"I'll accompany you." Max followed her out.

Uncle Bartholomew remained on the settee, staring after them.

Lina stumbled to the courtyard and drew a cleansing breath, hoping to help settle her stomach. "I despise him."

"Those are strong feelings."

"I have no doubt he hired those men." There was no use concealing her thoughts from Max any longer.

"Though possible, it's a serious accusation."

"He wants my money—my father's money. He is ruined and in debt, and so is Hamilton. He wanted me to marry Hamilton, and I almost lost my life when I refused. It doesn't take much to put two and two together."

"Are you serious?" Max was genuinely startled.

"Why would I lie?"

"If you refused Hamilton, why were you with him at the party?"

"It was the only way they would let me see Mateo."

"Ah...I must say that I don't like that Hamilton fellow."

"I don't either, but I like Bartholomew even less. He wants me dead."

"Without proof, it's all hearsay."

"Whose side are you on?"

Max stepped closer and lowered his head to speak in her ear. "You must remember that when someone is acquitted of a criminal charge, they can't be charged with it again. There must be overwhelming evidence to go after them. You only get one chance to convict."

Was it his sound reasoning or proximity that calmed her nerves? Maybe both. Being back at Blackwater agitated her more than she had expected, and she needed to stay on task. She reminded herself that her awful ordeal might be a blessing in disguise as she might now have Max's help, and the possibility of getting her assassins' confessions to bring down whoever was behind it all. "I suppose you are correct. But tell me, why did you lie? You didn't find me at the west border."

"For various reasons."

"Such as?"

"First, I wanted to see his reaction. Second, if he is the mastermind behind the attack, my story will cast suspicions on the honesty of his men. I'm sure they've given him an account of the events—"

"So, you do suspect my uncle? Apart from what I just told you, what else do you know about him?"

Max ignored her questions. "Third, if he trusts his men, he'll think I lied because I'm on to something. And hopefully that will prompt him to be extremely cautious about your safety."

"Or to exterminate me faster," Lina retorted.

The gardener came striding around the corner with Dexter in tow.

"Ah, Mr. Krammer, you are right on time," Max observed. "I hope he didn't cause too much trouble."

"He wasn't too happy to be in the stable, but a good breed is always strong-willed," Mr. Krammer said. "I fed him some hay and carrots, and he cheered up all right."

A breeze swept the grounds, and Lina moved closer to Dexter, shielding herself from the cold.

Max patted Dexter's forehead. "Thank you, Mr. Krammer. I see you understand horses. Do you help with them around here?"

"Occasionally, but Fred, a boy from the neighboring farm, is in charge of them."

"I imagine they are good riding horses?"

"You can say that, though we retired two of them. They have bad legs, you know. The other three are in pretty good shape."

"Who rides them?"

"Fred does to keep them in shape, and he enjoys it too. Sir Bartholomew doesn't ride. He prefers the car."

"I'm sure the horses don't mind. He's quite heavy," Max said matter-of-factly.

Mr. Krammer pursed his lips, clearly suppressing a laugh.

"My aunt used to ride quite a bit," Lina stated.

"Oh, yes, she used to compete in Bristol. If I may say so, she was a devil of a rider, but time has a way of slowing us down," Mr. Krammer said. "I was glad to see her teaching Mateo how to ride. The little fellow revived her love of riding."

"And what about you, Mr. Krammer? Do you ride?" Max inquired.

"Well, yes, of course."

"Often?"

"Anytime I get a chance."

Max guided the gardener away from Lina and spoke in a hushed tone. She couldn't make out their words until Max said, "Mr. Krammer, it's been a pleasure speaking to you. Thanks again for taking good care of Dexter."

"Ah, he is a good boy." Mr. Krammer pulled out a few pieces of carrot from his pocket and gave them to Max. "For the ride home."

"I see he's already won you over." Max chuckled.

Mr. Krammer stroked the horse's neck and strolled away.

"I better go before Eleonor chases me with the tea," Max joked, and mounted Dexter.

"I'm surprised she isn't out here already," Lina joked back.

"If it weren't that I'm already in enough trouble as it is, I would kiss you again."

The way he looked at Lina made her bones feel like they were on fire. "Goodbye for now."

"I'll see you soon."

The horse shifted away from the house.

"Max, wait." Out of the blue, Lina remembered Max's order to the tailor.

He tugged the reins, and Dexter halted.

"You haven't told me which color of fabric you picked for your shirts."

"The burgundy and navy blue—just like the beautiful lady suggested."

With that, Max turned Dexter and rode away.

CHAPTER 19
EVIDENCE

Lina awoke to the sound of voices but stayed motionless, listening.

"She's been asleep all afternoon," Annie noted.

"After what she's been through, she needs it," Mrs. Lester responded.

"Thank heaven the lieutenant found her. Now, think about that. What are the odds?"

"Luck favored her this time."

"You can say that again," Annie agreed. "And in more ways than one."

Lina suspected she referred to Max's good looks.

"Yes, his timing saved her for sure, though the doctor had to redo the stitches," Mrs. Lester observed. "Let's plan on bringing supper up here. The less she moves about today, the better."

"Dollie is making soup with some special herbs. She says they will have Lina back to full health in no time. Speaking of soup, what happened with the Swedish bread?"

"What?" Mrs. Lester seemed confused by Annie's words.

"Surely you haven't forgotten," Annie said in an incredulous tone. "You went to town right before the storm to get the ingredients."

"Oh, my. I did forget. When Lina went missing, I'm afraid I lost track of everything I was working on."

"Is Dollie going to make it?"

"Well, I suppose I forgot to ask her to." The housekeeper let out a short laugh. "I must mend this at once. Come on, let's get back to the kitchen."

The door closed, and silence settled in. Lina opened her eyes and saw she was in her bedroom. She felt lonely and adrift, not knowing where to go from here. She missed her parents in a way she hadn't before—a part of her had died with them, and no matter how much she tried to revive it, she knew her life would never be the same. Until now, she hadn't allowed herself to deal with the pain of their loss, but that was changing. She reflected on the vision of her parents she'd had when she was being drowned. It had seemed very real, and somehow, they had helped her stay alive. Although the memory intensified her yearning for them, instead of dismissing it, she embraced it. *They were right there with me. Wherever they are, they are aware of me. I'm not alone.* With those simple words, her heart and mind overflowed with peace.

In her vision, her parents had also asked her to care for Mateo. Lina longed to hear him laughing at something that had delighted him, or to feel one of his sweet hugs. Her decision to send him to High Point was still almost impossible to live with, though it was the only thing she could do under the circumstances. Would she have to wait an entire year before getting him back? No, it was too long. There had to be something else she could do to expedite the process of identifying her father's murderer. And hopefully, regain her freedom in the process.

Her thoughts jumped to Max. He had conquered part of her heart, and that part now ached for him. She would never forget the way she felt in his arms, but he was hiding something from her. Annie was right. The odds that he was in the right place and at the right time were nearly impossible. What did he know? What was he after?

With a sigh, she moved on to contemplate the dilemma of the disembodied inhabitants of Blackwater. Ruby lived in torment, ever searching for her son. Tommy aimlessly roamed the house but was seemingly unaware of his mother's presence. Lina couldn't imagine being permanently separated from Mateo, not knowing where or how he was. Their short separation was unbearable enough, and at times, it tore her heart. Poor Ruby. In that instant, Lina understood the woman's affliction. The two had wandered the house for years, neither Ruby nor Tommy able to rectify their conundrum. They seemed at the mercy of fate, or worse, a living person such as herself, who might or might not find a way to succor them. Suddenly, Lina's misfortune seemed minor in the face of their plight. If she couldn't solve her problems, perhaps she could do something to solve theirs.

Night found Lina wide awake, staring at the chandelier from her bed. Last she checked, it was one o'clock in the morning. That's what came of being confined to the bedroom all day long—a restless night. Her body was still sore, but it was more discomfort than pain.

Like an electric current, sudden giggling coming from the corridor traveled her body, pricking every nerve. *Tommy*.

The attic floor creaked overhead. Ruby was also on the move.

Another nerve-racking giggle was followed by a tap at the door.

Lina exhaled sharply. She had been holding her breath as dread spread through her. With the dead, one never knew what would come next. She fixed her eyes on the door, expecting Tommy to come through it at any moment. In fact, why hadn't he already? The tapping came again, and with a pounding heartbeat, Lina left the bed. This was her chance. Even if she failed to find his body, she had to try to bring his spirit to his mother. Perhaps she could somehow bridge the barrier between them, and they could find each other.

Lina had just wrapped a hand around the doorknob when a loud noise from the attic made her reconsider. She was certain Ruby had sent something crashing to the floor. If Ruby thought Lina was after Tommy, she might unleash her wrath on Lina, but there must be a way to make her understand. She pulled the door open and stepped into the candlelit corridor. Tommy scurried through the shadows up ahead, giggling as he went.

"Wait," Lina called. "Come back."

To her delight, Tommy stopped. Silently praying he wouldn't go away, she neared him.

"Tommy, where are you going?"

He shrugged, much like Mateo did in answer to her questions.

"See this?" Lina turned her head so he could see the bandage on it. "I was hurt and lost in the woods, but I found my way back."

He cocked his head to the side.

"I know you were also hurt. Tell me, how did that happen?"

His little body trembled as if the memory pained him. He turned and ran toward the staircase.

"Please wait." Lina dashed after him.

He hesitated by the banister.

It was time to test her theory. "Tommy, are you looking for your mum?"

He averted his weary gaze from hers, and in a dejected tone, said, "I can't find her. She's left me."

At that moment, Lina understood the weight of the sorrow he carried. A weight born of years of isolation, longing for a life once lived and now lost. His grief tugged at her heartstrings, a surge of tears burning behind her eyes. She wanted to tell him Ruby hadn't abandoned him, that she was desperately looking for him, and that she was steps away. But none of that would do any good if he couldn't see her, and she wasn't sure that could come to pass. Careful not to further harm his fragile soul, she suppressed her emotions and tactfully said, "I might know where she is." Yet, just as she said it, the anxious palpitations in her chest warned her that this wasn't a good idea.

"You do?" Tommy beheld her with intense distrust. If this backfired, he could become a fierce enemy. Coming and going as he pleased under the shadows of night, he could make her life a living hell.

But there was no turning back now. "Follow me." In semi-obscurity, Lina slipped down the candlelit corridors, keeping Tommy in the corner of her eye as he trailed behind. The urgency of knowing he could flee at any given moment fueled her to move faster despite her aches. Soon enough, the stairway to the attic appeared in the gloom. She placed a foot on the first board, and the chilly silence warned her that Ruby awaited her. She climbed, ignoring the image of Ruby flying down the steps in fury that formed in her mind. At the door, she looked down and saw Tommy at the landing. She signaled for him to come up. "Your mum is in here."

Tommy didn't move.

Without any help from Lina, the door opened into blackness. Among the dormant shapes, Ruby's eyes appeared like blazing coals. Though the woman was eerily still, her dark energy was almost palpable. It carried a ravaging force that attached to Lina's body, immobilizing her. In that instant, she had no doubt Ruby had the power to tear her apart inside and out—to extinguish the very light in Lina's soul.

Turning her attention to Tommy, Lina encouraged in a shaky voice, "Come up here. She is waiting for you." And to the woman, she said, "Ruby, Tommy is here to see you. Please think of him. Do you remember him?"

Tommy ascended the stairway in what to Lina seemed like never-ending slow motion.

"Come on, Tommy. Come on." Lina felt sick with fear over Ruby's presence, the red eyes boring into her.

Tommy climbed the final board and stood next to Lina.

Lina vehemently said to his mother, "Ruby, please focus. He is right here. Right here. Can you not see him?"

The woman shrieked.

Undeterred, pointing to the woman, Lina said, "There she is, standing by the crates. Can you see her?"

Tommy's face clouded with confusion.

"Can you see her?" Lina pressed.

Tommy inched into the gloom, cocked his head to one side, and, for a brief instant, Ruby's eyes lost some of their ferocity. She inched closer, one step, two steps. Lina quivered uncontrollably as the distance between them closed. And Lina grew aware of her vulnerable position—right at the top of a steep staircase.

"Mum?" Tommy said faintly.

Oh, please, see her!

The woman took another step. Lina remained petrified, unable to tell if Ruby's rage was dissipating or about to explode. Then, as if someone had slammed a door shut, a blast of wind came from somewhere on the floor below. Lina broke free from her paralysis with a gasp and a startled jump. Tommy instantly vanished.

"Tommy, wait! Come back," Lina pleaded in despair.

Ruby emitted a blood-curdling wail and launched herself toward Lina. Producing a scream of her own, Lina bolted down the steps. Her feet hit the landing and pounded down the passage. She reached the main corridor, and a yard or two ahead, Tommy rematerialized. Lina halted beside him, catching her breath.

"Tommy, I'm sorry. I'm sorry. I don't know what startled us, but did you see your mum?"

Instead of replying, Tommy pointed toward the end of the passage where the candlelight was swallowed up by the darkness.

"Is that your mum? Can you see her?" Lina scanned the space and saw a silhouette so enmeshed within the shadows that she almost missed it.

Tommy shuddered and shook his head.

The figure swiftly shifted and headed opposite her. The way it moved told Lina it wasn't a ghost. It wasn't Ruby. She looked back at Tommy, but once again he was gone.

Lina rushed after the newcomer, determined to find out who it was and why they were prowling about at this hour. Apparently, she wasn't the only one breaking the rules.

"It was cold—really cold..." Tommy's voice echoed in Lina's head.

"Tommy, where are you?" Lina came to the connecting corridor. There were no signs of Tommy, but she saw the mysterious figure scurrying ahead.

"Why didn't she like me?" Tommy sobbed, his voice haunting the passage.

She? Lina stopped mid-stride. Though she still couldn't see him, she asked, "Tommy, what did you say?"

Tommy didn't respond, but his anguished sobbing—a raw gut-wrenching expression of his suffering—reverberated from every direction. It was as if his agony, trapped in the walls, the floors, the ceiling, had suddenly been released.

Distraught as she was, Lina had to stay on task. She had to catch up with whoever moved in the shadows. Shadows. Now that she wasn't pursuing the ghosts and had Max's support against her uncle, she hit the switches as she ran down the hallways. But the light was always seconds behind her quarry. Here and there, she caught glimpses and heard footsteps, until she came to the service staircase that led to the main floor. She leaned against the railing, looking down. It was deserted.

Somewhere in the distance, a rooster crowed as Lina descended and dawn inched its way through the high windows. Her legs cramped as she reached the landing and veered in the kitchen's direction.

"Good gracious! What are you doing here?" exclaimed Maggie as she collided with Lina, the tray in her hand crashing to the floor.

Lina took a sharp breath at Maggie's sudden appearance, words escaping her.

A look of irritation crossed Maggie's eyes. "Were you looking for something?"

Yes! Ghosts and killers! Lina thought with some irritation. "I was on my way to the kitchen for some milk."

"Through here?" Maggie questioned.

"Yes, through here," Lina lied. The main stairway was a more convenient route, and they both knew it.

"Hmm." Maggie picked up the tray and walked away, shaking her head.

Lina stared after her—tall, stern, and white as a ghost. Could Maggie have been the figure she had been pursuing? If yes, she could have simply pretended to be here by coincidence to avoid detection.

"*It was cold—really cold ...*" Tommy had said. Had he alluded to his death? "*Why didn't she like me?*" he had also said. If his death hadn't been accidental, could he possibly have been speaking of his killer? If he was, then the killer was a woman. And if that were the case, not one but two murderers inhabited Blackwater, for surely her uncle had had a hand in her father's death.

"*To this day, I'm not sure why they stopped seeing each other. Maggie won't talk about it, but I suspect it might have had something to do with Stanley. Maggie wasn't too fond of the boy,*" Lina recalled Dollie's story about Maggie's lover, George, and his son, Stanley. Maggie had a history of disliking children. Perhaps the candles that she so faithfully lit in the attic could be to appease her guilty conscience. But what if Tommy had been speaking about his mother? If he thought she had abandoned him, he might have assumed she didn't like him.

But then again, anything could be possible, but it did not mean it was the truth. Nevertheless, Lina felt quite positive about two things— whoever had been lurking in the shadows brought unwanted memories to Tommy. Tommy, in turn, had warned Lina about her presence. Lina had the impression that that person had intended to cause harm, but when the element of surprise was removed, whoever it was fled.

"Fascinating," said Eleonor to herself, not having heard Lina coming into the library.

"What is?" Lina inquired.

"This book." Eleonor looked up and showed her the cover of *Cards on the Table*. "It was worth every shilling."

"Did you just finish it?"

"I know. It took me a while, but I was too distressed these past days to enjoy reading." Eleonor smiled warmly from her chair. "It's a novel that requires one's full attention. It has four suspects, and any of them could be the murderer. Nearly impossible to guess."

"Did you guess it?"

"If I may say so, I did." Eleonor beamed with pride. "But tell me, darling, how are you feeling?"

"Quite better." Lina came to the window. The sun reflecting off the snow-covered grounds had produced a brilliant day. "Although, I must admit I couldn't have done it without Dollie's soup."

"And rest. You mustn't do too much. You need to focus your energy on healing." Eleonor got to her feet. "Oh, don't forget the constable is due to stop by midmorning. I'll sit with you if you'd like during his visit. Reliving those awful memories might not be easy."

Simultaneous feelings of gratitude and contentment enveloped Lina's heart. Embracing Eleonor, she said sincerely, "Thank you for being here for me."

"Oh, dear, we'll get through this together," Eleonor said with teary eyes.

Mrs. Lester walked into the room. "Excuse me, Mrs. Eleonor. May I speak to you about the menu?"

"Well, of course," Eleonor responded.

"I'll leave you two to it." Lina left the library, having already decided to talk to the twins. It was an overdue discussion. She could gauge their reaction to the Joneses' story if nothing else.

Dollie, Maggie, and Mr. Krammer enjoyed their morning coffee in the kitchen.

After greeting them, Lina settled at the table next to Dollie. "Aunt Eleonor told me who the maid was. The one I asked you about a while ago," Lina spoke at once. Perhaps the twins would share information now that Lina knew the woman's identity. "It was Ruby Jones. My aunt also told me about Ruby's tragic story—the disappearance of her son and her demise."

Dollie swallowed hard, and her gaze dropped to the table. Maggie's face hardened. Was it disappointment or anger that passed through her?

Mr. Krammer jumped from the chair as if a fire burned unattended somewhere. "I ought to get back to work." He placed his cup on the sink and left for the outside world.

"What's wrong with him?" Lina stared at the now-closed door.

"He wasn't fond of Ruby—" Dollie informed.

"I must say, I'm impressed that you remember Ruby," Maggie interjected. "You were a child when she worked here."

"True, but some people have a long-lasting effect upon others." Though Lina hadn't met the maid when she was alive, her ghost indeed impacted her life.

"Hmm ..." Maggie's eyes narrowed on Lina as if questioning the latter's truthfulness.

"What was Mr. Krammer's quarrel with Ruby?" Lina addressed Dollie.

"Well," Dollie started. Maggie looked sternly at her, but Dollie went on, "Ruby had a strong character. She enjoyed giving people orders and often came across as arrogant—as if she were worth more than any of us."

"I think that's enough," Maggie said, abandoning her seat.

"Ah, there is nothing wrong with telling the truth," Dollie retorted passionately. It was evident that Dollie hadn't been fond of Ruby either. "The fact is that Ruby pestered Krammer about his work nonstop as if the grounds were her own. She had endless ideas for embellishing the gardens and wanted Krammer to bring them to fruition. And I must say that most of her ideas were impossible for one man to carry out alone. And that's not even considering how vast the grounds are and how much work it requires to keep it under control. Oh, indeed, he detested Ruby."

"It sounds like a terrible situation," Lina opined.

"It sure was for Krammer," Dollie asserted. "Maggie and I didn't pay much attention to Ruby. Though, I must say that she often came after us about our cooking skills."

"That came to a halt quickly when we threatened to resign," Maggie declared from the sink with a triumphant laugh.

Lina was startled by Maggie's display of emotion. She couldn't imagine a feud between Ruby and Maggie, but she had the inkling that Maggie would win.

"I remember the day when Ruby insisted that Krammer dig up the hedge of rose bushes he had just planted, just to move them two feet away," Dollie recalled. "He was so enraged that among some cursing, he said she needed a dose of humbleness. That was the only time I heard him speak like that."

"I bet he regretted wishing her *humbling* when Tommy went missing," Lina reasoned. Losing a child would bring the bravest parents to their knees with grief.

"Well, well, well." Mrs. Lester popped in from the hallway. "How are the pastries for teatime coming along?"

"Oh my," Dollie exclaimed, throwing her arms in the air in discontent. "I haven't even started the dough."

"You better get to it then," Mrs. Lester advised. Teatime was hours away, but the pastries would take about that long to make.

Mrs. Lester pulled out the day's menu to review the pastries list with the twins.

Lina remained on the chair. *Ruby was a controversial woman. Mr. Krammer disliked her very much, but so did Dollie and Maggie.*

Lina built the hearth's largest fire to date and lit a five-arm candelabra before snuggling into bed. Her thoughts traveled back to that morning. As expected, Constable Wilson, a short, older fellow with a thick black beard and mustache, took her statement. The affair had been easier than expected, as the constable was a well-trained man who didn't dig too deep or linger too long. After her interview, Bartholomew had walked Wilson out and spent a considerable amount of time with him.

Her mind jumped from her failure to discover anything to incriminate her uncle to the dilemma of the dead. She groaned, disheartened by not knowing what else she could do to help them. There had been a moment when she believed Ruby and Tommy had connected in the attic, but there was no way to be sure, and it didn't seem likely that Tommy would trust her again. Who was she fooling? How would she help others when she couldn't help herself? She didn't even know who was out in the corridor watching her last night.

Her mind wouldn't quiet down. It kept jumping from the dead to the living, from one question to another, from one problem to the next. And sometime during the process she fell asleep.

Lina's eyes flew open at the subtle groaning of floorboards. In a flash, she was standing beside her bed, straining to hear. The doorknob rattled. Unable to enter, the uninvited guest backed away. Lina exhaled, releasing some of the tension in her neck, but soon she perceived another noise—a clicking sound that came from Mateo's bedroom. This was no ghost. Door locked or not, a ghost would have come in already. Lina took the candelabra from the mantelpiece and blew out the candles. Armed with the metal object, she slid through the connecting passage and, standing next to Mateo's bed, identified the source of the noise. Someone was picking the lock.

Panic arced through her as she wondered if she would survive the night. However, flesh and bone she could fight. She might not have a chance against them, but she would surely try. She glided across the room to maintain a position of advantage, her fingers gripping the candlestick tighter as the door opened. She had to be quick. One hard blow to their head, and she'd run for help.

A tall figure stepped in, and Lina dashed forward, the weapon raised high in the air. In a split second, the intruder turned, seized the candelabra, and, stepping behind her, wrestled her into a position where she could neither move nor speak, his hand muffling her mouth.

"Shh, Lina. It's me, Max," he announced in a calm voice.

Though she heard the words, amid her panic and confusion, it didn't register.

"Lina, it's Max. It's all right. Shh, shh."

Max? She ceased her struggle.

"I'll let go of you, but don't scream, all right?"

Lina nodded, and he released her. Though she couldn't see him clearly, she recognized his outline. "Max?"

"Yes, just me." He held her tightly. In the safety of his arms, the accumulated emotions of the past days crashed down on her, and she began to sob. He soothingly held her head against his chest. "I'm sorry. I didn't mean to scare you."

After a moment or two, Lina commanded herself to get a grip. But then her mind began racing again, and she let out a string of questions. "What are you doing here? How did you get into the house? How did you know where to find me?"

"I promise I'll tell you later, but we need to go now."

"Go where?"

"To the police station," Max said.

"Wait—what?"

"I tracked down Bill and took him to the constable. You need to identify him before I drag him to London."

"I only saw the face of the other man," Lina said.

"Will you recognize his general appearance? His voice?"

"Yes," she answered with surety. "Did he say who he works for?"

"Not yet, but he'll talk soon enough."

"Why are you taking him to London?"

"Orders. We must hurry. Please, get dressed. We need to be back here before sunrise. No one can know about this."

Perhaps it was the residue of the shock that slowed her understanding, but she felt overly muddled. Max had somehow managed to enter the house undetected, she was now supposed to visit a man behind bars in the middle of the night, no one was to know about it, and the man was bound for London. Nothing made sense.

Seeing her hesitation, Max asked, "Do you trust me?"

"Well..."

"Just trust me this once, then."

Lina traveled the passage to her bedroom, and with only the light of the hearth, she changed into her riding clothes.

"Wear a heavy coat. It's quite cold," Max said from the passageway.

Once she was ready, they hurried down the corridors and exited the house into the frosty world outside. The crescent moon hovered over the distant treetops, its light barely enough to guide their way. They crossed the snow-covered yard while a stinging breeze whipped their faces.

"Almost there," Max encouraged.

Lina made out Dexter's form among a cluster of trees, and as they approached, he snorted and stomped his hooves.

"Hello, boy. It's nice to see you again." Lina patted his forehead.

Max untied the horse and helped her mount it. Then he settled in behind her, tightening his grip on the reins, and pressed his heels against Dexter's sides, nudging him into a trot. Lina hid her face in the lapel of her coat to block the freezing wind. The urgency of the matter became evident as Max continuously pushed Dexter to increase his pace.

Constable Wilson awaited them outside the two-story station that had once been the residence of a well-known family. Their last heir had donated it to the town, and it was quickly put to good use. The police had converted the back of the structure into a cell equipped with a couple of beds and strong iron bars.

"If you would, follow me, please," Wilson instructed in a low voice.

They entered the reception hall, and Max addressed Wilson. "Remember, this visit never took place, and the prisoner was never here."

"There is nothing to fret about, Lieutenant." In passing, Wilson retrieved a truncheon from a desk.

They came to a cell where a man lay face down on a makeshift bed. Wilson fiddled with the lock, and soon the door swung inward. He stepped inside. Preferring to have the bars between them, Lina stayed in the hallway with Max beside her. Her stomach churned at the sight of the muddy boots on the floor near the prisoner, her mind jumping back to her terrifying encounter with the men, the images still vivid.

Yes, this man was Bill. She had looked carefully at his footwear as he taunted her from his horse. The short black boots had three square buckles in front, and the laces were too long. He'd tied them around the tops of his boots several times.

Wilson ran the truncheon back and forth against the bars. "Mr. Robinson, you have visitors. Get up."

In response, the man grumbled angrily but did not change his position.

Wilson struck the weapon on the bars again. "Get up!" When the man ignored him again, the constable poked him a few times.

"Not even in jail can one be at peace," complained Robinson.

Lina gulped at the sound of his voice.

Robinson rolled off the bed and stood defiantly, taking in the disturbers of his peace. His swollen, bruised face sported a black eye and bulging eyelid. His gaze jumped from Lina to Max to Wilson, then back to the first, where it lingered. Though Lina hadn't seen his whole face before, there was no way under heaven she would forget those eyes, embedded in her mind like a dreadful curse as they were.

The impulse to spit out a few not-so-pleasant words tempted her, but there was no need to waste her energy on such a man. She simply said, "Yes, it's Bill, one of the men who attacked me."

"I don't know what you are talking about, miss," Robinson challenged.

"Get him ready. I'll be back soon," Max said to Wilson. And grasping Lina's hand, he guided her out.

They mounted Dexter, and as the horse walked away, Max leaned forward, placing his chin on Lina's shoulder. Listening to his soft breathing, she felt her attraction to him collide with her distrust of him. She couldn't deny that Max had been her savior in more than one way, but her trust was in short supply. Bray's betrayal didn't help. Now, more than ever, she wished she knew Max's involvement with her family and what he was after. And though she wouldn't admit it, what bothered her most was that Max wouldn't fully confide in her. She could only hope that when the time came to change that she wouldn't be disappointed.

Truth, Lina said to herself. *That's all I want.* She couldn't remain idle in hopes that Bill would betray his employer and solve her problems. Even if he did, and she could free herself from her uncle's dominion, it didn't mean her father's murder would be solved.

"*Bartholomew has gone to the pub,*" Eleonor had said.

Defying the constraints of careful planning, she propelled into action. Ever since she had searched her uncle's office, she had regretted having done a lousy job. She needed to correct that. There were many documents in there—some of which might be useful in her quest to put the man behind bars. True, he might have destroyed incriminating evidence, especially after some of the papers went missing. But there was only one way to find out. She moved quickly through the passages with purpose and determination.

She stepped into Bartholomew's office and secured the door behind her. The saddened eyes of the creatures displayed high on the walls seemed to follow her. She rushed to the window and drew the drapes. Daylight bathed the room. Lina moved to the desk and pulled open the first drawer. She brought out a stack of papers. It was going to be an arduous task. She turned one piece after another, meticulously analyzing them. It took longer than she'd expected to finish the pile and return it to its place.

She pulled out the contents of the second drawer. It was packed to the brim. Again, she flipped through all sorts of documents: Real Estate;

Stock Exchange; Businesses in India; and, as far as Lina was concerned, a hoard of other insignificant information. She thrust them back into the drawer and focused on the third one filled with folders.

The first few folders were fruitless. With a sigh of exasperation, Lina turned to another one. It contained several lists of names and addresses of people related to Bartholomew's social and business life. She then noticed a list that deviated in its format. It had several columns: Names; telephone numbers; occupations; and dates—the latest had been recorded last week. Lina plunged onto Bartholomew's shabby chair to study the paper. If she wasn't mistaken, the names were Italian, German, and Japanese, and their occupations were military-related. Why would her uncle have such a list? Why would he contact these people? She had no clue, but considering that the world was on the brink of a global war, it had to be important. And since Bartholomew had no ties to the government or the military, it shouldn't be in his possession. Could this have something to do with the papers Max had in his cabin? She would find out. She folded the paper and buried it in her pocket.

She picked up another page and couldn't believe what it contained. Sentence after sentence, she read a detailed timeline of the night her father was assassinated. Bartholomew had even recorded the activities of the household. Why? Had he written it to ensure he had a perfect alibi?

Her gaze swept over it again, and she saw a detail she had missed. It left her dumbfounded. Was it an accusation, complicity, or a trap? If it was the truth, then once more, Lina's world was turned upside down. But she wouldn't jump to conclusions—she needed to be cautious not to be deceived.

Whistling, loud and clear, broke the silence, bursting from outside the office. Lina erupted from the seat. She stashed the paper in her pocket and did her best to gather the rest in the folder. She dropped it in the drawer and rushed to leave.

"Jasper, Ruppert, come on, boys," Bartholomew called from the other side of the door.

In her state of mind, Lina couldn't come up with an excuse for being here, not when the door was closed. He would see right through her, and she couldn't risk losing the papers she had stolen. They had to reach the authorities. In a heartbeat, she pressed her fingers to the molding on the wall, and the panel cracked open, exposing the hidden niche. Lina scrambled inside. It was dark and stuffy in the narrow space. She sat on the dusty floor, hoping to calm her breathing and stop her body from shuddering.

Bartholomew's heavy footsteps crossed the office, followed by the complaining of his chair under his weight. "Ah, boys, it's been a long day," he said to the dogs. "You are lucky you don't have to worry about life. All you need is someone to love and care for you—and you got that. If only I would too..."

One of the Ridgebacks emitted a short, warning bark.

"What is it, boy?"

The dogs sniffed just outside the niche. They knew she was here.

"Wait," Bartholomew grunted. "The lamp is off..."

"*But the room was bright,*" Lina thought. The drapes. "*I forgot to close them.*"

"I smell a rat," Bartholomew growled, and the panel flung open.

Before Lina could react, he seized her arm and hauled her out of the niche.

"You are hell-bent on making mischief," Bartholomew fumed. "As if we didn't have enough problems as it is."

"Mischief? No," Lina fumed back, shocked at the audacity that came over her. At last, she supposed she had had enough. "What I'm hell-bent on is discovering who killed my father!"

"You would do well to leave it alone." Bartholomew slammed the panel door shut with a force that shook the room.

With a growl in their throat, Jasper and Ruppert moved from behind their owner to stand in between him and his niece. Then, they did something that shocked Bartholomew more than it shocked Lina if that were even possible. They turned to face the man, barring him from reaching his niece.

"How could you?" Lina sputtered. "He was your brother."

The ferocity in Bartholomew's eyes diminished, giving way to unexpected awareness. He knew that she knew. He shot a glance at his desk.

Lina had to leave; the urge was almost unbearable now. She had to protect the papers in her pocket at all costs, and she was no match for him.

"You stole something from me. Didn't you?" he accused.

Lina retreated a step.

"Give it back, or I'll take it back!" he demanded with rage. The vein in his neck pulsated extra hard while his skin turned crimson red, the color expanding to his face.

The Ridgebacks' soft gurgling grew louder, and they flashed their teeth at their owner.

Lina didn't have to think about it twice. She bolted out of the office.

CHAPTER 20

FREED

There was only one thing on Lina's mind. She had to share what she had discovered with the authorities. She dashed across the foyer, amazed that her uncle hadn't come after her yet. In passing, through the door's sidelight she saw two black cars entering the courtyard.

"Who is that?" Lina wondered aloud as she halted by the glass.

"I'm wondering the same thing," Mrs. Lester said as she suddenly surged into the foyer. "I saw them from the library window."

The tension in Lina's body eased, her previous anxiety suspended at the sight of the newcomers. She hoped their presence would provide the time she needed to escape Bartholomew's wrath and get the new-found information to the police.

With her usual attention to neatness, Mrs. Lester took a moment to smooth out her already well-pressed green wool suit. With each stroke of her hands over her jacket and skirt, the insignificant wrinkles vanished, solidifying her self-assurance. She squared up her shoulders and unfastened the door.

The women stood on the threshold as six men exited from the vehicles, leaving the drivers behind. Chief Inspector Cook from Scotland Yard introduced himself. He was younger than Lina would have expected, with red hair and intelligent green eyes. Max came next, and two police officers followed, escorting Bray Hamilton.

Lina took a step back as Bray came into the foyer. The harshness of his hands, the foulness of his breath, the lust in his eyes—it all came back to her. But at that moment, he looked defeated. That Bray was in custody didn't surprise Lina. He was one of those men who, one way or another, eventually ended up in jail. What puzzled her was that the police had dragged him to Blackwater.

"Miss Laroche, correct?" The inspector addressed Lina.

"Correct, Catalina Laroche."

"We are here about the matter of your father's murder. Some new evidence has come to light."

Lina knew she heard correctly, but the words felt surreal, the timing impeccable. Could it be that the truth would be revealed at last? Would it match what she had conjectured from Bartholomew's papers? She glanced at Max. His face was unreadable, his body stiff.

"I'll fetch Sir Bartholomew and Mrs. Eleonor," Mrs. Lester decided at once.

"Mr. Hamilton has asked to speak with you in private," Inspector Cook said to Lina. "It will be brief. Right, Hamilton?"

"Right," Bray answered grudgingly.

"Miss?" The inspector required an answer.

"Very well." Lina drew reassurance from the police presence. Bray had no choice but to stay in line, and considering the circumstances, it might be worth listening to him.

"Accompany them," Cook ordered two of his men.

Lina ushered them to the drawing room.

"Come on, chaps. Give us some privacy," Bray said to the officers. "I'm not about to jump out the window."

Reluctantly, the officers stayed just outside the door, keeping watch on their detainee.

"The inspector said this would be brief," Lina reminded Bray unceremoniously. "I'm listening."

"I see you haven't forgotten or forgiven me."

"Should I have?"

"All right." Bray sighed. "I'm going to be locked up for some time, but for whatever it's worth, I wanted you to hear the reason from my own lips."

"At this point, why do you care what I think?"

"Because I fell for you," he confessed rather swiftly. "I have never wanted a woman more than I wanted you. Your rejection might have had something to do with it. I'm not used to that, but—" he cleared his throat "—I love you."

Lina was incredulous, but something in the sincerity in his gaze and the tone of his voice left her befuddled. The all-confident Bray Hamilton had felt the sting of rejection. Considering the many hearts he had broken, a dose of his own medicine was fitting.

"Aren't you going to say something?" Bray asked.

"I'm not sure you want me to."

"Of course, I do."

"Right, then. The truth is that I don't think you know what love is. You exploit your good looks and family name to take advantage of women. I could never be romantically involved with you, for you lack one incredibly important but basic thing—integrity." Lina felt great satisfaction to have expressed her thoughts in such a truthful manner.

Bray's face reddened—whether in shame or anger she didn't know. Either he didn't agree with her, or he was truly embarrassed by his past behavior. Hopefully it was the latter, but, like Annie had said, a wolf could change its coat but not its character.

"Remember the day we searched the attic?" Bray quickly moved on from the subject of love.

"What about it?"

"I found Bartholomew's documents and hid them inside my shirt."

"You took them? Why?" She remembered the interval during their search when Bray had gone suspiciously quiet. Now she knew why.

"Greed. I knew from Bartholomew how valuable they were. I was going to sell them to the highest bidder, inside or outside the country. I suspect he was about to do as much. The night at the count's house, I propositioned the general with the bloody papers. It was all hypothetical, but I suggested I could produce them in exchange for political leverage.

All I gained was a prime place on the military's radar, and now that I'm going to prison, I want you to know the truth about your father."

"What do you know about my father?"

"He suspected Bartholomew stole the documents from your flat. I think he wanted to convince Bartholomew to return them voluntarily. Your father still would have kicked him out of Blackwater but would have spared him going to prison. That's why he came to Coleford."

"What are the documents about?"

"The men outside the door won't let me divulge any information, but let's just say they contain matters pertaining to national security."

The list in my pocket must be related, Lina thought. The urgent calls in the middle of the night, her father's deep preoccupation, and his sudden trip to the manor—it all fell into place.

National security. The general. Max. Of course, his mission was to find those papers. That was why he was in the forest. That was why her father's name was on the file in the cabin. "Where are the documents now?"

"The Secret Service has them. They caught me before I could sell them."

"Thank heavens." That was the first good news she had heard in a long time. "My father can rest in peace now." He must have felt guilty, so guilty, to have lost them. Even worse, the betrayal of his own brother must have driven him insane.

"I'm telling you this to make it clear that while I stole the documents, I had absolutely nothing to do with your father's death."

Again, she found sincerity in his words. He would never be an admirable man in her eyes, but at least she was spared having to deal with Bray as a murderer. "I appreciate you telling me this."

Bray smiled, clearly pleased, though Lina didn't think his confession anywhere near praiseworthy. It was merely a small patch on a large wound.

"I imagine you brokered a deal with the police to lessen your punishment," she reckoned, his smile quickly fading.

"I did what I had to."

Lina shifted to the door.

"Wait," Bray called. "Tell me...Who gave me the blow at Count Easton's?"

"Mrs. Lester."

"Ah. I would have never thought Lester to be that strong."

It was his biggest flaw—underestimating the worth and strength of women.

"Take him to the car," Cook said, encountering them in the corridor. "The rest of us will meet in the library."

"Yes, sir," an officer answered.

"Wait a minute," Bray complained. "You want me to miss all the fun. Let me stay."

"Hamilton," the inspector snorted, "I have had enough of you," and signaled to the officer to proceed.

Bray muttered a bunch of complaints about his mistreatment as he was guided out. Lina had the inkling that Cook had separated Bray from Bartholomew in case things got heated. One would be easier to contain than two.

Lina and Chief Inspector Cook passed his men now posted outside the library to join Bartholomew, Eleonor, Max, and Mrs. Lester inside. Mrs. Lester excluded herself from the group, preferring to hover by the bookshelves, her expression grave. Lina stood alongside her aunt, wondering why the housekeeper was part of the meeting in the first place. Eleonor's eyes were moist, and her small frame quivered a little— the accumulated emotions of the past decades had been churned up.

"Now that we are all here, let's get this over with so you can leave my house," Bartholomew growled, moving about in irritation.

Cook didn't seem fazed by Bartholomew's stature or demeanor, but that might have had something to do with his personnel nearby. "We are here to execute two warrants."

"Go on, then." Bartholomew's eyes narrowed at the inspector.

"Sir Bartholomew Laroche, you are charged with espionage and treason for stealing and plotting to sell government information." Cook produced a paper from his pocket and extended it to Bartholomew. The latter refused to take it.

"Espionage and treason, of course," Lina whispered.

"Preposterous! You have no proof!" Bartholomew let out a mocking laugh.

"Mr. Laroche, let's not complicate matters," Cook advised. "We have Mr. Hamilton's statement against you. You first stole the documents from Sir William and were in the process of selling them when Hamilton took them."

"Hamilton?" Incredulity crossed Bartholomew's eyes. It was obvious he hadn't anticipated Bray's betrayal. His gaze darted at Lina, and he scoffed, "I would like to see you prove that."

"That won't be a problem," Max stated. "The person you were negotiating the sale with was me."

"I... I..." Bartholomew stuttered. His world of lies started to collapse, and he couldn't construct a defense fast enough. In exasperation, he paced the perimeter, tugging at his mustache. The other men tensed at his movements, but he returned and, scrambling to regain ground, said, "I have done no such thing."

"We have a detailed record of your communications," Max stated. "That's enough proof in and of itself to convict you."

Bartholomew glared at Max. His neck and face turned crimson with rage, but surprisingly, he remained still.

Lina extracted the papers from her pocket and extended the one containing the list of foreign names and numbers to Inspector Cook. "I found this in my uncle's office. It might be of help."

Cook scanned the list. "Indeed, this is of great significance."

Bartholomew now glared at his niece. Lina couldn't celebrate her triumph just yet. Not until the second paper she had stolen was explained.

The inspector further said, "If espionage was the only reason we were here, I would be glad indeed. Sadly, the second warrant is for the murder of Sir William Laroche."

At Cook's pronouncement, the room grew silent though everyone was on the verge of explosion. The accused readied to snap at the accusers. The accusers readied to subdue the accused. Justice was here, and Lina hoped that, in the end, it would bring peace to her and Mateo. Eleonor placed her arm across Lina's back, in a reassuring gesture.

Bartholmew broke the silence. "You can't blame that on me. I had nothing to do with it." The threat of a murder charge had him recoiling like a snake being thrown into the fire.

"We'll determine that later, but for now," the inspector turned to Eleonor and said, "Eleonor Laroche, you are under arrest for the murder of your brother-in-law, Sir William Laroche."

Eleonor's breath caught in a sharp gasp.

"You'll be transported to London to await the inquest," Cook added.

"What a sham!" Eleonor exclaimed. "This is an unforgivable disgrace on Scotland Yard."

Cook nodded to Max, and the lieutenant spoke. "The death of William solidified our suspicions about the classified documents' whereabouts. Bartholomew and Eleonor Laroche appeared to have unshakable alibis for the night of the murder. Bartholomew was at a farm with a broken-down car and was later driven to the train station by the farmer. According to the staff, Eleonor had taken a sleeping draught and retired for the night. Not only this, but there were no other cars at Blackwater at the time."

"Well, there you have it. You said it yourself. It couldn't have been me," Eleonor asserted in a triumphant tone.

"Not so fast, Mrs. Laroche," Max regained control of the conversation. "I was on the same train as William when he was killed. At the station, I was running to get on the motor bus when I saw a woman on horseback circling the station. Considering the lateness of the hour, I found it a bit strange. When we met in town, I had no doubt you were that woman."

Max's look of bafflement upon meeting Eleonor was now justified— he suspected her of being the murderer all along. And of course, Max's insistence that Lina not condemn Bartholomew so hastily made sense. Lina looked at Bartholomew. He stared at his wife as if in a trance. For the first time in her life, Lina saw him disarmed, his demeanor attesting to his innocence in his brother's death. Though Lina had suspected it as soon as she'd read her uncle's timeline, as the truth was confirmed, she felt out of orbit, her perception of reality a total distortion. Struggling to place things in their proper order, she searched her aunt's eyes, desperate for some indication that the woman was innocent. But in them, Lina found a trace of malice she had failed to see before. She stepped away from Eleonor.

"I also found this." Lina handed the inspector the second paper. "I believe he wrote this timeline to discover who the killer was—and he did."

Cook read, "Eleonor had enough time to ride to the station, kill William, and return to the house before anyone got wise. She must have tampered with the car—that's why I saw her earlier in the day coming from the car's direction."

"You knew," Lina reproached her uncle. "How could you have remained silent?"

Bartholomew didn't respond.

"It's all hearsay." Eleonor's voice escalated, her eyes clouding with anger. "You have no case against me."

Undeterred, Max went on. "Well, Eleonor, Mr. Krammer would disagree with you. That night, he noticed a horse missing from the stable. Assuming Fred might have taken it, he didn't think much of it. But he saw you, Eleonor, returning the horse."

Innocent, harmless Aunt Eleonor had killed Lina's father. Now that the scales of darkness had fallen from Lina's eyes, things made sense. "Yes, I agree," Lina accused. "You are a skilled rider and had ample time to accomplish your goal. You went as far as to convince Annie that you had been asleep when in truth you had just gotten into bed."

Whatever power had contained Bartholomew thus far released him, and he choked. "What have you done, woman? Even when I feared it was you, I'd hoped it wasn't."

"Be quiet, you fool!" Eleonor shouted viciously.

"As if you weren't up to your neck already," Cook addressed Eleonor, "Bill had much to say about you."

"*You*? You sent the men to kill me too?" Lina sputtered.

Eleonor didn't need to respond; her eyes said it all.

"Furthermore, our witness," Cook signaled to Mrs. Lester, "heard you speaking on the telephone with the men, advising them of Miss Laroche's whereabouts the day she was attacked. You'll also be charged with the attempted murder of your niece."

Lester's sudden trip after Lina left the house...Lina held the housekeeper's gaze inquiringly.

"It's true. I overheard the conversation and went to town to ask Lieutenant LeBlanc, whom I trust, to search for Lina," Mrs. Lester informed, leaving Lina totally baffled.

She knew Max? How? Lina looked at Max for an explanation.

"We'll explain later," Max said.

Cook called his men into the room. "Get them out of here."

As the officers approached the criminals, Eleonor pulled a gun from her pocket, bringing the room to a standstill.

"Think this through, Eleonor," Cook said. "You cannot get away. Don't make this any worse for yourself. Put the gun down. Just put the gun down." Even as he spoke calmly, he signaled his men to retreat.

Ignoring Cook's pleas, Eleonor pointed the weapon at her husband. "You beast of a man! I will put a hole right through that heartless body of yours. You brought poverty upon our heads and disgraced our name— and for what?" She laughed, a maniacal laugh that made Lina's flesh crawl. "Answer me, Bartholomew. For what?"

"Eleonor, for heaven's sake, put the gun down. Let's not make things worse. We still have the right to refute the charges." Bartholomew searched Eleonor's eyes, and his face contorted with fear.

Lina had the insight that he'd had plenty of encounters with this darker version of his wife.

"Refute the charges?" Eleonor scoffed. "I will hang, but it will be a relief to the hell I've lived in since marrying you, Sir Bartholomew Laroche. You have loved your addictions more than anyone, including yourself. Yes, I killed William. I did it because of you, you wretched fool! William was on to you. He was coming to remove us from Blackwater and cut financial ties. Money, oh yes, all I had left in this world was the comfort of good living, and I wasn't about to give it up."

Eleonor terminated my father's life. She also hired Bill and his companion to get rid of me. She is the cold-hearted killer. A second of utter clarity hit Lina. The scattered fragments of information fell into place, forming a cohesive picture that had eluded her for so long. That night in the corridor, Eleonor had been the person lurking in the dark, hunting

Lina. Tommy knew Eleonor presented an imminent danger and had warned her. His words came so clearly to her mind that, for a moment, she wondered if he was in the room and had just spoken. "*It was cold— really cold...Why didn't she like me?*" He had been speaking of Eleonor. She was the one behind his death. But why?

"You know what happened to Tommy," Lina said to Eleonor with irrefutable conviction. "Tell us."

A sardonic smile crossed Eleonor's face. It was clear she possessed the secret key to unlock Tommy's mystery.

"Eleonor?" Rage replaced Bartholomew's previous fear as he looked at his wife. His eyes blazed with an intense fire, betraying the turmoil within. Eleonor had committed horrendous crimes, but the possibility that she had done something to Tommy stabbed his very core. "I was a fool not to have seen it before. What did you do to the boy?" His voice, sharp and thunderous, echoed with indignation.

Eleonor took a stronger stance, gripping the gun with renewed determination. Max placed a hand on his pistol and maneuvered Lina to the side, shielding her with his body. Cook brought his right leg forward as if readying to pounce on the menace.

"Oh, I'll tell you all right," Eleonor answered Bartholomew. "You think you got away with killing my unborn child, but I had the last laugh. You destroyed my soul that day, so I destroyed yours." Her grief, not having adequately healed, had turned into hatred. And that hatred, having festered over time, grew into unspeakable evil. She viewed Bartholomew as a murderer for causing the end of her pregnancy. The day when Lina had witnessed their quarrel outside their quarters, Eleonor had accused him of as much.

"What are you saying?" Bartholomew braved moving a step closer.

"Don't you move!" Eleonor held the gun a little higher and cocked it. Bartholomew froze. "You had an affair with that wretched woman in town. Oh, yes, I knew all about it. Did you think I was stupid? She bore your child. How ironic—you got the very thing you deprived me of. And as if that wasn't enough, you brought them to the house. How could you have been so insensitive? Every time I saw you with the boy, so affectionate and caring, I was disgusted. It was a cruel reminder of what

I had lost. He should have been mine, not hers. You thought you were so clever, but I always had the upper hand."

Now that all the cards were on the table, Lina put two and two together: Bartholomew was Tommy's father. The story Eleonor told Lina about Bartholomew's relationship with the boy was a lie, a grotesque picture of her husband designed to mislead Lina. The evil woman had gone so far as to insinuate that Bartholomew was behind Tommy's disappearance, but he hadn't detested the boy, he'd loved him.

"What did you do to Tommy?" Bartholomew's hands fisted—gun or no gun threatening him—he was ready to strike Eleonor. Cook shook his head and raised a warning hand at Bartholomew.

"I killed him," Eleonor confessed coldly. Her words hung in the air as everyone tried to process them.

In that instant of total shock at the inhumanity of Eleonor's actions, the room darkened as if someone had closed the drapes and night had fallen. Lina glanced at the others. No one seemed to notice except Eleonor, whose face distorted as Tommy appeared inches away from her. Their gazes connected. She could see him.

Tommy looked different than before. His brown shirt and trousers were dripping wet, and his hair was pulled to the side, revealing a bruised face. His eyes were sunken and sad. His white hands hung beside his body, devoid of life.

Tommy spoke to Eleonor. "Tell them where you put my body so I can go to my mother."

And so it was. Ruby couldn't reach her son until his remains were recovered. Finding his body was the bridge after all.

"Tell us where you buried Tommy," Lina demanded, knowing that the others were unaware of the ghost.

Eleonor's eyes clouded with tears. Lina couldn't understand. Were they a result of fear or remorse?

Tommy clenched his jaw, and his hands fisted as he raised them toward Eleonor in a threatening manner. "You won't have sleeping powder in prison, and I'll visit you every night until you die," he threatened, his whole being darkening. Tommy must have terrorized Eleonor's nights, trying to get her to confess. The medicine she took wasn't because of Bartholomew but because of the hauntings. The amount didn't seem so excessive anymore.

"The wretched creature," Eleonor cried out. "He is in the pond."

"The pond? Impossible. We found nothing there," Bartholomew refuted.

"You fool. I threw him in after it was searched."

Simultaneously, Bartholomew lunged at Eleonor, and the latter pulled the trigger. The giant man stumbled backward, then collapsed to the floor. Inspector Cook ran to him. And as fast as he had come, Tommy disappeared.

Eleonor pointed the gun at Lina. "You couldn't stop poking around. You knew he was in the pond."

Max launched at Eleonor, and yet another shot rang out. This time, Eleonor fell to the ground with a terrifying wail, her weapon dropping beside her. She cradled her bloody hand.

"Well, that wraps up the afternoon," Mrs. Lester said in a calm voice, lowering the gun she had used to shoot Eleonor.

Max kicked Eleonor's gun out of reach and helped the injured woman to rest against the sofa.

"I wouldn't be surprised if it's the same revolver used to kill Sir William." Mrs. Lester collected Eleonor's weapon and handed it to one of the officers.

Mrs. Lester did have a gun after all. Lina contemplated the housekeeper, not believing what she had just done. Who was this woman? She wielded the firearm even better than the pipe.

"We need a doctor immediately," Cook told one of his men, and, leaving Bartholomew, he inspected Eleonor. "She can make it to the infirmary in town. You and Lester go with her," he ordered the other officer. "Come on. Let's move."

Max snatched the cloth runner from the credenza and, tearing Bartholomew's shirt open, pressed it against the wound. Lina rushed to kneel beside her uncle, her ears still ringing from the shots. Though she could hear the people hustling around and Max breathing hard, the world momentarily stopped. It was just Bartholomew and her. His large, round eyes were no longer angry. Somehow, even with his physical pain, he looked at peace. Much like he had in the picture in his room. He grabbed Lina's hand and held it to his side. "Forgive me, child. Do forgive me."

Lina struggled to contain the burning tears. The poor man had wasted his life. One too many drinks and he'd lost his senses and hurt Eleonor. One mistake had resulted in a life of suffering for so many.

"Don't speak, sir," Lina prompted.

"No, dear child. Don't call me sir. Call me uncle, though you deserve better." His eyes went unfocused.

"Please, stay with me," she said, sensing his life slipping away.

Bartholomew forced his gaze onto hers. "Lina, I am sorry for everything I've done to you, but you must know I had nothing to do with your father's murder. I didn't like him because he was always right, but I loved him. And I did not know anything about the attack in the woods."

Lina glanced at Max, who nodded in confirmation of Bartholomew's statement. "Shh, save your energy. We'll discuss it later."

"There is no later." Between spasms of pain and sharp breaths, he went on. "Yes, I suspected Eleonor killed William but had no proof. That's why I wanted you in your room at night and why I was glad to send Mateo to school." Bartholomew broke into a deep sobbing that crushed Lina's heart. He was a flawed man, but she had misjudged him terribly. And there was no time to rectify that. "I should have never taken those bloody papers from your father. He would be alive if I hadn't. I'll take the blame to my grave."

"He is losing too much blood." Max applied more pressure to the wound.

Cook, who had listened to the conversation, dashed out of the library, shouting, "Did we get a hold of the doctor yet?"

"I'll find Tommy's remains, and he'll have a proper burial," Lina said to comfort the dying man. Though, she had already decided to do it for Tommy's sake.

"Thank you." Bartholomew smiled faintly. "I don't have much, but what I have is yours now. Including Ruppert and Jasper."

"I'll make sure they are well cared for." Lina smiled back and found herself saying words she never thought she would. "Be at peace. I hold no grudge against you."

"You are brave and strong, just like your mother. You'll do just fine in this cruel world, just fine." Bartholomew closed his eyes. "Do know that even when I didn't show it, I was happy when you returned unharmed... I was happy." He took a final breath and let go of Lina's hand.

Blackwater felt desolate without Bartholomew, Eleonor, and Mrs. Lester. Even the ghosts had ceased their activities. Lina approached Bartholomew's empty office, feeling a pang of nostalgia for the man. He must have found a measure of joy in his son, Tommy. And Ruby must have thought Bartholomew to be a wealthy man and Tommy the inheritor of his father's fortune. Of course, Eleonor, who had fought tirelessly to hold on to whatever they had left, would never have allowed it. Tommy's fate was sealed from the beginning.

Lina paused at the threshold. Jasper and Ruppert lay side by side near the desk as if comforting each other. They had hardly left the room since their master's passing. They raised their heads, acknowledging Lina's presence, but soon returned to their mournful state.

It was so awfully quiet. In the stillness, Ruby's words came back to her. *"My conduct will be irreproachable and worthy of all praise."* Even trapped in her anguish, Ruby must have had times when her inner light was stronger than the grief that obscured her understanding. Ironically, those times might have been the most wrenching as she faced her failure to find Tommy. Now that the truth had finally been exposed, would Ruby find peace? Would she be reunited with Tommy?

Lina moved into the office. "I'm sorry he is not here." Crouching beside the dogs, she caressed their backs. She was still tense around them, but somewhere along the way, her interactions with Jasper and Ruppert had taught her to control her dread of large breeds. "We'll go for a walk later today."

Jasper and Ruppert sighed and dropped their heads between their paws. Just like their master, they were a little rough around the edges, but there was a soft spot in their hearts.

She resumed her march to the library, waiting patiently for the police. Now that the weather had finally warmed up, they tackled the enormous task of searching the pond. As soon as Tommy's remains were found, Lina would return to London to be near Mateo. Mateo loved school and had decided to stay there, but they would spend the weekends together.

Lina marveled at how life could change so drastically from better to worse, then back again. Just a few months ago, she couldn't have imagined feeling hopeful and excited about the future. And while Oxford was still a possibility, she decided, after witnessing Mrs. Lester's triumph with the pipe and Max's decisiveness in action, to join the pilot program for female agents. Females who could gather information and carry out sabotage and other covert operations would be a great asset to the nation. But no matter where her adventure led, she would never again be fearful of what lay ahead, for she knew that miracles were always possible, and that joy could be found when one least expected it. And from time to time, she felt the same peace she felt in the pool of icy water, when she had been drowned but somehow comforted by her parents, who watched from somewhere in the hereafter.

The Secret Service. The words brought peace to her heart, for Lina already had a wonderful mentor—Mrs. Lester, who was an undercover agent. William had placed her at Blackwater to retrieve the classified documents, and Lester had fabricated her obsession with lighting candles to facilitate her nightly searches. However, as the search went on unsuccessfully and the government pressured William, he traveled to the manor himself, hoping to persuade Bartholomew to return them.

That wonderful agent, Jane Lester—she was the one who'd let Max into the house the night he took Lina downtown to identify Bill. And of course, she had kept a close watch on the household and protected Lina. Lina smiled; she hadn't made it easy for Lester with her nightly adventures. She made a mental note to send Lester a large package of Woolworths Buttered Brazils. As it turned out, they were indeed Lester's weakness. Although the candy jar in her bedroom was full, Lina later discovered that Lester had two others in the kitchen pantry. And as for her gun—of course, she kept it on her person.

Eleonor—she had been adept at presenting one face to the world while shielding her true identity. She thought she had gotten away with her crimes, but Tommy had taught her an unforgettable lesson. She had killed him, but she couldn't get rid of him. Lina sighed. It would be a while before she could wrap her mind around all that had transpired. For now, an inquest would decide Eleonor's fate. If she claimed insanity and the jury believed her, they might spare her life.

Bartholomew—Lina wished she'd have had a little more time with him. Time without all the lies and secrets—time to get to know her real uncle, the one hidden beneath his addictions. But as it was, she would have to cling to the memory of his last minutes alive when they had truly connected. His funeral had been a private, but beautiful affair, and Lina was grateful to have parted ways amicably.

Her thoughts jumped to Bray. Poor devil. He'd gotten burned by the fire poker and received a severe blow to the head—the latter compliments of Lester. Well, he'd had it coming. He'd been sent to prison alongside Bill. Bill's companion was still at large, but Lina was confident that sooner or later, the police would catch up to him. Max's decision to send Bill to London was justified as both the military and Scotland Yard wanted to protect him as a witness for Eleonor's conviction.

Through the window, Lina noticed a car enter the courtyard. *Max.* His visit wasn't unexpected, but still her heart throbbed. She heard the front door, and soon Max surged into the library in a well-pressed blue uniform. And along with him came the sense of security she loved. At once he enfolded her in his arms, and she welcomed his closeness.

"How are you holding up?" he asked softly.

"I'm all right."

"I'm sorry that bringing the charges against them took so long. We had a heck of a lot of circumstantial evidence, and we needed a confession. We knew they might talk if we exposed them in front of each other. We speculated there were things each might not know about the other."

"That was brilliant, but tell me something ...were you really on the same train as my father when he was killed?" She'd wondered since Eleonor's arrest. It seemed too much of a coincidence, even though he was already working on the case.

"No, I wasn't. We had a witness who saw a female rider at the murder scene. He described Eleonor perfectly, and when I saw her with the bags from the tack shop, my suspicions intensified. I pretended to be the witness, hoping to scare her into a confession."

"And it paid off."

"Thankfully."

Another uncertainty surfaced, and Lina let it out, "You weren't at Mateo's school visiting someone else. You were there to check on him."

Max nodded. "We ordered the school not to release Mateo to anyone before letting us know. We wanted to make sure he was safe."

"Thank you."

"I heard you are returning to London." Max pulled her closer.

"As soon as we find the boy's remains."

"I was not expecting that. I thought we knew everything about Bartholomew and Eleonor."

"Secrets and sins—they multiply," Lina lamented.

"Yeah, I guess so. But with them gone, you must be lonely around here. This house is immense."

"I still have a few people, plus Ruppert and Jasper." Lina felt a surge of gratitude for the staff, whom she considered her friends. For the time being, Dollie would enjoy the break from the grueling cooking schedule; hopefully, Maggie would lower her guard and enjoy life a little more. And who knew, maybe even find another suiter. Annie had accepted Lina's invitation to work at her flat in London. It wasn't the French Riviera, but Annie was thrilled to move to the city; Mr. Krammer would now care for the dogs and transfer the ground's maintenance to Fred— whom Lina had hired to work at Blackwater full time.

"Ruppert and Jasper?" Max asked.

"The dogs."

"Ah."

"Besides, Mateo is coming for the weekend," Lina said.

"How is he doing?"

"He's resilient, though I must admit I'm grateful he wasn't here these past days." When Lina loosened her hold on Max, he responded by tightening his arms around her.

"I heard you applied to the Secret Service."

"Indeed, you are well-informed, Lieutenant."

"You'll be a great agent. We might work together someday."

"We might."

"Lina, I'm disappointed to say that I've been assigned to a case up north."

"So, you are moving on." Her statement held more than one meaning.

"For the time being, yes."

"Max, I'm truly grateful for what you have done for Mateo and me." She looked away, hiding her longing to express many things—things that would remain unsaid for now.

"It was a pleasure." He smiled. "Listen, I'll be back in London in late spring. I'd love to spend some time together and perhaps show you my flat."

"I'd like that."

Max lowered his head until his lips touched Lina's. She matched the fervency of his kiss, reassuring him that she'd accepted his offer.

Lina watched as the divers, under the direction of Inspector Cook, dragged a metal crate to the edge of the pond, along with vestiges of rope and large rocks that once had been attached to it. She turned away as the men opened the makeshift coffin. The collection of horrifying images stored in her mind was enough to last a lifetime. She didn't need to see Tommy's remains.

"A child, all right. Sad, indeed," Cook mourned. "And more rocks to keep the box underwater."

Lina inhaled and exhaled deeply. It was done. She could now lay Tommy to rest beside his mother in the Coleford Cemetery. Eleonor had been clever. The heavy box had sunk, most likely tangled with debris, and meshed with the bottom of the pond, an assurance that his body would never surface. Considering its size, she suspected Eleonor must have used her horse to haul it here.

Cook neared Lina with a grave expression. "We found this with him." On his gloved hand rested a deteriorated toy. Though it had been underwater this long, thanks to the treatment Mr. Snow had applied to the wood, it was still recognizable.

It was nothing short of a miracle. Lina's heart ached for Tommy. This must have been his favorite—the passenger car. Had he dreamed of going on an adventure?

"May I have it when you are done with it?" she asked the inspector.

"I don't see why not."

Lina planned to visit Mr. Snow. Considering the recent events, she hoped he wouldn't mind making a whole new train for Mateo. The old one, along with the passenger car, would go with its owner to his new grave.

Under a bright sun, Lina and Mateo strolled the lawn hand in hand. They were set to return to London Sunday night, leaving the house staff in charge of Blackwater. The siblings planned to visit often, especially to check on Ruppert and Jasper.

"I have something to tell you," Mateo said sheepishly.

"What is it?"

"You know the pond drawing I sent with Max?"

"Yes, I still have it."

"The boy I drew is Tommy, not me."

"I suspected as much."

Eleonor had paid particular attention to that drawing. The boy playing with the toy train near the pond was dressed like Tommy. She must have thought as much. And Lina's determination to find Tommy's body, combined with Max's involvement, drove her to have Lina killed. Eleonor must have feared that if his body was found inside the box, the investigation would be reopened. More so, seeing his son's remains,

Bartholomew would have gotten the truth out of her, and the repercussions would have been swift.

"And one more thing," Mateo said softly.

"Yes."

"Promise me you won't be upset."

"All right." Lina looked at him sideways. "I promise."

"I stole an envelope with papers from sir's office and hid it in the attic."

Lina stopped midstride. "You did?" Well, that explained how it got there.

"I did."

"Why?"

He shrugged.

"Don't fret. You aren't in trouble." Lina playfully ruffled his hair. "The envelope was found and returned. Now, tell me why you hid it."

"Tommy told me to do it. He didn't say why."

"Hmm."

How much did the dead know about the affairs of the living, and to what extent could they interfere? What was Tommy's motive for hiding the documents? Did he know of their importance? Or was he just being mischievous? Lina couldn't say, but he wouldn't have been able to do it without Mateo's help. Maybe, just maybe, the dead's boundaries ended where ours began, and for them to trespass, we had to allow it—be it for good or evil. Whatever it was, she was satisfied that there was more to life than met the eye.

"Look, Lina, look!" Mateo pointed to the far side of the pond.

As if mirroring the siblings, Ruby and Tommy stood at the tree line, holding hands. Ruby wore a blue dress, and Tommy wore a white shirt and trousers. Their faces glowed with joy, all darkness gone. Lina felt a profound peace. At last, they had been reunited.

"She is the maid I followed to the attic," Mateo said. "Is she Tommy's mum?"

"That's his mum."

"I found him crying one day," Mateo recalled. "He said the house was too big and he couldn't find her."

"Well, they are together now." When the appropriate time came, Lina would have a thorough discussion with her brother about the Joneses, including how they were related to her and Mateo.

"He looks very happy." Mateo waved at his ghost friend.

Ruby nodded slightly at the siblings. Tommy waved back, beaming, as they sauntered into the woods. Lina smiled, sensing that Tommy was off to the most wonderful adventure of his existence.

Thank you for reading! Did you enjoy? Please add your review because nothing helps an author more and encourages readers to take a chance on a book than a review.

And don't miss more from Marcia Armandi with THE GHOSTS OF LEWIS MANOR available now. Turn the page for a sneak peek!

Also be sure to sign up for the City Owl Press newsletter to receive notice of all book releases!

SNEAK PEEK OF THE GHOSTS OF
LEWIS MANOR

Brockenhurst, the New Forest, England, 1942

As the train creaked into the station, my thoughts remained on the incident that had landed me here. I was not sure when I first became aware I could see the dead. In my nineteen years of life, they had hovered around the edges of my awareness like a faint melody heard from another room. When I was younger, they'd blended with the living well enough—the girl in an old-fashioned dress in the park who'd ignored my invitation to play, the old man with a blank look who'd stood on our porch one moment and was gone the next. The sightings were rare, and as an adult, I treated those old memories as dreams. That was, until the war started. The overwhelming number of disembodied spirits roaming the streets of the city could not be ignored.

Thankfully, most spirits—at least those *I'd* encountered—seemed oblivious to the world of the living, completely absorbed with whatever it was they did. They paid me no heed, and though seeing them had been slightly disconcerting, I considered them mostly benign. That was, until the boy called for my attention.

Being deceived to the point of endangering my family made me realize I might have to look more closely at this ability, for if I failed to comprehend what lay beyond the veil separating the living from the dead, I could find myself on the wrong side of it. The thought was grim. For if I were to ever understand the supernatural world, I would have to step farther in. But as I considered the possibility, goose bumps crawled up my arms, and fear of the unknown made me think better of it. I decided to brush away the uncomfortable thought as the train finally stopped, and I rose to gather my belongings. After all, I was here to escape the ghosts.

Alighting from the train, the first thing I noticed was the sky. Compared to the hellish brew of London, it was vast and endless— paradisal to behold. Yet dragging my suitcase across the platform, I felt the part of a vagabond, a refugee from the land of the dead. Piper sniffed the air, which had the refreshing scent of recent rain.

The other travelers brushed past me, impatiently trying to get on with their journeys. Feeling a little of that impatience myself, I readjusted Piper in my arms and took a fruitless lap around the station, avoiding the puddles as best I could. The groundskeepers of All Hallows, the Goswicks, were supposed to fetch me. But no one appeared to be looking for me.

Within minutes, I was the only person in sight except for the clerk behind the ticket window and a man wiping the water droplets off a black car in the parking lot. "Excuse me, sir," I said to the clerk. "Is there a way to call for a cab?"

His dark eyes rose to meet mine as he put down the pipe he had been smoking apparently nonstop, for he stood in a cloud of fumes. "How far are you going?"

"Burley. I understand it is a neighboring town?"

"That's correct, and Albert Craven"—he pointed at the man by the car—"offers local transportation." Looking at his wristwatch, he added, "You might want to speak to him right away. He usually leaves about now."

"I'm most obliged, sir."

Mr. Craven was a middle-aged man with a thick mustache and bushy eyebrows. Folding the cloth in his hand, he took a step back from his vehicle—an unmarked, older car I would have never guessed to be a cab —to make sure he hadn't missed any water spots. Piper growled as we approached, capturing his immediate attention.

"Good afternoon, sir. The clerk told me you are a cab driver. I'm in need of a lift to Burley."

"Indeed, I am." He extended his hand to me. "Craven, miss. Albert Craven."

"Seraphina Addington." I met his strong grip with my own.

"Burley, you said?"

"Yes."

"Not too far from here, about five miles. We can be there in a jiffy."

"Thank you." I was relieved, hoping that once I reached the Goswicks, I would regain a bit of that security which came from belonging somewhere.

After the incident in London, Father had contacted General John Lewis, an old comrade of his from the Great War, and accepted his previous offer to let me stay at his country house, away from the chaos of the conflict. Prior to becoming a general, John Lewis had been a familiar face, the image of an uncle in my mind. He was a wealthy and influential man but also acquainted with grief, having lost his wife at a young age and never remarried. Of course, we hadn't seen him since the war broke out.

"If you'll permit," the man said as he hefted my suitcase into the boot of the car. I settled into the back with Piper snuggled against the folds of my blue dress, which Mother insisted I wear, arguing that it matched my eyes and contrasted with my brown hair. I had acquiesced only to avoid an unnecessary confrontation on the day of my departure. Under any other circumstances, I would have worn slacks despite her disapproval. She was one of those who clung to the past, shunning twentieth-century styles.

The car left the station, making all sorts of racket and complaining of long-needed maintenance. The roads were lined with thatched-roof cottages that sat far back from the street, some with hydrangea hedges, others with evergreen shrubs. When we reached the end of the paved streets, Mr. Craven turned onto a rural road guarded by trees of every shape and sort. Through them, I caught glimpses of meadowland flowing through the ancient yews. It was breathtakingly green.

I was surprised to feel the unexpected beauty and calmness of my surroundings flood me, the contrast with what I had left behind startling. The war had taken so much from us, and we had quite rapidly adjusted to its ugliness—the sky dotted with black-and-red clouds of smoke as if heaven itself cried over the world; the explosions of the bombs followed by the shattering of windows; the mangled corpses; and for me, the spirits of the dead who walked aimlessly amid the rubble.

The New Forest, brimming with life, reminded me that our world was still beautiful, our people resilient. The war would end, and we would rise stronger and rebuild all that had been lost. Now that I was away from my family and needed a steadiness to allay my fears for them, I resolved to hold on to this belief more than ever.

Piper rearranged herself on the seat as we bumped along the muddy road. I ran my hand reassuringly through her fur, steadying my emotions at the same time. No doubt she would prefer the country to the air raids, which spared no one, tormenting humans and animals alike.

Apologetically, Mr. Craven explained, "The main road to Burley gets particularly nasty after a rainstorm. You must forgive me, but I'm taking a detour. A longer route through the forest. We don't want old Harvey getting stuck in the mud—no, surely not."

The car has a name. I smiled.

Up ahead, trotting gently along the roadside, a group of soldiers on horseback headed in our direction. Mr. Craven steered Harvey to the side of the road, if *road* was the proper name for this patch of mud in the woods.

"That's the Mounted Home Guard," he informed proudly. "They are volunteer soldiers operating out of Breamore. Great lads, they are. We also have both British and American troops stationed here, but thankfully, no bombs have fallen yet. Well, apart from Southampton, that is. The port is a target, but we've been spared farther inland."

"That's a mercy from heaven. Let us hope it remains like this." I had seen firsthand the erasure of history, brick and mortar, paper and binding. Hundreds of years destroyed in a matter of minutes.

"Where in Burley are you staying? Where should I let you out?"

"I'm not sure how to find it. I'm afraid I don't have an address."

"Don't fret, miss. In these parts, places have names. That's how we find them, not by numbers or anything like that."

"The name escapes me at the moment, but I'm a guest of General Lewis."

"Oh, I see. He is well known in the region—he owns the Burley mansion. The largest structure in the region." Just as he said that, a new thought seemed to startle him. "Wait, are you certain? The mansion currently serves as a military post—soldiers coming in and out all day. Not a good destination for a young lady, if you know what I mean."

The straightforward honesty of country folk was something I could get used to. "Agreed. No, I'm not going to the mansion. I understand the general owns a country house as well."

"You aren't speaking of All Hallows, are you?" His gaze found mine through the rearview mirror. For a split second, a shadow of disbelief crossed what I could see of his face.

"Yes, that sounds about right. I'll be staying there until things settle down in London."

He reached to loosen the collar of his shirt as if it suddenly strangled him. "That could be a long time...a long time indeed, to be in a house like that."

Was there something wrong with the house? Leaning forward, I asked, "Mr. Craven, what do you mean, 'in a house like that'?"

When he took longer than needed to respond, I knew he would not disclose the truth; however, I kept my gaze on him through the mirror until he did answer.

"It's one of the oldest houses in the region. Hundreds of years of history, you understand. I'm afraid All Hallows's fame will live forever. But it has been deserted since..."

"Since when?"

"An awfully long time...I didn't think it was habitable anymore."

"For my sake, I hope it is. But why is it famous? I imagine there are plenty of old houses around here competing for fame."

"Actually...since I've never been to the manor, I'm afraid my opinion wouldn't be an educated one." He cleared his throat, obviously unhappy with my questioning.

"I would still like to hear it."

"It's better that you wait to hear it from those familiar with the place." These last words he said with finality, putting an end to the subject.

His reason for not sharing was simply an excuse. Just as I considered pressing him further, the car slowed to almost an idling stage, but I couldn't see any reason for it. Piper lifted her head as high as she could, ears pointed, eyes wide open, in response to the unexpected change.

"Is anything the matter?"

"Miss, I thought you were going downtown. The manor is on the outskirts, and the roads are impossible during this weather. I'm afraid all I can do is let you out in town. Maybe you can spend the night there— rethink things?"

Rethink things? What did I have to rethink? Even if I wanted to stay in town, I had no money to spare. "Surely the roads can't be any worse than the ones we've traveled on."

In a faltering voice that betrayed his businesslike approach, he replied, "If the car gets stuck, it would be days before I could get any help. So, no, I can't drive you there." He glanced at the lowering sun. "No one would, at least not until tomorrow."

I said the first words that came to mind. "You must be having a laugh." I imagined Mother's response to such boldness, but after all, I had not come this far just to come this far. "There must be another way. Tell me there is."

He thought for a moment or two. By the way he fidgeted in his seat, I could tell he fought whatever idea he considered. At last, he let it out. "There is, but I don't recommend it. The forest is not safe for a woman to go about alone."

"It involves walking, then?"

He moved his head in assent.

I turned his words in my mind. There were areas in London where women felt unsafe to travel alone, daylight or not. I'd had to traverse them a time or two. This couldn't be any worse. *I should have brought Mother's frying pan.* I had seen her chase away several solicitors with it. It worked wonders.

"Walking Piper and I can handle. We just need directions."

He frowned as if saying, "*The foolishness of this woman will get her in trouble,*" but aloud, he said, "I can drop you off at the edge of Oker field. The manor is not far from there." He paused and then suggested yet again, "But I must insist that staying in town is a wise choice." The assertion made me want to successfully brave the trail to All Hallows all the more.

"I'll take my chances."

With a severe expression of disapproval, Mr. Craven pressed his foot on the gas pedal. Harvey picked up speed, and at length, we came to a lane free of trees on one side. I leaned against the window to observe wild ponies roaming freely in the fields. If ponies were the type of threat my driver was worried about, my biggest challenge would be to keep Piper's excitement under control. She did not like anything, apart from her own kind, that had four legs, and she made sure they knew it.

The more I focused on the scenery, the more ponies I saw. "Oh my. There are so many of them."

"They belong to the commoners," Mr. Craven informed. "They have the right to graze their animals in the forest. A good thing too. The ponies and the cattle help maintain the landscape."

The vehicle made its way deeper into the woods, and soon the ponies were but a distant image. I was about to ask Mr. Craven how much longer we had when Harvey produced a jerking sound and came to a halt in the middle of nowhere. There were no houses in sight, just a welded wire fence guarding the meadow. Beyond that was a thickly wooded area. It was so still it didn't seem real.

I noticed Mr. Craven's hand tremble as he looked at his wristwatch. But the hour appeared to calm his nerves, for he said, "Oh, good." I imagined he meant that the remaining daylight was good enough for me to make the journey on foot. I certainly hoped that was the case, for time could be treacherous when moving against it.

With unexpected agility, he sprang from the car as though a fire burned unattended somewhere and opened the back door for me to follow suit. I stepped out and immediately felt my shoes—my nicest pair, meant to accompany the dress—sink into the wet ground. Piper jumped down after me.

"Remember, cross the field and go straight south through those trees. You'll see the manor soon enough." He flipped the boot open and quickly set my bag on the grass. Piper barked at the rushed handling of our property. "May I suggest you waste no time."

Civility, though I wasn't feeling it at the moment, called for me to say thank you. I handed him a few bills to cover the ride. He stashed them in his pocket without counting them.

"It's not too far. You'll be all right," he said, as if willing it to be true. Without further ado, he was back in his car. Harvey made a sharp turn, and with surprising speed, Mr. Craven drove away.

Don't stop now. Keep reading with your copy of <u>THE GHOSTS OF LEWIS MANOR</u> available now.

Don't miss more from Marcia Armandi with THE GHOSTS OF LEWIS MANOR available now.

Seraphina must choose the lesser of two evils—the ghosts that haunt her or the murderer who hunts her.

Born with a rare ability—or curse, Seraphina can see and hear the dead. During the early days of the London Blitz, she is confronted with hundreds of lost souls wandering the streets.

As the war escalates, her parents send her away to the home of an old friend in the English countryside to preserve her sanity. But there are monsters lurking in the hallways and the surrounding woods of the mansion, not all of them are ghosts.

Seraphina must use her gift to help solve the gruesome mysteries of Lewis Manor's past in order to prevent her own murder in the present.

Please sign up for the City Owl Press newsletter for chances to win special subscriber-only contests and giveaways as well as receiving information on upcoming releases and special excerpts.

All reviews are **welcome** and **appreciated**. Please consider leaving one on your favorite social media and book buying sites.

Escape Your World. Get Lost in Ours! City Owl Press at www.cityowlpress.com.

ACKNOWLEDGMENTS

My deepest gratitude to Lisa Green. Thank you for your patience, hard work, and priceless advice in bringing *The Haunting of Blackwater* to publication.

And a huge thanks to the entire team at City Owl Press for believing in me as an author. It is my pleasure to work with such fantastic people.

ABOUT THE AUTHOR

MARCIA ARMANDI was born and raised in Argentina. She is a soccer fanatic and loves listening to tango. Marcia studied International Family History Research and Writing.

After decades of compiling personal histories, she has developed a profound gratitude for the strength that can be found in families. So it is that through her fiction, Marcia explores the meaning of love and loyalty in times of fear, war, and finally, death.

facebook.com/ArmandiMarcia

twitter.com/MarciaArmandi

instagram.com/marciaarmandi

ABOUT THE PUBLISHER

City Owl Press is a cutting edge indie publishing company, bringing the world of romance and speculative fiction to discerning readers.

Escape Your World. Get Lost in Ours!

www.cityowlpress.com

facebook.com/CityOwlPress

twitter.com/cityowlpress

instagram.com/cityowlbooks

pinterest.com/cityowlpress

tiktok.com/@cityowlpress

www.ingramcontent.com/pod-product-compliance
Lightning Source LLC
Chambersburg PA
CBHW021342060726
47498CB00020B/1487